Stephanie DosSantos

TALIN
AND THE TREE
THE ELIMINATION – BOOK 2

BlackDog BrownDog Press

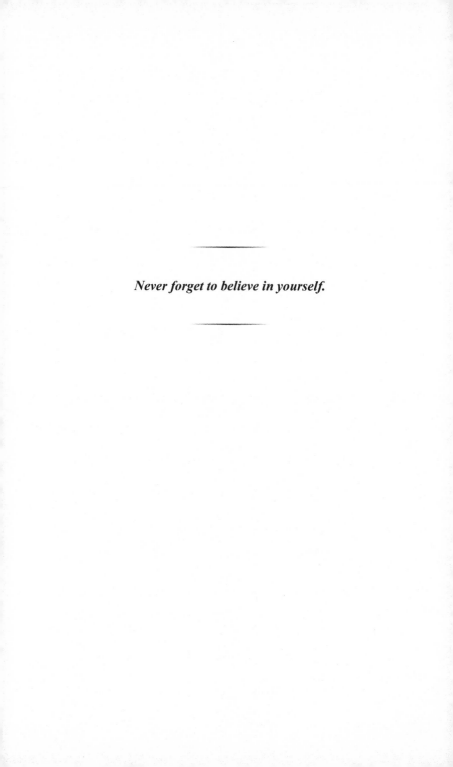

Never forget to believe in yourself.

CONTENTS

PRONUNCIATION GUIDE

Names in this book are derived from the Caribbean area. Some names relating to the folklore characters have French or African roots. The following guide may help readers to correctly pronounce them.

Talin - Pronounced with a short 'a' sound, rhymes with "gallon".

Papa Bois - Pronounced with a silent 's' sound, as in "bwah".

Mama D'lo - Pronounced as a contraction, as in "duh low".

Onca - Pronounced traditionally with a soft 'c' sound, but for purposes of this story and the character's traits, it is pronounced with a hard 'c' sound, as in "on kuh".

Vieux - Pronounced with a silent 'x', as in "vee oh".

Javon - Pronounced with a soft 'a', such as "juh vonn".

THE REALM

The Barrenlands

The Theater

The Grove

The Sphere

The Mountains

The Cemetery

The Meadow

The Lake

Jumbie

The Shelter

The Ruins

The Ocean

The Gorge

N

W E

The Fire Marsh

The Temple

TALIN
AND THE TREE

Stephanie DosSantos

A SEARING PAIN SET TALIN'S ANKLE ON FIRE, AS IF THE DEVIL himself had latched onto it. His attempts to grab the roots and vines as they passed overhead were useless against the incredible force yanking him down. The inside of the tree's trunk glowed a sinister orange. His eyes stung, and he could smell his own burning flesh. Dirt fell into his mouth as he screamed.

Dragged into the Realm, Talin clawed at the ground desperately struggling to escape the jaws of Onca, the fiery big cat he'd tangled with just days before.

"Help!" he screamed to anyone as the attack continued. A vicious snarl erupted from the cat as it whipped Talin's body about, sending whirling clouds of dust around the base of the tree. Onca's fangs pierced so deep, Talin was sure they had struck bone. Looking past the fiery feline behind him, he saw Papa Bois just out of reach.

"Onca, release him! Now!" Papa's voice boomed with a menacing tone Talin had never heard before. But it did not appear to intimidate the cat at all.

Oh no.

Talin's body was whipped again, like his dog used to shake its stuffed toy. His screaming continued.

The cat held Talin tight within its jaws, not letting go.

"Release him!" Papa commanded again and Onca finally relinquished his mighty hold on Talin, nearly spitting him out like some vile substance. Papa was holding a spear in his hand, raised high above his head. It looked like it was made of ice.

Talin scurried toward Papa like a frightened bug. Onca slowly circled the pair, his head low, shoulder blades popping up above his top line as he alternated his stealthy steps. Talin could smell the musty smoke rising from the flames that covered Onca's spotted body. When he flicked his tail, embers flew through the air then settled into fiery drops on the dusty path. He snarled.

"This is no Healer. He's just a boy, Papa."

What?!

Talin could not decide if he was shocked that the cat was speaking or was offended by what it said. Onca's voice was deep, low, and everything evil. He kept circling, eyeing his prey. The light emanating from him was so intense it nearly drowned out the moonlight above. Talin's eyes continued to sting from the heat billowing so close to him.

"He is your new Healer, you will respect him and follow his orders." Papa said.

The cat laughed a hearty guffaw. "I will not. He is not suited, nor ready, to take me on."

"As father of this forest Realm, I am commanding you to leave the boy alone—"

"Ah, you call him a boy yourself—"

"Age has no bearing in this matter."

"Ah, but it does, sir Papa..." Papa and Talin slowly circled with the cat, mirroring his movements, never allowing their backs to be exposed to the dangerous teeth, claws, or fire. "It does."

"How?" Talin joined in the conversation trying his best to stand tall, puff his chest, and look more intimidating than he really was.

His nerves were evident despite his bravest voice, and he stumbled on his painful foot.

"Ah, the boy can speak for himself can he?" Onca teased.

"Onca, as Healer, I command you to stand down."

An evil laugh erupted from deep within the cat's chest, "You command *me*? Me, Onca, the great exalted one?" Onca lashed out with a flaming paw, claws exposed, coming dangerously close to Talin's flesh. "You and I are not so different. *I* have been a great Healer, just like you."

He's a Healer?

Onca must have seen the confusion on Talin's face. "Oh? You mean you didn't tell him, Papa?"

"It has not been necessary."

"Well, it seems necessary now, doesn't it?" The cat continued to pace around them. "I see you were at my lair recently— uninvited." His words rumbled like distant thunder.

"The Temple does not belong to you, Onca. It belongs to all who inhabit the Realm."

"Well then, that would include me. And seeing how there aren't that many of us left, I have claimed it, as you know." Turning his head toward Talin, he said, "The boy is quick, I give him that," then stared deeply into Talin's eyes, "but he lacks the stamina and strength a Healer needs."

"With time, Onca, just as you once learned," Papa replied.

"Fine!" he roared. "Let him learn, *then* I will challenge him. And I will win. And he will lose— or die. Then I will take my rightful place here as ruler!"

The cat made a stealthy 180-degree turn, facing Talin. "And you. I will follow you. You will not rest."

Onca turned away and fled into the trees, the sound of crackling flames diminishing with a trail of smoke into the forest.

. . .

"HOW IS YOUR ANKLE?" Papa asked.

As if on cue, the pain surged like a giant wave, bringing Talin to his knees. "I don't know, it feels like it's still burning." The adrenaline rush had dulled the pain for only a short time.

"Come."

Papa led a limping Talin to the edge of the Lake. "Step in."

"But you said stay out of —"

"Step in. You are Healer now, it is safe."

I'm the Healer...

Talin reluctantly obeyed. The cool water was refreshing, yet more painful to the bite. Blood oozed from his wounds; four fang marks to his ankle, two on the inside, two on the outside. Talin felt certain the wounds bore into the bone.

The water began to ripple gently across the lake. A school of colorful fish circled his lower leg, swimming furiously around it. The bubbles forming from the fish in the now pinkish-water began to cloud the view of his foot. Flashes of color popped within the bubbles.

"What are they doing?" he asked Papa.

"Healing."

Talin couldn't believe what he was seeing. It was like watching a cyclone of fish winding around his leg, a blur of every color in the rainbow. Then as suddenly as the fish began their furious swim, they dispersed back into the Lake. The water cleared and he was no longer bleeding. His ankle felt warm and tingly. The pain had subsided, but was not completely gone.

Wow.

"Better?" Papa asked.

"How did they do that?!"

Papa didn't answer, as if the question didn't need answering or Talin should know that this was a normal occurrence.

"Step out."

Papa guided Talin to the shore and asked him to sit while he removed aloe from his own pack and applied a generous amount to the wounds. Talin winced. Papa wrapped the ankle in various leaves and secured them with twine, as he had previously done for Talin's scraped knees.

"You'll want to rinse that tomorrow and reapply it."

Nodding, "Ok, do you have any more?" Talin said, "My pack was soaked when Dewain pushed me into the Falls."

"Absolutely."

Talin took a deep breath. "So, what was that all about?" He tilted his head back towards the tree.

"Onca? He is upset. He wants to rule the Realm."

"You won't let him, right?"

"No."

"Good." Talin seemed relieved.

"You will."

"Wait, what?"

"You won't let him."

Talin was rendered speechless. He had just been bitten by an evil spirit animal that barely obeyed Papa Bois' great power, how was he supposed to stop him? Dewain's Induction had just spiraled into an Evocation, while Talin was still learning what his role as Healer even was, and now he had to control a fire-breathing jaguar spirit. How much worse could this get?

He didn't want to know.

"Papa, what did Onca mean when he said he used to be a Healer?"

"Exactly that."

"Come on, a flaming jaguar was the town Healer?" He nearly rolled his eyes.

"He wasn't a jaguar back then. Now he is between two worlds and has taken on spirit form."

"Does every Healer do that?"

"No."

With a single word, Talin's hopes of seeing his great-grandfather in the Realm one day were mostly crushed.

"Healers who have not made their peace are in a type of limbo. Healer Hunte never wanted to let the title go, or pass along his power."

"Who?"

Papa offered a hand to Talin to help him from the ground.

"You should go home now to check on your family."

"But you said I was needed here."

"I did."

"Then I should stay."

"But now you are injured. Rest your wounds, return as soon as you can and we'll continue," Papa said, placing a hand on Talin's shoulder, "Healer Talin."

Then he motioned for Talin to go.

Carefully ascending the roots, Talin looked down as often as the moonlight would allow, assuring no orange glow crept up behind him. Using mostly his upper body strength to navigate the vines, he maneuvered himself within the twisted mess, now charred from fire.

As he emerged from the tree's trunk, he could smell the burnt earth from Onca's wake, or it could have been from the extinguished torches of the Induction ceremony, perhaps both.

Peering over a root, he checked to be sure that no one had returned after the police left Dewain's botched Induction. Everything was clear.

Talin gathered the trash bags he'd filled the night before and walked home with both a sore rib and ankle.

————

LEAVING THE TRASH BAGS OUTSIDE, he limped up the back porch, where he could hear his mother and Marisha whispering in the kitchen about the evening's events. Quietly, he opened the screen door. The house still smelled of warm, sweet cocoa.

"Talin, where have you been?" His mother stood from the table, advancing in his direction, "I asked you to come straight ho—"

He saw her eyes meet the banana leaves. "Oh Lord, what happened to you? You went back in the tree didn't you? I thought I had made myself quite clear you were to come—"

"Mom, I'm ok."

"That is not the point young man."

"I wasn't going to go, but I—"

"But you did. Healer or not, you are still my son, and you will obey the rules of this house first. What happened?"

The pendants around Talin's neck shook, the vibration causing a clinking sound. His mother nearly screamed, falling back into the kitchen chair.

"Stop that!"

"I didn't do anything."

Marisha went to comfort her. "It's ok, Mrs. Williams. We're safe with Talin now."

His mother was still clearly spooked, probably full of adrenaline herself after the Induction, he thought. She had, after all, been willing to take on a slew of drunken men with her machete to defend him not long ago.

"I'm sure Talin can walk me home tonight," Marisha looked up at him. "Maybe you should stay home and relax," she said, turning back to Mrs. Williams.

"Sure," he paused with concern in his voice, tipping his head towards the living room, "will you be ok by yourself Mom?"

She nodded, "He left for the bar in the middle of the raucous," then turned to the leftover glass of juice she and Marisha were sharing.

"I won't be long, I promise," he told her.

. . .

HE STEPPED outside to escort his friend home. They stayed on the main roads sprinkled with sparse street lights.

"I'm sorry I didn't believe you about being Healer," she said, "it's just that—"

"It's ok, I was pretty surprised myself."

"Really?"

"Yeah. Everything happened so fast."

Talin glanced at the front windows of people's homes with their lights still on at the late hour, wondering if anyone was peering out of them. He wanted to hold Marisha's hand—for safety—but didn't. Then she jumped at the sound of a growling alley cat, likely in heat.

"You ok?" He chuckled.

"Yeah, I guess I'm just still a little jittery," she said, a shy giggle beneath the words.

Talin wondered how high she'd jump if it were anything bigger than a kitten and looked cautiously over his shoulder.

"I'm sorry about Dewain," he said, referring to the injury he'd caused Dewain.

"Oh, don't be silly, he's—"

Talin stopped and turned toward her. "No, really, he's family and I hurt him—"

"To save your goats." She smiled at him, staring into his eyes.

Talin felt a flutter in his chest. Her eyes seemed to sparkle under the streetlight. He took a deep breath and smiled sweetly back then kept walking. "Come on."

WHEN THEY APPROACHED HER HOME, all the lights were on and the echoes of a tense discussion charged the outside air. He saw her hesitate.

"I really should get inside, will you be ok on the way home?"

"Yeah, I'll be fine," he said, patting the knife still at his side.

"Ok, thanks." She leaned in to hug him goodnight and he

hugged her back. Then she ran to the porch, cautiously opening the front door. All Talin heard was Mrs. Dyllon shouting, "Where have you been all this time?! If you were at that Induction, you will be grounded for life miss..." her voice trailing off as he envisioned her chasing Marisha to her room. Hiding behind a bush along the sidewalk, Talin listened to the conversation inside. He saw silhouettes of Marisha's parents through the window. It was cracked just enough for him to hear bits of their discussion.

"She needs to stay away from him, she'll tell him!" her father said.

"No, she won't. She knows better at this point."

"What if she does and the entire town finds out?"

"The entire town likely already knows," Mrs. Dyllon said, "Plus, they think it's Healer Dyllon anyways. Just stick with that."

"They've probably forgotten the other stuff by now."

What? What stuff?

Talin desperately wanted to stay and eavesdrop, but he'd promised his mother he'd come straight home. He'd already disappointed her once tonight and didn't want to get caught up too long. He turned quickly to jog home, hoping Marisha's parents did not step outside if the conversation escalated. Wasting no time getting back, he wanted to avoid all contact with people.

———

BACK HOME, he finally disposed of the trash bags in the receptacle. Inside, his mother was not in the kitchen. Her empty glass of juice sat on the table next to the tin foil-covered pan holding the remainder of his birthday cake.

What a birthday, he thought.

Feeling his ankle burning again, he went upstairs to shower. His mother's bedroom door was cracked and the lights were out. Hearing her breathing peacefully, nearly snoring, he left her alone.

In the bathroom, he undressed and started the water in the shower. He sat on the side of the tub and unwrapped Papa's handiwork from his ankle. It was a ghastly sight. Blisters had formed around his ankle, and streaks of black and blue bruises had popped up all around the puncture wounds. The rest of his lower leg was more red than his worst sunburn and blanched white if he touched it.

His hair was a sticky, sweaty mess from his shove off Dive Rock at the Falls and his body was covered in dirt and dust from climbing out of the Realm. He couldn't believe Marisha had hugged him tonight, twice.

Marisha...

He laid the pendants on his towel and stepped into the gentle spray of lukewarm water. Any warmer and he would have likely felt stinging bullets of pain across his leg and ankle. He made his shower as quick as possible, but his mother's lavender and vanilla body wash had never felt so good.

When Talin returned to his room, he slipped the pendants around his neck for safe keeping. Crossing to the window, he looked out at the tree. The breeze was soothing, but a hint of lighter fluid still mixed with the salty air.

Seated at his small desk, he propped his ankle up on the bed and used the previously opened bottle of aloe to coat his burns. He wrapped the ankle with an elastic wrap and colored bandana.

Plopping into bed, he rested his foot on a pillow and laid down, staring at the ceiling. He was exhausted. His mind bounced back and forth between being shoved off the outcropping at the Falls, nearly drowning in the Sluice, saving the goats, Marisha's hugs, and her parents' cryptic conversation he'd overheard. Each event threw a different emotion at him, stealing away precious minutes of sleep he desperately needed.

What would Healer Kingston think of last night?

Sleep was elusive again this night as Talin tossed and turned.

His ankle slid across the bed sheets, awakening him every few minutes it seemed, throbbing in pain.

TALIN'S ALARM clock was the sunrise. Forcing himself out of bed, he put on a shirt, tucking the pendants safely underneath. Hobbling to the bathroom to change the dressing on his ankle, he smelled breakfast.

Tenderly stepping downstairs, he tried not to limp, and prayed his stepfather wasn't home.

"Morning," he announced.

"Oh, good morning!" she said, spinning around from the stove where she was scrambling eggs. "Eggs this morning?"

He shook his head as usual. It would be cereal and toast. A small bit of leftover fruit he'd brought back from the Realm seemed appropriate as he gathered everything and sat down at the table.

"Marisha made it home ok last night?" she asked.

"Yeah, she's good."

I think.

She sat down to eat with him and both remained awkwardly silent for the first half of their meal. Her fork clinked against her plate and his spoon in his bowl. A bird chirped from the porch.

"So, how often do you need to go back to the tree? Is this going to be a daily occurrence? Every time you go, it seems you get hurt, and after last night, there's no telling what else is—"

"Mom, I'm ok."

"You don't look ok. Last night you were a complete filthy mess, everyone wanted to hurt you, grown men wielding knives at you. Marisha was so overwhelmed she passed out, and now...now you're limping from whatever happened after I left." It was obvious she was frightened. He wondered how much she truly slept. "And now the whole town will be talking about it and asking me a million questions. I won't know how to answer when I'm at work. The law is now involved, our property is a target for violence, not to mention your father and what he thinks about all of—"

"Mom," he interrupted her, even if it was only to allow her a chance to take a breath. "I don't know what's going to happen. I am figuring this out just like you are. But Papa will help, we'll get through it."

"Speaking of Papa helping you, what happened to you last night?" She asked, pointing at his ankle under the table.

"It's just a scratch, it's nothing." He didn't want to alarm her further.

"Scratches don't make people limp, smelling of aloe with their foot wrapped all the way up to their calf."

He stared at her, not wanting to answer and increasing her anxiety.

"What...happened?" She emphasized both words.

He had to tell her. There was no more hiding the things he had done, or would soon be called to do. If he expected her to trust him and allow him to become an adult, and the Healer, she had to know. Taking a breath, he mentally prepared himself.

"When we saw Papa last night, he told me I was needed in the Realm, then Marisha passed out. When you left...I went to get my pack by Jumbie and I really was going to go home, but Onca grabbed me and pulled me into the tree."

"Who?"

"Onca, he's a jaguar—"

"A jaguar?! What in the—Jaguars do not live on this island."

"I know, but they used to in parts of the Caribbean and the Realm isn't exactly like...*here*." He left out the small detail of this particular jaguar being engulfed in flames.

"I told you weeks ago there will be no more stories or lies in this house young man—"

"I'm *not* lying! You didn't believe me at first that I was Healer, then you didn't believe that Papa Bois was real, and now you've seen him with your own eyes. I've told you stories about the Realm," he said, although he had conveniently left out many of the more dangerous ones. "You've even ate fruit from the Grove, and now I am telling you there is a jaguar spirit that I have to deal with on top of dealing with the Dyllons. I don't know what else you want to know if you won't believe a word I say." Then his temper started to bubble. "Shall I tell you about the times I've nearly drowned in the Sluice?" She gasped. "Not once, but twice. What about the times Papa threw fireballs at me or sparred with me with our weapons while I hung on the edge of boulders or I ran barefoot across the boiling Fire Marsh or—"

"Enough!" she stood from her chair. Talin could see the terror in her eyes. "This is *not* what a Healer has done in the past, *not* what your great-grandfather did, and there were no stories about death defying circus feats or—"

"That you know of. Times are different now, Papa even said. It's different."

"Is that so?"

"Yes, everything is different." His eyes stared deep into hers, pleading with her to settle. "Is he home?" he asked while tipping his head towards the office.

She shook her head.

Thank goodness. If he was home he would have certainly made his way to the kitchen by now in a violent rage.

"So what does *he* think of all this?" Talin thought he knew, but...

She sat back down. "He doesn't know yet."

"Even after you left the house last night with a machete?"

"He heard the ruckus and left before I went to the tree. He hasn't been home since." Oddly, this worried Talin. Obviously, he would have been relieved to be rid of the man from the house. "He likely already knows by now or someone at the bar will certainly have told him. He comes home later and later. Some nights he hasn't even come home."

Where is he going?

He could see the anxiety growing in her eyes. "Maybe you should stay somewhere else for a little while," he encouraged, "just until some of this blows over a litt—"

"No. I'm not leaving you here and we aren't barging in on anyone else to let—"

"Just for a little bit, I'll be fine. I can stay in the Realm with Papa and maybe you could stay at Marisha's—"

"I will go nowhere near that family right now," she said, her voice stern.

"What's wrong with Marisha's? You like her parents."

"It's too close to the extended family, with all this," she waved her hands, "going on right now."

"Mom, especially with this going on right now. It would be safer for you to stay away a little while—"

"I *said*, I will not stay with the Dyllons." Her demeanor had changed in an instant. He could only wonder if it had anything to do with the conversation he'd heard the night before.

"It's not like it's Dewain's parents or anything, gee," he mumbled under his breath.

"Young man! You will not mention that family right now, do you understand?" Her hand smacked down on the table in front of him. It was shaking.

Talin was shocked. She had defended the Dyllon family before and always cared deeply for Marisha. She had never acted like this.

"Yes, ma'am." He stared in disbelief. "It was just an idea."

"A bad one at that. Keep coming up with ideas like that as Healer and no one on this island will trust you."

He did not understand. "What does that mean?"

"It's for another time, Talin, not right now."

"No, I think it's a good time right now because I don't understand, and I need to know a lot of things!" His voice was the most mature it had been since the conversation started, or ever. Completely confused, he needed to know why she was suddenly so defensive. "Tell me why it's not a good idea to be around the Dyllons except for the fact that I am Healer and Dewain isn't, and his family is going to be upset for awhile?"

"He threatened us last night Tali—"

"Dewain and his father did, not Marisha or her parents."

"You don't think that if one or both of us are at their family's house they won't show up causing trouble?"

"Marisha wouldn't let that happen, and *that's* not the person I am worried about hurting you. She can talk to her parents, they would understan—"

"No, Talin. They would not, they will always support their family first, as do most. I'm quite certain we are not welcome right now."

"But you're a family friend, why wouldn't they help you?"

A tear escaped her eye.

"What?" he asked. It was clear there was more to the story.

"I really can't tell you."

"Why not? I'm not a kid anymore! I'm trying to think of a way to help, so how about no more secrets from me and no more from you?"

He leaned forward across the table, reaching for her trembling hands, looking into her brown eyes. "Why can't you spend some time with the Dyllons for a little while?" he whispered.

"It's not them, it's your father."

"Yeah, I know, and if you are at Marisha's you'll be safe there from him—"

"Not that father, Talin," she interrupted.

"What?" he pulled back into his seat. "What do you mean my father? Who is he? What's going on?"

"Do you remember the man at the Induction last night who waited afterwards with Dewain and Amos?"

Adrenaline rushed through his body, starting from deep within his chest. "Is that...my dad?"

She explained the story.

"Talin, when I was younger...Anya and I were best friends, we grew up together." Talin's eyes grew large. "And...I fell in love with her brother, Javon."

Javon...

"He wanted to marry, but I wasn't ready." Her voice cracked. "Well, the marriage ended quickly and messy."

Anya is my aunt?!

He couldn't help but remember the way he'd been treated by her at the library with Marisha.

Talin had waited many years for the news about his father, then found it hard to stay focused on what he was hearing. Questions filled his mind at a record pace. Did Anya know who he was? Had she seen him in town since he and his mother returned from overseas? How could she treat family that way? Had Talin waved to his father walking to or from school or seen him at the market?

"Then you came along," his mother continued, "and I had a falling out with both of them." Her eyes were the source of a fountain of tears now streaming down her face.

Talin felt sick to his stomach, no words came, and he felt like he may have a panic attack. His mind was buzzing, reminding him of the over-ripened plum he'd eaten during his first trip into the Realm. This was not at all how he envisioned the conversation unfolding.

"What?" was all he could whisper.

"Talin, I'm sorry I didn't tell you sooner, but with everything with the Evocation and the Induction, I didn't think it was the time to talk about it. We were all so focused on different things."

"So, then Anya knows who I am?"

She nodded, wiping her cheek. "I've tried to keep you away

from her since we came back, but...for years she's known about you, but not actually seen much of you. I'm sorry, this is not how I wanted you to find out."

"I'm sure she *really* hates me right now."

"I don't think she hates you. She was just convinced it was her son that was to be Healer with their history. She probably hates me more because of her brother."

Crossing to her, he leaned down to hug her in the chair, "It's ok Mom."

Sobbing now, she grabbed his arms, holding onto him for what he thought felt like her life. Her fingernails dug into his skin so much he forgot about his sore ankle.

"Did she know about great-grandpa?" he asked.

She nodded. "Just enough."

THE THINGS that had occurred over the last several weeks were now starting to fall into place. Healer Dyllon had chosen Talin's great-grandfather to be Healer. So, clearly, the family had been friends of one another for a long time. But now, Dewain's family believed it was their 'turn' to have a Healer again. Talin couldn't help but think that Aunt Anya had threatened him in the library just to persuade him from attempting to be a possible heir. She seemed desperate for her son to be Healer and not her ex-best friend's child.

Talin worked up the courage to ask another question.

"Did you leave the island to get away from my Dad?"

"No. I left to get away from Anya."

What am I going to do now?

"Mom," he sighed, then whispered, "does Dewain know?"

"I don't know. He might." She tried to dry her tears and pulled Talin in front of her to face him, and he knelt in front of her like she was his queen. She had always fiercely protected him, and he'd always worshipped her, despite the forehead kissing. She was infinitely patient and caring, wise, kind, and strong, but now she seemed completely broken.

"Does Marisha know?"

"I'm not sure. She could have told them both over the years. I really don't know."

The answer crushed him. Now, he was dying to know if his best friend with the jet-black hair and angelic eyes knew he was related to her.

2

THE FOLLOWING MORNING, TALIN'S WORLD HADN'T STOPPED spinning. Events began to blur, complicating every memory. With no idea how to move forward, with the community, Dewain or Marisha, he now wondered which people knew who he really was and who didn't. Did Dewain not like him because of who he was or simply because he just didn't?

Talin needed to talk to someone. His mother hadn't emerged from her room, likely trying to calm her shattered nerves, he assumed. Marisha was likely grounded for going to the Induction and forbidden to speak with him the rest of her natural life. That left only Papa.

TALIN CRACKED his mother's bedroom door, leaving her as much privacy as he could, "Mom?"

"Yes."

"You ok?"

"I'm fine," she said.

"I need to go see Papa—"

"Talin, please—"

"Mom, I promise I'll be ok. I just need to ask him some questions."

He heard her sigh, "Ok." Hearing the reluctance in her voice, he felt she wanted to protect him, but with his new role it was probably extremely difficult for her.

"I'll be back."

He grabbed the pack and its contents from his closet and headed out the back door, tucking the necklace under his shirt.

JUMBIE WAS MAGNIFICENT AS EVER. It was as if the canopy had grown and filled in overnight. A gentle breeze rustled the outer leaves. The air was fresh and void of spilled rum. The sun glistened off the ocean below. Best of all, there were no goats to cut from the branches.

Talin climbed over the root to the portal and removed his knife from the bag, securing it on his hip. He strapped his pack to his shoulders and checked the wrap on his ankle, then pushed into the soft bark. He tipped backwards, but did not tumble over. Grabbing the first vine he felt, he gently controlled his descent into the darkened trunk all the way to the ground below. He pushed through the vines and into the Realm.

Another beautiful day awaited him. The ducks swam peacefully on the Lake. The sky was blue with minimal clouds and everything else was as emerald green as he remembered. Thankfully, Onca was not in sight, but Talin kept his head up and remained on high alert as he made his way to the Sphere to find Papa. Through the lush forest, and the Cemetery's gently rolling hills, he paced himself.

AT THE ENTRY to the Sphere, Talin removed his shoes and stepped over the porthole's circular frame of limbs—shoulders back with confidence. The area looked just as it did the first time he saw it, open and clear, free of vines, boulders, or odd agility obstacles. The blades of the weapons on the wall caught the morning beams of sunlight. There was only Papa Bois, seated atop the single boulder on the edge of the Drop.

"Welcome, Healer Talin." Papa motioned his hand for Talin to sit with him.

"Bonjour, Papa."

"Bonjour. You're back so soon?"

He sighed. "Yeah..."

"Is your foot healed?"

"Well, it's better, but it's not back to normal yet."

"You should be strong and ready anytime you enter the Realm."

"Yes, I understand, but...I needed to talk."

"I'm listening."

Talin stared into the turquoise water below them, wanting to explain the entire backstory and conversation he'd had with his mother, but cut straight to his point.

"I found out who my father was."

"And?"

"Did you know who he was?"

"Ah, Javon Hunte. I did."

"Why didn't you tell me?" he raised his voice.

Papa lifted his hand to settle Talin. "At the time, it was not important—"

"But it *was* important! He was at the Induction for Dewain! He's *related* to Dewain! Did you know my mother and his mother used to be best friends?"

He nodded, remaining calm.

"And that means that me and Dewain are *related*!"

"It does."

"And..." Talin settled his tone, but his voice nearly cracked.

"And?"

"That means me and Marisha are related, too," his voice was solemn and filled with disappointment.

"Ah, Marisha," he began, "you like her." His tone was half a statement and half a question.

Talin nodded with a silly grin on his face, his cheeks turning a hibiscus rose color on his tanned face. "Well, you know. She's...my best friend."

Papa smiled, almost chuckling.

"This will not change your friendship, I assure you—"

"But—"

"Are you ready for the day?" Papa swiftly moved the conversation on, not dwelling on Talin's concern.

"No, not really."

"What do you need to be ready?"

"Why didn't you tell me who my father was? What am I going to do around Dewain now?"

"First," Papa paused, "you are the Healer and will act accordingly around Dewain. He is, as you say, family as well. But you need not worry about him. Pertaining to your father, it was not important to know at the time, and was not my place to tell you. There was much to learn. You could not be distracted."

"Well, I'm distracted now, that's for sure."

"A perfect time to start then..."

"What?"

Papa walked to the wall. "Choose your weapon."

"Now? Are you serious?"

"Quite."

Why?

This was Papa. Always pushing, always testing. Whenever Talin had doubts that he could not complete a task or was too exhausted to continue, Papa pushed harder. Papa Bois always made the point that Talin had to be ready, make quick decisions, and persevere, no matter what was happening around him.

"Fine," he mumbled and stomped to the wall. He grabbed the machete, one about the same size that his mother had used to break up the Induction.

"Why the machete?" Papa asked.

"Felt right." Talin took his defensive stance, weapon raised and ready. "Are we going to do this or not?"

"It reminds you of your mother."

Talin rested the weapon at his side. "Seriously, what does that mean? You read minds now or what?"

Just then Papa lashed out with a ball of fire, distracting Talin, evident by his weapon's slow deflection of the flame. Papa swiftly grabbed the knife from Talin's hip and rendered its sheath empty.

"Stand down!" Papa commanded with Healer Kingston's knife in hand.

Talin looked down at his side, his mouth ajar.

"But—"

"Attention! Never let it wander!" He tossed the knife back to its rightful owner. Talin caught it, resheathing it on his side. "You need to focus if you are to defeat Onca."

Onca.

He'd momentarily forgotten about Onca since hearing about his biological father. A subtle, warm throbbing sensation in his ankle reminded him of the threat.

First Dewain, now Onca.

He dropped his head, but his eyes looked up toward Papa, "And how am I supposed to do that?"

"By being ready."

"For what?"

"Anything."

That's helpful.

Papa took a small sword from the wall and held it in the ready position in front of Talin.

"What does he want anyway? Is he a man, jaguar, a spirit, shapeshifter, or what?"

"All of the above, and he wants the Realm."

"The whole Realm?"

Papa nodded.

"I don't get it."

Papa lowered his weapon and motioned for Talin to do the same. "Onca is a spirit. But he once ruled as Healer, like you."

"I remember him saying that."

"He did not choose his successor. He was released from his duties and banished beyond the mountain range." Papa nodded toward the west, where Talin had seen the white peaks across the Lake. "But he has made his way back to the Realm."

"Why?"

"To defeat you."

"But, why was he banished?" Talin had barely registered Papa's latter statement.

"He led with malignity and heinousness. He was ill-tempered and abused his position."

"But someone had to have appointed *him*."

"Yes, but it was a poor decision."

"So, why challenge me now and not the other Healers?"

"What makes you think he hasn't?"

Oh.

Talin stared.

"He has chosen you because he could not defeat the great Healer Kingston."

"What?"

Papa lifted his weapon to Talin. "Are you ready to defeat the former Healer Hunte?"

"Wait, who?"

What did he just say?

Papa lashed out towards the young Healer, with more aggression than he ever had previously. Talin raised the machete and deflected the blow, then tossed the heavy blade aside, taking hold of his personal weapon. He moved in fast, advancing toward Papa, causing the old man to stumble. But he slowed his attack, not wishing to harm Papa.

"You do not stop when aggressing or defending!" Papa yelled. Talin doubled his effort, placing a hand on Papa's raised wrist and holding his blade to the old man's chest with the other.

"What did you say Onca's name was?!" he nearly screamed the words in Papa Bois' face.

"Well done, stand down."

Talin's own heavy breaths were all that filled his ringing ears. He had attacked in anger, and Papa had let it go. In shock, he froze, his stance solid as ice, but he was unable to pull his thoughts, or his body, away from Papa or what he'd said.

"Stand down!" Papa ordered again, raising his voice. His unarmed hand pulled Talin away from him, nearly tossing the boy to the ground with surprising ease.

Talin settled but stood tall. Staring at Papa with adrenaline coursing through this body, his fists clenched. "Who is Onca?" he asked again.

"Onca was Healer Hunte."

Hunte. The name echoed in his ears...

"You just told me that's my father's last name."

"It is."

"No, it was Dyllon, remember? My mom's ex-best friend's brother's family. The Dyllons." Talin shook his head, squinting his eyes as if it would make it easier to work out the cruelly twisted connections. "*How* is Onca related to my father?"

"He is your great-grandfather."

"No, that was Healer Kingston!"

"You asked about your father's side."

Talin stepped back and shook out his tingling hands, trying to dismantle his mounting nerves. "No, no, no, I don't understand."

"It's quite simple."

Talin shook his head. *No, it's not simple!*

Papa continued. "Let's get into the details later, right now you need to—"

"No, let's get into them right now. I need to know what's going on. Why am I here?"

"You are the Healer. Healer Kingston chose you."

"I got that part. Why does Onca—" he caught himself, "my great-grandfather want to kill me?"

"Kill is a strong word."

"He said himself he would defeat me or I would die!"

"Ah, yes, you're right, he did."

"What does he want from me?!"

"Onca wants the Realm as he likely cannot reclaim the title of Healer. Getting you out of the way would satisfy his thirst for revenge."

Talin worked out the ancestral family tree, again, as best he could in the short time. He knew both he and Dewain not only had connections to Healers, but were related to the same Healers, and they each were heirs to the title.

Was the family keeping score? He didn't know but it was all his gut kept screaming to him.

"What did Healer Hunte do that was so terrible?"

"Onca. He is no longer to be referred to as a Healer."

"Ok," he said, nervously twirling the knife in his hand. "But you just called him that." Talin figured it was a test, but Papa ignored his comment.

"He was a hunter, took more than what was needed. He felt entitled, made rules that benefited only himself. He did not protect people, nor things needing his protection. He knew no humility, no empathy, no compassion. Shall I continue?"

"No. So, who was Healer first? Dyllon or Hun— I mean, Onca."

"Onca. Chosen by Healer Clarke. But Healer Dyllon was the one who challenged and banished Onca."

"But, Healer Dyllon chose my great-grandfather Kingston."

"And he made an excellent choice...as did Healer Kingston."

Talin tried to smile, but it was difficult. He fought to make sense of the information rushing at him. The family ties, the lineage. Who was Healer Clarke?

"But if Onca is a spirit now, does that mean Healer Dyllon had to..." he struggled to use the word "*kill*— ".

"The Dyllon family is good," Papa paused, not answering the killing question directly, "for the most part."

A sinking feeling filled the pit of Talin's stomach. Nausea set in.

"The two dueled frequently within the Realm, but his death was not at the direct hand of Healer Dyllon. One does not just simply execute another Healer," Papa continued. "After his banishment, Onca never returned to the surface above. His disappearance was the subject of many stories."

"What really happened then?"

"Healer Dyllon led with honor. He was caring to those around him. He brought integrity and favor to the family."

"No, I meant Onca's disappearance."

Papa quickly changed the subject. "You must be ready to challenge Onca." Turning away, he walked to the Drop. "Are you ready to continue?"

"But I haven't— "

"No time. Details are not important right now. In order to defeat Onca, you must outwit him."

"How the heck do I outwit a spirit? Give him rice to count or knots to untie?" Talin's voice was saturated with sarcasm.

"Much more simple."

Talin looked blankly, expecting a scolding from his mentor.

"Onca uses fire to his advantage. People are fearful of it. What douses fire above?" He pointed above his head.

"Water." Talin said, staring into the Drop.

"Yes."

"Please don't shove me in again!" Talin jumped back.

Pap's laughter broke the tension. "No, you must choose to use the water."

"What?"

"Be comfortable with the flames. Be prepared to fight fire with fire, and if you fail, extinguish him with the sea." It sounded so matter-of-fact as he said it, like a fireman dousing a house fire with a high-pressure hose.

"Splashing a cat with water, got it, sounds easy enough." Talin said.

"I assure you it is not."

Great.

"A simple concept, but not easy. He will lie in wait for you if you take safety in the water. So if you are scared, you will live in the water like a fish. He is fast, stealthy. He will stalk you. He may follow you out of the Realm at night and disguise himself."

"So what do you mean fight fire with fire?"

Papa produced his trademark fireball from within his cloak and a twist of his wrist.

"With this." The ball hovered in the air between them.

"But—"

"Are you ready to play with fire?"

Whoa.

"Um...I...uh...I don't—"

"Ah ah ah," he shook a finger at Talin.

"But you said I couldn't do magic."

"You are a special case." Papa winked. "Small exceptions can be made."

What?! Wow!

"My mom is gonna freak out when she finds out I'm—"

"Stop worrying about your mother!" Papa interrupted, but caught his tone quickly. "At least in the way you are worrying. If you want to help protect her, you must learn. You have matured and she must let you go as well. You cannot stay a child forever. It is every mother's heartbreak." Talin's own heart splintered hearing the words. "You have many other people to worry about now, not just your mother."

THE FIREBALL FLOATED between the men, as if waiting for a command. Talin looked past it into Papa's eyes which were fixed upon the ball of light.

"Raise your hand under the fire."

Talin was too afraid to move a finger remembering how quickly the flame had grown out of control when he blew on it while being warmed in the Shelter after the blood rains.

Papa gently guided Talin's trembling hand toward the flame. "Close your eyes."

Talin hesitated, but did as instructed, his palm tingling from the intense heat.

"The fire is not hot. Feel it cool and soothing near your skin."

"But—"

"Shh. Concentrate."

Talin held his hand as still as possible. It still trembled. He pictured the soothing water of the sea against his skin when he stayed out in the sun too long, the way a cold glass of juice freshly squeezed by his mother felt in his hand and against his parched lips, and the relief of the shade beneath Jumbie's branches when he sat next to Marisha. Talin's hand slowly relaxed and a smile began to form on his face as he recalled the images, especially Marisha's.

"Good, that's right. Can you feel the difference?"

"Yes."

The flame was still hot, no doubt about it, but the fear related to it was diminishing. His hand did not touch the flame, he held it an inch or two below, allowing the heat to escape. He opened his eyes.

"Keep your hand below or beside the flame to guide it. Never above." Papa winked.

Talin nodded. Again, Papa moved Talin's hand, to the left and to the right. The fireball followed. Then up and down. Talin was in complete awe.

"But, it's like the fire knows that your hand is there, not mine."

"Very well then." Papa withdrew his hand away from Talin's. He nodded, signaling Talin to command the flame himself.

Talin licked his lips and took a breath. First, he moved his hand down and away from the flame, and it followed! Talin nearly laughed in delight. Then he moved his hand left and right. His half-grin turned into a full-on smile as he watched the fireball mirror his movements.

"Slowly," Papa said, "try a circle."

Talin carefully raised the ball in a clockwise motion, completely fascinated with himself.

"Now, bounce it."

"What?" His focus left the flame and met Papa's eyes.

"Just a gentle toss up, a few inches."

Forcing his hand upward, he pushed the miniature inferno into the air, and quickly pulled his hand down and away. Again, the flame followed. A hearty laugh erupted from within Talin. "Ha! Whoa! Did you see that?"

"I did."

Talin made the flame bounce a few more times and even changed hands mid-toss, catching the flame in the opposite palm. Talin's laughter continued.

So much easier than climbing rock walls or drowning in the Sluice.

"Now, throw it at me," Papa instructed.

"What?"

"Throw it."

"But, I can't thro—" The flames then shot up nearly a foot, just as they had when Talin had blown into the flame, and he jumped back from the intense heat. The fireball hovered in the air, waiting.

"You can. Come and throw the flame."

Talin approached again with caution.

"Calm yourself, control your thoughts. The flame is only warm. You must remain in control at all times."

"It's so hot."

"That's what aloe is for."

"Huh?"

"Go."

Talin refocused. He envisioned the soothing warmth of a beach bonfire on a cool evening, the feeling of his mother's oven door left open after baking her famous Black Forest cake, and the warm summer day when he laid on the beach with Marisha after his wave diving lesson.

Steadying his stance, he carefully moved his hand between himself and the flame, then pushed it forward towards Papa, unconsciously blowing the air in front of him like blowing out his birthday candles. The flames shot up into the air as it slowly moved forward. Papa bounced it back like a beachball.

"That's all you have? Again."

Talin pushed it back, his eyes not losing focus on the floating object. Papa sent it volleying back several times as Talin learned to control the flames. The force of Talin's push steadily became stronger as his confidence grew, but his skill was nowhere near Papa's impeccable control of the ball.

Papa Bois then scooped up some water from the Drop with his bullhorn and doused the flame with crackling sizzles and pops. Talin's jaw dropped as he watched the tiny blaze spark and smoke, turn to ice, then drop from its position in mid-air. It landed with a thud on the grass below.

"How did you do that?!" Talin exclaimed. A dry-ice like fog emanated from the baseball-sized mass, which now resembled something like a hailstone that he'd only seen on TV.

"There are things you should know about fireballs."

I guess!

"First, always be in control and know the weapon's limitations."

"It's a weapon?"

"Of course. Anything can be a weapon." Talin was listening closely. "As you've learned with different blades, they all have different uses, depending on the situation. Fire in this particular instance, from various sources, can be used against Onca."

"But he is already engulfed in flames. What's one more?"

"You must use it in conjunction with water. Everything has positive and negative energy. It's about upsetting the balance in this case."

Fire cannot turn into ice...

"But how do I *make* a fireball?"

"Any flame will do."

"But you pull them from your cloak. I can't do that."

"You can't?" Papa teased. Talin shook his head, still not sure of what to think of Papa's sense of humor. "You may pull from any source of fire or an ember."

"I can't just grab something that is burning."

"Why not?"

"Seriously? I'm not like you. I'll get burned!"

"We can fix that."

Talin's eyes widened at the words, wondering if Papa was attempting another joke.

"Or you can use this," Papa said, reaching into the bag on his shoulder and producing a fine powder, the darkest of gray, almost charcoal black, in the palm of his hand.

"What's that?"

"Firedust."

"That's not real."

"Isn't it?" Papa asked while he stepped away from Talin and threw the powder into the air with the force of a White Squall. The powder ignited in an instant, forming into hundreds of glowing embers that drifted on the wind. Papa caught one in his hand, then protected it from the breeze and blew into his cupped hands. When he opened his hands, a fireball had formed and then hovered, just as the ones he'd pulled from his cloak did. "It is from deep within the earth here– and Hosea Preserve."

Talin was shocked. Hosea Falls was indeed an incredible place, as Marisha had shown him, and apparently produced extraordinary things he knew nothing about. He wondered what other secrets Hosea Preserve held and if anyone *else* knew about firedust.

"Wow, so is that what you pull out of your cloak?"

"Sometimes. Firedust is from the old volcano that forms the side of the mountain at the Falls, but any ember can be caught." He shoved the newly-formed fireball in Talin's direction.

Holding up his hand, Talin blocked the ball from coming too close to his face, and it hovered respectfully.

Papa smiled, "Have you ever had a campfire on the beach?"

"Sure. A couple times." Talin pushed the ball back at Papa.

"Every ember has potential. It's just waiting for direction. Now, douse the flame."

Talin went to the Drop and bent down to scoop some of the water into his cupped hands. He carried it to the fireball, taking care not to spill much. He threw the water at the flames. It sparked and sizzled, then formed a solid ball of ice and fell to the ground. It was quite a bit smaller than Papa's first sizable hailstone.

"Not bad for your first attempt." Papa said. A smile crossed Talin's face from the compliment. "Now, take the dust and make your own fire." Papa sprinkled a pinch of the particles in the palm of Talin's hand. Talin recalled learning about the old volcanoes that formed the island thousands of years ago, but they had lay dormant for as long as anyone could recall. He felt like this was bringing it back to life and he loved it.

Curling his fingers up, just enough that the dust didn't spill out of his hand when he tipped it sideways, he prepared to hurl the powder as hard as he could into the air.

He took a breath, and swung his arm out.

The dust burst into tiny glowing embers drifting in the wind. Talin was mesmerized.

"Well, you'd better catch one," Papa said.

Talin stepped forward to grasp an ember, the closest one to him. It felt like when he used to catch fireflies in the UK as the flame bounced around in his clasped hands.

"Now, make it grow."

Blowing gently into his hands caused the fire to burn hotter and larger quite quickly. He let it go. The tiny flame, about the size of a marble, gently drifted down.

"Quickly, grab it before it hits the ground."

Talin shook his hands of nerves, then reached again for the flame, placing his hand below the flickering ball just before it hit the grass. It hovered in his palm just as Papa's fireball had a short time ago.

Wow.

Talin blew gently toward the tiny ball once again and the fire grew to the size of a golf ball. He caught Papa's smile from beyond his view of the flame.

"Throwing the firedust, that's how you should always throw a fireball. Now, send it to me," Papa said.

Talin pushed a cushion of air behind the ball, sending it to Papa Bois. The larger the fireball became, the lighter it appeared to be than the air around it.

"Why doesn't it fall when it's bigger? Before, it was falling, not floating, when it was smaller and lighter."

"Embers seek out air currents to follow. You have to give them direction."

Being one who loved science, Talin's confusion was plainly expressed on his face as he thought about how this seemed completely backwards to the laws of physics and gravity.

"The ember is lighter than air. It is easily carried into the wind where it is extinguished or it is instructed where to go. If you recall your beach bonfire, multiple embers escape and then disappear because you did nothing with them."

"Ok, but this ball is heavier and so it should just fall faster, even before you turn it to ice."

"But you've captured it. You commanded it, giving it life, purpose and direction." Papa winked.

"It's fire. It can't think." Talin snickered at the ridiculousness. Still, none of it made sense, but then again, he was in a place that hadn't made much sense from the start.

Papa held out his arm presenting the Realm around him, like a game show host revealing the contestant's newly-won prize. "But everything is different here."

Boy, isn't it?

"So, I can only throw fireballs within the Realm?"

"No."

"Then I can do party tricks at home?" He laughed.

"Absolutely not! You are the Healer now. Act accordingly."

Talin quickly humbled himself, but he desperately wanted to show this to Marisha and be able to practice his new skill when he was not in the Realm. But, would those backwards physical rules apply above too? Or was the firedust special just because it was magical?

Papa shoved the fireball back at Talin with great force. "Douse it!"

Talin ducked to avoid the flame then turned around to see it slow its trajectory past him and hover, as if waiting for another command from one of them. He half-expected it to make a boomerang motion and come flying back at him. Talin marched to the edge of the Drop, scooped up water into his hands and carefully carried it to the flame and splashed it.

Sizzling smoke erupted as the ball, again, froze to a solid block of ice and fell to the ground.

"Remember to use your weapons appropriately."

"What?"

"You've created a new weapon." Papa motioned to the frozen snowball.

"What do you want me to do with it?"

"You'll think of something." Papa walked towards the Grove. "Hungry?"

"Very."

They entered the Grove to pick their favorite snacks. Papa chose mango, Talin an orange. Returning to the work table in the Sphere, they cut the fruits using the knives from the wall. Papa handed Talin a wooden cup for juice. Talin cut his orange into small quarters, hand-pressing his own juice with the nearby mortar and pestle, then poured it into the cup and took a sip.

His eyes lit up instantly.

"Is it not well?" Papa asked.

"Wait!"

Talin ran to the three balls of ice that lay melting on the grass not far away and gathered them up. Returning to the work table, he crushed the ice into smaller chunks with a mallet and dropped them into the cups.

Instant ice-cold orange and mango juice were served.

"Well done," Papa said with a smile.

It reminded Talin of sharing the coldest fresh juices with his mother and Marisha after school. Wishing he could have shared many of those times with his father brought his thoughts back to the present and his family history.

Papa and Talin took their usual resting place on the boulder at the edge of the Drop. Talin had not thought about who Onca actually was since being distracted by his fireball training. He began asking questions again.

"So, let me make sure I got this straight, Onca is also my great-grandfather, yes?"

"Correct."

Talin swallowed a gulp of sweet orange juice, wiping his chin as it dribbled down. "He seems evil. Is he really going to try and kill me?"

"Likely so." Papa's answer was just as direct, causing Talin to catch his breath again.

"Why does he want to kill his own family?"

"A number of reasons. Power. Revenge. The Realm."

"But does he want to come back as Healer? Can he even *do* that?"

"He could, but he knows it would not work to his advantage. It's been too long. The Realm would be better. But he would take either option. Being Healer would get him closer to his desire in the Realm."

"So he wants to overthrow you and not me?"

"Both."

"But he can't do *that*, can he?"

"Anything is possible if we are not prepared."

"You said he challenged Healer Kingston. Did he try to overthrow you before?"

"He has not directly challenged me for the Realm, as of yet, if that is what you are asking. But it's coming. I will need a strong Healer by my side to defeat him. Can you do it?"

Talin hesitated, "I'll try."

"There is no—"

"There is no try, yes, I know."

3

TALIN EMERGED FROM THE TREE AFTER A DAY OF REVIEWING weapon work, progressing with his firedust training, and learning more bits about the history of Onca. The afternoon sun was well overhead.

His head ached, still absorbing the startling news regarding his new, twisted family ties—no earthquake needed to rattle his nerves.

LEFTOVER CAKE SAT on the table as he entered the house and he dove into a hearty piece, the cherries tasting a bit more tart than usual.

As he finished his slice, he caught a whiff of rotten egg but couldn't pinpoint the source. The kitchen was in its normally spotless state, no unwashed dishes in the sink. Opening the fridge, he found no damaged eggs from his mother's morning gather. Inspecting the rooms on the main floor, he found nothing.

Then he heard it.

Heckling outside the front of the house, the subtle thump of what sounded like small hailstones, which the island had never seen. All his senses were on high alert. Peeking out of the partially opened window, Talin saw Dewain and his posse pelting eggs at the front of the house from the modest lawn of weeds.

Those better not be from our coop.

"You will never be Healer!"

"Go back across the pond, you don't belong here!"

"Thief! You will pay!"

Thief?

"It belongs to me and if you don't give it back, I'll just take it!"

"Dewain is Healer!"

"Don't even think of going back to the Falls!"

What?

"Oooh, mommy had to come save you with a butcher knife!" Laughter followed. "Coward!"

On and on the insults came, along with the eggs dripping their foul stink down the partly opened window and oozing mustard-color yolk onto the sill. His stepfather wasn't home to chase off the boys with his own butcher knife and Talin knew better than to confront the group alone. It was better to lie low inside the house, charading that no one was home. Talin hadn't noticed if anyone was watching him take the trek from Jumbie to the house, but now he assumed they had been.

Rule number four, pay attention—and everywhere, not just the Realm.

He moved carefully to check that the front door was locked and then checked the back porch.

Would they really be so bold to come in?

Gathering a few towels from the kitchen, he returned to the living room to place them on the floor underneath the windows, keeping the stickiness dripping down the wall from ruining the carpet below. As Talin stood up to close the window, an egg came sailing through and cracked open on the back of his head. He muffled his surprise to avoid being detected.

"Come out. We know you're in there!"

"Chicken!"

"Oh no, the chickens!" they teased, "I can't *eat* the chickens!"

More laughter.

He was not about to come out. Talin considered the possibility that Dewain, in fact, did not know they were related. Would a family member really treat another so badly? Talin wasn't so sure Dewain would care either way. After all, he had seen how his mother was treated by her own husband.

Talin chose to wait out the assault as long as he could, double checking that all the open windows had been shut. Within a few minutes, the boys outside seemed satisfied with the damage they had caused or ran out of eggs. None of them dared enter the chicken coup to pilfer more ammunition. Their calls could be heard fading out in the distance as they headed toward Jumbie.

Don't you dare, Talin thought.

He watched as the group dangled from the limbs like monkeys, cackling, yelling and laughing, most certainly discussing their "successful" raid on the Williams' home.

Talin waited to leave the house until the ruffian trespassers had left the back property. He didn't bother calling the police. He had to pick his battles, and he knew full well more were coming. He cleaned up bits of egg that had made their way inside the windows, and lit a few of his mother's favorite candles to cover the rotten odor. Talin concluded that the boys must have brought the eggs from home, his mother never let them sit in the coop past morning.

Going outside, he grabbed the garden hose and sprayed as much egg off of the house as he could. Although, rinsing the gooey mess only made matters more difficult, especially on the windows, which streaked a putrid milky foam. The only thing that would have made it worse would have been sprinkling flour or chicken feathers on top. He was grateful they hadn't thought of it.

After he was done rinsing, he tried his best to clean the windows with glass cleaner. Those on the ground floor cleaned up well, but the second story proved more difficult to reach. Precariously leaning out his mother's bedroom window, he attempted to shine it streak-free before anyone came home. Any damage to the house would be dealt with swiftly by his stepfather's belt or worse, no matter who caused it. Mr. Williams would most certainly find a way to tie it to Talin and the tree anyway. Once finished, he blew out the candles and retreated to the shower.

GETTING DRESSED, he wrapped his healing ankle, tucked the necklace back inside his shirt and went downstairs to check on things. His mother was unloading fresh groceries in the kitchen before dinner, and his stepfather was back in the office.

"Hi, Mom. Do you need help?"

"Oh, thank you, dear. Could you put away the ice cream, please?"

"You got ice cream?" The excitement was evident in his voice.

She smiled.

"Well, we had leftover cake and it just didn't seem right without ice cream. I can't believe I forgot it before."

"Thanks, Mom." If there was anything better than leftover birthday cake, it was leftover birthday cake with vanilla bean ice cream.

He finished helping with groceries, then folded the brown paper sacks to store as his mother began to prepare the evening meal.

"So," she asked below her breath, "how was today?"

He glanced towards the office, the door was shut.

"It was good."

"What did you do?"

He didn't want to answer, but he had promised. No more secrets.

"Threw fireballs." He said it so matter of factly, she seemed to miss the words.

"You what?"

"Yeah," he said, shrugging as if it was no big deal.

She leaned in close to him, her voice still low. "What do you mean threw fireballs?"

"Just like it sounds." He flashed a confident smile at her. She didn't answer, a concerned look on her face. "It's ok Mom. I'm not seven anymore."

Judging by her expression, Talin didn't think his joke made her any more confident about the situation. "Sorry." He made a conscious effort to avoid future snarkiness. Papa had said he was Healer now, and to act like it.

"Mom, I need to ask you something."

"Ok," she said, as she pulled pots and pans from the cabinets.

"But I can't right here," he said, tossing a glance towards the office.

"Can it wait till after dinner?"

"Yes, ma'am."

TALIN HELPED PREPARE THE CASSEROLE.

"Did you clean today?" she asked him.

"Clean what?"

"The house. It smells like lemongrass."

"Oh, yeah, it's your candle."

He left out why he had cleaned the house.

"Thank you."

"You're welcome, I kind of had to."

"What do you mean?"

He hadn't meant to let the last part slip out and didn't answer right away. "It just...needed to be cleaned, that's all."

"Why? I clean this house every day." She turned towards him

with a hand on her hip, looking just like Marisha when she'd scolded him not long ago. "What happened?"

His stepfather emerged from the office to get his pre-dinner drink. Talin let out a cough, "Excuse me," and turned to wash his hands in the sink.

"What's for dinner?" Mr. Williams asked.

"Rice and a casserole."

"What time?"

"About an hour. I'll come get you," she told him.

He filled his glass with spiced rum and calmly returned to the office, shutting the door behind him.

Why was he feeling so content?

"So..." she said, turning back to Talin, waiting for a reply.

"I washed the house."

"What do you mean you *washed* the house?" She tilted her head curiously.

"Like, the outside of the house."

"Then why would you burn candles *inside* the house? What's going on?"

"Dewain egged the house," he said, then he quickly turned to fill a large pot with water. "Do you want me to start on the noodles?"

"He *what*?"

"I cleaned it up."

"I told you things were not—" she stopped mid-sentence. "You're lucky your father hasn't found out about this, young man."

"He's not my father. We've been through this."

His mother didn't answer, but Talin recognized the scolding look on her face. "And speaking of him, where does he live? Because I'd like to talk to him."

"Talin—"

"What? I just want to talk to him."

"I don't think that's a good idea."

"Why?"

She turned to the cabinet and removed a bag of noodles. "Good idea. Here, why don't you start on the noodles. I didn't have a chance to make them, so I bought packaged."

"Why do you hate him so much? It's the man with the rum you should hate."

"Talin Boyce," her voice stern, "you will not speak to me like that *ever* again, do you understand?"

Talin knew he was wrong, and quickly remembered he was going to try not to be snarky. It hadn't lasted long, but the topic had been boiling inside him for far too long.

"Yes, ma'am."

It was apparent to Talin that, although his mother had finally disclosed who his father was, she would not likely partake in the conversation Talin wanted to have after dinner. At least not willingly. They had both agreed to no further secrets, but now he wondered if it was going to be harder for her than him.

Does it really matter if she knew about Healer Hunte? he wondered.

It did to him.

WHILE THE CASSEROLE WAS BAKING, Talin's mother tasked him with feeding the chickens. It was a mentally conflicting chore for him. Talin loved caring for animals and found it relaxing to see them pecking away at crushed corn, but it made him uneasy knowing why. Many of their lives would be cut short once he fattened them up. Their lives were in limbo and he sympathized with them on a certain level. Although he wasn't in danger of being someone's evening supper, he was in danger of being hunted, but the chickens had no idea they'd soon be killed. He glanced up in Jumbie's direction wondering how he would ever balance the two worlds.

"Talin," his mother called from the back porch.

"Coming."

HE AND HIS mother sat together on the back steps.

"You wanted to ask me something?" she said.

"Yeah, but you probably don't want to talk about it."

"I just don't think it's the best time to recontact your father."

"That's not what I was going to ask."

"Oh?"

Taking a deep breath, he asked, "When you were with my dad, did you know his grandfather was a Healer, too?"

She looked confused. "How did you know that?"

"Papa Bois told me."

She stared out at the tree. "What else did Papa tell you?"

"You mean about Healer Dyllon taking his place?"

She lowered her head with a heavy sigh. "Yes."

"He told me Healer Hunte was banished."

"That is how the story goes apparently."

"Well, he's back."

"Who's back?" she asked.

"Healer Hunte."

She whipped her head toward him. "That's impossible."

"Do you remember the jaguar spirit I told you about?"

Fear was apparent on her face as Talin tried to continue. "Healer Hunte was banished to the Realm, but as a spirit, and now he's back—"

"No. No, that is impossible." Panic was creeping into her usually soothing voice.

"Mom. It's true. It's the jaguar that hurt my ankle." Her eyes fell to his injured limb. "But they call him Onca now and he wants to—"

"Kill you." She finished the sentence for him.

"How do you know that?" He sat back, acting as if it were the first time he had heard about the threat to his life.

"He challenged your great-grandfather as well."

"You know about that? How come you didn't tell me all this stuff?"

"I'm sorry, there's just so much that has happened recently. I wasn't sure if it was the time. All these years I had hoped you would be Healer but was so afraid, then I didn't believe it, I didn't want to bring it up, then Anya's husband...but you needed to learn first, and..." Her head was in her hands in disbelief. "I can't lose you, Talin."

"Mom, if I am going to be as safe as I can be doing this, then I am going to need to know everything you know about our family and the Healers. I need to be ready."

Her hands dropped from her head to both knees and she rubbed her palms nervously.

"Ok." Taking a deep breath and keeping her voice low, she began. "Your father and I were very young when we were married. Again, I wasn't ready to get married, but I did anyway." She continued rubbing her palms and was slowly rocking forward and back.

"When I was pregnant with you, I began to have dreams that you were going to be the Healer. I thought I was just stressed.."

A premonition?!

Talin listened intently. She explained that the very day she found out she was pregnant the dreams began. They'd come at least once a week the entire pregnancy. As his delivery neared, she would dream almost daily. She described them in vivid detail. At first, she dreamt that her grandfather stood at the end of her bed in the middle of the night, telling her that her child would be the next Healer. She didn't believe it.

After Talin was born, the dreams went on until he was about two years old and became more detailed and terrifying. She saw him burning in a fire, people screaming, and she was unable to help him. She didn't know how this particular dream ended, as she would always wake up in a panic, running to the crib to check on him.

"And around that time, I finally told Anya about the dreams because they were becoming more intense and..." She rubbed her eyes, her hands starting to shake ever so slightly. "That's when things really got messy and I had the opportunity to study in England, so I left. It was safer that way."

"How did things get messy?"

"It was like Anya completely changed overnight. She refused to speak to me. There were threats made against me...and you—"

"From who?"

"The Dyllons. Amos specifically." A single tear escaped, rolling down her cheek and over her quivering lip.

Talin was confused.

"After things settled in England, and I met Robert, it was hard to come back here, but my mother needed me. Robert thought it would be a permanent vacation." She shook her head, eyes closed.

"The dreams stopped when we were in England?"

"They subsided for a time after we left here, and then stopped. But the closer we got to returning, they started again. Even more intensely than before."

"Do you have them now?"

Opening up more, she'd said most of the dreams came to her while she was taking care of her mother, but again, thought it was related to stress.

"This time I only told my mother about them, realizing there were too many coincidences to just be stress. She was the only one who seemed to understand. But her memory had already started failing her, so I don't know how much she really understood."

His mother continued, saying Robert had become more irritated with her. He told her she'd spent too much time away from home and it was one of the reasons he began drinking so much. He'd tried to stop. She explained that Robert truly thought he'd be living a dream life in the Caribbean. But relaxing on the beach, taking cata-maran tours, and deep sea fishing trips were not what happened. Robert sat waiting for her to come home tired and exhausted from being a full-time caregiver every night. He'd even accused her of having an affair and not being with her mother. They were growing apart.

Knowing how Robert felt about the island folk stories by that time, she tried ignoring the dreams, willing herself to believe the community rumors about the Dyllon family being next in line as Healer. "I didn't want to risk tangling with the Dyllons bringing everything up again," she said.

Eventually, she had to place her mother in a local care home when her needs became too overwhelming. When his mother's visits became less frequent to the care home, the dreams, too, began to subside...until the Evocation.

"So, I guess you can't ignore fate," she whispered.

Piecing the stories together, Talin remembered how his mother had reacted, not believing him the day he told her he was Healer. Was she that frightened of the Dyllons and what they would do?

"Anya doesn't know the dreams came back?"

"Goodness, no. We haven't spoken since I left the island after we were threatened."

"What exactly were the threats?"

She shook her head again, obviously not wanting to answer.

"Mom, I need to know. It's important now."

A heavy sigh escaped her lips before she spoke. She wiped a tear from her cheek.

"When I first told Anya about my dreams, she seemed shocked. She said she had them, too, when she was pregnant with Dewain."

What?

"She said it was common for families who have had Healers to think their child will be the next and, if that were true, I'd have different dreams, not the same ones over and over. She was convinced Dewain was the next Healer, as he was born first. She told me to ignore them and the tree would decide anyway. The next day, Mr. Dyllon stopped by the house..." Her words trailed off.

The familiar clinking of ice dropping into a glass sounded behind them. She waited until they heard the office door shut again to continue. "I'd never seen Amos in such a way before. He said Anya had never been my friend and she was just being nice since her brother liked me for so long. If I interfered with their family legacy, he would send the Heartman for you."

The who?

"It just didn't make any sense. I'd never heard him speak this way before or seen such evil in his eyes. It was best for me to leave to keep you safe. I packed that evening while you slept and we left the next morning."

"Who's the Heartman?"

"Papa Bois hasn't told you?"

He shook his head.

"He's an evil spirit, in the body of a man, who carves the beating heart out of children's bodies. He gives them to the devil and in return is granted longer life."

"Oh mom...that's not tru—"

"It is! You are the Healer. And you need to be aware of these spirits, just like the Old Hag or La Diablesse, if you are going to protect the island! The Heartman sometimes takes the life of adults, but children are much easier targets."

"Ok, but you really can't be serious on that one."

"Oh? And a fiery jaguar is real?"

She had a point...

Trying to understand her point of view, he thought about how she had been young and impressionable at the time, maybe seen as an overprotective, crazy single mother with her premonitions and dreams. But there was a time, not long ago, he hadn't believed any of the legends either. Now, Papa Bois was the closest thing he had to a father-figure.

"So, what else do you know about the family Healers?" he asked, trying to change the subject.

"Both of your great-grandfathers were Healers. But...no one likes to talk about Healer Hunte."

"Why? What did he do?" He knew generalities from Papa but wanted to see if his mother had any additional details about the stories.

"I suppose Healer Hunte made poor decisions."

"Like?"

"His power. Being in charge. From what I recall, everything was about him, not the people, not the island. It caused lots of problems. That's when Healer Dyllon stepped in. The Dyllons are good people in that regard."

He let out a laugh, quickly stifling it after what he was learning tonight.

Dewain acts like he wants to follow in Onca's footsteps.

THE TWO STARED at Jumbie in silence. The evening trade winds carried salty air from the ocean across the old cane field and his mother took in a deep breath. Talin's hair blew into his face and he brushed it back behind his ear. Tree frogs began to sing. The sound of waves crashing onto the shore drifted from beyond the hill. Dipping behind the tree, the sun was nearly at the horizon over the sea. The water glistened and twinkled as the tide rolled in.

"What did my Dad think of all that?"

"About Healer Hunte? He was embarrassed, but he was a child when it happened. He told me he was told the story his family wanted him to believe growing up."

"And what was that?"

"Mostly stories revolving around Healer Dyllon and how

wonderful he was and how horrible the Huntes were and not to mention his name, or that they were related. It hurt him growing up. I think it's one of the reasons Anya liked Amos."

"Why?"

"She thought by changing her name from Hunte to Dyllon, it would associate her with a good Healer."

Oh...

"Did your dreams predict anything else about me?"

"I don't recall predictions other than you being Healer, but that recurring dream about you in a fire..." She dropped her head.

"That would be Onca then."

"No, it was a real fire. You were trapped...and I couldn't save you. You were a teenager, about the age you are now. You were in a ball of flames, like a cyclone. I could only scream. Other people were screaming. But you...you were quiet. I was sure you were dead."

Talin gazed at his mother. Tears had welled up in her eyes again, but didn't escape.

"In your dreams, do you know who the next Healer is after me?"

"No dear...that's up to you."

Talin caught his breath.

"I'm sure Papa will guide you in that regard...when it's time."

"When do you think I do that?"

"Shantel!" a voice interrupted. "How much longer for dinner?"

"Not much longer dear. I'm getting ready to check," she answered.

"I'll go set the table," Talin said, hoping that his willingness to help in the kitchen would keep the peace tonight.

He opened the door for his mother, and she rested her hand on his cheek as she passed by him. Another clink of ice in Mr. Williams' glass resonated from the kitchen.

THE FOLLOWING DAY Talin completed his chores after breakfast then sat on the back porch staring at Jumbie. Deep in thought, he tried making sense of the family dynamics and his mother's dreams. He wanted to talk to Marisha, but his stomach flipped at the thought. It was too much, too soon, trying to retrain his mind that his bully, and his best friend whom he adored, were now both his relatives—had always been. His mother was related to the most respected Healer in recent history and his father related to the worst. His emotions were a tangled mess.

Even though his mother confirmed she knew both sides of Talin's family's history related to his new role, she couldn't provide many additional details or guidance on how to proceed. He needed more information. The only other person who knew everything for sure was Papa.

Talin had just been to the Realm, and was leery of returning so soon with an angry, fire-breathing jungle cat on his trail. Although his ankle was recovering and the pain had nearly subsided, he showed a noticeable limp when he was overly tired. Watching British nature documentaries had taught Talin that predators, especially wild cats, could score an easy meal by hunting wounded and slower prey. He didn't want to attract any more attention than necessary, but wasn't accomplishing anything above ground at the moment. Then he wondered if daily trips underground were part of his responsibilities, Papa hadn't said. How often was he supposed to go?

He decided to return to the Realm.

Gathering his pack from his closet, he left the house without a word. On the trail, his steps were full of determination and a new confidence. His pace steadily met the anticipation of the new challenge ahead.

He was going to sort the truth, stop Dewain's effort at overtaking him as Healer, and conquer Onca once and for all.

4

———

TALIN PEERED THROUGH THE VINES AND ROOTS BEFORE CAUTIOUSLY entering the Realm. The morning was clear and sunny. With no sign of Papa or Onca, Talin started the hike to the Sphere, rehearsing his questions on the way, fully expecting a new physical challenge as soon as he arrived that would take the place of his fact-gathering discussion.

AT THE PORTHOLE, he removed his shoes and leaned in head first, chin up, and stepped onto the grass, thick and soft beneath his feet. As he'd suspected, the Sphere had been transformed. It looked like a jungle gym of ropes and vines—for spiders.

What now?

Strung from one wall to the other, the strands were tied at various intersecting points and spread in every direction within the training area.

Talin carried his pack to the wooden table along the wall and removed his knife. He strapped the blade to his side, leaving the pack on the table, then turned to further inspect the obstacle hanging above him.

At the center, above the Drop, it looked like a giant spider had spun its web straight across the Sphere. Only this spider had to have been much larger than an average human. Surrounding the perfectly symmetrical center of the web was a random assortment of asymmetrical shapes formed by the criss-crossing rope-like vines, resulting in larger openings further away from the tightly spun ones at the center. It appeared quite rugged, but looked like the hanging vines that he once climbed here had gone completely haywire.

I'm gunna have to climb that.

He studied the area, the web's angles, and some of the lower dangling ropes that, certainly, were there to allow him to ascend up to the web. He tested their strength and elasticity with a light tug. Like the vines he had climbed previously, some were stiff, others more pliable.

"Good morning, Healer Talin." He heard Papa's voice from across the Sphere. He stood at the porthole to the Grove.

"Bonjour, vieux Papa."

Papa smiled and bowed his head to Talin, then met him at the boulder.

"You are back soon."

"I wanted to talk to you about some things."

"No time for talk." He motioned to the ropes around them.

"I knew you'd say that. Really, I just need a few minutes."

"What is your worry?"

"I need to know what happened to Healer Hunte."

"Onca." Papa reminded him.

"Yes, sorry, Onca. When he was Healer, what exactly happened?"

"Can you climb to the center of the web?"

"Papa..." Talin began, "probably, but I need to know this first."

"Climb and talk. We waste time standing still." Papa motioned for Talin to start. "Go."

Here we go again.

Talin climbed onto the boulder and grasped the nearest hanging rope, pulling on it to test its security. "You're going to tell me what happened then, right?" he asked, glancing back.

Papa nodded. "Go."

Talin easily climbed several feet up the rope, then wrapped his hands around a chunk of knots on the web. Swinging his legs up and over the rope into an inverted position, he dangled like an unco-ordinated monkey. When he situated himself awkwardly atop it, he stretched out over the rope's intersection with a sigh. Lying on his belly, he looked down through the holes at Papa.

"So? What did he do?"

"Onca's soul has not settled."

"Ok, and?"

"Cross the inner web."

"Grrr," he protested. He'd hoped for more than a single sentence answer. He needed specifics. Carefully rising to balance all fours on the ropes, Talin tried climbing to the center of the web. The contraption shook beneath his body. Bouncing as the vines and ropes sagged, he flipped upside down again. Holding on tight, he wrapped his legs around the vine to keep from falling. It took twice as much strength to right himself.

"So what did Healer Dyllon actually *do* to Onca?" he called down with a grunt while scuttling toward the middle of the web.

"He won the Elimination."

Talin's head whipped back, throwing him off balance again. "The what?" he said, hanging precariously from the web. "What is *that*?"

"A trial when one Healer challenges another. Keep climbing."

A trial? Why?

Talin kept climbing toward the web's center, calling upon his memory of how both monkeys and lizards navigated through the trees. Creeping closer to the middle, each of Talin's limbs absorbed the bounces separately. It wasn't graceful. But, climbing up all of the swinging vertical vines in the Sphere not long ago had definitely prepared him for this task. He picked up his pace as he approached the outer edge of the web's tightly woven center. The entire structure swayed like a hammock. He could only imagine what happened at this so-called *trial*.

"So, what happened at the Elimination?"

"Healer Dyllon won."

I got that part...

A frustrated grumble erupted from Talin's throat at nearly the same time his hand touched the inner web. The web immediately bled out a substance similar to warm bubblegum stuck to the underside of his shoe on a hot summer day. His growing pace had come to a messy halt, stranding him on the edge of the innermost and outer web.

"Onca will challenge you. Soon." Papa continued, "You must be ready for anything."

The more Talin struggled to avoid the off-white colored goo, the more it adhered to him as he tried to free himself from the life-sized arachnid's entanglement.

"What *happens* at the Elimination?" He continued to push Papa while desperately, and unsuccessfully, attempting to get to the web's center and render the chore complete.

He'll probably make me crawl back through this muck and rinse off in the Sluice!

"A series of challenges, designed to prove the strength, character, and abilities of a Healer." Papa paced back and forth below Talin, eyes to the ground.

Talin thought he would call for him to come down, only to instruct him to climb back up, faster. But Papa didn't give any instruction and Talin was rightfully and genuinely stuck this time, feeling like he was cocooned in a wad of chewing gum.

"Can you get to the center?" Papa asked.

"No, I'm stuck."

"That's too bad. The papaya is wonderful this morning."

Papa crossed to the table and began to make himself brunch from fruit he had brought in from the Grove. Talin looked down, seeing several papaya piled in a bowl and Papa slicing them one by one. The clunk of his knife struck the butcher block table. Talin was sure he could smell the sweetness drift into the air, and his mouth began to water.

"Could you help me down, please?"

"No," Papa replied simply, then went to sit on the boulder with his chopped fruit.

Talin's frustration was growing, but the more he squirmed, the more he found himself involuntarily clinging to his trap. The only thing that would make it worse would be a human-sized spider arriving to devour him.

"Hey!" he called down.

"Mm?"

"There's no spiders in the Realm, are there?"

There had already been half-human serpents and a jaguar spirit to greet him at the end of previous excursions, so it made sense in his mind that he would meet an eight-legged creature today.

Papa swallowed a bite of papaya and had a laugh.

"Well, is there?!"

"Come down for brunch."

"I. Can't. I'm stuck!"

"You are never stuck." Papa said, taking another bite.

Talin's temper flared. He twisted and writhed against the web until there was little left of him that wasn't cloaked in gooey globs.

He's really not going to help me this time? I could hang here all day!

In fact, Papa barely looked up to see what progress, if any, Talin had made in escaping his snare.

"I can't believe you aren't going to help me!"

"I won't always be around to help you. You must learn to be resourceful." Papa's voice was calm.

Yeah, well, I haven't got any resources against goo, I only— hey wait!

Talin carefully twisted his arm to his side, finding that the slower and more deliberately he moved, the less the web oozed of its petrifying concoction, and was able to reach the knife on his hip.

"Yes!"

Talin started cutting away the trap confining him. After each cut, his body fell slightly lower than before as, one by one, pieces of the web gave way underneath him.

Clinging to only a few strands, he double checked which pieces he'd slice next to avoid plummeting straight into the Drop—somewhere he really did not want to go again.

"Ah, I see you've learned resourcefulness have you?" he heard from below.

Holding onto the last piece of web, Talin hesitated to make his final cut.

Papa looked up at him. "Healer Dyllon battled Onca fearlessly," he said, stepping away from the boulder. "It was mostly a fair and equal battle. But in the end it was his boldness that set him apart."

Talin hung precariously with one arm directly over the Drop. Staring into the ominous and beautiful turquoise water, he didn't want to let go. He knew he'd rather not hang all morning either, wearing out his shoulder. But there was nowhere else to go, unless he traversed through more goo to get to one of the hanging ropes.

"When it was time for the Fire Summons, Healer Dyllon turned the flames towards Healer Hunte. Hunte was unable to fight them off. It burned him so badly, the damage was irreversible. Then he was banished to the Barrenlands, beyond the mountains."

"He *what*?"

"Theoretically, he could burn forever."

Who banished him?

Talin bounced and swayed from the elasticity on the final strand of web. Carefully switching hands, he tried to save his grip strength, while more gelatinous secretions oozed down his wrist and covered his arm. He couldn't hold on much longer.

"If one is to defeat Onca again, he must not only be resourceful, but bold."

Bold.

Talin thought about his most pressing choice. He could either cut himself loose from the web, falling into the Drop to be flushed away by the Sluice, or climb back up the web making his way to an edge and climb down, likely getting stuck again in the process, maybe even becoming a meal for a giant spider he hadn't met yet. As much as he hated it, the Drop was the quicker—and bolder, choice.

Rule number five. Make a decision.

Clutching his knife, he swiftly sliced the rope above his grasp and fell.

Talin splashed into the pool below like a cannonball and the waters began to churn. He quickly resheathed his weapon.

Remaining as calm as possible, he worked on controlling his breathing: slow and steady. Closing his eyes, he gathered his thoughts. The water spun faster, the force pushing him to the edge of the pool. He knew what came next: the water forming a funnel beneath him, then pulling him down into darkness.

Opening his eyes, he looked for Papa's reaction. His hand was outstretched from the edge of the pool as Talin spun past him.

"Reach!" Papa Bois yelled.

On Talin's next pass by Papa, he stretched his tired arm as far as he could and grasped the old man's hand. The catch had been enough to sweep any strong man off his feet, and into the turbulence with him—but Papa was no ordinary man, and stronger than several of the strongest combined. A bit of sticky goo didn't hurt either.

The Drop's suction fought against him, threatening to send his shorts into the Sluice. Talin held onto Papa with every bit of strength he had as the water crashed into him, tossing and twisting him from the force. Papa Bois leaned back, pulling Talin from the water with ease.

On the pool's stone-lined edge, Talin winced from his battering.

JOINING Papa for refreshments was always welcome after a physical challenge. Teaching and learning always accompanied a snack or a meal. And Papa Bois was right, the papaya was amazing today.

"What's the Fire Summons?" Talin asked.

"One of the challenges of an Elimination."

"What are the other challenges?"

"Earth Ritual and Water Rite."

"The elements?"

Papa nodded. "The Healer must be in touch with the natural world around him in order to protect it."

"What happens in all the challenges?"

"It changes."

"How come?"

"The elders set up the matches."

"So, do the Healers know about them ahead of time?"

"Some could, depending on their relationship with the elders."

"So, is this where Onca wants to challenge me?"

Papa didn't answer.

"I can just see this flaming cat talking with the elders about me," he laughed. "I bet they freaked out when they heard him talk."

Again, Papa didn't answer, which likely meant he knew more than he chose to say. Talin composed himself. "Well, I guess I need to know what the Earth and Water challenges have been before because Onca is likely going to win the Fire Summons, seeing how he is made of it. So, is it two out of three wins, or what?"

"Winner takes all."

Oh.

"Usually." Papa added.

Suddenly, the papaya wasn't settling so well in Talin's stomach. "Ok, you said Onca was banished to the Barrenlands. But, you also said the Temple at the Fire Marsh was his. So where does he really live?"

"Onca has been banished, he is not to inhabit the Realm except the Barrenlands. But Onca never follows rules, never has. His attempt to overtake the Realm, when your great-grandfather was Healer, included setting fire to the Temple. It doesn't officially belong to him, but he frequents the site. Over time he's become more brazen, venturing out more, taking what he learned of the Realm as Healer, and then calculating how he can overtake it or destroy it."

"Wow," Talin whispered. "Well, I should probably see the rest of the Realm then? And these…Barrenlands."

"Not yet."

"But if I knew—"

Papa's finger went up. "Rules," he reminded. "It is more important right now to prepare to battle Onca. If you can defeat him, you can defeat anyone. And if you find yourself in the Realm having lost your way, the spirits will guide you to where you need to go."

Talin thought about who else Papa might be referring to when speaking of defeat. Did he mean Dewain?

"So, the elders decide who wins the Elimination?"

"Yes."

"And that person remains Healer?"

"Yes."

"But why would anyone want Onca back as Healer?"

"I don't believe it's Onca they are rooting for."

Dewain?

"Did Healer Dyllon actually turn Healer Hunte into a spirit?"

"Have you had enough to eat? It's time you do some healing."

"Well, I..."

"You need to go home. Speak with your father."

My dad?

"You'll need your mind clear if you are to defeat your adversary."

"But I thought—"

"It will be soon."

"What's soon?"

"Challenges. Return when your mind is clear so that you can focus."

"How am I supposed to find my dad?"

"Be resourceful." Papa walked towards the entry porthole. "Good day, Healer Talin." He bowed to his student and disappeared through the opening.

5

TALIN ENTERED THE HOUSE MID-AFTERNOON.

"Mom!"

He found his mother sewing in her bedroom. The sewing machine at her work station sat in front of the window giving her natural light to work by, along with a view of the neighborhood comings and goings. The window was partially open, letting in a gentle breeze despite the heat of the day, but the ceiling fan helped disperse the warm air. On her bed, next to her chair, were stacks of lace, thread, and various ribbons. Her project consisted of brightly colored cotton material and linens flowing off of her lap, spilling onto the floor.

"What are you making?" he asked.

Looking up, she smiled. "A traditional dress," she said, fluffing the material in front of her. "For your Induction. You get your own, proper, Induction don't you?"

"Oh." Thinking only about battling a wild cat in the coming days, he hadn't thought much about his own Induction. "What if you're not allowed to go?"

"Don't be ridiculous. It is tradition to have Inductions at the tree, and I will not be run off my own property while overseeing such an important event for my son. I'll go where I please." He could finally hear the pride in her voice replacing the fear. "So, dear, how was your day? Your clothes look damp, did you go swimming?"

"Oh, um," he looked down at the shirt that was just barely sticking to his chest. "I took a quick dip. But I had a question."

"What's that?" She looked down at her machine as it began to whirl and the needle mended two pieces of red and white material together.

"I need to talk to my dad."

The machine stopped.

"By your father, you mean..."

"Javon."

"I just don't think that's—"

"Mom, *please* tell me where he lives. Papa suggested I speak with him."

"Papa Bois?"

"Yes, I just have so many questions, I can't concentrate on what I need to do before..." he paused, "the Induction."

He had promised no secrets, but he wasn't hiding anything. He knew Papa had wanted him to have his own Induction, but he was more focused on the imminent threat to his personal safety from Onca and wanted his father's side of the family story.

She held her breath before answering. "Why don't you meet him somewhere in public, not his house?"

"Why can't I go to his house, to talk in private?"

"Public may be better, safer."

"What do you mean safer?" He couldn't think of anywhere that was more dangerous than the places he had already been below ground. Her comment made him feel like the dog he'd left behind in the UK when she wanted to introduce it to the new neighbor dog. She had said that meeting on neutral ground was best to avoid any

skirmishes. A trip to his father's house couldn't be all that dangerous, could it?

She fluffed the fabric again. "Javon lives near the Dyllons. I just
don't want you running into anyone who would cause you any trouble." She pulled at the loose threads hanging off the edge of the
material, eventually choosing to snip them with her scissors.

He hated hearing her answer, being on the island so near to his
father and never knowing it. He'd likely seen him walking down the
street while he and Marisha went to and from school or the library.
He might have even called out "Good morning" to him.

"I'll be ok. Is it close to Marisha?"

She lowered her head, clearly not wishing to share the information.
"The address is 342 Orchid." Then she turned back to her sewing.

"Do you know if he would be home right now?"

She shook her head.

"I really need to go, Mom." Stepping into her room, he hugged
her in her chair. "I'll be home for dinner."

The whirring sound of the machine faded behind him as he left
the room and closed her door. He dropped his backpack in his room
but strapped the knife to his hip, covering it with his untucked shirt.

HE'D SEEN Orchid Street before but never actually walked down it.
It was only two blocks from where Marisha lived. Looking much
like the other streets in town, it was lined with simple concrete and
wooden homes, some unfinished and in the never-ending process of
construction as islanders raised funds to continue adding on additional rooms and floors whenever they could afford to. Stacks of
cinder blocks sat in driveways, wheelbarrows at the sides of homes
and in unkempt yards, waiting to be used. Windows hung open,
inviting the tropical air inside, free to rush past the metal bars

installed to deter theft. The occasional dog barked at the end of a chain as Talin walked down the street.

Continuing down the road, he looked for the house numbers. 310...318A...322...336.

"What you doing 'ere?" a voice behind him belted.

Turning, he saw Dewain walk out from behind a parked car that had the hood propped open with a large stick. He was flanked by the same two friends that had accompanied him to Hosea Falls.

Talin kept walking, trying to ignore them, avoiding any interaction, focused on getting to 342 in as direct a manner as possible. His eyes darted back and forth to the house numbers.

"I *said*, what you doin' 'ere?" Talin heard feet scuffling behind him, kicking up dirt as the pace quickened. A second later, a fist grasped his shoulder, spinning him around.

He stood face to face with Dewain.

"Stop it!" Talin said.

"What ya gonna do 'bout it?"

The other boys' best children's voices chimed in. "Oh, poor Talin, all alone." The hood of the car crashed down as one of the boys grabbed the stick holding up the hood and walked toward him, backing up Dewain.

"Stop, I'm just walking!"

"Well, while yer just walking by 'den, 'dis is mine!" Dewain reached for the necklace around Talin's neck, grabbing the leather strap and twisting it in a fierce attempt to choke him with it. Coughing, Talin reached for his neck with one hand, and his knife, discreetly tucked under his shirt, with the other.

"Oooh, he's got a knife!" the other boys chuckled, alerting Dewain.

One of the teens grabbed Talin's arm that held the knife, twisting it behind his back and held him still for Dewain. A punch to Talin's gut made him lose his breath. He gasped, holding onto the knife with all the strength he could muster as the boy tried to pry his fingers from around the handle. The strap around Talin's neck tightened further.

Dewain pushed himself up into Talin's face. His voice was low and menacing. "You can stop 'dis nonsense right now." Dewain's free hand reached into Talin's shirt to grab the pendants. Clasping them inside his palm, he shoved his fist in Talin's face, shaking it.

"I'm da owner of 'dis necklace so hand it over." Dewain yanked at the strap, but it held firm. Tugging again, he became more upset when the necklace did not break free.

The boys encouraged Dewain, "Cut it off with his knife!"

"Ya, use his own knife!"

Talin could only imagine what Dewain would do holding a knife against his throat. Attempting to free himself from the boys, Talin realized they were much stronger than the web he'd been caught in earlier in the day. He wasn't strong enough to fight them off alone. He had not heeded the Rules of the Realm, number four to be exact. Above ground, it mattered just as much to never lose focus, especially cutting through Dewain's own neighborhood.

"Awe, the Healer can't help himself?"

"Poor thing, he looks like he's gonna pass out."

"Good! We'll just take the necklace when he does!"

"What happened to your super powers now?"

Seeing stars, Talin could feel his last breath unable to escape, and a lightness filled his head.

"Dewain, let him go!" a voice ordered from across the street. "Go on, get out of here before I tell your father!"

Papa?

It was at that moment Talin heard Dewain scream, "Ahhh, my hand!" and release the necklace while the other boys gasped, calling out about something burning or burnt.

Ears ringing and dizzy, Talin fell to the ground. He heard feet shuffling across the street. The yelling continued. His vision was blurry. Someone was at his side, shaking him, "Hey, hey, wake up. Are you ok?"

Talin blinked as the blood rushed back into his head and his vision came back into focus. A slender but muscular man was kneeling next to him in the street.

"Good God, boy, why are you carrying that knife?"

Talin couldn't believe he'd held onto it.

Trying to help him sit up, the man asked if he was hurt.

Talin cleared his throat. "I, I think I'm ok." His voice was scratchy. The man rested a reassuring hand on Talin's shoulder, giving him time to gather himself, then stood up.

Talin looked up, his rescuer extended a hand to help him stand. "Come with me, let's get you some water."

"Thank you, but I need to go."

"I want to make sure you are ok, then you may be on your way." The man eyed the pendants around Talin's neck suspiciously, then guided him, a firm hand on his shoulder, straight up the front steps of 342 Orchid.

6

Talin's heart quivered inside his chest as he read the house numbers emblazoned beside the front door. The man placed his hand on the knob to open it.

"Are you...Javon?"

The man turned, "How do you know my name?"

Talin didn't know whether to cry, scream, hug the man, run away, or freeze in his tracks. He was finally there, and had no idea what to do or say. He returned his knife to his hip. Did his father really not know who he was?

"Mom told me, and I heard her call you that at the Induction."

"Please, sit down," Javon said, ushering Talin inside and motioning to the couch in the living area. "Let me get you something to drink."

Javon went to the kitchen while Talin plopped on the couch, still catching his breath. The home was simple. The concrete floor, painted a shade of terra cotta and sealed with a clear shiny sealant, was covered with strategically placed, brightly-colored rugs, likely locally made. Carvings of coconut trees and a beach scene capped the ends of the wooden bookcase across from him, obviously the work of a master. Various trinkets and hand-carved figurines of local sea creatures, stained multiple colors, adorned the shelves.

Javon returned to the living room and sat across from Talin in a sturdy plank chair with vividly hued cushions, no doubt inspired by the other traditional island decor surrounding him. The wood creaked as he sat. Javon leaned forward, handing his guest a cold plastic bottle labeled 'Wata'.

"Thank you." Talin cracked the lid and took a small, nervous sip.

The house was quiet except for a fan near the window helping to usher fresh air into the room, gently blowing the cream window treatments inward. Canvas paintings of island nature scenes hung to either side of the window. Talin's knee bounced as his eyes darted across the room.

"Why are you here?" Javon asked.

"To see you."

"You're Talin, yes?" He pointed to his own chest, referring to Talin's necklace.

Talin nodded, hoping for at least a smile, but the only thing he'd received so far was his estranged father helping him get out of a scuffle with Dewain, which he definitely appreciated. It would have to do for now.

"How come you never came to look for me?" he asked his father.

"Who said I didn't?"

Talin had never thought about it this way before.

"I suppose your mother doesn't know you are here?" he asked.

"No, she does."

"Really? What does she think about that?"

"She didn't think it was a good idea right now."

"Why is that?"

"Because of the Induction."

"Well, that is over so what else does she think now?"

"Well..." Talin paused, wondering how much he should tell his father. "I'm going to get my own Induction, since the other one..."

Talin didn't need to describe it, his father was there—supporting Dewain. Talin was well aware Javon had seen him rush in to save the baby goats, injuring Dewain in the process. He'd seen the Evocation while Talin was in the tree, the glowing pendants around his neck from Healer Kingston and, of course, his mother sprinting to the site, wielding her husband's machete and ordering the crowd to go home. Javon had seen all of it.

He must think we're crazy.

"So, you only wanted to meet me?"

"Well, that, and...can you tell me about Healer Hunte and what happened to him?"

The conversation had quickly turned to a business meeting, the business of being Healer. A heartfelt reunion clearly wasn't on the agenda. There was no warm embrace, no missing of one another after so many years, no questions about how the other had been.

Maybe he doesn't really want to know me...

"Can you be more specific?" Javon asked.

"Why was he challenged?"

Javon leaned back in his chair. "How much has your mother told you about me?"

"Not much."

"You do know my family connections, yes?"

Talin nodded, his brow beading with perspiration. The circulation in the room was poor even with the fan. "That's why I'm asking."

"You're not safe here," Javon said, getting up to go to the door. Talin was sure he was being prematurely ushered out without answers, without anything. "Dewain will be waiting for you when you leave." He locked the front door. "You need to go."

"But I just *got* here." Talin stood up. "Are you not going to tell me anything? About Healer Hunte, me, or Mom, or—"

"Not here."

Javon guided him again, his hand firmly on Talin's shoulder, this time through the kitchen to the back door. He tucked Talin's necklace back into his shirt for him.

What is going on?

Talin's father led the way through the backyard and over the chainlink fence. Walking swiftly down the alley behind the house, trying not to attract attention, his father took them an entire five block route. Five blocks further from home, past the street market lined with vendors selling everything from fresh goods out of coolers under portable umbrellas and pop-up tents, to imported items mass marketed for souvenir-seeking tourists.

"Where are we going?" Talin asked.

Javon didn't stop until they got to *Matthew's*, a local seaside cafe overlooking the ocean. His father entered, nodded at the hostess and made his way to a corner table in the rear of the restaurant.

Sounds of clinking silverware on plates and laughter from the guests in the room filled the space. Ice was poured in a glass at the bar, a sound he was well familiar with. The chunking sound of the blender as it buzzed to life was interrupted by his father's voice.

"How is your mother?" he asked, leaning across the table, keeping his voice low.

Talin stared, confused.

"Your mother, is she ok?"

"Yeah, she's fine."

"Welcome," the waitress said, placing two menus in front of them. "What may I get you to drink?"

"Coffee, please. What would you like?" Javon asked him.

"I...didn't bring any money."

"It's no problem. Order what you like," he encouraged. Talin was generally never one to turn down a meal, but was embarrassed he was not able to pay for it.

"Just juice, please."

"What kind?" she inquired cheerfully.

"Mango."

"Alright." She made notes on her notepad. "So who did you bring with you today, Javon?"

It was clear he was a regular, which explain why he had walked right by the hostess when they entered the restaurant.

"This is Talin."

"Well, it's a pleasure to meet you, Talin." She gave a genuine smile and nod, then turned to get the drinks.

"Come here a lot, huh?"

"You look like your mother."

Talin shifted in his seat.

"But you have my chin."

"So, is it true why Mom left?"

His father sighed and leaned back. "Your mother and I married after she became pregnant with you. She wanted to wait, but I thought it best to be wed before you were born. Some months after that, she and Anya started to argue."

"About what?"

"You."

Talin stared back.

"She said she couldn't be around my sister or my family anymore, needed to get away. Far away."

"Only because of me?"

"Amos didn't make things any better, arguing with me all the time."

The waitress returned and set the drinks on the table. "What may I get you two for lunch?"

Javon had not even touched the menu and answered, "Jerk chicken, please."

"Your side?"

"Plantain."

She turned to Talin, "Will you be having the same?"

"No, thank you. I, uh, I don't eat chicken."

His father tilted his head.

"No chicken? Where you from, boy?" the waitress teased.

"Could I just have some plantains and vegetables, please?"

"Of course," she said, transcribing the order before gathering the menus and heading back toward the kitchen.

"Why don't you eat chicken?"

"Just don't like it," he shrugged, not wanting to explain his reasons, then sipped some juice.

"So why did Amos argue with you?"

"To keep your mother quiet."

"About what?"

"Her dreams." Javon took a breath, his eyes focused on Talin's. "Your mother told me that she dreamt you were the next Healer. It was burned into her heart." He lowered his voice to avoid being overheard. "She cried herself to sleep, awoke with nightmares of you burning alive. When she told Anya, Anya didn't believe her. Anya told her it wasn't possible because she'd had the same dreams about Dewain being Healer, and there could not be two women given the same dream. She eventually convinced your mother it was Dewain who would take the position next, as he was older."

Oh no.

"It went on for months. Then one day she packed and left. And she took you with her."

The story was eerily familiar. A few details were conflicting from what his mother had said, but the common thread had been the Dyllon family.

"The Dyllons know who I am then?"

"They do."

"Dewain, too?"

"Perhaps. But I don't spend much time around them, unless I have to. Maybe they did not discuss it with him as he was still young, and since you and your mother left maybe there was no need. But, he has been groomed his entire life expecting to be the next Healer, that I do know."

"But it's been so long since there was a Healer, how would anyone know that there would even still be one?"

Javon took a long sip of his coffee.

"Traditions such as this don't just disappear." He paused. "Your mother knew for certain before the day you were born."

Talin wasn't convinced she was completely certain after hearing she fled to another country for their safety.

"Did you believe I was the Healer?"

Javon explained that he did, but after Talin and his mother moved away for such a long time, he didn't think they would ever return. He supported Dewain by default.

The sounds of the cafe drifted away as Talin focused on his father's words. "Your mother's history and mine are proof you could still be Healer."

"But Dewain has family history too, so how did you know who it was?"

"We didn't. Until the Induct—the Evocation."

Talin wore proof he was the Healer, so he still could not understand why the Dyllons persisted. There were so many witnesses at the ceremony. Certainly, people believed he was Healer now, didn't they?

"Did Amos threaten you?" Talin asked.

"Years ago. Anytime we discussed the possibility of you being named, he was threatening to me. He threatened with violence, with Obeah."

The Heartman...

Talin wondered just how much he was like the man sitting across from him.

"But now, it is clear you have been named." Javon said.

Talin's eyes stared down at his glass of juice. "Do you still love my mother?"

Javon smiled. "I care about your mother very much."

"But you don't love her."

"Why did you really come to see me?" Javon's eyes drifted away from the conversation to the other guests in the restaurant, a few pointing fingers in their direction.

"I wanted to meet you."

His father readjusted in his seat, still watching the others. "How did you find me?"

"Mom gave me your address."

Javon looked surprised. "Did she?"

A plate of steaming vegetables was placed in front of Talin, but the strong spices from his father's chicken overpowered Talin's meal that had been sautéed in a butter and pepper sauce. Both he and his father broke into the fried plantains first.

Like father, like son.

"It's good," Talin said.

"Best in town."

The two ate their meal in relative silence, as the guests around them hushed their conversations to uncomfortable whispers.

Mid-meal, Talin gathered his nerve to continue asking questions.

"I need to know about Healer Hunte."

A small cough while swallowing a bite of spicy chicken accompanied his father's answer.

"Again, how do you know about Hunte?" he asked, clearing his throat and taking a drink of his coffee.

"Papa told me."

"Who?" he said, taking another sip.

"Papa Bois."

Javon nearly spit out his drink, sending him into a coughing fit as he tried to breathe. His face turned red as he reached for the pitcher of water on the table.

"You ok?" Talin asked, standing to lean over the table. Customers turned to stare.

Javon nodded, motioning for Talin to sit down. Composing himself, he cleared his throat. "I'm sorry, you said you heard about Healer Hunte from *who*?"

"Papa Bois."

Talin could tell by Javon's expression, he thought his long lost son was crazy.

"So," he paused, "it is well-known my grandfather was Healer, but not for long. Why do you ask?"

Talin laid it all out. Retelling the story Papa had told him about Healer Hunte taking more control than was needed, taking advantage of his role, and not helping the community. "He was banished to the Barrenlands, I think by Healer Dyllon. But I need to know how. How he won the…Elimination."

Javon cleared his throat again, shifting once more in his seat. "We need to go." Javon raised his hand to signal the waitress. She nodded, cautiously approaching the table.

He definitely thinks I'm crazy now.

"Have a good day, Mr. Hunte," she said under her breath, handing him the check. She glanced at Talin without a word, retreating to the kitchen in a rush with her head down.

Javon tossed more than enough Eastern Caribbean dollars on the table. "Let's go," he said, making his way swiftly to the exit.

Talin sensed all the patrons were keenly aware of their sudden departure. They kept their eyes down, failing miserably to hide their stares, but making no direct eye contact with him. No one spoke. The hustle and bustle of the restaurant stopped.

OUTSIDE, Javon kept a brisk pace in the opposite direction from his house.

Good, headed back closer to home.

"What's going on? What happened in there? Where are we going?"

"Keep your head down, don't attract any more attention, and for God's sake cover up that knife," he ordered, referring to the handle of Talin's blade, which was exposed by his untucked shirt creeping up. "Why are you carrying that anyway?"

"Protection."

THE TWO LOST THEMSELVES IN AN ADJOINING MARKET, WEAVING IN and out of vendors and shoppers, and cutting through less-traveled alleys. Javon checked repeatedly for something, or someone, over his shoulder, pushing Talin's senses to an even higher alert.

"Could you please tell me where we are going?"

"Shh... stay with me."

They continued on their trek out of the busyness of the downtown area and up a gentle hill until they reached the old church of St. Barnabas on the edge of the neighborhood. The exterior walls were aqua-green limestone and wooden shutters hung to either side of the arched stained glass windows that framed the main entrance. Contrasting red brick made up the corners of the structure. After years of enduring the sea air, the church had definitely seen better days. Still, the flowering vines climbing the facade and manicured landscaping outside made it a gem of a building. The rooftop was raised to a point and a circular opening at the top of the gable displayed the church's bell that rang every Sunday calling the community to church services. Javon entered through a side door.

The air inside smelled stale.

"What are we doing here?" Talin whispered.

"I help on Sundays, but I come here often."

"Why?"

"Quiet."

It was the same reason he'd spent so many hours high in Jumbie's branches.

Long, narrow wooden pews flanked the centered aisle. They appeared to be oak or mahogany, handmade with simple details on the ends and stained a dark umber, highlighting the natural grains. He ran his hand along the wood, smooth and worn. A hint of lemon was the only fresh scent, leading Talin to think someone had just dusted.

"Sit." Javon said.

Talin sat next to him staring straight ahead at the simple altar, made of the same stone as the exterior, partially draped with a white linen cloth. The pale walls, mostly bare, stood in stark contrast with the dark wooden support beams lining the ceiling..

"It's so small," Talin said, used to the large ornate churches in England. He hadn't spent any time inside a church since being on the island.

"Would you believe it was smaller? This was originally a schoolhouse. But it was converted many years ago."

"Papa would like it."

Javon's mouth opened, but no words came out.

"What?" Talin asked.

Javon hesitated. "Papa?"

"Yeah, he said any building can be a temple."

"Ah, yes. Indeed."

"So, are you going to tell me why we had to run off so fast?"

"We weren't safe anymore in the cafe."

Talin rested back into the pew. "Well, no one was trying to choke me. But, seems everywhere I go now someone is telling me I'm not safe."

"Did you not see the people staring? Word is out."

"About what?"

"You."

"What about me?"

"That you are overtaking Dewain as Healer."

"I'm not overtaking anybody." Talin leaned forward again. "Papa told me I was Healer, and even my great-grandfather proved I was."

"But the community has been fed that Dewain is the next Healer. They believe it. My sister knows you live on the island but does not want to be around you to bring any attention, positive or negative, that would detract from her Dewain. Do you understand?"

"I guess." He really didn't. Dewain sure spent a lot of time around him, though, bringing negative attention quite frequently with his many bullying attempts at school, and egging the house.

"Even I believed it was Dewain," his father continued. "It was passed down to me a long time ago that I was related to the next Healer, but the same was said of Amos. At first, we both believed it was our own children. But, when you were gone for so long, it started to make sense that it would be Dewain, as we were both related to him. Neither of us thought you would return."

"Do you believe it's me now?"

"Of course," he said with a proud smile. "There are those on the island who think you will be like Healer Hunte, heavy handed and forceful, since you came back without warning, and then at the Evocation...well, those same people believe that Dewain will be like Healer Dyllon, well-respected and loved, overthrowing Hunte."

"Dewain is the one acting like Hunte," Talin said, thinking the exact opposite of what his father had just suggested. "So, what *happened* between him and Healer Dyllon?"

"It is in the past. You should not worry about that now and focus on your own path to being Healer."

He sounded an awful lot like Papa Bois. Talin turned to squarely face his father. "I *need* to know. Do you know, or not?"

"Why you so focused on the past, boy?"

"Healer Hunte...I mean, Onca, has already threatened to challenge me."

"What?"

"It's true. It's not in the past anymore."

"But who is Onca?"

"Healer Hunte."

"Now you talkin' crazy-talk, boy."

Talin pointed to his recovering sore ankle. "Do you see this? This is from Onca, the former Healer Hunte. I need to know the past so I can make sure it doesn't happen to me in the future. He has threatened to overtake the Realm, and kill me."

His father's eyes grew large and wide. He glanced around the church suspiciously. No one had entered while they talked. It remained empty, except for the warm-colored sunlight streaming in through the stained glass, bits of dust floating through the air.

Javon leaned in close to Talin. "That's impossible, and ridiculous. It's a fact the community believes the Healer to be Dewain, but there have been no threats to your life, boy."

"But Onca doesn't live here."

"Why do you keep referring to this Onca?"

"Healer Hunte is no longer a Healer, he is in spirit form after being banished. His name is Onca now."

His father blew a breath out through his pursed lips. "Pssssh. If you are going to be Healer, boy, you had better stop talking like that."

"Like what? It's true! You don't believe me? Out of all people, I thought you would help me, but I thought wrong. I'll be going now." Talin got up and walked to the rear exit of the church. "Thank you for lunch," he said without looking back.

"Talin, wait!" Javon called out.

Talin turned. "Why?"

"I believe you." Javon was standing.

"No, you don't."

"I do," he confessed. "Please sit."

Talin had wondered for several years who his father was and how he would react if he ever met him. The afternoon with him was not turning out anywhere near to what he had imagined. He'd hoped for a hearty hug, an 'I missed you', or conversation asking to keep in touch. He wanted to spend time with him catching up about life and learning how much he might be like his father. He wanted someone he could truly call 'Dad'.

Reluctantly, Talin walked back to the pew, but didn't sit. Arms crossed, he waited.

Taking a cleansing breath, Javon sat down. "Healer Hunte was challenged to an Elimination by Healer Dyllon, before Dyllon was named Healer, of course—"

"What is the Fire Summons?"

"It sounds like you already know what happens."

"I know the name, not what happens, or exactly how Healer Dyllon won."

"It is different for each Elimination, and there has only been two that we know of. This challenge in particular was fairly straightforward. The two were directed to walk over hot coals then through a wall of fire without being scalded by the flames."

Straightforward?

Images of Hollywood stuntmen covered in protective lotions and sporting puffy fireproof suits filled Talin's head.

"The man uninjured was the victor." Javon said.

"Were they allowed any props or preparation?"

"No, what do you mean?"

"Did they have any special...skills?"

"Like what?"

Talin searched for the words. "Magic or powers?"

Javon chuckled. "Sorcery it is not. The Elimination is strictly fought with each man's mental and physical strengths. Some

Healers have been spiritual leaders, but they're humans, not magicians."

"Then how did Healer Dyllon change Hunte into a flaming jaguar?"

"What?"

"Papa said Healer Dyllon turned the flames on Hunte and he was burned. Sent to the Barrenlands."

Javon's eyes blinked. His face held no expression.

Talin sat next to him and waved a hand in front of his face, "Hello? Did you hear me?"

"I heard you," he whispered.

"Did you know that?"

"Yes, but after the Elimination, no one saw Healer Hunte again." His voice was quiet and reminiscent. "He ran into the woods, fully engulfed in the flames. Screaming. But, he wasn't in animal...spirit form. The elders followed to see if they could render aid, but he was never found." Javon's dark face appeared a shade lighter than moments before. He stared through the pew in front of them. "Talin? Have you truly seen Healer Hunte?"

"Onca. Yes, of course."

"How do you know he is threatening you?"

"He told me," he said, pointing back to his ankle.

Javon placed a hand on the pew to steady himself. He swayed slightly in his seat.

"Hey, you ok?"

Javon blinked and shook his head. "Yes, I'm fine."

"You don't look fine."

"Tell me. The Realm is real?"

"You know about the Realm? Yeah, it's very real."

"You've been there?"

"I go all the time."

"How?"

"Through the tree."

"The silk cotton?"

Talin confirmed with a nod.

Javon looked intensely at Talin. "You must not let the spirit of Healer Hunte escape from the tree." His words held desperation.

"Ok...I'm working on that part. You have any ideas?"

"The Hunte family...we are not evil. And you must prove that you are stronger than Dewain, bring back respect and honor to the family name. You cannot lose."

Yeah, 'cuz losing means possibly dying...

Javon grabbed Talin by the shoulders. With a gentle shake, he looked into his eyes. "You *cannot* lose. Do you understand?"

Talin couldn't speak. The only thing he could think about was his mother's dreams since before he was born. He couldn't help but wonder if her dreams about not being able to save him from a fiery inferno were a premonition, just like her dreams of him becoming Healer. His heart raced within his chest, hoping history was not about to repeat itself. Why was his father being so persistent?

THEY SAT silent in the small sanctuary for a while. Talin's other questions for his father had completely evaporated. He could think of nothing but a battle with Onca. More questions than answers would soon follow, he was certain.

"You should go. I'll walk you home," Javon said.

"I'll be ok, I think I know the way from here."

"It's not safe."

Everybody keeps saying that.

The last thing Talin wanted was someone seeing him being escorted home like a grade schooler for protection. "I have my knife."

"About that knife. Where did you get it?"

"My great-grandfather made it for me," then he caught his words, "my...other great-grandfather."

"I see." Javon walked to the side door in which they entered, motioning for Talin to follow.

Wishing no disrespect towards his father after their first meeting, he did as instructed.

"You really don't have to walk—"

"Not to worry. I'll stay back the last block. I'd hate to have your mother greet me again with a machete in her hands."

8

SAYING GOODBYE HAD BEEN EVEN MORE AWKWARD THAN SAYING hello. There was no hug, no handshake, no physical displays of affection. Talin's father had asked to meet again, but they had not agreed to a time or place. He could safely assume it wouldn't be at Javon's home or anywhere public, given the way the cafe patrons had taken note of them as they left. His father had said to be safe and to give his best to Shantel, then simply turned and walked away, leaving Talin to fend for himself.

The last block home was long and lonely. He hadn't learned much more information than he had before meeting his father, but it opened the door for more conversations.

Talin dragged his feet along the road, kicking small pieces of rock and asphalt ahead of him. A neighborhood cat screeched nearby, startling him and forcing him into an acute awareness of his familiar surroundings.

Pay attention.

He took note of every neighbor out hanging the wash, tipping back a cold beverage on the porch or smoking alongside the house, and Mr. Browne's black and white dog barking at the end of his chain. No one seemed to be bothered by his presence, as they had been at the cafe.

BACK HOME, he heard the banging of pots and pans from inside the kitchen. The air smelled sweet, carrying the scent of curry, cinnamon, and garlic. His mouth watered.

"Hi Mom," he said, entering from the back porch.

Pulling the sweet potatoes from the oven, she welcomed him home with a smile.

"Why don't you get cleaned up before dinner?"

"Yes, ma'am."

Talin did as instructed then enjoyed an amazing meal before bed. She didn't ask about his time with his father, and he didn't offer.

HIS MIND DWELLED ONLY on his father's instructions, "You must not let the spirit of Healer Hunte escape from the tree."

Why?

Onca had come dangerously close once already when he grabbed Talin's ankle and pulled him below after Dewain's Induction debacle. Subconsciously, Talin reached to his ankle, rubbing the bite wound. It had nearly healed.

What does Javon know that I don't? Why won't he tell me?

Up until then Talin had only assumed Onca had been banished to the Barrenlands, occasionally wandering the Realm— unable or unwilling, to survive in the world above.

Caught between two worlds, Talin wasn't sure how to proceed. In the morning, there would be another early trip to the Realm.

THE CROW of the rooster and clucking chickens awoke Talin early. Willing himself awake, he sat up in bed to stretch. He'd had a peaceful night's rest and quickly gathered his pack, knife, and leather bag. Tip-toeing past his mother's room, he made his way down the stairs. Leaving the house, he was careful not to slam the screen door.

The sun had crested over the treeline, casting a brilliant glow across the old cane field. Speckles of the morning's golden light flickered between Jumbie's leaves in the distance.

Keeping the pace of an easy, unhurried jog to the tree, Talin felt his blood pumping.

"Morning Jumbie," he whispered as he arrived, securing his pack and crawling between the great roots. He pushed his shoulder into the bark, grabbed one of the inner vines, and descended into the dark with great control.

WHEN TALIN EMERGED from the roots, the sun had already risen high above the eastern forest and had begun its dance across the rest of the landscape. Talin knew which way to go.

As he passed by the hundreds of crosses in the Cemetery, he wondered again about the pendants on each one. Were they all past Healers, someone else, or a mix of both? He stopped to study several charms more closely.

I wonder if my great-grandfather is buried here. But I have his pendant, so it wouldn't be here...would it?

He made it a point to ask Papa. They hadn't talked about the Cemetery since Talin tripped, just outside this very forest, during his first visit into the Realm trying to run from Papa himself. Talin chuckled at the memory. Now he ran to Papa in times of trouble, trusting him completely. He was curious to know if Healer Kingston had been afraid of Papa the first time he met him. Did Healer Kingston ever think that the Dyllons would be lashing out so forcefully against him now? How would he feel about people hardly believing there would even be another Healer after several generations with the title left unfilled?

Continuing on, he kept his head up the rest of the way to the Sphere, checking over his shoulder and in the shadows for any hint of a blurry mirage within the leaves, hiding a smoldering big cat. He thought the light refraction might tip him off to any danger, but he saw none.

Reaching the Sphere, Talin left his shoes and pack at the porthole, but took his knife, and entered— ready for action.

No one was there. The giant web was gone, no ropes or vines dangled from above. No spiral of boulders towered around the Drop. Only the stone on the water's edge, the wall of weapons, and the massive wooden work tables were there. But on the skirt of one of the tables hung a sheet of paper, held in place with a small carving knife sunk into the tabletop's facing edge. Talin removed the knife, returned it to the wall, and read the note.

> *"Go to the Theater.*
>   *Papa."*

The Theater?

He couldn't recall which way the Theater was. Leaving the note on the table, he went to the porthole leading to the Grove. Peering out, rows of ripened fruit hanging from the trees tempted him, but he didn't recall ever leaving the Sphere this way. He'd only entered to get fruit and return. He had no idea what lay beyond the Grove. Returning to the main entry, he retrieved his belongings outside the training area. Looking around for anything familiar, he saw bits of a landscaped stone pathway to the west, partially covered with undergrowth.

Oh, yes...

Tying his shoes to his backpack, he started walking the familiar swirling patterns of the stones. They radiated a smooth, crisp coolness underfoot. The path was lined with the most lush foliage he'd seen yet, perfect camouflage for a jungle cat. Hibiscus flowers, birds of paradise, and frangipani bloomed around him. At the end of the trail, the pavers crumbled into the moat that surrounded the crooked center platform. The rock wall backdrop had crumbled further since the last time he'd been there.

Although today, an enormous tree had erupted from the water, stretching upward and disappearing into the sky. Its tall, ribbon-like roots covered the stone stage and plunged into the surrounding moat. The intricate carvings in the stage were mostly covered by the root system.

It looked strikingly familiar.

"WELCOME, HEALER TALIN," Papa said, seated on one of the stone benches that in the grass across from the stage.

"Bonjour, Papa."

Talin took a seat next to him. "Why aren't we in the Sphere today?"

"It's time to prepare for your Induction."

"But I thought—"

"You would like a proper Induction, yes?"

"Well, yes, but—"

"Then you'll prepare."

Talin had thought his crashing of Dewain's supposed Induction had, in a twisted sort of way, already been his own. Still, his mother had been right and he was excited to have his own.

Turning his attention to the magnificent tree in front of him, he asked, "Is that..."

"It is."

An exact replica of Jumbie's massive roots, thick canopy, and sprawling buttress towered in front of them. Talin had learned early on not to ask *how* something appeared in the Realm, only why. And as soon as he asked the question, he usually had already answered it.

"Why can't we just prepare by the real Jumbie outside of the Realm?"

"There are a few resources we have here that you don't have above."

"Like what?"

Papa motioned to the moat where bubbles were forming. A splash erupted at the surface, thrusting a jewel-encrusted Mama D'lo from the water and sending waves across the moat. She landed on the shore, propping herself up on her hip and smoothing back her hair away from the serpent that conjoined her.

"Mama D'lo!" he jumped out of his seat and rushed to the water's edge.

"It is a pleasure to serve you again, Healer Talin." She respectfully bowed her head, as did the snake.

"How did you get here from the cave?"

She winked at Papa.

"Everything is connected, remember?" Papa reminded him.

How far does the Sluice go?!

"Oh, yeah, of course. So what are you doing here?"

"Whatever Papa requires, I imagine."

"So let's get started shall we?" Papa said.

"Now?" Talin asked.

"Little time."

"But I had questions before we start."

"No time."

"But—"

Papa raised a finger as to scold him and command attention. He walked to the edge of the moat.

Again, really?

"Mama D'lo, could you summon the fish please?"

"My pleasure." Dipping into the water, she disappeared as quickly as she'd appeared.

"Fish? Why fish? I don't want to go swimming again."

"Just in case of injury."

"Injury?"

Talin's gut flipped on itself.

"Talin, are you familiar with Jumbie's branches?"

"Yes."

"Each one?"

He nodded. "Of course."

"So familiar, you could climb them blindfolded?"

Terrifying visions of himself climbing the look-alike tree while blindfolded swept over him. He hesitated with his answer.

"That's a no." Papa said, answering for him, and reached into his cloak pocket.

No, no, no, not a blindfold...

Papa gently shook out a bundled material, allowing it to unfurl, revealing a brown and white stripe-like pattern. He then refolded it into a length just long enough to wrap around a nervous teenager's forehead and wide enough to fully cover said teenager's eyes.

"You're serious?"

"Always." Papa presented the bandana in his open palms with respect. "This is a piece of material from your great-grandfather's burial vestments. You should wear it proudly."

Just when Talin was ready to revert back into a childish argument about his task, he thought about what his great-grandfather would think of him right now. It was time to step up.

A deep breath escaped him as he took the material in his hands. Running his fingers over the heavy cotton-type textile, he knew it was most definitely handmade.

Sparing him no time to appreciate the material, Papa took the wrap away and tied it around Talin's head. The knot pushed uncomfortably into the back of his skull.

"Ouch!"

Talin was then instructed to climb the tree as high as he could go.

"But it's on the other side of the moat!"

"It is."

Talin felt everything but the pride he was supposed to feel as he squatted down onto the grass, hoping to get things over with as quickly as possible. Scooting carefully on his bum to feel for the water's edge, he slipped and plunged straight into the water with a splash.

"Awe, come on!" He pulled the bandana up on his forehead as he surfaced.

"I suggest you get moving."

Talin wanted so badly to talk back. *Yeah, or what?!*

He knew better. He also knew to move when told because something sinister might be on his trail. Swimming across the moat, he climbed onto the stone platform, soaking wet.

It's too early for this.

Pulling the bandana back down over his eyes, he cautiously stepped towards the tree, so as not to trip on any loose rocks from the crumbling stone backdrop, feeling every pebble under his bare feet. He held his arms out in front of him to avoid bumping into a root. Feeling the first one, he slowly walked along the wall-like structure, using his hands to navigate the space. Then he quickly became aware of not only the feel of the bark under his fingers, but the sun on his skin, the sound of the birds chirping in the distance...and a gentle splashing not far away.

Probably Mama D'lo, he thought.

Please be Mama D'lo...

Talin had crept over the lower roots so many times to gain access to the treetop, he assumed it would be second nature to move among them now, but things were completely different without sight.

Awkwardly climbing onto one of the roots, he leaned over it to keep his balance and not topple down the opposite side. With his belly to the bark, he clung to the root, arms and legs hanging over each side. He moved at a snail's pace, completely opposite of the night when he was chased by his stepfather in the pouring rain. Right now he couldn't outrun a sloth, as Papa had described him once before. Reaching out, he felt for the subtle bumps and low hanging branches that would help propel him into the lower limbs, but it was more tedious than he thought.

Inching his way up toward the trunk, his brow had already started to feel uncomfortably warm. Sweat dripped from his forehead, running down to the bandana. He debated wiping the beads away and "accidentally" pushing his blindfold up where he could just peek out.

Thinking twice, he kept crawling.

Bumping into a branch, he grabbed hold, pulling himself up and stood more upright, finding his balance.

"Climb on." The instructions came from behind him. "Speed will come, and it will need to come quicker. Secure yourself on the branch."

What is the point of this?

Talin crept out, feeling the branch sag under his weight. It wasn't the strongest he'd been on. Wondering where in the tree he actually was, he reached for the bandana.

"Ah, ah ah..." Papa scolded.

A splash, seemingly below him, caused his heart to quicken.

"Mama D'lo?"

No one answered.

"Papa?"

No one answered.

What's going on?

Talin was frozen with fright.

He reached out with one arm, arcing it above his head and in front of him, hoping to feel the next branch up. There was none. Talin scooted back down the branch, thinking he would need to be closer to the trunk to find a different branch to perch himself on.

"What are you doing?" Papa called. His voice came from above.

"Um...I'm going back to try and find a different branch."

"Climb down."

"What?"

Pap instructed Talin to climb down out of the tree, leaving his blindfold on.

Papa began giving additional instructions.

"You don't know the tree." Papa's voice sounded behind him.

"Well, I..." he reached for his blindfold, thinking he would get a break from the drill.

Papa's hand met Talin's, stopping him. "The blindfold stays."

"But I can't see the—"

"You must prepare for every possibility."

"That's impossible."

"You will try."

He heard Papa circling him on the platform, tiny stones quietly crunching beneath his hoof. "I will remove your blindfold, but only for a moment."

The footsteps continued to circle him.

How does he move around so fast?

"You must study the tree as quickly as possible, committing every detail you can to memory."

It sounded like he was going to learn first hand about people with photographic memories.

Papa pulled the blindfold up to his forehead, and Talin stared straight ahead at the tree. "How long do I have?"

His eyes were again covered by the blindfold. "About this long."

"Wait!"

"No time. Climb."

"But that wasn't enough tim—"

"Quickly."

Talin stepped forward slowly, arms ahead of him. His hands followed the subtle curve of a root where he felt a familiar indentation that he'd used as a step to climb up. Pulling himself up carefully, he draped a leg over each side as if riding a horse, leaned forward, and began to scoot.

"Faster." Papa said.

"I don't want to fall!"

Trying to picture himself in the tree and recall the path he'd used so many times before was proving difficult.

I got like three seconds to study the tree. It's not enough...

The thought distracted his focus.

"Your Induction is right around the corner."

Talin turned his head toward Papa. "What? When?"

"Keep moving."

Hoping Papa would continue to reveal more details as he did when Talin was climbing the spider web, he started moving faster. Slipping, he caught himself across the root.

"Come down." Papa said.

"Again?"

His blindfold still covering his eyes, he scooted backward down the root. Sliding a leg over the edge, he hung off one side from his fingertips. He allowed his feet to touch the crumbled stone below before letting go.

"Can I take the blindfold off?"

"No."

Figures.

"You must be ready for anything from Dewain at the Induction."

"I know."

"I'm not sure what he will try to do." Papa lifted the blindfold. "Study it. Quickly."

Talin focused on the tree. His eyes darted about as he tried to memorize the roots, where the branches split off the trunk, and any familiar handholds he had used before. Then as quickly as the blindfold came off, Papa pulled it back down again.

"Are you ready?"

Talin took a breath. "Yes."

Papa's hands met Talin's shoulders, spinning him in several circles. "Go."

Wait, what? That wasn't supposed to happen.

"But..."

Just when he thought he could make some progress, Talin was disoriented as ever.

"What if your rival is closing in? Go!"

Slightly dizzy, Talin stumbled in the crumbled stone. He heard a large splash again and water rushed over his feet. Small rocks and pebbles pelted his ankles, the force of the water pushed him slightly off balance.

What is that?!

It felt like a tidal wave swept over the platform as Talin was thrust into a root. But he had no idea if it was where he had remembered one to be, or if he was off to one of the sides of the trunk. Splashing continued. The water rose a few inches higher, now halfway up his calves. The rush of water spilling over the edge of the platform into the moat filled his ears as he tried to imagine what was happening and why. It didn't matter, he had to climb before the water rose higher.

He pulled himself up onto the root, straddling it, hoping it was the most center one he'd just envisioned. His feet slid across rough, prickly bark on the side of the root as he tried to shift into an upright position. The spot was large, with an unnatural indentation.

Is that?

He paused, feeling the spot with his foot, flexing his toes. It was the scar his stepfather had left with his machete.

He knew exactly where he was.

Pushing off the root, he stood slowly and balanced. Reaching out, he felt a sturdy limb and grabbed it. Using his upper body strength to hold on, he swung his legs up, and latched onto the limb with bent knees. Hanging upside down, he started climbing up, away from the water below him, just like he had when trying to get away from the drunken man's machete that stormy night. He struggled to pull his body weight up and over the limb so he could sit atop it and catch his breath. The sounds of rushing water were diminishing.

Repeating the process, he stood up, leaned against the trunk and searched for the next limb that sprouted from it. Finding it quickly, he envisioned the tree in his mind and started climbing as soon as his hands landed on the next branch, and the next, and the next. It wasn't the fastest he'd climbed in the tree, but it was faster than he imagined it would be blindfolded.

How high up was he supposed to go? He decided to climb into the canopy until Papa told him to stop. There was no discussion, no questions, nothing but silence and the sounds of his grunts as he lifted his body weight higher. And the birds, an occasional splash from the water. The wind rustling leaves in nearby trees and the—

"Well done. Come down." Papa said.

"With my blindfold?"

"Yes."

He now realized it was probably a good thing he was practicing in a Jumbie-replica, out of range of his mother's view, especially with his vision hindered by the blindfold. She might've had a heart attack.

Still might.

Talin cautiously retraced his steps in reverse. It had been easier to come down than go up, maybe because he recognized the route. He wasn't sure.

. . .

PLANTING his feet on the ground, he felt wet, sandy grit under his toes. He reached for his blindfold, lifting it to his forehead.

Papa stood next to him on the barren platform. The pieces of broken stone from the half-crumbled wall had been swept away, only puddles of water remained in the grooves of the intricately chiseled platform, glistening in the bright sun. Talin was now able to see more of the carving on the stone stage.

A creepy looking creature was in the center. Half creature, half human. Its puffy face was contorted and horns sat atop its head, fangs protruding from its mouth. Several rings surrounded the design, each filled with a unique pattern of their own that further separated into different sections to complete the ring, like a circular spider web. Talin couldn't see all of it due to the tree roots, but the entire stage was covered in the intricate carving.

Wow.

"Is this a sundial?"

"Of sorts."

"What's that?" Talin pointed to the creature in the middle which was holding something odd in his hand.

"An old god from centuries ago."

"What's he holding?" Talin tilted his head and squinted at the ground.

"A human heart."

"What?!"

"No need for alarm."

Talin laughed, "Yeah, right!"

"It is only a reminder."

"Of what? An evil god I am going to meet and if I can't defeat him, he'll rip my heart out?"

"Again. No need for alarm. It is a reminder that all things are connected and to protect the world we have around us. We will be our own demise if we do not care for what surrounds us, starting with our own hearts."

How Papa came up with the flowery prose, referring to the monster holding a human heart dripping with blood, he'd never know, but he did know Papa had been around a very, very long time. There was likely some kind of truth behind it.

"So, this god will rip out my beating heart if I don't protect...what, the Realm?"

"Don't jest. The Realm and its inhabitants may not seem real to you still, but I assure you, there is no room for mockery here."

"Sorry." He didn't question further, as he had his own past to deal with instead of worrying about an age-old god that likely didn't exist anymore. Or so he hoped.

"You should not just care about the Realm, but the world above. We are all connected," Papa continued. "There is much you will learn as Healer. We've not yet begun."

Yet? If climbing rock walls, swimming in the Sluice, escaping from jaguar spirits, getting stuck in life-sized spider webs, and climbing 50-foot tall vines was *not yet* starting training, what on earth was he doing? And what on earth *would* he be doing when training really did "start"?

Talin looked around the Theater and the neatly laid out semi-circle of flat stone benches facing them, sitting atop a perfect carpet of emerald grass. Lush mahogany and palm trees formed natural walls surrounding the open-air amphitheater. There wasn't much more to it.

"Papa," Talin said, "The last time I was here, you said my great-grandfather was probably here. Is he buried in the cemetery, or is he...here?"

Papa paced along the edge of the stage, hands clasped behind his back. It took him a moment to answer.

"Healer Kingston was...his body was buried in the great tree's crypt. But his soul separated from his body when he passed. Your great-grandfather still lives."

Talin's eyes widened.

"But not in the physical way that you and I are speaking now."

Talin's shoulders slumped and hopes of meeting his great-grand-father were crushed. Papa continued.

"When we die, well, mortal beings...your soul separates from your body and lives on elsewhere."

"Where?"

"Everywhere."

Talin felt the eye roll coming, but didn't allow himself.

"Is his body in the cemetery?"

"Yes."

"And the coffin?"

"Likely gone. It's been three generations."

"Did you bury him?"

Papa nodded.

"So, you took the necklace, and all his clothes?"

"It is a duty I have had for many years. I serve many purposes to keep balance between the Realm and above."

Talin knew that the knife, bag, necklace and bandana Papa had given him all came from the same source. Now he wondered where the feathered headpiece and the robe Healer Kingston wore in the photo were. Would he get those, too?

"Did you take things from other Healers?" Talin asked.

"No need."

"What do you mean?"

"All the Healers in the past had been chosen while they were alive, and before the Healer who named them passed. They passed down their own relics. You were...a special case."

Oh.

"So who gave *you* your...job?"

"I have been here since before there were Healers."

Wow.

"Who else is in the cemetery? There's so many graves."

"Healers past, sometimes their family, elders, visitants and voyagers—"

"Voyagers?"

"Those from above who have been granted special access to the Realm, but are not Healers themselves."

"Wow! Really? Like who?"

It was the first time Talin had heard that others "from above" were able or even allowed to enter the Realm, much less be buried there.

"We do not have time to discuss the intricacies right now. But, I imagine there's only one grave you care about."

Talin nodded.

Together, they walked to the Cemetery.

9

ENTERING THE CEMETERY, PAPA LED HIS STUDENT OVER THE GENTLY sloping hills. Moving off the path, they made their way into the tall grass, past many grave markers.

"Pay attention. Keep your head up." Papa instructed.

Talin wasn't sure what he was to look out for, likely Onca hiding in the grass, blending in with the speckled orbs of light that danced across the field. Even with the possibility of being hunted, Talin felt peace here.

They trekked into the tree line, further than Talin had explored before.

The crosses grew more sparse, as well as the light. Then in the shade, below a tree with hundreds of thorny spikes covering the circumference of the trunk, was a marker.

"Here lies Healer Kingston. I will give you time." Papa said.

"Time for what?"

"Paying your respects." Papa turned and walked several yards away, watching the tree line beyond the gravesite like a sentry.

"Why does the tree have so many thorns?" he asked Papa.

"Monkey-no-climb."

"Monkey what?"

"It is a very young silk cotton tree, like your Jumbie. But it has lost its thorns long ago. Have you not heard the locals call it monkey-no-climb?"

Talin shook his head.

"The monkeys do not like the thorns, most of the animals do not. Pay your respects, we can't stay long."

Talin looked down at the marker. A tree trunk erupted from the ground, forming the shape of a cross - simply but finely carved. The pendant hanging from the middle was a brilliant green gemstone tied on with rusty wire.

"What's the stone?" Talin called to Papa.

Papa Bois only raised a finger to his lips.

Talin quietly sat down in the grass in front of the marker, not sure what to do. No one close to him had ever passed away. Having only been to one funeral before, in the UK for his stepfather's father, he knew he should probably stay quiet and respectful.

But it's not a funeral. Am I supposed to say something?

He didn't speak his thoughts aloud, he simply sat in awe of the cross in front of him, wondering why the green stone, the size of a golf ball, had been chosen for the marker. Papa had told him the pendant on his own necklace had been made from rock, a symbol of infinite strength, but he didn't understand the jewel. Jewels were for girls, pretty and sparkly. It looked more fitting for someone such as Mama D'lo, not a strong carpenter-turned-Healer. Was it just a stone that happened to be green? He thought a red or even a yellow would be more appropriate, more masculine. Maybe they ran out of other colors for his marker, as no two decorations were the same, and there were, literally, hundreds of graves. And why was he buried so far away from the others? Why under the branches of a silk cotton tree?

A few minutes passed while Talin thought about what he would say to his great-grandfather if he'd been standing right in front of him. He had so many questions.

Did you throw fireballs? Did you swim in the Sluice? Did Papa Bois make you do all the stunts he is making me do? Do you know Mama D'lo? Thank you for the knife.

Most importantly...

Why did you pick me? What do I do?

Things are different now.

Getting comfortable, Talin sank lower into the soft grass. There was a certain sense of peace here, a different peace than Hosea Falls. Talin reached out to touch and inspect the green gem.

"Talin!" Papa yelled. Onca leapt out of the trees with a roar, straight toward Talin, but pounced on Healer Kingston's grave instead. Flocks of birds scattered from the treetops. Falling back, Talin rolled away and drew his knife.

Papa Bois was at Talin's side immediately, standing between him and the snarling cat. Onca dug his powerful claws into the ground.

"Onca! You will leave this sacred ground!" Papa commanded.

A deep laugh escaped Onca. "Sacred? Nowhere is sacred." He began circling his prey. "Don't be alarmed. I thought it proper if the boy really wanted to meet his great-grandfather...how about here, how about now?"

"You're not the great-grandfather I was thinking of." Talin said.

Onca let out another evil laugh, "Oh? I see you know our connection, boy. And a sense of humor, too..."

"I'm not a boy."

"No? Either way, I don't care, but I can help you meet your precious Kingston Boyce," he roared. An outstretched paw swiped at Talin. "I see you aren't fond of me. No matter. I'm not fond of you either."

"Onca, this is not the time nor the place for any challenge!"

"No? It's only the boy. No one to cry out to for help. No trickery. And he's already in the Cemetery, I'd be saving you burial work. I think it's perfect."

Papa reached under his cloak, pulling out a fireball that briefly hovered above his palm. Quickly turning it to ice, without water, he thrust it at Onca. The cat dodged it, avoiding a direct hit to his core, but a loud crack and sizzle were followed by Onca spinning around, snarling at his hind-quarter. Black smoke swirled into the air, rising from his hip.

"Your bag of tricks is running out, Papa Bois. It's time the boy and I dueled. Stop dragging it out."

"There will be no such duel!"

The cat continued circling slowly, with the smallest hesitancy in his back leg.

Did Papa injure him?

"You and I both know you won't always be around to save him."

"Onca, stand down! Leave this place, or—"

"Or what? You'll toss another fireball? You can't hurt me with fire. And you think a little block of ice is going to do any damage? You've known me long enough," he growled. "You know your time is limited. Just make it easy and give yourself and the boy up— no duel, no damage."

"Never. I'd say that is one of your tricks. If you are as powerful as you say, let the boy train, then come back for a fair fight. Only a coward would surrender to you."

"I'm not a coward." Talin added, almost growling himself.

"Hmmm, we shall see." Onca changed the direction of his pacing. "Papa, I'll give you that last request. It might be a good show."

"You are dismissed, Onca."

"You cannot dismiss me! I leave when I'm ready and will return when I am ready! Just make sure the boy is...ready as he can be. It won't matter."

On Onca's final circle around them, he flicked his tail over Healer Kingston's grave marker, setting it on fire. Digging into the grass atop it, he left deep claw marks in the soil, then leapt into the treeline and disappeared.

Talin jumped toward the tree stump, pulling the bandana from his pocket, and swatted at the fire in an attempt to extinguish the flames.

"Quick! Put it out!" Talin yelled.

Papa stepped forward, pulling Talin aside.

Papa leaned toward the fire, took in a slow, deep breath, and exhaled. His breath was a white cloud, reminding Talin of exhaling on a cold winter day when he lived overseas. The cloud swirled around the cross like a cloudy day and the flames slowly diminished. The haze of smoke evaporated into a fine mist that fluttered to the ground, settling peacefully onto the charred stump, like glitter in a snow globe.

The fire was out.

"How did you do that?!"

Papa Bois didn't answer.

"It was like a dragon, but in reverse!"

The stump was burnt around the edges of the carved cross, but the hanging gem was unscathed. The marker was far from ruined, nothing he couldn't fix with some sandpaper, steel wool, and a little bit of time. He refused to let Onca win. But he'd need to come back and take care of it another time.

Turning to Papa, the questions flowed without pause. "What did he mean by a show? When is he coming back? How much time do I need to get ready? *Your* time is limited, what does that *mean*? And how'd you turn the fireball to ice without water? Can I do that? Did it really hurt him—?"

"Stop." Papa lifted his open palm.

"Sorry."

"Onca will take advantage when you are most vulnerable, as you saw today. Always pay attention."

I know, rule number four.

It had always been the hardest for him. Talin was beginning to wonder if he would be able to relax or let his guard down ever again. It wasn't sounding promising. Life had definitely changed. It would never be the same. Ever.

"To answer your questions...I can turn the fire into ice. You cannot— not without water. Second, if Onca is unable to surprise you when you are most vulnerable, he will happily make a spectacle of it any other time. Next, it will take a lifetime to train you, but we will do what we can to prepare—"

"You mean this is never going to stop?!"

"You made a decision! Our entire lives we never stop learning. We grow, we change, we evolve. If we don't— we are dead. And we all have limited time, even me."

"But– I thought you're immortal."

"Souls are immortal. In the way that those above believe. When we die, our souls leave our bodies and our body returns to the earth. But the soul never dies. One is never truly gone."

Talin stared blankly, "But, you said you were hundreds of years old."

"I am."

Completely confused by the things he'd just heard, Talin stood motionless. Why had Onca said that to Papa?

"We must train now." Papa said, changing the subject.

"But—"

"You need to be ready for your Induction."

Oh yeah.

"You've had enough time here?" Papa asked.

"Well, I had some questions."

"Quickly."

"What is the green stone on the grave?"

"Emerald."

"Why that?"

"You don't know?" Papa's brow was raised.

Talin shook his head. "No."

"I thought your mother told you about the Preserve?"

"Hosea Preserve?"

Papa nodded. "Yes. Healer Kingston planted many of the trees there and worked to protect the area from mining."

"Mining? Like for coal?"

"Emeralds."

Ohhh...

Talin suddenly understood why the area had been such a 'hot sweet potato' as Marisha had called it. Of course a rich Hollywood elite would love to purchase the property. Not only was it the most gorgeous, and peaceful, place on the island, but it was worth a fortune—literally. He swallowed hard, looking down at the emerald. It must have been worth half-a-fortune alone. Just hanging out in the open, anyone could have taken it—like the visitants or voyagers that Papa had just mentioned. Was that where Mama D'lo found many of the jewels that she decorated herself with? How many more emeralds were buried deep within Hosea Preserve? What other jewels were there? Did Healer Kingston plant a preserve on it to hide the fact that there were minerals there worth more than the island itself? How many other people knew about its secret? But before Talin could ask more questions, he was interrupted.

"It's time to head back to the Theater."

More climbing...

They would always be short on time, so wasting no more, Talin used every second to ask questions and learn everything he could regarding the history of the Realm, slipping in questions whenever he had the smallest of opportunities.

"So who did you say these other people in the graves are?" Talin asked as they started their walk away from Kingston's resting place, back to the Theater.

"Besides Healers or their families, there are visitants and voyagers. Both mortals from above, who've been granted special permission to enter the Realm. But voyagers are those who enter the Realm and never leave."

"They all died here?"

"Voyagers did. The others requested this be their burial ground or were those who had nowhere else to go, like those with no place to live or disowned from their families."

Talin wondered if Papa himself had buried them all, and what a feat that must have been. But, the man possessed magical abilities, so maybe it wasn't as difficult as he'd imagined.

CROSSING BACK onto the path leading to the Theater, Talin was enthralled with the fact that other people could enter the Realm, and he continued pressing Papa about who could, when, why, and how. Did they all enter through Jumbie's portal? What did they do while they were here? Did they have to keep it a secret? Could anyone enter or did you have to be invited? Was there a limit to how many visitants could stay and for how long? But after passing through the sea of crosses, Talin had one other pressing question. *How did they die?*

Papa slowed his walk, approaching the crumbling rock trail at the edge of the moat. "Because of the nature of the Realm, visitants must be kept to an absolute minimum, and under the utmost secrecy. Most are invited, but not always."

"Who invites them?" Talin was itching to show Marisha the Realm, proving it exists once and for all. "Can I invite someone?"

"Most visitants are family of Healers and have a reason to be here."

"Like what? Marisha is...family." He stumbled on the word. "She's...related to Healer Dyllon—"

"She has no reason to enter the Realm."

Hearing he would not be able to share the Realm with Marisha made his heart sink. She'd already been so close when she pressed her hand into Jumbie's softened bark. Why couldn't she just press harder, like he had done? What kind of reason would one need to enter the Realm?

"It's time to work." Papa said.

Deflated, and his inquiry session abruptly over, Talin stared at the look-alike tree across from them. He wondered how fast he'd need to climb this time around.

"What would you like at your Induction?" Papa asked.

"I'm sorry?" he said, caught off guard.

"Your Induction, Healer Talin."

Talin had thought about this some time ago, but now was afraid to say what he truly wanted after just being shot down with his request to allow Marisha into his new world. Scared to ask if she and his mother could attend his Induction, he stumbled on his words.

"Um...I, I dunno."

"Shall I decide for you?"

"No, I mean—"

"We must make decisions for ourselves, Talin. Never let others decide what is best for you. This is an Induction that will be remembered for many years. I imagine goats will not be present, but you must decide what you want and how you wish others to perceive you. As long as it is within the rules."

Talin knew exactly what he wanted, but had to muster the courage to ask. It had been against the rules for generations. The worst that could happen would be Papa saying no. Right?

Without wasting more time, he blurted out his number one request.

"I want Mom and Marisha to come."

"Done."

"Really?!"

That was easy.

"Of course. What else?"

He thought quickly.

"No goats."

"I was right," Papa said with a smile.

"Well, at least not for a sacrifice."

Papa smiled and nodded, listening as Talin described the perfect Induction in great detail.

Thinking about what his most elaborate celebration might look like, he would ask for everything he could think of until Papa said no. Ribbons and lights from the tree branches, festive music, singing, local dancers, lots of food, and no alcohol.

But Papa did not say no to a single request.

"I will make sure Jumbie is ready for you."

Talin smiled. His chest swelled with pride.

"Now," Papa continued, "you must climb."

10

Marisha was sitting atop a tall root when Talin crawled out of the portal.

"What are you doing here?" he asked, surprised to see her alone, much less perched atop a root. It was the closest he'd ever seen her to Jumbie, except for the time she ran in a panic after pressing her hand into the portal.

"Wanted to talk." Her voice was quiet.

Talin dusted himself off of loose dirt. "K, about what?" He led the way to the crooked church bench, but Marisha didn't follow.

"Don't you want to go over here?" he asked her.

"No, can we stay under the tree?"

*This **is** unusual.*

"But maybe on the back side between the roots? I'm not supposed to be here," she confessed.

"Oh, yeah, right."

He picked a spot on the opposite side of the tree that within the next hour would have the best view of the setting sun over the ocean. "How'd you know I was here?"

"You weren't home. Where else would you be?"

Talin sat in the dirt, inviting her to sit next to him. It was the perfect spot for hiding from parental eyes. Their shoulders nearly touched in the narrow space.

"Have you been waiting here all afternoon?" he asked her.

"No, not long. When you come home, it always seems to be just before sunset or right after dark."

"How would you know that?"

"Your mom told me."

Oh.

"What happened there?" Marisha pointed to the abrasions on his shins.

"Oh, nothing."

"Talin, what happened?" she pressed, her long hair falling onto a shoulder as she tipped her head.

"Just scratched myself climbing a tree is all."

"Hm. Must have been some tree. You're good at climbing."

At least he didn't have to work anymore to convince her about the Realm being real or being Healer.

"Yeah, well it's different when you're blindfolded."

"What?! Why would you do that?"

"Because Papa said to."

She huffed. "So, if Papa asked you to jump off a bridge, would you?"

He didn't answer, but smiled and let out a quiet laugh. "You sound like your parents."

"Seriously Talin, why would you do that?"

"I needed to."

"Why?"

"Training."

"I thought you were done with that. You're Healer now."

"Nope, it's only just started." Not wanting to scare her, he wasn't sure he wanted to mention Onca's threat, and changed the subject. "So was there anything special you wanted to talk about?"

"Nothing in particular really. Just needed to be out of the house."

"Did something happen?" The last thing Talin remembered was hearing her mother scold her after the Induction. "Were you in trouble for being at the Induction?"

"Yeah," she sighed, "my parents argued two days straight."

"About the Induction?"

"No. You."

"Me?"

Marisha tilted her head dramatically, "Really, Talin?"

"Well, what did they say? What happened?"

Marisha quietly told him the story of her parents arguing about what other people would think of the most recent Evocation at Dewain's Induction and the events that brought it to an abrupt end, meaning Talin's run in with Dewain.

"They told me people were beginning to wonder who the real Healer was, don't you read the paper?"

"No, I've been...in the Realm."

No one from the paper had approached him, or his mother as far as he knew. So it was obvious people had only heard one side of the story.

"They said to be quiet, that the Dyllon family really needed this," she said, apparently referring to needing a Healer in the family.

"Need it, why?"

"Status, I guess. Maybe they think the title will hide the fact that Anya and Amos don't have much. Never did. The Dyllons aren't the wealthiest family on the island. I think it really bothers them."

Recalling the run down neighborhood Talin had found himself in when attacked by Dewain, he realized that the Dyllons not having enough money might make sense to some people. Not to mention his father had walked right into the restaurant later in the day as a regular, seemingly well-treated before Talin had shown up with him, and plopped down a stack of bills that covered more than enough for their meal and the waitress' tip.

But money hadn't mattered to Talin, and no one was paid to be Healer, as far as he knew. Marisha's father was Amos' only brother, why would it bother her parents so much who the Healer was?

"Would your parents believe I was Healer if there was a second Induction?"

"You mean one especially for you?"

"Yeah."

"I thought Dewain's—" she shook her head, "but it's already happened. The tree shaking and…I think that's why so many people are confused."

"Well, I guess it proved I was Healer at the end of the night, but still Papa said I would get my own Induction."

"Really? When? Can I come?" She sat up a little straighter.

Talin smiled, seeing her so excited for him. "He said you and Mom could both come."

"Really?!"

"Yeah, I wouldn't joke about that."

Leaning forward, she wrapped Talin in a tight hug, then abruptly pulled away. "Oh, um," she blushed. "Sorry, I just got excited. I'm really happy for you, Talin."

He smiled. "It's ok." But now he was starting to feel awkward thinking about their family ties. "How come you never said we were cousins?"

Looking as if the blood had drained from her cheeks, Marisha slumped back against the tree. Her eyes looked distant. "What?" she asked, as if she hadn't heard him.

"Come on, Mom filled me in and Papa told me, too. Seems I am the last to know about everything lately."

"I…but we're just friends."

"And *cousins*. Don't play dumb. And that means Dewain is my cousin, too. Wouldn't you think that'd be important for me to know all this time?"

"About the Induction," she changed the subject. "I really want to go but my dad and Uncle Amos won't be happy. I may need to just hide out somewhere and watch from a safe distance."

"Marisha, answer me."

"I don't think we should talk about that right now."

"Well, you wanted to talk, so let's talk."

"My parents forbid me to see you anymore!" she blurted out.

Talin paused, not expecting that.

"Why would they forbid you to see *family*? I know Dewain's Induction didn't end the way everyone wanted, but that's not my fault! My great-grandfather chose me to—"

"It's *really* complicated at home, Talin." He stared, not understanding the sudden change in her mood. "Always has been," she added with her head down. "They don't like it when I hang out around you, even at school. I can't even go to the Falls anymore on my own, unless I sneak out or lie about where I'm going. I'm sure they send Dewain to spy on me."

She went on to say that she'd been told it looked bad for her to be hanging around him, and sent mixed signals to the community, when the Dyllons were making it clear that Dewain was the Healer. Her parents believed she'd helped placed doubt in the minds of the community. They said she needed to be supportive of her family, and that meant keeping her distance from Dewain's perceived threat.

She didn't want to talk about it anymore, and he wanted to know why. What else was she hiding? More importantly, what was the Dyllon family hiding? Seems everyone was hiding something.

. . .

THE ROOTS WOULD SOON CAST a shadow over them when the sun began to set over the sea. Bits of golden light reflected in Marisha's dark eyes.

"So, if you aren't supposed to be around me, how are you going to get to the Induction without your parents finding out?"

"I'll sneak out."

"That's original. You've thought about this already?"

"Well, I'm not going to ask permission if that's what you mean. Just be ready for trouble when everyone shows up."

Talin sat up straighter. "What kind of trouble?"

"I'm not exactly sure. Everyone keeps their voices down when I'm home."

"Who's everyone?"

"Dad, Uncle Amos...Dewain."

"Dewain? He goes to your house?"

She nodded. "He brings friends sometimes."

"So, trouble at my Induction...figures. Do they know a date? Papa hasn't even told me yet."

"You don't know when your own Induction is?"

"No. He just said 'soon'," Talin said, air-quoting Papa.

"I guess you better pick a date then. They all seem to think it's happening soon, too."

Talin wondered if he could even do that. Papa had said he needed to make decisions for himself or others would do it for him. Were 'others' going to set up an Induction, pretend to welcome him with open arms and then—

"What do you think would be a good day?" he asked her.

She shrugged. "But the sooner you figure it out, the less time they have to prepare to screw it all up."

Good point.

"Look," she said, standing up and brushing herself off. "I really should go. Let me know when it is somehow."

"Ok." He stood with her, "but I'm sure you'll hear about it at home, too."

Talin didn't have a chance to say goodbye or question her further, as Marisha turned quickly and disappeared around the root. Peering over, he saw her dart past the old church and down the trail toward the beach.

Talin seriously considered returning to the Realm rather than continuing home. Marisha's news left him with a sense of urgency to schedule a day for his Induction—or at least ask Papa. He had already seen some of the damage that Dewain and his family could inflict, and the longer he waited, as Marisha said, the more people Mr. Dyllon could persuade to join in the trouble-making. If Talin wanted the celebration to be as drama-free as possible he'd need to act fast. But he wanted to make sure he was ready.

And what would his mother think?

Papa's words, *"Stop worrying about your mother,"* echoed in his mind. But he needed to worry about her. He felt responsible for so many things. Yet, there was so much more he was getting ready to take responsibility for. Being Healer was starting to get complicated, and he'd only just begun.

So, sitting under the tree, waiting for the sun to set, he followed rule number five—and made a decision.

———

TALIN PUSHED the vine growth out of his way, re-entering the Realm. In the dusk light, he was careful to check the shadows for anything suspicious. Still unsure of where Papa spent his evenings, Talin set out for the Theater, where they'd last met.

STANDING at the edge of the moat, Jumbie's doppelgänger still remained, but Papa did not. Talin decided to check the Sphere.

At the porthole, Talin peered in. Near the boulder, Papa lay in a woven hammock that hung from the ceiling.

Talin quickly kicked off his shoes before he entered.

"Papa?" he said quietly, hoping not to startle him, "are you awake?"

"I am."

Talin approached.

"Why are you back so soon?" Papa asked.

"I really need to talk to you about the Induction."

Papa raised a brow, but remained still in his hammock.

"I need to know when it is. Is it still soon?"

"What's your hurry?"

"Well, I talked to Marisha and she said the Dyllons are planning trouble and I don't want to give them anymore time to—"

"When would you like it?"

"You mean I can pick?"

"Of course."

Talin hesitated, not knowing when an appropriate time would be. Why hadn't Papa told him this earlier? They'd discussed everything but the timing, but he didn't expect Papa to be so accommodating. "Well, when do you think a good time is? I want to be ready."

Papa's voice was calm. He didn't appear panicked or rushed. "Tomorrow."

"Tomorrow?! But that's too soon!"

"You asked."

"Well, then...maybe a few days?"

"Will the weekend be ok for you?"

"Ok, sure." The words escaped him before he even realized it.

Papa sat up in the hammock. "There is much to be done. Go home and inform Marisha and your mother, but keep the date quiet otherwise."

Talin nodded enthusiastically.

"Can you see about getting your ribbons and decorations for the tree?"

He could.

"I will take care of everything else."

"But how are you going to plan all of the other things from down here?" he asked, referring to the dancers and musicians and all the other details they'd previously discussed.

"I'm a shapeshifter, remember?" Papa said and winked. Talin's heart flipped inside his chest. "Hurry home, and return tomorrow, early if you can."

"Thanks, Papa!"

Talin turned and left the porthole, throwing on his shoes and running down the Cemetery path to Jumbie.

THE SUN WAS SETTING in glorious oranges and purples across the horizon. Talin took a deep breath of the refreshing sea air, looking over the glistening ocean. Not wanting to waste any more time, he ran up the worn path to home, bursting through the back door. The screen door slammed behind him.

"Mom!" he called, then heard grumbling from the home office.

"Some people work in the evenings. Keep it down!"

Talin had been so excited to discuss the Induction with his mother that he'd nearly forgotten his stepfather's random schedule in and out of the house.

"Sorry. Is mom home?"

"Upstairs."

HIS MOTHER WAS PROPPED up against a fluffy stack of pillows, reading in bed. Her nightstand lamp cast a golden light across her face. A pile of colored material, in the process of being transformed into her Induction dress, sat next to the sewing machine.

"What's going on, Talin?" Her book dropped down to her lap. "You missed dinner."

"I'm sorry. I was with Papa."

"Oh," she took a breath. "What did you do today?"

"Is your dress done?"

"Not yet. In a few more days maybe."

"Will it be done by Friday?"

She sat straight up, holding in a gasp.

"Papa said you and Marisha could come to my Induction."

"This Friday? In three days?!" She clutched her chest.

"Well, he said this weekend, and ceremonies seem to always be on Fridays, so I think—"

"Well, there's no time to waste then!" She leapt out of bed, headed for the sewing machine. Pulling the chair up to the desk, she started fluffing the materials and turned on the machine. The built-in light illuminated her needle and thread.

"Who is going to be there? Oh my goodness, is there going to be an announcement soon? Hopefully your fath— Robert, will be out that night..." She shook her head. "He usually is lately." Then she grabbed the white lace trim she was preparing to sew onto the skirt. "Do you like the color?" she asked him, holding the lace up beside the cherry-red and white plaid-patterned madras cloth.

Red was the dominant color but it had a touch of yellow, too. Picking up a brilliant canary-yellow satin ribbon, she held it between the lace and madras, telling him she was going to hand-stitch it between the two at the hem to bring out more of the yellow.

"Then I'll have a matching yellow sash for the waist."

It was obvious she was quite proud of her work.

"Yes, I like it. It's bright."

"Yes, well, I wanted something traditional but with bright colors! What are you going to wear?" she asked him.

He hadn't given his own wardrobe any thought at all, but hoped he didn't have to wear red.

"Oh, I'm not sure."

"Well, if you need me to make anything, you need to let me know right away."

"Ok, I will, but I don't need anything special made, I don't think, but...I do need some help with the tree."

"The tree?" She turned away from her project to face him. "With what?"

"Can you help me decorate Jumbie?"

"Well, I...of course. What do you need?"

"I was hoping we could hang ribbons or something from the branches. I need to ask Marisha, too, but she may not be able to help."

A smile lit up her face. "Sounds festive. Certainly I have some spare ribbons around here." Leaving her seat, she began rummaging through the trunk at the foot of her bed. "If not, I can run to the store tomorrow and pick up something nice."

"Mom, you don't have to spend any money."

"It's ok, I don't mind. It's a special occasion."

It was a nice change for him to see her happy about his new role and less afraid than she had been the last few weeks. But he could only imagine how that could rapidly change when Robert found out about everything.

"Have you told...anyone about me?"

"What do you mean?"

"Well, when someone," he cocked his head toward the door, "finds out about me not just spending time at the tree, but actually inside of it, don't you think there's going to be a prob—"

"Talin," she interrupted, "how about this?" She pulled out a roll of solid red satin ribbon.

Red...

"Mom, you're going to be ok, right?"

"Maybe I could layer the yellow ribbon on top of this one."

"Mom..."

"Yes?"

"Did you hear me?"

"I heard you." She continued to rummage through the trunk looking for more ribbon.

"And?"

"I'll figure it out."

"It's in three days. What if it doesn't go well?"

"I'll figure it out."

Knowing what his past trips to the tree had meant for her, he wasn't convinced. When taking away Talin's cell phone and binoculars didn't work to keep him home, Robert turned to Shantel to take out his frustrations, physically. It wasn't long ago that she'd suffered a black eye from the hands of her own husband, while protecting Talin. He knew she would always protect him—and worry about him, especially now. Being bullied by Dewain, although not pleasant, had proven to be nothing compared to some of his trips into the Realm. Knowing how his mother worried whenever he came back injured from various training scenarios with skinned knees, burned hands, or nearly drowned in the Sluice, he wondered what she would think when it came time to fully fill in Robert. Would she again be in danger being on the receiving end of his anger? More so, would Talin be able to protect her? Talin didn't want her worrying anymore about her own safety because of his new role.

"You know he's going to find out when he hears all the music and we aren't here," he suggested.

"Music? Oh, what kind of music? I thought it would be traditional or fancy but...a little more reserved." She seemed to be avoiding his question.

"Well, Papa said music and singing and dancing."

"Oh." She sat back onto her heels in front of the trunk.

"What?"

"So, it's going to be like the others?"

"Without the goats."

"Of course," she whispered.

Her sudden change in demeanor concerned him.

"Are you ok?"

"Oh," she shook her head and looked up, "I'll be fine honey. Why don't you try and find something festive to wear and I'll finish up gathering ribbon by tomorrow. Then we can talk more."

11

As instructed, Talin returned to the Realm as early as he could. The sun had just risen when he pushed through the vine growth. Orange and golden rays crossed the Lake and Meadow, the glow was perfect camouflage for Onca amidst the morning shadows.

Seeing no signs of the cat, Talin secured his pack and set out for the Sphere. The air was still, birds were chirping, and the fruity smell of frangipani hung in the air. Staying acutely aware of his surroundings for any unwelcome surprises, he noticed a dark figure on the far side of the Lake.

A lone black horse was grazing in the Meadow, its mane and tail so long it was difficult to see where they ended in the tall grass.

Wow.

He wanted to get a closer look, but hesitated. Knowing this place, he might get more than he bargained for. Going around the lake might also scare it away or cause it to charge, so Talin stopped, admiring it from a distance. He made a clicking noise with his tongue to get its attention.

The horse lifted its head and looked in Talin's direction, ears perked. It didn't make any noise or try to run, only stood, looking absolutely majestic in a sea of green all the way up to its belly. Sparkles of golden light seemed to bounce off its black back. Talin could have stared at it all day, but Papa was waiting, so after a few moments he continued down the path. Before entering the forest, he looked back across the Lake. The horse was gone.

ENTERING THE SPHERE, there weren't any unusual obstacles to climb or jump on. All the weapons were in their place along the wall. Maybe they were going back to the Theater today.

Papa entered through the opposite porthole, his arms full of fruit. Noticing Talin, he bowed his head.

"Good morning, Healer Talin."

"Good morning, Papa."

"Would you care for some juice?"

Papa met Talin at the table and they cut fresh oranges. Talin used the mortar and pestle to extract the juice.

"Were you able to secure your arrangements yesterday for the Induction?" Papa asked.

"Yes, mom is going to help decorate Jumbie."

"Very good, and Marisha?"

"I don't think she can. Her parents won't let her near me." He took a gulp of juice. "You said don't tell anyone about the Induction, so will there be an announcement somewhere, or is anyone going to show up?"

"It's already taken care of."

Oh...

Oh no.

"But how will I know how many—"

"Let me focus on the details. You focus on protecting yourself. Those who need to know have been notified."

"Are the Dyllons invited?"

"You need to focus on other things, not the Dyllons. Are you ready for today?"

Talin took a deep breath. "Yes."

"Can you climb to the top?" Papa gestured towards the top of the Sphere.

"There's no ropes."

"There are plenty of things around you to get to the top," he said, motioning with his hand, referring to the wall of trees surrounding them. The trunks and branches formed a type of lattice work, arching inward the higher they came to the open circle at the top of the dome.

"Oh, ok." Talin turned and walked toward the entry porthole, planning to climb the Sphere from outside.

"The entry is blocked." Papa said.

"No it's not. It's fine." As Talin leaned over to exit the Sphere, his back was met with a burning thump. "Ow!"

Fireball.

"What was that for?"

"I told you the entry was blocked."

"But it's not bl—"

"For this drill, you will act as if the portholes are not here."

Ohhh.

"How am I supposed to climb to the roof then?"

Papa did not answer. Then the answer came to Talin.

"Wait. I can't climb from the *inside*."

"Why not?"

"I'll fall where the trees start bending in. I can't hang on upside down!"

"You told me you were ready. Are you not?"

Talin grumbled and walked to the wall nearest him. Tilting his head up and back, he searched for branches that were small enough to grab but sturdy enough to hold his weight when they sagged. There was a mixture of dried, dead branches and lush, fresh green ones. Each posed their own risk. Breaking a branch would send him tumbling to the ground. The freshest greenery would bend under his weight with no way to climb back up. Both options left the possibility to start the drill all over again. And once he met the curvature of the branches overhead, he knew the second half of the climb would require all upper body strength. Pushing with his feet would be impossible. Having climbed many ropes in this very training area, he tried to change his mindset.

Taking a breath, he reached out to a branch and tugged, testing its sturdiness. It held. Pulling his weight straight up the wall, his foot felt for a root to balance himself. Limbs cracked as he placed his weight on them. Face to face with a wall of green interwoven roots and branches, he tried to concentrate and think ahead.

Placing one hand above the other, he gently checked the sturdiness of each limb before allowing it to bear his weight, slowly ascending until he was about fifteen feet up the wall. The first part of the climb wasn't so bad. Then, as he suspected, the creaking limbs started to sag under his weight. They began to arch inward with a good thirty-five feet for him to reach the top of the Dome.

Talin was grateful the bark was smooth. He supposed it could be worse, riddled with thorns and crumbling dried shards of bark. Staying focused on his ascent, he looked for the next branch to grasp.

Water splashed below in the Drop and Talin turned his head to look.

All he saw was choppy waves sloshing about.

"Papa, what was that?"

A bird screeched, flying past him and out the top of the Dome.

The Drop was usually calm until something, or someone, fell into it. Whatever it was, was large. Or sounded large.

"Keep climbing," Papa said.

. . .

BUT THE CLIMB was easier said than done. The wall he was climbing was gradually transforming into the ceiling. Gravity tugged at his feet as he progressed until he could no longer make contact with the more vertical wall with his lower limbs. He was now dangling from only his hands, and soon it might only be his fingertips.

It was like hanging from the monkey bars of a jungle gym, only this jungle gym wasn't horizontal. And not nearly this high in the air. He began to shift his weight by swinging his legs slightly to gain some momentum and grabbing a branch a few inches above him. Moving in short arm lengths, he covered several feet this way with relative ease, until his shoulders began to ache and his palms grew hot from the friction of his hanging weight.

No encouragement came from below, but Talin didn't dare utter that he couldn't complete the task. If he fell now, he'd land in a crumpled heap on the ground nearly thirty feet down.

Don't fall. Don't fall.

His ankles, at the least, would surely be broken, putting a hard stop to his Induction. He did not want that. Being more than half-way up to the Dome, there was no going back. Recalling the amazing view he and Papa had shared the last time he climbed to the roof, he was desperate to soak in that view again.

Focusing on each handhold helped, and he celebrated internally each time he clung to a new branch. The curvature of the wall finally morphed into the ceiling, becoming horizontal, like the more familiar school monkey bars, and the strain on his shoulders eased up slightly. Swinging his legs again gave him the last burst of momentum he needed to reach the opening above the Drop in a short amount of time.

It took a few more swings to throw the weight of his legs up and over, onto the edge of the roof. Talin expended every bit of his remaining strength to push up with his arms and collapse onto his back atop the flat surface.

He wanted to scream and cheer, but was too tired. No sound escaped except his heavy breathing and a quiet moan.

"Very good, now come down," he heard from below.

What? Right now?

He hadn't even caught his breath or sat up to take in the view he was looking so forward to.

"Ok, I just need a second," he said, trying not to sound irritated or obviously exhausted.

"No time."

Of course there's not.

Talin quickly righted himself to look out over the Realm. Past the Lake, in the Meadow, stood the black horse. Its head down, it grazed in the grass alone.

"Talin!" Papa called, distracting him.

"Coming!"

Talin crouched on the edge of the Dome, looking over and feeling a pinch in his stomach. He carefully sat on the edge of the opening with his legs hanging over the Drop, and looked at his reddened palms. He wondered if the climb down would be any less painful. It had to be easier than the climb up.

"It's time to jump." Papa said.

"What?!"

"You need to jump."

He can't be serious.

Talin's heart nearly stopped. He shook his head and backed away from the opening.

"Ohh, no. I'm not jumping."

"Why not? You jumped from the boulder. Same thing."

"No, it's not! This is twice as high!"

He knew what would happen as soon as he landed in the Drop— if he survived striking the water from nearly fifty feet up. Visions of every bone shattering in his body flashed through his mind, then the fear of screaming as he hit the surface and sucking water into his lungs instead of air—suffocating till he drowned.

"I've seen the island cliff divers. If they can do it, and from much higher up, so can you."

"They've been trained!"

"And you're training now. Jump."

"Papa—"

"Talin. You've leapt from the boulder, leapt at Hosea Falls—"

"Pushed!"

"It's not that much higher. Quit babbling and jump."

He couldn't think of a way out of this one, and Papa had used the term 'babbling' like he was a toddler. He could swing his feet over and start climbing down like a monkey, but he was afraid of the reprimand Papa would give him when he reached the ground— if he reached the ground in one piece. Fireballs could be thrown his way, Papa could magically change the structure of the Sphere, causing him to fall anyway or any number of unusual and dangerous things. He also knew if he was hurt, Papa could help heal any injuries he had, but he wasn't sure drowning counted in that—and he didn't want to test the theory to find out.

Make a decision.

Be bold.

He took a breath...and jumped.

The air rushed past him, his hair flying above him, his arms and legs flailing as he fell. He had only moments to grab his nose and twist his body in a way that would let him land in the water feet first...

As he hit the surface, his hand was ripped away from his nose and he descended deep into the Drop. His ears popped but his left ear burned with severe pain. Feeling intense pressure around his chest, he held out his arms and legs to slow his speed and began swimming ferociously to the surface. The bubbles were muffled around him.

Again, he was unable to swim against the strong current and was quickly pulled down lower, then flushed in the opposite direction, still unable to control his own direction in the Sluice. With his ears ringing and his lungs burning, he was quickly propelled out of the water to the surface.

Gasping for air, Talin erupted in a coughing fit, gagging, and attempting to stay afloat. Wiping his eyes, he looked around. He was back in the Lake. Releasing a maddening yell, the sound was muffled in his left ear like it'd been stuffed with cotton. He slapped the water with his reddened palms.

Ow!

A neighing sound drifted from across the Meadow.

Startled, Talin turned.

The black horse was at the edge of the Meadow, staring directly into Talin's eyes.

Barely treading water, Talin tried to swim in the horse's direction. Pain had returned to his previously injured rib and ankle. Then another coughing spell spooked the horse, causing it to bolt, its exceptionally long black mane and tail flowing behind it.

As Talin reached the shore of the Meadow, he dragged himself out of the water and struggled to stand on his throbbing ankle. He was unable to see where the horse had escaped to as the grass was so tall it reached his chest. For all he knew, the horse could have simply laid down, completely disappearing, and he'd be none the wiser.

Exhausted, Talin turned around hoping to see Papa Bois magically appear on the opposite shoreline.

What was the point of all this?!

Climbing, leaping, jumping, swimming, fighting. He thought he was supposed to be healing. The only thing he'd really learned about healing was in the apothecary class, learning to mix local herbs and natural plants. There had to be more.

Papa was not waiting on the shoreline.

Talin knew from previous drills he could hike back to the Sphere or take the Sluice. But, he didn't know how to take the Sluice from the Lake to the Sphere, and he wasn't sure he wanted to with a reinjured rib and ankle. He was not about to ask Papa how to return through the Sluice just yet either–because he'd learn. Right now, he might end up at Hosea Falls, even further from where he needed to be. Limping on his weakened ankle, further than what was necessary, was also not a wise choice with Onca on the prowl.

Glancing back one last time into the Meadow, Talin began to walk from the far side of the Lake back to the road that led into the Cemetery and beyond. It was a long, painful trek. He constantly looked over his shoulder and through the trees. Being easy prey at this point, limping along, he needed to make it back to Papa's healing hands if he was going to make it to the Induction in one piece.

Entering the Sphere, Talin watched as Papa prepped another glass of juice and approached him quietly.

"Papa..."

"Ah, you've returned."

"I need your help."

"That's why I am here, to help you," he said, dropping a pinch of bright yellow powder into the glass then handing it to Talin.

"No, really. I hurt myself from the jump."

"I imagine it was the landing, not the jump?" The words were muffled in one ear, but Talin understood the joke.

"My rib and my ankle are really hurting again. Can you fix it?"

"I may be able to help a little bit. Drink. Then I'll take a look."

"What did you just put in it?"

"Turmeric."

Talin had learned a bit about turmeric earlier, recalling it helped with inflammation. "Did you know I'd be hurt?" Staring into his glass, he took a sniff.

"It was obvious when you jumped you were out of control. We'll need to work on that."

"What?" Talin's head whipped back up at Papa Bois.

"Go ahead, drink."

Talin didn't want to drink his orange juice laced with bitter turmeric. The smell was a blend of orange and ginger, which wasn't so bad in itself. It was the acidic aftertaste he knew was coming. But wanting to feel better for the Induction, and knowing he would need to be at his best, he took a large gulp of the concoction. Surprisingly, the orange juice overpowered much of the musky, peppery bite from the spice, but not all of it. His nose wrinkled as he struggled to get the remaining juice down.

"Come lie on the boulder." Papa said.

Talin lay on his back, as flat as he could, the boulder pressing an uncomfortable arch into his flanks.

"Close your eyes and breathe."

He could hear Papa warming his hands together as he did in the Shelter. Calloused, warm hands then pressed into the left side of his chest.

"You are holding your breath. You need to breathe."

Trying to relax as best he could with a giant rock stretching out his back, he exhaled, willing his entire body to loosen up and sink onto the stone.

Papa's hands pushed firmly in a rhythmic motion. His thumbs seemed to pinpoint the exact location of the pain. Talin winced. The soothing motion continued for several minutes until Talin finally relaxed and noticed the area starting to feel numb.

Papa's hands slowly lifted their healing pressure, but remained just above Talin's chest. Talin couldn't feel Papa physically touching him, but somehow sensed he was still there and not finished with his work. He didn't move until instructed.

"Better?" Papa asked.

"Yeah. A lot." Talin exhaled like he'd just received a massage from the island's one and only award-winning spa. Papa offered an outstretched hand to help him up. Talin felt only a minor pinch when bending forward to sit upright.

"It's not perfect and you will need to protect it from injury for a time." Papa instructed.

"Thanks, Papa."

Papa bowed his head respectfully. "Now, the ankle?"

"It's just a little sore, not like my rib. But I can't hear very well out of my ear. Can you fix that?"

"The fish will help with the ankle. The ear I cannot help with."

Happy to hear his ankle could be helped but disappointed knowing his hearing might suffer for a while, Talin asked, "So, do we need to go back to the Lake to see the fish?"

"No need." Papa raised his hand over the Drop and the water began to spin.

"I don't want to go down the Sluice again!"

"Shh."

Talin watched as the glistening blue water transformed into a swirling blur of reds, yellows, greens and even purple.

"Is that the fish?!"

The water settled and stopped spinning when Papa lowered his hand. "You may sit on the edge now."

Talin moved to the edge of the Drop and dangled his feet below the surface. Hundreds of small, colored fish began circling his ankle, making their own cyclone of water around it. His foot began to tingle.

As quickly as the school of fish organized and began circling, they slowed and moved away, darting about in the pool as if they were playing. Talin sat in awe, admiring the colors, patterns, and color combinations of each individual fish. One by one, they swam away deep into the Drop.

"How do they know to come to you?"

"We are all connected, Talin."

"Is there anything you can't do?"

"Raise the dead."

Talin let out a laugh at what he thought was Papa's sarcasm, but seeing his face, he realized Papa was not joking at all.

"Oh. You're serious? For real?"

"For real."

Hearing this blunt answer, Talin had learned the answer to his earlier question and consciously made it a point to follow all the rules of the Realm, to the letter, for his own safety. From this point on he'd pay keen attention to his surroundings, remaining alert to anything that may cause him harm underground. He certainly didn't need to risk a tangle with Onca without Papa by his side. Realizing he wasn't much safer above ground with the Dyllons' threats against him than he was below—it was more important than ever to pay attention to the things Papa Bois was trying to teach him. He easily could have drowned in the Sluice, more than once, and when Papa had asked him early on to practice his swimming with Marisha...he hadn't. And now that she was forbidden to even be near him, there was no way he could be on the public beach or in the waves with her. Plus, the thought of not being alive to protect his mother was unbearable.

"It always bothered me. I can live almost infinitely, heal the sick and wounded, shapeshift, and possess magical abilities. But I cannot help those once they have left this world." His voice was low and quiet as he stared into the Drop.

"Was there someone you couldn't save?"

Papa looked up from his gaze, "I believe your hearing will return to that ear, given time. But right now you have very little of that to prepare for the Induction, so I suggest we keep moving before your pains return. Shall we continue?"

The way Papa Bois had spoken made Talin uncomfortable.

"Well...Ok," he stumbled on the answer. He got up and stood next to the old man.

"First, you should learn a proper water entry."

Water sentry?

"I'm sorry, what?"

"Attention, Talin. You must focus."

"I'm trying, I can't hear out of that ear very well and it hurts," he said, rubbing his left ear.

Papa turned to face Talin. "Since you are going to be spending a large amount of time within the Realm, you should learn a proper water entry."

Talin's eyes widened.

Oh no, he means dive! But, certainly not from that high up!

"There are many places here where the skill could prove useful," Papa continued.

Talin stared. Heights had not exactly been his strong suit in recent weeks and he wondered what other environmental hazards awaited him within the Realm.

"But, I can't jump from—"

"Rule number six! As Healer, you must have confidence. You cannot show weakness. You will no longer use the term *can't* in such a context."

Why does he have to sound just like my mother?

"Do you understand?"

"Yes." Talin's voice was soft and hushed, definitely not exuding much confidence.

"Let's start with that. Speak up after you've made a decision. You don't sound confident. You sound like a lost puppy."

Yeah, just like I couldn't outrun a sloth...

"Yes, I understand." His voice was louder this time.

The thrill of his adventures was fading. Talin had loved learning so many things about his great-grandfather, and was grateful he'd been encouraged to find his biological father, although his first meeting was not what he had expected. The Realm had proven to be a great escape from some of the more unpleasant realities above. His newfound title made him think he could do anything and finally be accepted by others, but the reality of mastering it and understanding its bigger importance was much more than he expected. The Realm and its problems were real. Papa was real. Even Marisha and his mother had seen him with their own eyes. Talin couldn't help but recall the looks on both their faces upon seeing Papa Bois after Dewain's failed Induction. His mother was stunned, Marisha had fainted.

The man standing in front of him had seen generations of real Healers before him. Talin had not even graduated high school, had never met his great-grandfather, and was expected to fulfill a role he hadn't believed even existed several weeks earlier. He'd made a choice to accept his title after nearly drowning in the Sluice, without knowing what else lay ahead. But his own belief in himself was fleeting at best, especially during times when he was injured. All this only served to remind him, again, that Onca was very real, too.

"You had confidence with Marisha when you walked her home after the last Induction. Where did that go?"

"How'd you know that?"

A tomcat's rough growl sounded from within the man's throat, but his lips never moved.

Talin's mouth dropped open. "That was you?!"

"I still need to keep a close eye on you." Beginning to pace in the grass, Papa redirected the conversation. "Now, you must practice, manage your time, pay close attention. And, you are injured again so it is more important than ever you become proficient and confident at all your skills. Do you understand?"

"I understand." He answered, standing a little straighter.

"Very good, as we will not visit this discussion again."

Gulp.

"Let's start from somewhere you are comfortable."

THEY ENTERED the Theater from the stone path. Jumbie's double remained untouched at the stone stage, roots flowing off into the moat. The sundial was cleaned of dirt, from the last tidal wave that had nearly swept Talin away with it. Roots covered a portion of the designs on the outside rings of the carving.

"You are comfortable in the tree?"

"Yes."

"Climb the low branch here over the moat."

Easy task...for now.

Talin climbed up the branch Papa chose, tenderly supporting his weight when stepping on his sore ankle, unable to risk another injury. Straddling atop the branch, he asked, "What now?"

"Jump."

"From here?"

Papa nodded.

The branch was about ten feet above the water. Without hesitation, Talin stood and jumped off the branch feet first into the moat. Surfacing, he swam to the edge of a root snaking its way into the moat. He climbed the root back up on the platform.

"Now, the next branch higher up." Papa said.

I see where this is going.

Climbing up past the first branch, Talin found a launch point a few feet higher, just far enough to the side that he wouldn't crash into the one below him.

"Jump from here now?" he asked, looking into the moat.

"Yes."

Talin stepped off the branch, falling into the water and landing in a seated position.

Ouch.

"I see the problem," Papa called when Talin surfaced. "It's not the height that is your problem."

Yeah, right.

"It's your entry into the water, as I thought. Have you ever dove before?"

"I'm on the track team, not the swim team."

"Running won't be your strong point either if you don't protect yourself and that ankle. The higher you go, the more out of control you are."

Well, yeah...

"You need to be tight when you enter the water."

"Tight?" he asked, climbing out of the moat.

"Stiffen yourself, like the dagger. Arms straight and down at your sides." He demonstrated the position for Talin. "Try again."

Talin went back to the same branch and looked out over the edge and jumped, pulling his arms in at his side as he drew in a deep breath. He dropped into the water with barely a splash.

Papa complimented him as he surfaced and instructed him to climb the next highest branch.

As Talin climbed higher, so did his anxiety. It was difficult to find branches that had clear paths to the water the higher he went, and he looked for branches on different sides of the tree. Now a little over twenty feet up, Talin was starting to feel pain returning, and he wondered if the cliff divers on the island ever worried about crashing into the sides of the cliff on their way down. Watching the next summer's Olympic high dive competition on television would definitely have a new meaning.

Hesitating on his branch, he was coached from the ground.

"Focus on your landing. If you hold your arms out, like a cross, while you are coming down, it will slow your fall. Be sure to tuck them in and be tight before going into the water."

Rehearsing the move in his mind, he envisioned the high divers...and the cliff divers...and jumped.

"Well done." He heard a woman's voice behind him as he surfaced.

Turning around, he was sharing the water with Mama D'lo.

"Thank you," he smiled. "Have you been here this whole time?"

"Not long, I heard splashing and needed to investigate. And, my! You were like a bird gliding out of the tree!" Her tail swished in the water.

"Mama D'lo," Papa said, "I may need your assistance in the coming days."

"Oh yes, Papa, anything a'tall!"

"Talin will be Inducted as Healer this Friday evening."

Mama clapped her hands in excitement while Papa motioned to Talin with his finger to exit the water. "Would you increase your patrols in the waterways should things get out of hand?"

"It would be my honor," she said and bowed, leaning over at the waist where her tail met her torso.

"But there's no water up there at Jumbie." Talin interjected, climbing out of the moat and pointing toward the underground sky.

"Anything can happen at an Induction." Papa reminded him. "Thank you, Mama D'lo. We will be finishing here soon. I apologize for disturbing you."

"Very well. No problem. Happy flying, Talin!" Mama called before diving under the water, her tail flicking behind and propelling her down into the moat. She disappeared beneath the bubbles.

"I'd like you to dive a few more times, Talin."

"Ok." His answer felt more confident knowing that Mama D'lo would have his back if anything were to go wrong.

"Go back to the last branch."

Talin made his way back up into the tree and walked out onto the branch.

"I'd like you to go head first this time." Papa called up.

"What?"

"Did you not hear, or are you questioning me?"

"Both," he said flatly. "You really want me to dive in head first? How deep is it? I really don't need to break my neck this time."

"You just watched a serpent swim away to another part of the Realm. I believe it's safe to say it's deep enough."

He had a point.

Talin had never dove anywhere head first—willingly.

He'd been shoved once, maybe just a few feet higher than where he now stood, and was wildly out of control. It was a miracle he'd not landed in a belly flop or flat on his back.

"I don't think I—" Talin caught himself. "I don't...know how to do that."

"Lean forward as you take off, arms out to control yourself, same as before. But pull them over your head with your hands together, palms flat, before you hit the water.

He wasn't liking the sound of that last hit-the-water-part.

"Remember to stay tight, hands flat against the water, elbows locked, straight like your dagger," he added.

Talin wondered if Papa ever had to do any of the stunts he was constantly asked to do. How did he know so much about diving? Maybe he watched the cliff divers more than Talin thought?

Balancing himself on the branch, looking down, he leaned forward, held his breath and pushed off. Pulling his arms straight above his head, he struck the water, legs toppling over backwards and his calves slamming against the surface.

He surfaced with a painful yell. "This isn't going to work!"

"Rule number six!" Papa yelled. "You didn't slow your descent with arms out, and you weren't straight enough entering the water. Try again."

"But Papa!"

"Again."

Talin pulled his body from the moat and carefully climbed back to the branch.

My legs hurt.

"Focus," Papa said.

Talin took slow breaths.

My rib hurts.

"Arms out, arms up."

He reviewed the fall in his mind.

This isn't the Olympics.

"Like a dagger," Papa continued.

At least I'm not blindfolded.

Talin leaned over, arms wide and let gravity pull him over the limb.

Striking the water with arms above his head, he plunged deep into the moat. It felt as if his body wouldn't stop. Pulling his arms out to his sides, he began kicking and swimming for the surface.

"Perfect, Healer Talin. Perfect." Papa said.

12

DURING A BREAK FROM THE AFTERNOON'S TRAINING, TALIN SAT atop the Sphere, one of his favorite places in the world now, and asked Papa, "What's going to happen at my Induction?"

He obviously had never been to a proper Induction before, at least not in its entirety, and he wasn't even sure what was supposed to happen. All he knew was which things wouldn't be happening this weekend.

"A lot of celebration mostly. You won't be required to do much."

"I don't have to give a speech do I?"

Papa chuckled. "No, not unless you want to."

Talin shook his head.

Looking out over the Realm, seeing the Meadow sparked his memory.

"Are there horses here?"

"There are many animals that make the Realm their home, but horses are not one of them."

"Then how did the black horse get here this morning?"

Papa Bois sat up straighter, all his attention on Talin. "You saw a horse this morning?"

"Yeah, after I jumped from here into the Sluice. I came up in the Lake and there was a big black horse in the Meadow."

"Why didn't you tell me?"

"I didn't think it was a big deal, and you said there was too much to do. So..." Talin shrugged.

Concern washed over Papa's face.

"What? Is something wrong?"

"Word travels faster than it used to." Papa answered quietly.

"What are you talking about?"

"I imagine the horse you saw was Thantos. Did it have a long mane and tail and three legs?"

"Three legs?! I don't know about that, the grass was too tall to see. But it ran off so fast there was no way it was missing a leg. A horse can't live on three legs!"

"It was riderless?"

"Yeah, just munching on the grass."

Papa rubbed his chin. "Very odd."

"What's odd? I mean, three legs is odd, and this whole place is odd," he said, motioning to the vast landscape around him, "but what's the big deal about the horse? He looked harmless. A horse can't do much with three legs anyways. They usually die, or people put them down."

"Thantos is generally only out at night, and usually not within the Realm. Word is definitely spreading about you. He must have come for the Induction. Many spirits and beings will be wanting to see."

This is getting weird.

"So...this horse, is a spirit or a *real* three-legged horse?"

"It depends who you ask. You see me as real, yet those above see me as a spirit. Know that Thantos is very real, but do not get close to him."

"Why not?" he asked, thinking of how the horse had spooked when he tried swimming toward it.

"His breath is toxic. Those that breathe it in become severely ill, many do not survive."

"A three-legged horse that can kill me with its breath?" He chuckled, then stopped. "You're for real?"

"If you have learned one thing during your time in the Realm, what would it be?" Papa asked in a most serious tone of voice.

"Um," Talin paused to think about what it was that Papa was after. "That things aren't as they are above."

"Correct. Never forget that. You are a human ambassador here. Many beings can easily overpower you."

Onca immediately came to Talin's mind as Papa continued. And how Papa could not save people from death. Now, there was a horse breathing poisonous fumes to worry about.

"You are the youngest Healer the Realm has ever had. This can be seen as a weakness that will be taken advantage of. I assure you. They know it will take time for you to learn the land, the rules, the history. So don't be surprised if you start to see more beings both in and out of the Realm. Not all wish you well."

This was all the more reason for Talin to be keenly aware of his surroundings at all times. The seriousness of what he was doing was sinking deeper into his gut. His stomach ached and cramped as the words washed over him.

So far, Talin's focus had been to learn how to defend himself from the biggest potential risks he could face at the Induction. Papa critiqued his use of weapons for defense, his climbing skills to escape pursuit, his ability to dodge and create fireballs and, of course, how to display more confidence. They'd covered improvisation and resourcefulness using the things you have around you to combat an attacker.

"How much more do I need to learn, and how long is it going to take?"

"It will depend on how quickly you can learn and retain the skills and information. And on how many beings will challenge you and how soon. And how many at a time. You will never stop learning."

They both sat silent for a few moments as Talin took in the spectacular view of the Realm. It looked so serene, so peaceful, lush and beautiful. Birds chirped, squirrels scampered up and down tree trunks. The breeze danced in his hair, carrying the sweet scent of a nearby frangipani with it. He was reminded of the first moment he stepped into the Realm, completely unaware of what incredible dangers lay hidden within such a pristine place.

Pulling his thoughts back to the original subject, Talin asked, "So, what's going to happen at *my* Induction?"

"Ah, yes." Papa cleared his throat. "Guests will arrive just before sunset. You should wait at the house with your father—"

"Whoa, wait. My father or... my stepdad?"

"Well, your father, of course."

"No way. My mom doesn't want to see him and my stepfather will—"

"Be just fine," Papa interjected. "I doubt your stepfather will even be home with the usual Friday night special at the pub."

"Oh, but Papa, I really don't think that will—"

"Well, if not at the house, you need to be nearby so your father can escort you in."

"My *dad* walks me in?"

"It is tradition. He is an elder and you are his son."

"My *dad* is an elder, too?"

"You didn't discuss this with him?"

"No...it didn't go like I thought it would. When I told him about Healer Hun—I mean, Onca, he left in a hurry."

"I see."

"I don't know if my dad will even be there."

"I suggest you wait in the tree line then. When the circle forms, you will be escorted to Jumbie's base and the elders will present you."

"The elders hate me."

"They don't all hate you."

That's comforting.

"The dancers will perform for you and offerings will be made to the tree— no goats, of course." Papa winked. "Then it's time for fellowship, relax and enjoy music and dancing, food and drink. The evening will close with a final dance and individual blessings to you. Quite informal."

It sounded perfect, but only time would tell if it would go down without drama.

"What do I wear? Do I have to have something special?"

"Wear what you are comfortable in. Make sure you can move freely in case of trouble. Keep your weapon accessible at your side."

For Talin, that meant his cargo shorts and a simple tee shirt. Nothing spectacular.

PAPA REVIEWED defense drills with Talin the remainder of the day, in a variety of familiar locations within the Realm. He attempted to keep Talin's pain at bay with healing treatments between the sessions, and Talin even learned to identify a few types of the fish that swam around his ankle in the Drop. Angelfish, blue tang, parrotfish and clown fish were easily identifiable, but there were others he'd never seen before such as cichlids, killifish, basslet and royal grammas.

INTO THE EVENING they focused their training in the Theater under the added shade of Jumbie's branches, as it would most closely resemble Talin's Induction.

"Can you climb with the blindfold again?" asked Papa.

Even with fatigue setting in, Talin mustered, "Yes."

Retrieving the crumbled wad from his pocket, he rolled it up narrow enough to cover his eyes.

"With respect, Talin." Papa said, taking the cloth from Talin's hands. He folded it neatly, pressing the creases with his fingers, and flattening it into a perfect narrow strip.

"Sorry," Talin said, "I'm tired."

"Not an excuse," Papa scolded, motioning for Talin to turn so he could place the blindfold over his eyes and tie it in place. "Climb as high as you can."

Stumbling, it took Talin a moment to find his place on the platform and feel his way to a familiar root.

"Stop." Talin heard. "Do you know where you are?"

"Yeah."

"Did you when I blindfolded you?"

"Well...no, I guess not. I had to figure it out."

Papa retrieved Talin by the hand and led him back to the starting point several feet away from Jumbie's trunk. "Rule number four." He briefly lifted the blindfold from Talin's eyes. "Even when you are tired."

Then he said, "Look," as Talin's eyes started to focus in the tree's direction. And just as quickly, Papa pulled the blindfold back down. "Now, climb."

Not enough time.

Careful to avoid tripping, Talin turned toward the tree and took several cautious steps until he bumped into a root and ran his hands along the bark. Feeling an imperfection full of splinters a few inches deep confirmed he knew where he was. He pulled his body weight up. Crawling on the root and making his way up to the trunk, he tried to hide his smile.

"Very good."

Papa had him repeat the exercise several times by starting Talin in different locations around the tree and spinning him in circles before letting him go. With each repetition Talin became faster and more confident, and he was able to climb quite high into the tree.

"You may come down now."

Please don't make me dive... please, don't make me dive.

"May I climb down?"

"Would you rather dive blindfolded?"

"No."

"Yes, climb down."

Filled with relief, Talin skillfully made his way down, and removed the bandana.

"Very good."

"Thanks."

"Now, go home and rest. You will need as much time as you can to heal."

"Am I not coming back tomorrow?"

"Return as early as you can."

Talin bid Papa goodnight and turned to make the walk back toward the Cemetery.

"Where are you going?" Papa asked.

"Back to Jumbie, to go home."

"You have a perfectly good replica here."

"Really? I can get back from here?"

"It's an exact replica," he said, winking. "Be aware of your surroundings."

———

THE SUN HAD SET when Talin returned home. Sneaking in the back door, he made it upstairs, avoiding his stepfather, without any problems. Robert was becoming more and more of a recluse. He hadn't even argued much or yelled at Shantel anymore, nearly ignoring her.

"Are you ok?" his mother asked from across the hall as Talin opened his bedroom door.

"Hi mom. Yeah, I'm ok."

"Come here a moment, please."

When Talin entered her room, she proudly gathered her material and held it up in front of her to display the progress she'd made on the dress.

"How do you like it?" She twisted from side to side, holding the bodice close and showing off the flow of the skirt.

"It's great!"

"I just finished. Worked on it all afternoon after work and I'm done early, so I have two days. I can make something for you. She tossed the dress on the bed. "Let me see," she said, grabbing the flexible tape measure.

"Oh, no, Mom. That's ok, I really don't need—"

"Don't be silly. *My* son will look proper for his Induction." She pulled the tape from his shoulder down to his waist. "Hm, you've grown."

She had made several articles of clothing for Talin when he was little, but it had been quite some time since she had completed something for him as a teenager.

"Mom, really, I just want to wear my shorts and a tee shirt."

"Excuse me?" she said. She sounded offended.

"Papa suggested I just be comfortable, just in cas—"

"I can do comfortable."

Stepping back, he tried to excuse himself, but she kept after him with the dangling measuring tape. "Mom, I really should shower now."

"At least let me make a nice shirt-jac or dashiki that you can wear with your shorts."

Talin had seen the traditional cotton shirt worn at local weddings and events, and it seemed to be loose fitting enough for what Papa requested but not so loose that it would be in the way. It even had pockets so that he could store small items, maybe some powders, herbs, or firedust.

"Ok, but make sure it's not too long on the side, so I can get to my knife."

His mother's eyes widened.

"Just in case," he reassured her.

"I'll make sure you have a slit on the side. What color?"

"Anything you like, Mom." Traditionally, the shirts were plain colors but in recent times had gained popularity with more vibrant and robust colors in their designs, which he was sure his mother appreciated.

"Just not red," he said.

She flashed a heartwarming smile. With her hands on his shoulder, she leaned in and kissed him on the cheek.

"You're right, you need a shower."

AWAKENED by the whirring of the sewing machine, Talin stretched out and rolled to his side, allowing himself to settle back into the bed. He had slept surprisingly well after his hot shower.

The smell of scrambled eggs and bacon drifted into his room, and he covered his head with the sheet to avoid it.

It didn't help. Talin rolled back over facing the window, squinting under the white bedsheet.

Why is it so bright?

Suddenly, he realized.

Oh no!

Throwing the sheet off his head, he sat up in bed and looked at the alarm clock. It was past nine. He never used his alarm, as most days he was up at sunrise on his own. Leaping out of bed, he caught his ankle in the sheet and tumbled onto the floor.

"Talin?" his mother called.

"I'm ok!"

He clutched his throbbing ankle and untangled himself.

Dang it!

His mother stood at the door. "What happened? Why are you on the floor?"

"Just tripped."

"Are you ok?"

"Yeah, I'm fine."

"I was wondering when you were going to get up."

"I'm late. I gotta go." He stood up, gently testing the ankle.

"There's breakfast downstairs, not just bacon and eggs."

Talin went to the closet to change his shirt and gather his pack. "Thanks, Mom. But really, I gotta go."

"You will slow down young man and have breakfast," she sternly instructed. "I am still your mother."

He knew that the longer he tried to argue with her, the longer he'd be stuck at the house. Conceding to breakfast, he went downstairs and made quick work of a bowl of cereal and grabbed a cinnamon sprinkled bagel as he dashed out the back door.

"I want to remeasure you for your shirt tonight when you get back!" she called behind him.

With a mouthful of bagel, Talin waved and nodded to her, and continued his brisk jog down the trail to Jumbie.

ENTERING THE REALM, he looked around, hoping to catch a glimpse of the mysterious three-legged horse. There was no horse in the Meadow. Instead, a row boat was floating in the middle of the Lake.

Further delaying his training to stop and investigate the random row boat would undoubtedly make Papa unhappy, so Talin wasted no time heading for the Sphere.

"You're late," a booming voice said.

Talin stopped and looked around. It was definitely Papa's voice and seemed to have come from the Lake.

"Papa?"

The old man sat up in the boat, apparently from lying down, then motioned for Talin to join him.

Why is he in a boat?

"You want me to swim over there?"

"Preferably. Unless you've learned how to fly."

Very funny.

Reluctantly, Talin tossed his pack on the bank, secured his weapon at his side and began the swim to the middle of the Lake. No intense waves surrounded him, no swirling of water trailed behind him. The day's training hadn't even begun and he was already soaked. The healing fish accompanied him in a school just under the surface. The water was the clearest he'd seen thus far and the temperature so perfect that he could have swum all day—which was exactly what he was afraid of.

"Climb aboard." Papa Bois said.

"Can you give me a hand?" Talin asked, hanging on the edge of the boat with a hand outstretched.

"No."

No?

"What if you are alone?" Papa asked.

"But, I'm not."

"Very clever." Papa extended a helping hand for Talin to climb into the boat. "Next time, you need to climb in on your own."

"Next time?"

With no effort, Papa tipped the boat to its side, pitching Talin back into the Lake with a splash— then let out a hearty laugh. "Don't be late next time."

Talin treaded water as Papa scolded him. "But you said come as early as I could, and I oversl—"

"Sunrise. Your usual time. Now, back in the boat."

On my own, I assume.

The ends of the boat curved upward, sitting slightly taller out of the water than the rest of the vessel. Wooden planks at the front and rear were secured across the width of the craft and formed the only seats. Talin positioned himself at the middle of the boat where the sides gently sloped down closest to the water. No rope, no chain, no makeshift ladder to climb in on.

The boat tipped toward him as he tried to pull his weight up, causing a rush of water to spill onto the floor. Only Papa's weight kept it from tipping completely over. Talin kicked underwater, propelling himself up and leaned over the side of the boat, then slumped onto the floor and sat up.

"A Healer should learn to be a little more graceful." Papa smiled.

"Very funny."

Papa chuckled. "Now, stand on the bow."

"On the end?"

Papa Bois nodded. Talin went to the front of the boat and stood on the seat in the bow.

"This is a good place to learn balance." Papa said and began rocking the boat from side to side. Talin swayed left and right, flailing his arms trying to keep his balance, but with the next teetering of the boat plunged back into the Lake.

"Back in." Papa said.

Talin swam to the side of the boat and lifted his body back up, draped his leg over the side and climbed in with a sigh.

"Again." Papa instructed.

Talin took his place at the bow. The rocking began again. With his arms outstretched, knees bending and flexing in alternating directions, Talin attempted to keep himself upright.

"Not bad, not bad." Papa lauded. "Can you go up on the edge?"

"You mean the very tip here?" Talin pointed to the front of the bow where the sides met at a point just beyond the wooden seat.

The wood that made up the sides were about three inches wide, narrower than a gymnast's balance beam.

Talin stepped up, bending over at the waist, attempting to balance with his hands on the edges as the boat steadied. Slowly, he stood up. Before Papa could even start rocking the boat, Talin over-corrected and fell back into the Lake.

He heard another laugh as he surfaced.

"It's not funny." Talin said.

"It is," he heard as the chuckle faded.

Again, Talin pulled himself up into the boat, wondering how long this drill would last. At least the water wasn't too cold or too warm.

Talin climbed back in, made his way to the tip of the bow, and balanced himself with each foot on either side of the narrow wood edge. He stretched his arms out slowly.

Papa started pitching the boat, slowly at first, then more vigorously. Talin didn't last long on his perch and found himself immersed again.

"Grr... really? Is this punishment for being late?"

"No, but I can make it so."

"No, no. That's not what I meant."

"Again."

Talin pulled himself up onto the side of the boat, the choppy water challenging his ability to re-embark. Moving up to the bow, he balanced himself on the edges until he found a rhythm with the waves and stayed upright.

"Very good!" Papa congratulated him. Are you ready for the advanced training?"

"Advanced? I thought being on the edge was the advanced part."

"Mama D'lo..." Papa called.

A mass of bubbles shot up from below the boat, causing it to shake and vibrate. Mama D'lo soon appeared port-side.

"Good day, Papa! Healer Talin," she bowed her head. "How may I be of service?" Her tail whipped in the water.

"Thank you Mama, it is time for Talin to advance his training in centering and balance. I believe you may be able to increase the difficulty for us?"

She winked and disappeared below the surface. Papa nodded to Talin to keep his place at the tip of the boat.

He inhaled deeply, unsure of what to expect. Raising his arms, he secured his stance.

Papa started the boat tipping to and fro. Talin compensated. The size of the waves around the boat increased, as they did when he had first entered the Lake by mistake, and stretched out to the banks. White caps lapped at the side of the boat just before he fell into the choppy waters.

"What was that about?"

"Again." Papa commanded.

Talin dragged himself back aboard the boat and took his stance once again. Papa rocked the still-unsettled boat as the white caps became taller, pitching Talin further than he could balance and careening into the rough waves. Mama D'lo surfaced and giggled. "That was a good one!"

"Yeah, yeah..." Talin grumbled. Mama dipped below the surface with a grin and a wink.

"Again." Papa said.

The drill continued until Talin's fingertips wrinkled like he'd soaked in the bathtub far too long. Mama D'lo had been overly delighted to send him flying into the Lake over and over. Finally, Talin stayed upright and onboard the boat without drenching himself. Then the water settled.

"Well done." Papa said.

Talin thanked him, his voice filled with exhaustion. Swimming always made him tired, but having to climb back into the boat each time he'd gone overboard quickened the onset of fatigue. Talin sat down as Mama D'lo surfaced with a chuckle, clasping her hands. "Oh my, what fun! What's next Papa Bois?"

"Don't wander far, Mama."

Great. Talin thought.

"Talin, would you mind rowing us back to shore?"

Talin grabbed the oars and tried his best to steer the boat back to the shoreline nearest Jumbie. The boat turned and bobbed and nearly spun in a circle.

"Have you never been in a row boat before?" Papa asked.

"No. Just inner tubes and things like that."

Papa kindly showed him how to propel and steer them back to shore. Mama D'lo gave a flick of her tail to push the boat along, making her own current.

The boat bumped to a stop along the shore. Stepping onto solid ground, Papa said, "Now, row back to the middle."

"On my own?"

"Yes, I've just shown you how."

Wanting to pass his "test", Talin centered himself in the boat and did as instructed, propelling himself back to the middle of the Lake. The water had thankfully settled. He turned to see if Papa was going to instruct him to row back, finally ending his drill.

"Now, stand at the bow," he hollered.

"Right now? The end of the boat will sink without your weight on the other end."

"Are you saying I'm overweight?"

"No!"

Papa chuckled. "You are not that heavy, and the boat will not sink. It is made from the silk-cotton tree."

Talin's heart beat a little faster. He knew the stories of using a silk-cotton tree's wood. It had to be blessed many times over before it could be used and be for very special circumstances indeed.

"How old is this boat?"

"As old as your great-grandfather."

Talin stepped up onto the front edge, sending the boat into a rocking motion, throwing off his balance. Catching himself from falling into the Lake, he toppled onto the floor of the boat instead, landing on his sore rib.

Ouch.

"You're not concentrating."

"I am!"

"You are thinking about your great-grandfather and if he also stood in this boat."

How did he know that?

"Talin, you are easy to read and kind-hearted, but you must also focus. Healer Kingston has been everywhere in the Realm that you have, and have yet to be. He has done many of the same drills. Not all, but times have changed. Clear your mind. Now, to the bow."

Talin got up and went to his post.

"Mama D'lo. Would you mind?"

"Not at all, Papa." She dipped below the calm water, but it didn't stay calm for long.

Oh no.

The waves began and Talin bobbed on the end of the boat. It wasn't long before he found himself swimming again. But the waves did not settle like they did before, allowing him to reboard his vessel.

They kept coming. And grew larger.

Crashing whitecaps splashed Talin in the face as he tried to swim to the boat. But it was pushed farther away.

"Mama, please stop!" he pleaded as he floundered to get to the boat. The faster he tried to swim, the further away it seemed to get. "Papa, make her..." he spit water from his mouth, "stop the waves!"

"Be resourceful." Papa yelled over the splashing.

Be resourceful? But I don't have anything to help me.

The waves increased in size and intensity and Talin was being battered by them. Already tired, he took a breath, submerged himself and relaxed under the water before surfacing again, trying to control his breathing.

It was more peaceful underwater than above the surface. He went under again and opened his eyes. The bottom of the boat was visible several yards away, or at least it appeared that way as he knew things were altered underwater. Coming up for a breath, he caught a glimpse of Mama D'lo's tail whip then disappear under the swells. He sank back down to avoid the repetitive pounding punishment from the surf and save his strength. Mama D'lo was swimming effortlessly under the water, then leapt out with glee. He could hear her muffled laughter as she plunged below. Her jewels glistened from the bits of sun that were able to break through the surface. She seemed absolutely delighted by her self-made entertainment, at Talin's expense.

She looks like a dolphin jumping around, just like Marisha looked when— wait!

Talin didn't have an object to 'be resourceful' with, but he certainly had learned from Marisha to swim under rough waves weeks earlier. It had been so effortless for her as well, saving her energy for the swim, not fighting to stay above the waves. That particular day she had finally believed him about Papa Bois and the Realm, she'd even taught Talin a single line of French that he often greeted Papa with, *Bonjour, vieux Papa.*

He hadn't tried diving underwater to get to the boat. He was making more work for himself fighting against the swells above the surface. Mama D'lo, on the other hand, was having a fabulous and effortless time.

Talin took in a breath and dipped below, kicking his legs and using large breaststrokes under the water. Coming up for another breath, he saw he hadn't made much progress, and the waves continued to crash around him. Back under, he tried submerging himself slightly deeper and pushed himself harder to gain more distance. He repeated the process several times until he came up and was able to flutter-kick his way to the edge of the boat and grab on with arms that felt as heavy as sandbags.

To catch his breath, he clung to the side for a time, the waves continuing to smash him into the solid surface. There was no weight for counterbalance and he didn't think he could climb in on his own without tipping the boat over in the rough waters.

"Can you stop the waves now?"

The waves did not stop. Mama D'lo called to him as she leapt out of the water, "Oh, splendid! You made it!" She dipped back below the surface.

If she's anything, she's definitely positive.

Bursting from the water again, she continued, "Can't you get in the boat, Healer Talin?" Back under she went.

Gathering strength, Talin attempted to pull himself up on the edge of the boat, but the waves tipped the vessel in one direction one moment and the opposing direction the next, preventing him from doing anything but hang off the side. He was certain the boat was going to flip, trapping him underneath. His rib couldn't take many more beatings into the hull before he thought he'd sink.

A sudden pressure butted against his feet, thrusting him out of the water and catapulting his body over the side. Landing with a thud on the floor of the craft, Talin stared up at the sky.

"Oh, what fun!" Mama called, sounding quite proud of herself. Then she peered over the edge at him, resting her chin on her crossed arms. "I haven't frolicked like that in a long time! Oh my, so good to know I haven't lost my touch." She winked.

"Yes," Talin stared in disbelief. "Good to know." Seasickness was setting in.

"My, are you alright? I've never quite seen someone with such tanned skin turn so green."

"Mama D'lo!" Papa called.

"Coming!" she chortled and swam to meet Papa on the shore.

Talin sat up in the boat, clutching his ribs, and trying not to lose his breakfast cereal in the Lake. As much as he wanted to be back on solid ground, it looked like a serious discussion was taking place between Mama and Papa, one he didn't wish to be a part of. The turbulent waters were settling down. Lying back and closing his eyes, he tried to control his nausea by focusing on his breathing.

"Row back, Talin!" Papa called from shore.

BACK ON SHORE, Papa grabbed the bow of the boat, pulling it a few feet onto the bank.

"Where's Mama D'lo?" Talin asked.

"Other responsibilities to tend to."

"She's in trouble for helping me, isn't she?"

"Mama D'lo is doing what she has been tasked to do, and that's to look out for you."

"So, she's not in trouble?"

"No trouble. But you need to learn to solve your own problems."

"I'm sorry, I couldn't— I mean, it was so hard to get back to the boat and I didn't ask for hel—"

"You solved the original problem, which is what I asked you to do. Come." Papa motioned for Talin to exit the boat. "Are you hungry?"

"Not really, to be honest." The nausea was not completely gone, but he knew he'd need to eat soon. Especially before more drills.

"We'll go to the Sphere to get you some ginger."

———

THE LEISURELY WALK to the Sphere, and the sensation of solid ground under his feet helped settle Talin's stomach. Papa retrieved fresh ginger, placing a small chunk in a mortar bowl. When Papa took his pestle to it, the sweet spice's distinct aroma filled the air.

Soon it was a flaky paste that he scooped into cups carved from old coconut shells. He filled them with tea from a nearby pitcher. Covering each cup with his palm, one at a time, he shook them.

"Drink," he said, handing one to Talin. "You should learn to meditate."

"Why? I can't defend myself from Dewain by just thinking happy thoughts. I need to review the weapons again, and then—"

"Meditation is not just thinking happy thoughts. This is why you must learn it. Your battle will begin with your mindset, so that it may end with a calmed spirit."

My battle?

Talin found it odd to switch gears from all the physical tasks that were thrown at him to the much calmer act of meditating. He had no clue how that would help him win his battles. One thing he knew for certain though, even though he didn't think he was the meditating type, Dewain certainly was not. Talin was willing to try, though, hoping it would at least settle his nerves in certain situations.

"This will help when it's difficult for you to find a way out of a situation and need to be—"

"Resourceful," Talin interrupted.

Papa smiled at his pupil and took a sip from his cup.

WHEN THEY HAD FINISHED their tea, Papa guided them back to the Shelter in the forest. Talin kept watch for flickers of orange light, especially while crossing the Gorge.

Entering the Shelter, they sat across from one another on the stone slabs. It was the first time Talin had been there since learning he had been chosen to be Healer after the blood rains, then once more when he was given the Healers' pendants, only to race away with them to Dewain's Induction. It was strange recalling the memories, it had seemed like ages ago. He shivered slightly, remembering the adrenaline running through him as the earthquake rattled the ground, the pain in his side after Dewain pushed him off Dive Rock at the Falls. What a sight he'd seen after he climbed out of Jumbie's trunk and saw Dewain preparing to sacrifice not just one goat, but a mother goat and her three kids.

Forget Dewain...

Even in the daylight, the forest covered the Shelter in a cloak of darkness. Only the tiniest bits of golden sunlight flickered through the cracked walls and across Papa's aged face. He lit them a fireball.

"This is a good place for learning. It is quiet, dark, private. Easy to focus. Meditation is a mental exercise. It will help you train your attention and awareness."

"Rule number four."

Papa smiled. "As you progress, your focus will increase, and your mind will clear of the distractions you hold."

Talin's mind was always buzzing with some sort of worry about all of the physical tasks he was doing or why. Sleep never came easily because his mind refused to slow down.

"How do I do that?"

"Begin with your stance, like in defense, but now open yourself up." Papa demonstrated for him, looking something like a Buddha. With knees bent and legs folded Indian-style, his one hoof was barely visible from under his cloak. He rested his wrists on his knees with palms up. Talin didn't think such an old man could be so flexible.

Talin copied the position on his bench.

"Sit up straight, but relax your shoulders. Posture is important. It is easier for energy to flow through you."

Talin readjusted as Papa continued.

"Now, close your eyes and focus on your breath. Slowly, in and out."

Talin took a few breaths, the deeper breaths causing some discomfort to his injured rib.

"Focus only on what is happening now."

Talin knew of only a few people who used mediation and he always thought it was ridiculous, a silly ritual encouraging people to believe in unrealistic internal powers. But Papa had not steered him wrong yet, so he decided to at least try. Attempting to focus on his breathing, he continually reminded himself to relax his shoulders. Papa said fewer and fewer words, guiding Talin through the technique. "Eyes closed...inhale...relax...focus...clear your mind..." his voice growing softer and quieter, like the Shelter had just expanded and Papa was suddenly fifty feet away.

Before long, Talin's attention drifted away from all he had to accomplish and focused on the soothing sound of Papa Bois' exhales. He squinted, peeked with one eye, curious to see what his mentor was doing. Papa sat more still than a stone statue. His face seemed peaceful and he looked more wise than he ever had. A faint haze surrounded him, almost a mist. Talin broke his concentration and opened his eyes to get a better look. It was difficult to tell if the haze was real, or if his eyes were merely tired, and he didn't dare break his pose to reach across and find out. Closing his eyes again, he attributed the odd haze to his fatigue.

Surrounded in silence, his painful ear resonated a high-pitched ringing. Being so water-logged today didn't help, and he was surprised he didn't feel blood trickling down to his jawline. Desperate for a distraction, he opened his eyes again, his gaze landing on the sizzling flame hanging in the air inches away, now shifting Talin's focus to the temperature of the room. It felt more like a sauna in the tropical heat, considerably different than the cool air that filled the space after sundown. Focusing on just one thing was proving more difficult than he thought.

After several minutes of sitting in silence, Talin's shoulders finally stayed relaxed. Grateful to not be climbing, swimming, or diving, he finally allowed his mind to drift to nothing, escaping the chaos of the last few weeks. No worry about getting hurt, being chased by Onca or dealing with Dewain. It was indeed peaceful. Meditation meant rest, and if he could learn something while resting, he was all for it, although he wasn't sure what exactly he was supposed to learn from it other than reducing his stress. Only one thing could have made it better—being in such a peaceful state next to Marisha at the Falls. Maybe this was what she was doing when she drifted off there. He was in no rush for the session to end.

"It's time to get back to work." Papa said softly.

"But we just started here."

"True skill in meditation comes with time, you will not master it in one session."

"I was pretty relaxed. I think I got it," Talin said as he uncrossed his legs and stretched.

"It is not just about relaxing. We will continue another time." Papa did not discuss it further. Instead he stood, extinguished the fireball and walked out of the Shelter.

But...

13

THERE WAS MUCH TO DO.

After a hearty lunch in the Grove, including a surprise variety of breads, greens, vegetables and rice, Papa ushered Talin into the Sphere.

Whoa.

The training area had been transformed over lunch, without a sound or Papa leaving his place during the meal.

"How do you do this?!" Talin asked.

All the elements Talin had trained on before filled the space— the boulders of ascending heights, the life-sized spider web, ropes and vines hanging from the full expanse of the ceiling. Talin's lunch dropped in his gut as he imagined what was coming next.

"It's nothing, really. Choose your weapon." Papa instructed.

"But I just ate."

"Choose your weapon!"

Talin went to the wall and inspected all the blades, but he didn't take anything. Instead, he turned to Papa Bois and said, "I choose mine," and pulled his great-grandfather's dagger from its sheath. If he was going to be threatened by Dewain at his Induction, he would only be armed with his own weapon. It was time to ensure he was skilled enough to use it.

Papa Bois pulled an even larger dagger from the wall and advanced toward Talin. Talin deflected Papa's blade with his own, side-stepping and then advancing on his challenger. The two exchanged blows with their daggers, circling each other in the grass, dodging the hanging jungle vines, and moving between the boulders. Sparks bounced off their blades as the metal struck the boulders from missed blows at their opponents.

"Climb!" Papa yelled, moving swiftly toward Talin.

Talin placed his weapon's handle in his mouth, freeing up both hands, and climbed up the nearest vine faster than he ever had. Below, Papa swapped his dagger for a machete then went to the vine Talin had escaped on, making a swift cut of the greenery. Talin was stuck above the old man on a much shorter vine than when he'd started.

"Wha you do at or?" Talin asked, still gripping his weapon in his teeth, garbling the words.

"Are you going to ask that of everyone who challenges you?" Papa cut another nearby vine shorter, then another.

Talin adjusted, securing his grip on the vine. He sheathed his weapon with one hand. "Well, no."

"If you must draw your weapon, you will keep it in hand at all times until the danger has passed."

When a fireball came flying at Talin, he tucked his head behind the too-small vine. The flame struck his shoulder. "Ouch!"

Taking hold of the dagger again, he was able to deflect the next fireball with it. And the next. "Stop!"

The fireballs did not stop. Talin was having a difficult time hanging onto his swaying vine and swiping fireballs away with his blade. There had to be a better way.

After another fireball, Talin knew he would fall if he didn't get away from the barrage. He gripped the dagger between his teeth again and began swinging on the vine. A moving target was harder to hit, but Papa had a sniper's aim.

Talin swung toward the closest boulder, leapt off the vine and onto the top of the stone. Steadying the majority of his weight on his stronger ankle, he saw the next fireball heading toward him. Lifting his hand as if he might catch a softball, he flattened his palm, and pushed the fireball back down toward Papa Bois. Papa hurled the flame back and Talin blocked it again, sending it toward his target with greater speed and intensity, the fireballs never making contact with his hand.

Two fireballs were launched toward him simultaneously, then three. Talin effectively blocked them all.

"Excellent! Come down." Papa said.

Having leapt between all the boulders circling the Drop not long ago, he knew there were very little handholds to climb down and it was too high to jump, especially with a still-healing ankle and rib. This had been Papa's plan— figure it out. Scanning his options, he quickly calculated the distance of a leap back to a nearby rope he hoped to slide down. Resheathing the knife, he checked that it was secure on his hip, swung his arms out and jumped.

Catching the rope, he wrapped his legs around it as quickly as possible, only slipping down a few inches. He carefully climbed down to save his palms from blistering and stood on the grass next to Papa.

"Very good. You are learning to combine your skills."

Talin thanked him, secretly hoping that swimming and diving weren't on the list of skills to review and combine. He didn't dare ask.

Changing the subject, Papa asked, "Have you thought about what your offering to Jumbie will be?"

"Oh, no. I thought the offerings were from all the other people."

"The tree and your great-grandfather have chosen you. I suggest you show your gratitude."

"What should I give? Animals are out, and alcohol is out. That's what people usually do, right?"

"You are the Healer of a new generation, a new time. You may start any traditions you wish. What you do will be recorded and may be imitated with future Healers. Remember...return, reclaim."

Nothing immediately came to mind. It seemed like the hardest decision yet. "Ok, thanks. I'll sleep on it tonight."

"Speaking of sleep, you will rest well tonight after the remainder of today's training."

Uh oh.

THE REMAINDER of the afternoon was filled with combining all of Talin's skills after each session; weapon work, climbing in (and on) the Sphere, scaling boulders, traversing across the sticky spider web, climbing the silk-cotton tree in the Theater, and of course, Talin's new favorite— fending off and creating fireballs with volcanic ash and floating embers. Papa continued to critique Talin and give instruction on how best to defend himself, demonstrating the movements, then challenging Talin with more intense scenarios.

Hot and tired, Talin requested a break. Papa suggested they take a walk—to the Lake.

THE BOAT REMAINED on the edge of the bank and Papa stepped in, taking a seat. "Let's go," he said.

"Can I have a break?"

"Yes."

Boarding the boat, Talin took the remaining seat. Papa grabbed an oar and shoved off from the bank. The Lake was smooth, the only ripples coming from Papa's leisurely paddling. It wasn't long until he handed Talin an oar.

"Now you steer."

Talin guided the boat in a circle all the way around the Lake, studying the scenery as he rowed past the Meadow and the Mountain range, the unusual buildings and oddly-shaped trees that lay beyond Jumbie's roots, as well as the blue horizon beyond that.

"Papa, what else is here?"

"One hurdle at a time."

"You'll show me, right?"

"No rush, Healer Talin, no rush."

Talin continued studying the landmarks around him, while also looking for other signs of life within the Realm. A few monkeys leapt between the trees, colorful parrots occasionally flew overhead, but there were no signs of a black horse, a jaguar, or other unexpected creatures.

The sun was dipping quickly behind the trees. It was nearly sunset when Papa said, "It's dusk. You've not practiced much in the dark."

Oh no... Talin gulped and turned to look at Papa, who motioned for him to take his stance on the bow.

Oh please, not again.

"But, you said I could rest."

"You have, but now it's time to work. If you are challenged by Dewain at the Induction," *you mean when I'm challenged,* Talin thought, "You will not have the advantage of daylight to assist you. You must know your surroundings. Your awareness must be at its peak."

"But, I practiced with the blindfold."

"It is different. There will be torches throwing shadows he can hide among, and smoke may cloud your vision. The flickers of light will distort your sense of distance. We will work into the night. There is no time left."

"But, my mom wants to measur—"

"To the bow! Focus! If you cannot master these simple tasks, you will be unable to protect anyone else around you."

Simple?

Talin had heard this reasoning before. Reluctantly, he went to the bow, stepped up on the edges and tried to balance himself, waiting for the boat to rock violently, agitating the water and everything in it. Attempting to clear his mind of his frenzied thoughts, he worked hard to direct his attention to the present, knowing his singular task was to train successfully.

Then maybe he could go home.

Closing his eyes, he waited...

Feeling the evening breeze blow across the Lake was refreshing. Taking a breath, he caught the scent of frangipani in the air. He heard the birds' songs gracefully fade away as the frogs began to take their turn. His shoulders relaxed. He was ready.

No waves came.

Opening his eyes, he saw he was alone in the boat in the middle of the Lake. His heart quickened.

"Papa?"

Everything was quiet. The sun had set and the surrounding trees were cloaked in shadows from the eerie glow of the moon.

The old man was not on shore, not in the water, and not answering Talin's calls. Was this another test?

Talin stepped down into the boat as the waves rolled in like a tsunami. The boat rocked wildly, and Talin dropped to his knees for stability. Grabbing the sides of the hull, he looked in every direction for Papa, but the only thing he saw was a blue-green glow covering the bottom of the Lake and growing brighter and broader, lighting up the water like a swimming pool at night. The waves cast fractals of light in all directions.

A large splash next to the boat startled him and a familiar dark-haired woman emerged from the turbulent waters.

"Oh, hello Healer Talin!" said a chipper Mama D'lo, the black serpent clinging snugly atop her head. "Back again?"

"Mama D'lo, can you make the waves stop for a moment, please?"

"Sorry, against Papa's orders at the moment."

"Orders? Where is he?" The boat bobbed back and forth as the woman held on with ease to the starboard side. Her long hair floating around her in the water, glistening in the moonlight like an oil slick. In the flickering light and rough waves, Talin still was unable to get a good look at where the woman's body ended and her serpent-like lower body began.

"He wanted to see you centered before the exercise began. Let's play!" Mama D'lo then made an impressive leap back into the water. The boat began to spin and bounce over larger and larger waves, threatening to throw him overboard.

No, no, no....

Again, Mama leapt in and out of the water. "Hold on Talin!" she called.

The boat spun faster, tossing Talin onto his back at the stern of the boat. The centrifugal force was similar to what he'd experienced in the Drop, except this time he was spinning in place—along with his stomach.

The deep blue haze of the moon reflecting off the trees blurred and whizzed past as he tried to focus on a single landmark to keep from throwing up. Unsuccessful, he careened over the side of the boat and into the water, filling it with his stomach contents.

Feeling something bump against his calf and hit his foot, he ducked under the waves and opened his eyes expecting to see Mama next to him —instead his knife was sinking rapidly to the bottom of the Lake.

He reached down, dizzy, and his reflexes too slow to grasp his weapon. The blade reflected bits of the colored light as it quickly descended.

Coming up for breath, Talin was struck on the shoulder by the boat as it tipped off a rolling wave, narrowly missing the side of his head. Frantically, he grabbed on. He and the boat spun about in the rotating waves, when Mama D'lo surfaced next to him.

"Oh, Talin, that was fabulous! You stayed on much longer than Healer Dyllon, and he was a fisherman. Used to boats, you know."

"I lost my knife! I lost my knife!"

Talin didn't appreciate the compliment, certain he was not cut out to be a sailor or a fisherman. Taking a gulp, he managed to keep additional stomach contents down as the swirling began to slow.

"A knife? Why do you have a knife?"

"My dagger! My great-grandfather's dagger! I need it for the Induction! It must have slipped out of the sheath!"

As the water stilled, Talin hung on the side of the boat with his eyes shut. The churning in his stomach not only due to the typhoon-like waves he'd just endured, but from the angst of losing his most prized possession. "Can you get it for me?"

"Why, I will try. The water is still pretty churned up here, you know."

"Yeah, I see that." He tried to be polite as a remaining rogue white cap struck his face.

"Hopefully it hasn't been sucked into the Sluice. Oh dear! Hard to tell where it could end up. Could be anywhere really..." She gazed off as if she were distracted and the reptile on her shoulder flicked its tongue at Talin. "The bottom of the Lake, Coral Cave, the Falls, maybe even the Theater, or the—"

"Mama, please!" he pleaded, as she continued discussing the knife's possible whereabouts.

"Oh, yes, so sorry." Then she dove under and disappeared.

The last waves settled and the Lake was calm again. Talin was anything but.

BACK AT THE edge of the Lake, Talin pulled the boat onto the shoreline and dropped the oars inside it. The aqua glow within the Lake was fading. Over the Mountains, the moon had risen. Lying back in the soft grass, he stared up at the stars that now lit up the night sky. A green shooting star darted across the expanse, twinkled then went dark.

Mama D'lo had not resurfaced with or without his knife and Papa Bois had not returned with any further instructions. He thought about going home, as his mother would surely be worried and still needing to check his measurements for the shirt-jac. She had one day left to complete it. It had been some time since she had last made him clothes and he'd had a growth spurt. Talin feared it would be too tight or too loose to wear comfortably without her double-checking her pattern.

His stomach continued to turn on itself so he checked his pack for ginger powder. Finding none, he laid back down to wait for someone and watch the stars. Thin clouds passed overhead, hiding and revealing the moon at random intervals. Talin often wondered if Marisha was seeing the same moon he was whenever he was in the Realm. Were they different moons?

He fretted about whether she would come to the Induction after leaving so abruptly the last time they spoke and telling him she was forbidden to spend any more time with him. Something didn't feel right.

A purple shooting star raced across the sky.

Wow.

A gentle wave washed ashore, catching Talin's attention. Mama D'lo slithered up on the shoreline, letting her tail swish back and forth in the water.

"Did you find it?" he asked, sitting up.

"No, not yet," she shook her head, "but I will. The Sluice must have taken it quite a ways."

"Must have," his shoulders slumped back down.

"I'm sorry, Healer Talin." Her voice lifted slightly as she continued. "But I know these waters better than anyone. There's no way it can leave the waterways, and I did have the Sluice quite riled up—"

"It's ok. I know you'll find it."

She bowed her head. "Goodnight, Healer Talin," she said, turning back toward the water.

"Wait! Where are you going?"

"Why, it's time to rest. Aren't you going to rest?"

"Yes, but I haven't heard from Papa and I really need to get home. I just don't want to go unless he has something else we—"

"Oh, so you aren't staying the night?"

"Staying the night? No. He didn't say anything about it and I don't have my knife to—"

"Well, he mentioned to me you were staying, but I don't think it's wise to lay here on the shore out in the open with Onca prowling about." She winked.

Onca...

"Oh...well, I..."

"I could take you to the Cave. Onca isn't fond of it. Or you could stay in the Shelter I suppose, I heard you know where it is?"

"But, the tree is right here," he said pointing behind him, "I could just go home."

"Maybe Papa has something for you early in the morning?"

"Well, I was late this morning. Is that my punishment? Make sure I'm not late again?"

"Papa isn't one for punishment. He is one for lessons," she said matter-of-factly.

Talin considered his options. He had one day until the Induction, he didn't want to risk upsetting Papa, and he needed to be as prepared as possible. He'd been completely exhausted from the day, and was nervous about oversleeping if he went home. He was already where he needed to be, but a wet soggy mess. He was not excited about climbing into the Gorge at night to get into Coral

Cave, assuming Mama had meant Coral Cave and not the cave that was tucked away behind Hosea Falls. And, either way, the Sluice was not his transportation route of choice to go anywhere. But the idea of hiking into the forest without Papa Bois, or his knife, to get to the Shelter wasn't high on his list either. He didn't dare venture off to somewhere new but couldn't think of too many other places to go within the Realm when he recalled rule number five—make a decision.

"I'll make frequent patrols of the waterways for you, whatever you decide."

"Thank you, Mama."

She bid him goodnight and gently swam away into the Lake. Talin pulled his pack over his shoulder and looked around for any signs on Onca, then headed for Jumbie's trunk. Hopefully his clothes would be dry by morning.

14

THE CALL OF BIRDS SIGNALED A NEW DAY AND SUNBEAMS BROKE through the vines. Talin stretched his legs in the cramped space and released a long yawn, inhaling the humid air. His head hurt from resting it against the inside of Jumbie's trunk during the night. It hadn't been restful sleep, but it was sleep nonetheless.

As Talin pushed through the vines, he looked around the Realm for any signs of life—Papa pacing, Thantos grazing, Mama D'lo having an early morning swim in the Lake, or Onca ready to pounce. Maybe no one was up yet.

Without his weapon, he was hesitant to leave his hiding spot. He checked his pack, trying to be resourceful. He found a small amount of firedust and placed it in his nearly-dried shorts pocket. It wasn't much, but it was something. At the bottom of the bag was his great-grandfather's carving knife. Being so used to carrying his dagger, he'd forgotten about the small blade, not much bigger than a pocket knife. Or it might have been that he was just too busy concentrating on his tasks that it went unnoticed. It was too slender to fit securely in the other weapon's sheath, so Talin tucked it away in the cargo pocket of his dirt-covered khaki shorts. He secured his pack and set out to the Sphere.

WHEN TALIN ENTERED THE PORTHOLE, the training area had been cleared of all obstacles, and instead, a large breakfast buffet was beautifully laid out on the work table. Exquisitely hand-carved wooden bowls and pitchers of all shapes and sizes overflowed with bread and pastries, greens, fruits and vegetables, diced potatoes, milk, tea, juices, and more. Sides of various spices and powders dotted the table. There were even pancakes with maple syrup, a bowl piled high with chunks of chocolate, and a small tabletop fire resembling a barbecue grill flickering at the end of the table.

Wow!

"Good morning, Healer Talin," he heard Papa say behind him.

"Oh! Good morning, Papa."

"Sleep well?"

"I slept. What is all this?!"

"The feast is in celebration of you." Papa extended his hand, inviting Talin to eat first. "There is a fire if you wish to warm something."

"It's all for me?"

"We'll share," Papa smiled.

With renewed energy, Talin grabbed a wooden plate, filling it first with all his favorites. Pineapple, banana, mango. A coconut shell cup held his favorite juice. Papa joined him on the boulder to eat as they watched the birds swoop in and out of the skylight and monkeys climb down the walls to snatch bananas off the table. Toucans hopped among the bowls, snapping their beaks on grapes, causing a few to roll onto the ground to the waiting iguanas. Neither Talin or Papa shooed them away. It felt like a picnic at the zoo.

Talin asked for seconds and Papa encouraged him to take what he liked; the rest would be fed to the animals, as if they weren't getting their fill already. Talin couldn't resist a pancake or two, fresh maple syrup and some sweet potato. There was no rush to train, no surprise drills, or any unwelcome guests. It was the best breakfast he ever had.

When his belly felt as if it was ready to burst, Talin laid back on the boulder and let out a moan.

"Where is your weapon?" Papa asked.

Talin was so enchanted with his breakfast entertainment, he'd briefly forgotten.

"Oh," he sat back up. "I lost it." He dropped his head. "It fell in the Lake last night when the boat tipped. Mama D'lo looked for it, but she couldn't find it. Can you get it back for me?"

"I patrol the forests. She patrols the waters. If it is able to be found, she will be the one to find it. You must be mindful at all times, in all scenarios to never let it leave your side."

Talin nodded, "I know, I'm sorry. The water was just too much. It must have slipped."

"What do you have for protection in the meantime?"

"Well, this morning I got some firedust from my pack and put it in my pocket."

Papa smiled, "Resourceful."

"And I have Healer Kingston's carving knife in my pocket." Pointing to the wall behind the breakfast table, "Do you think I could borrow one until I find mine?" Talin asked.

"If your blade is not returned by tomorrow, you may take one."

Talin thanked him.

"Do you have any final questions before tomorrow?" Papa asked.

He did have questions, some not directly related to the Induction. "Maybe one. You said my father walks me into the ceremony, but why didn't you tell me earlier he was an elder?"

"Family members of Healers past are usually asked to be elders. I thought when you talked to your father, he would have told you this."

Talin shook his head. "No. When I told him about Onca he got really nervous and left. Said I couldn't lose against Onca."

"He speaks truth. Your mother is tied to Healer Kingston, your father to Onca. But you are tied to both."

And Healer Dyllon.

"So there is much concern about how similarly you will rule—like Kingston or like Onca."

Is my dad concerned about how I will rule?

Talin recalled his father's words, telling him to bring back honor and respect to the Hunte family name. "But what about Dewain? Nobody seems worried about how he would rule."

"Tradition says you are Healer. There is no question, there are no doubts. But the Dyllon family has had other destructive motives in grooming Dewain as Healer. It's all the island has heard for years. People will eventually believe whatever is continually repeated to them," he nodded at Talin, "without someone to question it."

"Do you think the Dyllons really know it's me and now they are just embarrassed?"

"When one is raised to believe something so deeply, even though it is wrong and falsehoods are before them, they sometimes cannot humble themselves to change or make amends."

"Do you think they will ever change?"

"It's too early to know. That is a monumental task for a Healer."

"What do you mean it's a task for a Healer?" Talin fully understood that one individual does not have the power to change another, evident by his mother and stepfather's relationship.

"The community will now look to you. But they will scrutinize and judge every action, every decision, every word you speak or write. It is up to you to set a new example. Be firm, yet respectful and encouraging. Teach, but do not preach."

It was sounding like he would never be left alone, ever. Talin wanted to help others but not be in the spotlight. He was shy and quiet, mostly from the bullying he'd endured, and over time he'd learned it was safer that way. Dewain was better suited for the spotlight and all the attention. He relished in it. Maybe that was part of the problem, Talin thought. The power had gone to Healer Hunte's head and it obviously didn't turn out well for him...

"Do you feel you are ready?" Papa Bois finally asked.

Being honest with himself, Talin wasn't sure, but he took his time responding. Many people were counting on him to revive the legend. His mother had had premonitions about him and seemed happier again recently, more than she'd been in quite some time. His father's wish was to bring honor back to the family name. He was specifically chosen, before he'd been born, by his great-grandfather. What did Healer Kingston know that Talin didn't?

"Yes."

"Are you still in pain?" Papa asked, returning their empty plates and cups to the work table.

"Yeah, a little bit actually."

Papa suggested they go to the Theater, and allow their meals to settle and let the animals enjoy the remaining breakfast. Before leaving, Talin grabbed a few pieces of chocolate then covered the bowl with a nearby cloth cover.

"No chocolate for you," he informed the toucan hopping across the table toward him. Being that cocoa was a poor choice for dogs, he assumed it would also be a poor choice for the local animals.

DROPPING his pack near a stone bench at the edge of the moat, Talin hoped he wouldn't have to climb the Jumbie look-alike again.

"Come, lay on the bench. Let's work on your rib."

As instructed, Talin laid down, staring into the sky overhead, admiring the white clouds that seemed to extend forever—but couldn't as they were below the earth. How could this be?

"Close your eyes."

Talin heard Papa's palms rhythmically rubbing together. Large, warm hands then pressed firmly onto the left side of his chest.

"Breathe," he said.

A deep exhalation escaped Talin. The warmth of the sun helped further relax him and he allowed his mind to drift. His neck and shoulders relaxed, followed by his chest and full belly.

"In your nose, out your mouth," he heard Papa remind him. Focusing on his breathing, he settled into the present moment, feeling grateful for not having to climb the great tree blindfolded, relishing any downtime Papa would give him. Breathing in...and back out, again and again, Talin thought he might quite enjoy a daily meditation. He sensed his legs and arms feeling light as the sun's rays became warmer, penetrating his skin, and he drifted off to somewhere other than the Theater.

TALIN STARTLED himself awake with a snore. Sitting up on his elbows, he looked around. "Papa?"

He was sitting near Talin's feet on the long bench.

"I'm sorry, I think I fell asleep."

"You did."

"How long was I out?"

"Maybe an hour or two."

"I'm sorry, why didn't you wake me up?" The last thing Talin wanted was to be scolded by Papa, or worse, miss out on any last-minute drill that would help him be ready to challenge Dewain.

"You are tired. I've asked a lot of you. You deserve to be well rested for tomorrow."

Talin readjusted, sitting up on the bench, making himself comfortable. "Thanks." It had been difficult getting sleep the last few weeks.

"But, there is still work to do. Have you decided on your offering?"

He hadn't. "No, I was trying to think of something that won't be wasted or thrown away."

"Respectable."

"I remember the first time I came to the Realm, then came out and saw the goat Dewain sacrificed...it was so awful and smelled terrible, so I tried burying it." Papa smiled. "I'd thought about planting a frangipani then, because they smell so good—and to remember the goats. It'd be something just between me and Jumbie. So, maybe I could plant one?"

"That's a fine idea. A very kind gesture."

"Really? Do you think it's enough?"

"Absolutely. It's never about the size of the gift, it's the meaning behind it. You may want to only present it tomorrow, then return later to plant it. They can be tricky. Be sure it gets partial to full sun. Jumbie's branches cast a great deal of shade."

Talin began to think of where he might plant the frangipani at the site. A few ideas came to mind, but then the realization that he had no idea where to even get a frangipani overshadowed it. Did he buy seeds at the store or a potted plant at the nursery? Could he just cut a branch off an existing tree or take a piece from one in the Realm? He had no idea.

"It's time to review." Papa interrupted Talin's thoughts and directed his attention to Jumbie's base.

"During the Induction, I want you to stay near the tree at all times. You are most familiar with it. It will give you protection, a point of reference, and an escape route. If Dewain brings trouble, I highly doubt he will announce it ahead of time, so be acutely aware of your surroundings at all times."

Marisha already told me he's coming.

"Rule number four." Talin said.

"Yes, and do not forget rule number two."

"Don't scream for you."

"Correct. I will not be there to help you. At least not in the way I am able to here."

"What do you mean?"

"I am a shapeshifter, watch for me. I will not look how you see me now." Papa stood from the bench, straightening his burlap cloak, leaves falling from the folds of the material.

"What will you be then?"

"Whatever the situation calls for."

"But, I really want you to be there."

"I wouldn't miss it, Healer Talin." Papa bowed his head. "Now, cross the moat."

15

THIS WAS IT, HIS LAST CHANCE TO PREPARE. RISING UP FROM THE bench, Talin stood tall, balled his fists, and stretched out his fingers. He slid down the slope into the moat, swam across to the platform and climbed up. Papa asked Talin to close his eyes.

"Take the blindfold from your pocket and tie it on."

Nerves set in.

Here we go.

As instructed, he pulled the wet bandana from his shorts pocket, wringing out the water. The drops hit his feet and splashed onto the rock slab. Eyes still closed, he folded the bandana as straight as he could then placed it over his eyes. Tying it to the back of his head, he visualized his place on the platform, the position of the tree and its sprawling roots.

"Climb!" Papa's voice commanded from across the moat.

Talin turned and walked briskly to a root. As he placed his hands on it to judge where he was, water splashed. What felt like a tidal wave raced across his feet, and the platform tilted sideways, knocking him off balance. Stumbling into another root, he grabbed on, pulling his upper body up and over, not confident of his position in the roots. Waves crashed against him with stronger and stronger force, and he kicked a leg over the root to stabilize himself.

That's got to be Mama D'lo.

The platform tilted in the opposite direction, and he scraped his calf across a rough and all too-familiar landmark.

Ow!

Scooting up the root like an iguana, Talin climbed as high as he could— visualizing every hand hold and branch along the way. He gained confidence the higher he went as the waves subsided. Then the wind picked up, swirling around him. Limbs bounced and swayed in the gusts. His moat-soaked t-shirt flapped against his body like a torn, wet sail. Unfortunately, he felt like he'd been in this situation before.

"Higher!" Talin barely heard from below as the winds increased. Bits of sand, leaves, and other debris stung his body as they struck him. The wind howled in his ears. The only thing missing this time was the rain.

What is he doing now?

Talin was as high in the canopy as he thought possible, clinging to a branch in the wind and listening for further instructions. It was several minutes before they came.

"Come down!"

The windstorm did not subside until Talin had descended low enough, near the roots, but then the waves took over again, crashing into him from different directions. A distant giggle confirmed his earlier suspicions about the source of the swells.

She is having entirely too much fun with this.

Nearing the ground, Talin held tight to a root. As he neared solid footing, the platform tilted again, causing him to fall to the ground. With the next wave, he was washed into the moat's choppy waters.

Dang it! I was so close!

Talin bobbed in the crashing waves.

"Are we done now?" he called out to Papa.

"Yes, go back to the platform."

Pulling his blindfold down around his neck, Talin saw debris littering the grounds around him where he and Papa had been seated. The waves settled as he swam back to the stage. Mama D'lo breached playfully ahead of him.

"Well done, well done!" she said, then disappeared again into the moat.

Talin climbed out of the water and sat on the edge of the crooked platform. The tipping had stopped, the winds had ceased, and he was able to catch his breath. Small twigs, mud and leaves covered the area around Jumbie on the sundial's intricate carvings.

Papa remained on the opposite side of the moat as they talked.

"You did well."

"Thanks."

"You climbed quickly and confidently. You knew your surroundings and adjusted to the unstable ground. You may need to call upon those skills tomorrow. Are you comfortable with defense using your weapon?"

"Yes, but I still don't have my knife. Did Mama D'lo find it yet?"

"Not that I am aware. Would you like to review again using my dagger?"

"I think I should."

"Very well." Reaching into his cloak, Papa retrieved his own weapon and winked. "Don't drop this one," he said, then tossed it across the water.

Talin scrambled to his feet, barely catching it. It was larger and heavier than his own—and would have sunk quickly. He'd seen it in training before but had not been able to really admire its intricate details. The gold metal blade was about eight inches long with a wide cross guard. The carved ivory-colored handle was either animal horn or bone. The butt finely decorated with a design of silver and gold leaves.

"Wow, this is awesome."

"It does not need the fancy details to do the job. But it was a gift."

"Really? Who gave it to you?"

"Not important right now. Assume your stance. Step back!"

Lifting the knife, he focused on Papa, ready for fireballs or anything else the man was preparing to hurl his way. He stepped back, looking behind himself to avoid tripping on the smaller roots or debris.

"Face forward! You need to know where you are at all times. Never avert your eyes from your attacker."

Talin shifted his weight and slid his feet instead of lifting them to trip over something. He could better feel where the roots were without falling that way, especially when moving backwards.

Papa had skipped the fruit and gone straight to fireballs. They came in rapid succession.

"Left!"

Talin moved left.

Then right. And back.

Missing the first few balls of fire, likely due to the unfamiliarity with the extra weight of the borrowed blade, Talin was still able to quickly fall into a rhythm and deflect the remainder of the flames. The balls landed in the water with a sizzle or smoldered in mud puddles spilled across the area around him.

"Switch hands!"

What?

He hadn't practiced this before, but obeyed promptly, tossing the weapon to his left hand. He felt like he'd started training all over.

Just like Papa to make me start over.

Still, he focused. Fireballs flew in his direction, striking his body several times.

"Ouch! Wait, let me practice first."

"No practice. Your Induction is tomorrow. What if your dominant hand is injured?"

Talin swiped at the fireballs, turning the wide face of the blade toward them, blocking their trajectory to burn him. He'd not concentrated so keenly for some time and his weak arm tired quickly. It seemed Papa had a never-ending supply of fireballs. They kept coming. Some slow, some fast. Some hovering, then darting about and changing direction mid-air. For a full fifteen minutes, he sparred with the flames.

"Well done," Papa announced as Talin blocked the last fireball.

PAPA DIRECTED Talin back to the bench.

After crossing the moat, Talin returned the dagger, wrung out his shirt and sat on the simple stone slab, staring at the silk cotton tree.

"You're tired?" Papa asked.

"Yeah." His arm ached.

"And you are drenched. You will need your rest tonight. You should go."

It was early afternoon, an unusual stopping time, but Talin wanted to make sure he had been coached on everything he needed.

"That's it? We're done?"

"Never done. Just done for today."

"Do you think I'm ready?"

"You are as ready as you will be for tomorrow."

There was truth behind what he'd said. Talin knew there wasn't much more he could do in the next several hours.

Papa stepped in front of Talin and said, "It is customary I give a blessing to the new Healer on the eve of their Induction." He reached for the necklace around Talin's neck, held the pendants tight within his palm, then placed his right hand on Talin's shoulder.

He bowed his head and closed his eyes. Papa's voice was low and quiet.

"As the father and protector of the forest, may you, Talin, be blessed with strength and guided by wisdom as this Realm's chosen Healer."

Talin could hear the sincerity in his words. Bowing his own head, he stared at Papa's feet—one human foot, and one deer hoof. A sensation of warmth coursed through his body, and he wondered if his great-grandfather had received this same blessing.

"May the Earth, and the beings within it, watch over and protect you as you lead others. May you be filled with knowledge to make the choices and changes around you for the better, uniting broken spirits, and bringing back lost trust and respect for the position you now hold. And, when the time comes, may you make the best choice for your successor. May all of Nature, and the life within her, forever watch over you, Healer Talin."

Papa's hand gave his shoulder a firm squeeze. Talin opened his eyes and looked up at Papa, feeling refreshed—and very, very blessed.

"I will see you tomorrow," Papa said as he motioned for Talin to leave.

Talin stood up and gathered his things. "Thank you, Vieux Papa," he said with a bow of his head.

The old man smiled and returned the bow.

IT WAS NEARLY time for dinner. Talin was greeted by the aroma of cinnamon plantains wafting from his mother's frying pan. He'd never been so hungry, even after his sprawling, private breakfast buffet.

"Hi, Mom."

"Where were you last night?" She said coldly, stirring the

golden yellow chips and clanking the lid back on the cast iron skillet.

"I needed to stay overnight."

"I thought I was clear that you still live under this roof, and Papa Bois is not in charge of y—"

"I'm sorry. I'll talk to him about it. But, tomorrow is the Ind—"

"I'm fully aware." She tipped her chin up in the direction of the office.

Not being home much, Talin hadn't heard from his stepfather— to his relief. And he didn't dare ask about his stepfather's where-abouts. He didn't care anymore. If Robert had a tantrum, fine. Talin was learning that what he'd faced in the Realm, and was about to face, was much worse than his cranky, intoxicated stepfather. He'd also been learning it was his mother's place to work out the details of her marriage, which appeared to be falling apart faster than the current of the Sluice.

"Go to the shower before dinner, please. And don't leave that knife laying around."

Oh no, my knife!

Being so focused on his final training this afternoon, he'd forgotten to ask again if Mama D'lo had found it before he left for home.

As instructed, Talin went upstairs to put his bag away, change out of his wet clothes and clean up. A fast shower would ensure he made it back down in time for dinner, then see if he fit into what his mother had worked so hard for him to wear to the Induction. After that he would decide what he would take as his weapon, other than his pocket-sized carving knife. He'd returned Papa's knife before leaving the Realm and hadn't chosen another from the Sphere as they had discussed.

Even though he'd planned on getting to bed early, he didn't think he'd actually sleep. Tomorrow was a huge day. And according to Marisha, it was assured that Dewain would show up to stir trouble—and he still had no real weapon.

BELLY FULL, Talin cleared the table and helped his mother wash the dishes while his stepfather excused himself to the office. A sweet floral scent drifted behind him as he left the kitchen. It was a smell he didn't recognize, definitely not his mother's perfume. Robert didn't wear cologne and usually reeked of rum. Talin looked toward his mother, but her back was turned as she returned the dishes to the cabinet.

"Um, mom..."

"Yes?"

He tried not to think about the new fragrance, but it had reminded him about the offering he needed.

"Where do I get a frangipani?"

"The tree? Why do you want a tree?"

"It was going to be my offering for Jumbie tomorrow."

"Oh." She sounded surprised.

"Well, you might be able to find some cuttings tomorrow. It will be difficult to bring even a small tree with you. You don't want seeds?"

"No." Talin felt seeds were not significant enough. He wanted something more substantial. At least a started tree would be something tangible he could hold and present.

"I've already taken off work tomorrow, so maybe we could go early in the morning and find one before decorating Jumbie."

He'd nearly forgotten about the decorating.

"Thanks, Mom."

They finished putting the dishes away and his mother excused herself to go upstairs. Talin went to his room to think more about what weapon he could bring to the ceremony.

A machete was awkward. The butcher knife in the kitchen didn't seem as sturdy as he would like, but it would work in a pinch. Talin considered a trip to the shed to see what was lying around as one option, as well as an early morning trip back to the Realm to try and find Mama D'lo to ask about his knife.

"Talin, come here, please," his mother called from across the hall.

Talin entered to find her holding up his shirt in front of her. "Well, what do you think?"

The shirt-jac was light tan with gold, yellow, black and white embroidered trim around the collar and an open-style neck. Matching embroidery circled the ends of the short sleeves and two rows of the design ran across the bottom hem. It eerily matched the bandana passed down to him from his great-grandfather.

"Wow, I like it."

"Really? You like the color?"

"Yeah, it even matches my bandana."

"Oh, did you need a sash?"

"No, I have something already. Just a second." Talin excused himself to retrieve the bandana from his pack. It was still damp from the moat. Returning to her room, he said, "See?"

"How did you know this was the color I was using?"

"I didn't." Talin unfolded the cloth to show her the pattern.

She gasped when it was completely unfolded. "What is that?"

"It's from great-grandpa Kingston."

"But...how did you get that?" She asked, pressing a hand to her chest.

"Papa Bois gave it to me. See, look." He handed it to her to check the pattern against her handiwork. Ever so gently she held it, rubbing her fingers across the threads.

"Is it really—" she stopped herself.

He nodded. "It's from his burial robe."

She took a moment to admire the cloth, then abruptly asked, "Why is it wet?"

"Oh, I was swimming with it."

"In the ocean?"

"No, a moat in the Realm."

Please don't ask, please don't ask.

"Well, I assume you are wearing this tomorrow then?"

"I guess I can."

"There will be no guessing," she said sternly, turning back to her work. "Now, try on your shirt to check the fit. You didn't leave me with much time for alterations."

It seemed no one had much time to do anything recently. Talin slipped the shirt on, adjusting it. She closed the bedroom door so he could look in the mirror hanging on the back of it.

Wow.

It was perfect. It was comfortable and a little flashy. Two pockets near the bottom of the shirt would hold a bit of firedust nicely.

Covering her mouth, his mother watched over his shoulder. He could see her eyes start to glisten and water. "Do you really like it?"

"Mom. It's perfect."

"How's the fit?"

"It's great."

"Do you need anything taken in or let out?"

"No, really. It's just fine. It's not too tight or too loose anywhere," he said, opening up his shoulders and folding his arms across his chest, testing the fit. He lifted his arms and twisted in different directions to check how freely he could move. Turning to the side, he tried to see the back. More matching embroidery spread across his shoulders.. The gold threads caught the light in the room. They would really shine in flickering torch light.

Folding the bandana lengthwise, his mother stepped in front of him and tried wrapping it around his waist. "I'm not sure this will fit around you."

Talin took it from her. "I can wear it on my head," he said, and tied it around his forehead.

"That's not how you should wear a sash."

"But, that's how I've been wearing it."

After straightening the bandana, she fiddled with his shirt, double checking the fit across his shoulders and down the sides.

While trimming a few stray threads, the tears welling up in her eyes finally escaped and rolled down her cheeks. Talin wiped them away with a finger.

"You ok, Mom?"

She nodded.

"I just never believed this day would finally come."

BACK IN HIS ROOM, Talin removed the bandana from his head, and laid it over the sill of the opened window to dry. Staring out at the tree, he still wasn't sure what to bring as a weapon and reviewed his options again.

Returning to the Realm tonight probably wasn't going to be possible. It was looking more and more as if he would be using his great-grandfather's carving knife and anything else of substantial size he could find in the shed.

In his pack, he found a few herbs and remedies left inside. He tucked away the carving knife and slung the pack across his shoulder, and headed to the shed to give the knife a final polish.

TALIN SLOWLY OPENED the creaky door. Bits of dust floated in the air, sparkling in the setting sun streaming through the window.

Placing his bag on the work table, Talin looked around for something that would easily fit in his dagger's sheath or his pack. The pegboard on the wall held a variety of options and looked quite different from the weaponry wall in the Sphere. The blades in the Sphere were much older but had aged much better. Here, the tools were covered in dust, dirt and bits of rust and haphazardly hung on the wall.

Pliers, screwdrivers, and pencils had been tossed in an empty coffee can which sat on the work table. The screwdriver was an option, but it certainly wasn't good for blocking the blows he knew Dewain would throw. He'd seen his knife at previous ceremonies. It was slightly bigger than his own missing blade.

A hammer hung on the wall. It was a good size, but since he hadn't trained with a hammer, he passed, finding it too awkward. Although he thought the claw on it would be interesting to use. Next to the hammer hung the axe, dried chicken blood still on the blade, likely from use when the machete had been too dull to do the job. It was a bit too large, and he felt it would be too clunky to carry. An empty spot next to the axe usually held the machete, but it was outside near the chicken coup, waiting to be used on his stepfather's next feathered victim. It would be too obvious if he took it, his stepfather would notice immediately.

He kept looking.

Hedge clippers...definitely not an option. He'd need two hands to operate it. Rakes, shovels, and hoes leaned against the wall nearby. They wouldn't be appropriate either, too big and awkward. A large hand saw sat atop a pile of scrap wood and sandpaper.

Nope, not a saw.

There were not a lot of smaller tools he felt comfortable with. Realizing his dwindling options, he thought maybe he could swipe the butcher knife from the kitchen in the morning, without his mother noticing.

Talin turned his attention to the sandpaper and steel wool he'd used prior, pulled the metal stool up to the workbench and took out the carving knife.

Using the last remaining bit of golden light streaming through the window, he cleaned the blade of the last remaining rust spots with steel wool. A fine grit sandpaper gave the wooden handle a smoother finish. Tinkering with the knife kept his mind focused, helping settle his worry about the Induction. He was like his mother in this way, keeping himself occupied with a task. If all he had was the carving knife, so be it. It would be in the best shape he could get it.

Then, digging around in unmarked bins full of nails, screws, drill bits, wire, wrenches, and ratchets, he tried to find the sharpening stone for the blade. His stepfather used it fairly often for the axe and machete. Finding it in another bin filled with more old rusted tools, he went to work on his blade, testing its sharpness every so often on nearby papers.

When he was satisfied with his work, he put the knife back in his bag and closed the shed door securely behind him.

THE OFFICE WAS quiet when Talin slipped into the kitchen. The new foreign floral scent had disappeared. He made sure the butcher knife was in the drawer in case he decided to take it. When he went upstairs, his mother's bedroom light was already off. He heard a gentle breath that wasn't quite a snore. After placing his pack in the closet, he slipped into bed, hoping to fall asleep early.

As the excitement of what would happen kept him awake, for once he was able to sympathize with what Dewain might have felt in preparing to be inducted. Still, Talin knew he was the Healer. He just had to prove it to the rest of the island. The Induction was really going to be something.

16

A KNOCK ON THE BEDROOM DOOR RUSTLED TALIN FROM SLEEP. HE sat up in bed. "What is it?" His heart quickened.

Groggy, it took a moment for him to realize where he was.

"Talin, are you up?" his mother said, partially opening his bedroom door. "We need to get some errands done this morning,"

"Ok, just a minute."

Then he remembered.

The Induction is today!

He changed into comfortable clothes and met his mother downstairs.

"Good morning," she greeted him with a smile in the living room, looking for something in her purse.

"Morning." He rubbed his eyes. "Do I have time to eat something?"

"Yes. I was up early today. I got fresh donuts if you'd like." She pointed to the kitchen counter. Donuts were a treat his mother didn't often purchase.

The sweet smell of chocolate filled his nose as he opened the box, making his mouth water. The dozen chocolate-glazed pastries had not yet been touched. He grabbed two.

"Thanks, Mom."

"Fresh milk in the fridge."

Talin poured himself a large glass, as it didn't seem right to eat donuts without it. It was as special a treat as Papa Bois' breakfast buffet the day before.

Talin finished in record time, licking every last bit of chocolate glaze off his fingers and chugging the remainder of his milk, while his mother waited patiently on the couch. "Wash your hands, young man."

"Yes, ma'am."

THE CLOSEST NURSERY was about a twenty minute drive through the rolling hills of the neighboring town, giving them time to discuss how they were feeling for the day.

"Big day, eh?" she asked him.

"Yeah." Talin's stomach rumbled, but whether from chocolate or nerves, he couldn't quite tell. "I'm getting nervous."

"Well, I can understand that, but remember how special this is. Focus on that. Not just special for you, but the entire island." Her face lit up as she spoke, sharing reassuring words, reminding him of his great-grandfather and how extraordinary the day was going to be.

Then he thought of Dewain.

"What if Dewain shows up?"

"Well...he is family, and all on the island are welcome. Some people are going to show up expecting him to be named. But, they will see otherwise. Plus, there is proof if anyone tries to challenge it. Your letter and knife, the bandana...your pendants."

His stomach cramped. Maybe it was the sugar rush.

Talin hoped the day would be special and not ruined by his own family. But no matter what, it would surely be memorable.

He tried to focus on the advice his mother was lending him and match her confidence level. It had taken her so long to gain it herself. But she was right. There was proof. And Dewain had attempted to take it once already. Would he try again in front of a crowd?

THEY PULLED into the drive of the nursery. The car bounced and dipped across the gravel road, his mother trying her best to avoid the potholes. A sign with several painted wooden arrows, each pointing in different directions, helped usher them where they needed to go: Greenhouse. Orchard. Vegetables. Hay and Feed. Supplies.

His mother turned in the direction of the greenhouse.

Stepping out of the car, Talin's senses were bombarded by the strong scent of fertilizer. The bags were stacked near the parking area in front of the large greenhouse. Pallets full of potting soil warmed in the tropical sun. The greenhouse's windows were covered in moisture and he could hear the misters spritzing water onto the foliage inside. Careful not to trip on the highway of water hoses crossing the mulch footpath, they entered the building through the main door.

An employee, trimming dead leaves off rows of young potted plants, greeted them. "'Morning, may I help you find some'ting?"

Talin answered. "Yes, do you have any frangipani?"

Brushing his hands of loose dirt, the man removed his gloves, leaving them near the plant he was tending. "Yes, right over here," he said, leading them to an area filled with larger leafed plants and a stack of what looked like old discarded sticks, each almost two feet long. They were gathered in small bundles of two and three, tied with twine. The sticks looked like they had sickly green scars on the bark.

That's it? Just a stick?

"We have 'da cuttings and started trees. Diff'rent colors. 'Da pots start at $50 and the cuttings start at $30."

"How much are the...cuttings?" Talin asked.

"Two bundle is $30 and three bundle is $40. How many you need?"

"Oh, just one." Talin said, not wanting to burden his mother with additional expenses. She grew everything in her garden from seed, received a discount at the market she worked at, and did not spend extra money for luxuries such as a specialized plant at a proper nursery. She'd already made him a shirt for his ceremony, most likely spending more than her entire budget on the fancy gold threads and other embellishments.

"Well, we could do two. Two different colors would be very nice," his mother said, looking at Talin.

But, it's a stick.

"What color are the flowers of the cuttings?" she asked about the less expensive of the two choices.

"I have yellow, orange, and a red."

"But do they smell good?" Talin asked.

"Ah, yes, very fragrant," the man said.

Talin inquired further. "Do they smell the same or do they smell different?"

"'Da' yellow, a kind of peach. Da' orange, like fruity. The red, kind of like cinnamon."

Wow. All so different.

"Which would you like, dear?" his mother asked.

"Is that cinnamon on the stick?" Talin asked, pointing to a brown powder at one end of the cuttings.

"Ya, mon. It cinnamon. Help it to dry."

"Is that why the red smells like cinnamon?"

His mother elbowed him playfully.

The man chuckled. "Nah, mon, it's just how you do it. They all 'ave cinnamon when they are drying. Prevents infection to da' tree."

Talin was struggling to figure out how such a simple stick could grow into the beautiful frangipani trees he'd seen around so much. It looked like a stick he could have used to play fetch with his dog.

His mother asked again, "What colors would you like?"

Talin was planting the tree in remembrance of the goats and red reminded him of goat blood. Red was also Dewain's warrior color. He wasn't sure he wanted to pay tribute to that so he chose yellow and orange. Plus, they had sweeter, more traditional scents, as described by the nursery worker.

"Ah, good choice," the man said, "very fruity together. You need any 'ting else? Pots? Fertilizer?"

His mother declined and they met the man at the register outside the greenhouse in a simple outbuilding. Shantel dug through her purse again, handing over the thirty Eastern Caribbean dollars like it was an everyday occurrence. The man explained the cuttings were ready to be planted anytime.

Back in the car, Talin thanked her.

"It is the least I can do. This is a very special occasion."

Talin stared at the sticks in his lap. "So, how do I present these to Jumbie? They look so plain and boring."

"We can use some extra ribbon and wrap them up nicely, then come back tomorrow or the next day to plant them. I should have some leftover soil and fertilizer in the shed. I'll show you how."

BACK HOME, his mother collected her ribbons and sat at the kitchen table wrapping the cuttings in a variety of ways until one was to Talin's liking.

"How's this?" she asked.

"That's good. Not too girly."

"Ok," she laughed. "It's going to take a while to decorate the tree. Shall we start before lunch?"

Talin agreed, not knowing exactly what she had planned. "Do you know if Marisha is coming?"

"I saw her at the market yesterday and asked her, but we'll just have to wait and see. She doesn't want to hurt your feelings if she can't come. She said things were...complicated at home."

Yeah, probably.

"Let me show you what I got for the decorations," she continued. He followed her to the back porch where she grabbed a large plastic bag that she had cleverly hidden behind the dirty laundry basket, next to the washer and dryer. "I put it here so Robert wouldn't see it."

"Does he know?"

"About tonight?" She paused. "He knows you are being honored for something."

"So he knows."

"Well, not everything. But I'm sure he's heard the stories at the bar. He hasn't said much to me the last few days. It's better that way."

"You'll still be able to come tonight, right?"

"Nothing would cause me to miss this." She smiled and opened the sack. "I hope you like a lot of color." Pulling out an assortment of vibrantly colored ribbons on small spools, she set them on top of the washer. Some rolls were covered in glitter or sequins. Reaching back into the bag, she pulled out several sets of white lights strung on wire, the type you'd find decorating a covered porch.

"How are we going to turn those on?"

"The Reverend has a small generator and extra extension cords he's agreed to loan me this afternoon when he drops off the tables and chairs from the church."

"Is he coming, too?"

"I think he might. I wanted to have a good share of things done before he stops by. When he gets here, can you help me carry the tables and chairs to the tree? I don't think he should be carrying them that far and that's going to take a while as well."

"Sure."

She showed Talin more items she'd found to decorate the tables with.

"Mom, you shouldn't have spent all this money."

"Don't you worry about that," she said, putting everything back in the bag. "Most of it was on sale. Besides, this is a once in a life-time celebration, and if your fath— Robert, can spend his money on rum and—" she stopped herself. "I can spend mine on whatever I like."

Talin suggested they start decorating right then. She agreed, but insisted on making lunch first to take along, avoiding unnecessary trips to the house. She prepared small meals while Talin gathered the scissors, twine, zip-ties, tape, extra trash bags, and other items they might need for decorating. Tossing his pack over his shoulder, knife inside, he also grabbed the bag of decorations. His mother carried a small picnic basket and they made their way toward Jumbie.

It was a gorgeous day, nearly as perfect as the Realm. Not too hot, the humidity was at a tolerable level, and the breeze was mini-mal. Talin and his mother looked up at the great tree.

"I don't even know where to start," his mother said. "Do you have any ideas?"

"Maybe the lights first? Put them over where people might eat at the tables. Where will they go?"

"I think they should be here, off to the side." She pointed to the area nearest the house, opposite the old church ruins. "We will likely be dancing in the center here. But there should still be some lights there, too. I have plenty."

His mother obsessed over the details. They discussed whether the lights should be hung in a pattern or randomly draped in the branches. After climbing the tree and stringing one or two strands of the lights to compare, Talin preferred random.

"I prefer something more symmetrical. It looks more professional," a voice said from the ground.

Talin looked out from behind a thick branch, "Marisha!"

"Plus, you are looking down from the tree. Everyone else will be looking up from the ground." Marisha dropped a backpack off her shoulder.

Talin scrambled down from the tree.

"Marisha, thank you for coming," his mother said.

"You're welcome. I can't stay too long, Mom is expecting me home soon. I'm not supposed to be here. Dewain is probly spying on me right now."

"You're going to come tonight aren't you?" Talin blurted out.

"I don't know if I can. I want to, but—" she passed him her backpack. "Here, I brought more decorations. What do you need help with?"

"Talin and I can finish the lights later. Is there anything you brought that we could set up right now?"

"Well, I mostly have table decorations, so I can leave them here and help you fix whatever you need before the tables come."

"That's very kind of you," Shantel replied. "Well, we could readjust the lights and you tell us what looks best. Then we can start on the ribbons."

Together, the three of them moved strings of lights until they were to Marisha's liking, imagining how they would look at sunset. Shantel then opened several rolls of her ribbon. Marisha said the glitter was her favorite and that it would look best nearest the lights to reflect their color.

"Talin, how would you like the ribbon hung?" his mother asked.

"It doesn't matter." Talin was quickly losing interest in the task.

There were only hours left before the whole town potentially showed up to the production. It wasn't in his nature to be the center of attention and ribbons were the least of his worries.

"Yes, it does matter. Make a decision," Marisha said, echoing the words of Papa Bois.

"Ok, just let them dangle from the branches. Just don't make it too... girly."

Talin's mother pulled him aside, firmly grasping his arm. Under her breath, she whispered. "Young man. This is for you. Your great-grandfather chose you for this day. Marisha is trying to be helpful. And if you haven't noticed— she is girly. One day, you will learn to appreciate that. I suggest you start now."

Then speaking loud enough for Marisha to hear, she added, "Now, where would you like the ribbon hung?"

He looked at Marisha, waiting with her arms crossed. "Ok, hang them from the branches so they can blow in the breeze. Don't wrap the trunk, I may need to climb. Maybe save some for the tables, too."

Marisha grabbed the scissors and went to work cutting the ribbons in various lengths. Everyone helped hang them. Some dangled straight down, while others were able to be spiraled with the sharp edge of the scissors like an embellishment on a Christmas gift.

After cleaning up, they sat down to eat, except for Marisha.

"I really need to get home now," she said.

Talin got up to help her with her bag, "You'll be back tonight?"

"I don't know, I hope so. I'll try. But if I'm not, I want to hear all about it tomorrow."

As she turned to leave, Talin's hopes sank. Marisha's answer hadn't sounded promising.

"Talin, come sit and eat. We've still got to bring down the tables later."

"Not hungry."

"Talin…"

Joining his mother, he asked, "Do you think she's coming tonight?" and sat down, grabbing some chips and a sandwich.

She took a breath, "Well, what is meant to be will be. I imagine things at home are tense right now."

Yeah. She said that.

Besides his mother, Talin wanted more than anything to have Marisha at the celebration. She'd listened to him as he'd gone on about the Realm and taught him the folklore when he didn't believe the tales himself. She'd helped him learn to dive into large swells, greet Papa Bois with traditional words, and shared Hosea Falls with him. They shared more than friendship, they shared blood. It definitely wasn't going to be the same without her. He stared at the rainbow of colors that dangled from Jumbie's limbs.

His mother tried to reassure him, "I'm sure if there is any way she can come, she'll be here."

17

THE SUN WAS READY TO DIP BELOW THE HORIZON WHEN TALIN'S mother called for him from across the hall.

"Talin, are you ready?"

"Yeah, just a minute."

Talin pulled himself away from the window sill. He hadn't stayed at the tree to finish setting up after helping his mother and the pastor set up the tables. She'd sent him home to get a shower and start getting dressed, so he was excited to see the finishing touches she'd made with the table decorations.

Crossing the room and opening the creaky closet door, he grabbed his backpack. Digging inside, he removed the carving knife and placed it securely in his cargo short pocket. Disappointed, he knew it was all he was going to have for protection tonight. With his mother accompanying him, he doubted he'd be able to nab the butcher knife from the kitchen drawer.

Securing the pack over his shoulder, he paused to look at himself in the short mirror on the inside of his closet door. It was difficult believing this day had finally come after everything that had happened over the last several weeks. His stomach was in knots.

"Talin?" his mother called again.

Smoothing the material with his hands, he pulled down the shirt-jac and straightened it, stood tall and tried to compose himself.

HE CROSSED the hall to his mother's room, "Wow! You look great!" he told her, with a smile.

"You really think?" She turned to her side, posing in the hand-made dress. The red, yellow, and white plaid pattern flowed as she swished her skirt from side to side. A bright yellow satin ribbon was sewn atop a wider, deep red ribbon that hugged her petite waistline. The tail of a large bow dangled in the back. Her hair was pulled up in a turban-style headscarf, matching the dress' material. Fussing with her short, ruffled sleeves that made a straight line across her chest to her shoulders, she asked, "I don't know, sleeves on the shoulder or off?" She moved the sleeves atop her shoulders and back down again, looking in the mirror with indecision.

"Um, whatever you're comfortable with. It looks good either way."

"I'm sorry, it's not about me." She grabbed his shoulders, gently shaking him. "Wow! Look at you, so handsome! Turn around, let me see."

Talin turned.

"It's missing something. Where's your bandana?"

Talin took the now-dry bandana from his pack and handed it to her. She gently folded it and tied it around his forehead, the knot to the back. "Much better. You look... official now."

Turning him around to face her, she held his hands in hers. "Talin, I want you to know how truly proud I am of you today."

"Thanks, Mom."

"No, really. I didn't believe you and I'm sorry. It's just, all those years ago believing it was you, then to not only be threatened over it, but to have that dream taken from me so long ago...I can't believe

I ran from...never mind." She let go of his hands and untucked the necklace from underneath his shirt, straightening the pendants, so they now hung in plain view. "I could never be more proud of you than I am right now." She rested her hands on his shoulders and placed a gentle kiss atop his head. "We should get you down there. The guest of honor shouldn't be late. The people have waited too long. Don't make them wait any longer."

———

ON THE BACK PORCH, his mother grabbed the two frangipani cuttings, both fancily tied with red and yellow satin ribbons. Talin escorted her by the arm as they made their way down the trail toward the tree line across from Jumbie. She'd chosen to keep her sleeves up.

As they drew closer, he could make out the finer details of the ceremony area. All the white lights were aglow, the colored ribbons swayed in the evening breeze, glitter flickering in the light. The generator competed with the song of the tree frogs and the mumbling from the crowd. Those that had gathered underneath Jumbie's canopy wore brightly-colored costumes and held tall, lit torches. Voices called out as he arrived and crossed into the tree line with his mother.

"There he is!"

"Shhh!"

"It's almost time!"

"Get ready!"

"Here he comes! Here he comes!"

The crowd hushed as Javon entered the trees to greet Shantel and Talin. Nodding, he addressed Talin's mother first. "Evening, Shantel."

"Good evening." Her expression remained neutral, and she squeezed Talin's arm.

"Are you ready, Talin?" he asked.

"I think so."

"Thanks, Shantel. I can take it from here." Javon said.

She nodded, then turned to Talin, a tear escaping down her cheek. With her hands on his chest, she said, "This is your moment. Healer Kingston would be so proud." She hugged him tight. "I love you." She turned away, walked out of the trees and stepped into the crowd just feet away.

"Hi," Talin said quietly to his father.

"How are you?" Javon asked, looking official, wearing an elder's traditional gold and tan ceremonial robe over his clothes.

"Good, I think. I'm still not really sure what I'm supposed to do."

"I'll walk you through it. The crowd is still gathering, we can stay here a moment longer. Besides, I...have something for you."

Javon reached inside his robe. "I was at Hosea Falls last night gathering my thoughts for today, and I heard something splashing on the shore." Revealing Talin's knife, he handed it to him. "I think this belongs to you."

"Oh my gosh!" Talin took the weapon, looking it over for damage, but it was unscathed and looked brand new. "Wow! Thanks! It was at the Falls?!"

"It was such a loud splash I went to see what had happened and it was just sitting on the rocks at the beach entry. I'd seen you use it before."

Mama D'lo.

She'd found it. And found a way to get it to Talin, just in time. The biggest smile ever stretched across his face. Excitedly, he put it in its sheath and secured it. Now, he felt ready.

Drums began to beat.

"Maybe you can explain how it got there to me later?" Javon asked.

Talin nodded, nerves setting in.

"Stay next to me. You won't need to do much."

Javon pushed through the foliage and Talin followed, drums beating louder. The crowd, forming a circle in the area in front of Jumbie, applauded. There had to have been fifty or seventy-five people, all dressed in traditional red and white checkered quadrille dresses, or trousers and waistcoats of matching colors. The elders stood together, dressed similarly to Javon. With women in layered skirts and elaborate headscarves making up about half the crowd, it was definitely a historic moment for them and an Induction.

Scanning the rows of people as he stepped forward, he saw his mother standing near the base of the tree. Sporting the bright yellow sash helped her to stand out among the quadrille dresses around her. The entire area was superbly lit by strings of white lights and the guests' flickering yellow-orange torches as the sun finally dipped below the horizon and nightfall officially set in. A row of tables covered in white linens sat to the side, nearest the house. Folding chairs sat on either side of the tables, waiting for their guests to dine. A wide, glittering table runner and palm fronds ran the length of them with Marisha's tea lights flickering on top. Where was she?

At one end of the tables, a potluck of local foods was piled high. A cacophony of rice and beans, sweet potato, steamed pepper and carrot, fresh baked bread, grilled pineapple and mango scents filled the air. Glasses of hibiscus iced tea and ice water were being served by a young girl about his age from insulated coolers. Fruits and salads sat nearby the coconut rum cake with white drizzled icing, and bread pudding with pineapple and cherry glaze. The presentation rivaled Papa's celebratory breakfast. No meat seemed to be on the menu, which Talin appreciated.

He and his father arrived at the trunk of the tree as the drums stopped. All eyes were on them as his father addressed the crowd.

"As an elder in this community, I welcome you to tonight's celebration. The tradition of Healer has been with our island for hundreds of years. But, it has been three generations since our last

Healer, Healer Kingston Boyce, has served. Just when our community thought the tradition had withered away and died in recent times, fate and the spirits showed us it is very much alive. Now, Healer Kingston's great-grandson—my son—Talin Boyce has been chosen to fill this role." The crowd cheered, a drummer banged his drum.

"The responsibility of Healer is to be a leader, advocate, and spirit guide for our island's people and traditions, a protector of nature and all within it." He placed a hand on Talin's shoulder. "As we celebrate tonight, I already see a welcome shift in the traditions since Healer Kingston last served. Tonight, for the first time, we welcome our wives, our sisters, our mothers and daughters."

The women in the crowd clapped, whistled, and cheered. Talin beamed at his mother.

This isn't so bad.

"A new generation will breathe new life into this role. He will bring with him many more traditions, not only to this Induction ceremony, but to daily life on our island. To date, since records have been kept, Healer Talin is the youngest to be named for this title. The elders wish Healer Talin great success on this journey." More cheers and drumming erupted.

An older man with a gold stole around his neck stepped forward next to Javon to speak, the ends of the garment hanging just above the dusty ground as he walked. Opening a leather-bound book, he read aloud addressing the crowd.

"As senior elder of the Healer's council, I officially recognize and accept Talin Boyce, son of Javon Hunte and Shantel Boyce-Williams, as Healer."

"What does the boy bring to the council as proof for this selection?" a man asked from the rear of the crowd.

"Proof accepted is heir of the great Healer Kingston, kin of Healers Hunte and Dyllon, as well as possession of a Healer's relic. The council finds this to be of a genuine nature."

"What is the relic?" another man asked.

Several men throughout the crowd, all wearing matching stoles of various colors atop their traditional dress, shouted.

"Here, here."

"I've not seen the relic!"

"We wish to approach!"

"I am on the council and I did not approve this relic."

Talin whispered to his father. "Who is that?" Referring to the senior elder speaking to the crowd.

"Mr. George, from Azacca Farms."

Talin had heard this name before from his mother and glared at the man who had sold the goats to Dewain and his family for the previous two Inductions. Seems the island was a small place after all.

"Don't worry, I was given strict instructions. No goats," his father assured him.

"From who?"

"I don't know. Now, shhh."

"The relic is Healer Kingston's pendants," Mr. George answered the men, "as noted at the most recent Evocation." The men in the stoles talked amongst themselves and seemed satisfied by his answer.

Mr. George motioned for Talin and his father to be seated in two chairs near the tree's trunk as he continued the announcements. He introduced a troupe of musicians and dancers that emerged from the treeline opposite them.

About fifteen performers, not much older than Talin, entered the area with traditional island instruments: buleador, tamboras, steel drums, guitars, maracas, guiros and claves. The flamboyant, choreographed spectacle that followed was a feast for the eyes and ears. Dust clouds from the dry earth trailed the troupe's footsteps. The crowd swayed and clapped along, many snapping photos with their mobile phones.

The girls twirled in their dresses and leapt into the air. Stepping up to their partners' sides, they were then spun around with vigor. The dancing and tribal rhythms were a treat for everyone in attendance, but it was all to welcome *him* as Healer. At the end, the performers took a respectful bow in front of Talin and the crowd clapped and whistled.

Mr. George stepped forward again. "Now, we will present our offerings to the tree, as it has clearly helped us confirm our chosen new Healer as in years past. In doing so, we ask for safety from the spirits deep within it. Javon, father of our new Healer will begin, followed by all guests, then Healer Talin will complete the offerings."

Javon stood, stepped up to the trunk and reached into his pocket. Talin turned in his seat to watch. It was difficult for him to see exactly what his father held, but he gently placed the palm-sized object on the ground and bowed his head for a moment, then returned to his seat next to Talin. The guests were silent except for a quiet, respectful rhythm humming from the percussion instruments. Torches crackled in the night air.

Nearly every member of the crowd took their turn, one by one, quietly approaching the tree and placing their offerings at the base of the roots. Some brought small items, others larger. Talin watched as the pile of gifts continued to grow. Lit candles, oils, clutches of local flowers, pottery, bags of seeds, wood carvings and trinkets, and colorful material that might be used for making clothing or costumes. All the offerings had their own private meaning from the giver, but none were shared aloud. Even a knife was left. Remembering Dewain could crash his party at any given moment, Talin made a point of keeping an eye on the blade during the remainder of the ceremony. And out of all the people walking past him with offerings, none were Marisha.

"Now, our Healer will give his offering," Mr. George said.

Reluctantly, Talin rose from his chair, chest heavy, and walked to where his mother was standing, holding the two frangipani cuttings tied with ribbon. He took them from her and knelt at the base of the tree, gently setting the plain-looking sticks next to the many other offerings, all much more colorful and appearing more expensive and meaningful than his.

"You know why," he whispered to Jumbie so no one could hear. Returning to his seat, he felt all eyes on him.

Mr. George continued, "At this time, I invite you all to partake in food and drink to celebrate and welcome Healer Talin!" The crowd cheered.

"Wait! You forgot an offering!" A voice called from near the tree line. The crowd, looking surprised, turned their attention.

Dewain.

"How about mine?!" Dewain said as he dragged a bleating goat onto the dusty ground in front of the crowd, the rope taught as the goat tried to pull away. The crowd gasped. Talin's blood ran hot and his jaw clenched. Three other boys followed behind Dewain, dragging and prodding a second goat.

"Let's do this!" Dewain shouted as the other boys cackled and yelled, all pulling knives from their belts.

Talin leapt from his chair toward Dewain, his own knife in hand. Dewain spun around and their blades met. Sparks bounced off the metal. Dewain's gang took hold of his goat as he faced off with Talin.

Several in the crowd attempted to rush the boys, but Mr. George held up a hand—and said nothing. The crowd stopped their advance, leaving the two to duel under the torches.

"Talin, stop!" his mother screamed.

"Yeah, Talin, stooop!" Dewain mocked. "You can't stop it this time! What a pathetic offering. Sticks? Really?" He swiped with his knife, but Talin deflected it. "Is that all you can afford? You're supposed to be the *Healer*. Do you see my hand?" He showed Talin the burn mark on his palm, a half-healed scar in the shape of a circle that he'd received trying to steal the pendants from around Talin's neck not long ago, nearly choking him to death in the process.

"You'll pay for this." Dewain threatened.

Talin didn't give him the time or satisfaction of conversation, leaping over a large drum and shoving over one of the taunting boys, causing him to lose his grip on one of the goats. It ran into the crowd, dragging the rope behind it. Another boy leapt into the dirt to grab it, missing by inches. Talin stepped between the boys and the fleeing goat so they could not attempt to go after it a second time. Talin scanned the surroundings for Dewain, who was opposite him standing near the crowd, someone whispering in his ear.

Growing angrier, the boys grabbed the remaining goat as it kicked and desperately tried to escape. But, unfortunately, it was no match for the three burly teens now restraining it in the center of the circle. Two held the body and one held onto the short horns, pulling its head up to expose its neck.

"Go!" the boys yelled to Dewain. "Quick!"

Dewain ran toward them, "Hold it steady!" and dove for the struggling animal's throat with his knife.

Talin, just a bit too far to catch Dewain, threw his knife. It sliced the back of Dewain's calf, instantly sending him tumbling to the ground, just short of the struggling goat. Dewain howled in pain then grabbed his leg, screaming obscenities. Talin raced forward and leapt to retrieve his weapon. Landing on the hard ground on his belly, the two wrestled in the dust cloud. The noisy chaos from the crowd grew louder. Men yelled. Women screamed. Talin's rib ached terribly.

Talin jumped up, thrusting his knife at all of the boys, purposefully missing by the narrowest of margins. They scrambled, letting go of the goat. It, too, ran for the crowd and disappeared. Only then did Mr. George allow the crowd to step in and hold the boys back. Talin's father stepped up and placed a hand on his son's chest, gently guiding him in the opposite direction back to the chairs in front of Jumbie. "Ok, enough," he said quietly.

"You said no goats!" he yelled at Javon.

"I didn't bring those goats!" he spewed back under his breath.

Several muscular men, some holding weapons themselves, held all the boys, making them sit in the dirt to enforce the peace. Not one of the four teens dared move.

Mr. George spoke again.

"There will be no disrespect during the ceremo—"

"Yeah? Tell that to your 'new healer'," Dewain yelled, "he's wrecked two Inductions already!"

"Silence!" Mr. George raised his hand along with his voice. "You may sit quietly to observe this, or the elders will—"

"Will *what*?!" Dewain's father burst through the tree line, approaching and challenging Mr. George.

Oh no.

"Mr. Dyllon," Mr. George said, "the elders have discussed this at length. The last two attempted Inductions were not endorsed by the council, and if you or these boys cause any further disruption, you will be forcefully removed from this holy ground, as well as be permanently severed of your duties as an elder in this community!"

"The council must unanimously approve the Inductee, and *this* choice," Amos pointed a shaking finger directly at Talin, "I did not approve!"

"In the extensive history of this council, it has always been majority rule with all Inductees, and this one is no different. I am sorry if you disagree or are disappointed with the council's choice. Also, bear in mind the Evocation that was witnessed by a majority of the community, including yourself. Many of them are standing here in front of you." Mr. George reminded him, referring to Dewain's last Induction.

"Yes, because *my son* was in the tree!"

Mr. George, an older man with slightly shorter and thinner stature than Amos, stepped forward to face off with Mr. Dyllon, within grappling range. It appeared what he lacked in physical strength, he made up for by his knowledge of the council's inner workings, a confident presence and wisdom. He reminded Talin a little of Papa Bois, maybe even hiding some hidden martial arts talent or something more sinister behind a farmer's facade. Maybe raising goats was just a front.

"And what relic has your family produced, Amos?"

"*He* stole it!" Again, a finger was pointed at Talin as Amos started to pace in front of Mr. George.

"I did not!" Talin yelled, standing up out of his chair. "Dewain is the one who tried to steal it! Look at his hand!" Javon rose slowly, standing next to Talin.

Amos continued. "There is only one way to prove you and the council have made the wrong decision, and I will prove *that* to you." He pulled out a folded piece of parchment paper from his shirt pocket. "I'd hoped you would see it differently, but you *all*," he pointed to the crowd now, "have forced me to assert my power as an elder to call for an Elimination!"

The crowd gasped.

What? An Elimination...that's what Papa had said could happen with Onca—not Dewain!

Dewain smiled devilishly, blood still oozing from his calf dripping onto the dirt. No one had tended to him, as Javon had, when Talin's blade injured him once before.

"Not possible." Mr. George said. "An Elimination is for challenging a Healer who is no longer fit to serve. That does not apply here. In addition, you must have the seal of the senior elder, and that is me. I have not signed off on any such request, nor will I."

"Oh, but you did Mr. George, you did..." Amos sauntered even closer to Mr. George, face to face now, showing him the opened piece of paper and pointing to the bottom. "Plus, the mandatory signatures of two additional elders as witnesses."

Mr. George's eyes widened. "You have stolen my seal! What kind of Obeah is this?"

"I wouldn't call it stealing," he said, his smile as wide as Jumbie's buttress. "I challenge any elder here to come forward and question the official seal. See it for yourselves! Mr. George does not recall giving his approval in his advancing age, and now here, in front of all of you, he plays me as a fool. Make no mistake, he is lying to all of you!"

"That is not true!" Mr. George shouted.

The ground rumbled. The tree's leaves shook, causing the strung lights to bounce and flicker like the torches. Ribbons rattled above them. Again, the crowd began to talk, confusion on their faces. Talin's pendants began to vibrate and glisten.

Uh oh.

Dewain exchanged glances with his friends.

"The spirits know untruths have been spoken." Mr. George informed the crowd. He didn't look at all concerned that the earth below him could open and swallow him up at any moment.

"I see your sticks worked well keeping away the spirits!" Dewain laughed. "Nice going, Talin!"

Mr. Dyllon continued his rant, also not phased by the shaking below his feet. "Your seal is on the edict!" Slowly walking in front of the circle of onlookers, he shoved the paper under their noses to prove his point. "See here, fine guests! Look!"

Talin whispered to his father. "Is that real?"

"Amos!" Javon called, "I'd like to see that, please!"

Amos approached him, shoving the paper into Javon's chest.

The rumbling settled.

Whispers from the crowd continued.

Talin watched as his father read the paper, seemingly studying it carefully. Glancing at Mr. George and back to Amos, he returned the paper.

"The Elimination will take place Sunday," Javon announced, glaring at Amos. The crowd gasped again.

Wait—Sunday?! But, that's the day after tomorrow!

Talin heard the breath escape from his mother's chest. She looked faint. Someone held onto her arm to keep her steady. Discussion from the crowd grew louder and Dewain's maniacal laughter could be heard above the stunned guests. Javon nodded his head toward Mr. George.

Mr. George, again, raised his hand. "Quiet! Quiet!"

Everyone turned their attention.

"There is some discrepancy over the validity of the Elimination edict. But, as the father of the Healer has so…boldly announced, I believe this can be settled once and for all." He paused. "The Elimination will take place Sunday at sunset, beginning here at this sacred place. *All* are welcome to attend to serve as witnesses."

More gasping and discussion rushed through the crowd. Talin swallowed down a hard, dry lump in his throat as his mother sobbed uncontrollably nearby.

"The winner will be announced at the conclusion of the evening. After which time, there will be no further discussion on this matter. Do we have an accord amongst the elders present?"

"Here, here."

"Irie."

"Aye."

"Agreed," several in the crowd answered.

"So now, from this time until the Elimination, Talin Boyce will serve as Healer." Mr. George stared at Amos as he continued, "and anyone present not wishing to observe or participate for the remainder of this evening may excuse themselves immediately."

Dewain continued laughing and was addressed by his father. "Dewain, we go now. Only nonsense remains here tonight."

The men holding Dewain's gang at bay reluctantly released their guard. Struggling to stand on his injured leg, Dewain jerked his arms away from those holding him. "Enjoy your little pity party, Talin. Sunday night is the real show! *My* show!"

Mr. Dyllon escorted the boys back through the tree line. Two of the elders followed, Talin assumed to make sure they were really leaving the area.

Mr. George announced, "I apologize, Healer Talin, for the interruption. Now, where were we?"

Javon spoke up, "We should eat."

"Ah, yes," Mr. George refocused his attention, "so much wonderful food has been prepared for us to celebrate. Please gather around the tables, give thanks and enjoy the feast. And, give your congratulations to Healer Talin, and wish him well on this most recent development." Respectfully, he took a bow to the crowd, his stole brushing the ground.

A FEW GUESTS from the crowd reluctantly approached the tables, obviously shocked from what they had just witnessed. Talin's mother ran to him, grabbing his shoulders. Her eyes were red and filled with tears. "Talin! What are you going to do?!"

"Shantel, it's ok." Javon said, stepping between them.

"*You* did this!" She shoved him back. "You made this ridiculous announcement. You know as well as I do that Mr. George didn't give his approval! Why would you do this?!"

"Please, keep your voice down. People are watching."

"Talin is Healer," she growled, her voice lower. "Why would you just throw him to the dogs?! There's nothing he needs to prove anymore!"

"I know what I'm doing. Don't worry about it—"

"Don't worry about it?! This is my *son*!"

"And he's *my* son, too. Or did you forget?" he snapped back.

"Both of you, stop!" Talin said.

The three stared at each other.

"Let's go eat." Talin said, taking his mother by the arm and walking her to the tables.

SOME GUESTS WERE eager to approach, congratulating him on his new title. Others were shy and reserved, or looked too nervous to speak to him.

Starting to settle into the evening, tempers simmered between his parents and Talin was able to enjoy much of the food brought by the locals. All of it tasted like a world-class chef had prepared it. Still, nothing was as good as the fruit. He'd always been partial to fruit, but the guests were literally raving over it.

"Wow! This is amazing!"

"Shantel did you bring this from the market?"

"I need to know who grew this!"

"Now, this is what a melon is supposed to taste like."

"It's SO fresh!"

Pineapple slices, mango chunks, and bunches of bananas were the finest he'd ever tasted and rivaled the bounty from the Grove.

Wait. Only fruit from the Grove tasted like this.

Talin whipped his head, looking over his shoulder. He had not brought any fruits to the feast, so who did? Looking around, there was no sign of Papa Bois. And still no sign of Marisha either. Talin slumped back in his seat, picking at the remaining bits of fruit on his paper plate.

"Sit up straight," his father said, nudging him.

He sat up, not wanting to let his disappointment show.

"IF EVERYONE IS through with their meal, I'd like to continue with the celebrations this evening," Mr. George announced.

Leaving the tables, the crowd returned to the ceremony area and stood in their original circular formation, a few still holding onto finger foods or fruit.

Talin heard the cry of a goat from behind the tree's trunk. "Here, I've got it!" someone shouted.

No! Is Dewain back?

A slender young man gently led one of the goats that had run away earlier in the evening toward the crowd. Talin leaned in, hand on the butt of his knife.

Javon placed his hand on Talin's shoulder, holding him back. "Wait," he said.

The crowd remained quiet. The drums were silent.

"With a new Healer, comes new traditions." Talin looked up at his father as Mr. George spoke. "Today will be no different. Tonight, we remember, return to, and reclaim our history and our roots." Talin's eyes widened hearing the words. "We celebrate all living creatures around us. Please, bring the animal forward!"

Talin's full stomach flipped on itself. "I'm NOT hurting a goat," he sternly told his father.

"You won't." Javon said.

"Nobody else will either!" Talin snapped.

"Just wait."

The man with the goat stood in the middle of the crowd, relaxed. The rope around the goat's neck was loose and the animal stood, sniffing the ground, unafraid. A second person walked forward carrying a handful of flowers then placed a garland around the goat's neck. It was a lei made of frangipani blooms.

Mr. George continued his speech as the goat tried to eat the petals off its necklace. "Both Healer Kingston and Healer Dyllon protected the animals of the forest and the sea, as well as all of us who inhabited the island at that time. It is a tradition I suspect Healer Talin will continue."

Relieved, a smile crossed Talin's face.

One by one, several in the crowd came forward to bow to the

goat or place flowers at its hooves. One guest reached into her pocket. When she removed her hand, Talin saw it was covered in a yellow powdery substance. She drew a simple wave-like pattern with it on the goat's back then returned to her place. As close as Talin was, he distinctly smelled turmeric. Another guest simply approached the goat, placed their hand on the animal's head and whispered something to it Talin couldn't hear.

When everyone who wanted to approach the goat had done so, the man holding it approached the tree trunk, tied up the goat and quietly walked away.

"Now, we celebrate!" Mr. George proclaimed, followed by a cheer from the crowd. The musicians and dancers flooded the ceremony floor once again, encouraging the crowd to join them. The night air was filled with laughter and cheering, the sound of the ocean drowned out by the drums and other musical instruments. The flickering tabletop candles and bright lights stretching across the tree branches cast a warm glow on the guests' smiling faces.

"Come on, Talin!" His mother grabbed him by the arm, pulling him in to dance with her.

"Mom, I can't dance!"

"Don't be silly."

Twirling her dress and swaying to the beat of the music, she encouraged Talin to join in. He was happy to see that her tears had dried. She was truly trying to enjoy the moment. People waved at Talin, patted him on the back and nodded their heads in his direction when he made eye contact with them across the sea of guests.

The goat stood calmly, munching on grass and the frangipani, unfazed by the activity and loud music around it.

A girl about Talin's age wearing a low cut, flowing green and yellow checkered dress swayed up to him. Bumping into him, she flashed a smile and gave him a wink. Bending her finger and encouraging him to follow her, she disappeared into the sea of guests on the dance floor.

Marisha?

"Is Marisha coming?" he asked his mother, trying to keep tempo with her steps.

Leaning in to speak over the noise, she said, "I don't know honey, I haven't seen her yet. Try not to let it upset you. If she could be here, she wouldn't miss it. Something must have happened."

Something happened alright.

Disappointed she hadn't come, he struggled to make the best of it—even with the Dyllons' interruption. The news of the newly-announced Elimination weighed heavy on his shoulders.

GUESTS CONTINUED DANCING, frequently exiting the dance floor to visit the tables full of food and drink. Many grabbed finger foods so they could continue eating while dancing and conversing with friends. Lifting their cups in the air, they toasted to Talin from across the space. One such guest, wearing a green and yellow checkered dress, took a large drink, then blew a kiss his way.

During a pause in the music, one of the performers announced, "Quadrille!"

The crowd cheered and the guests split apart. Men lined up on one side of the area, women across from them. Steel drums began a light, steady rhythm as the men crossed the floor, offering a hand to dance with a woman on the other side.

Quadrille...

Talin recognized the name from school assemblies. The high school dance troupe performed the traditional steps in the gymnasium on special occasions or during pep rallies.

I hope I'm not supposed to know this.

Talin stood next to his mother with the women, near the tables, watching the parade of men choose a partner to dance with.

Then Javon approached Shantel with an outstretched hand. "Dance with me?"

She hesitated.

"To celebrate our son," he said.

"Go on, Mom."

Shantel took Javon's hand, stepping back onto the dance floor. Most of the guests now had a partner and stood facing one another, ready for the dance to start.

The musicians played a traditional melody as bodies began to sway in place to the beat. The women held their skirts out with one hand, swishing the material to and fro with the rhythm. The man who had announced the dance acted as the caller, naming the steps to take. Salute, step across, draw away, promenade left, and promenade right looked something like a Caribbean square dance. The men slowly twirled their partners in place, hands above the ladies' heads and waited for the next instructions. The dance had started with chosen partners, but soon the men shifted their positions and moved down the line to new lady partners one by one, completing the caller's steps each time. The women stood in place, and the men continued switching positions until they completed a full circle around the dance floor and returned to their original partner. Javon's smile was wide when he returned to Shantel. Her eyes avoided his, and she looked away swishing her skirt awaiting the next call.

The caller asked for claps, then stomping of feet. But while Javon's hands weren't busy with a dance move, he adjusted Shantel's dress, pulling a sleeve down off her shoulders. She jerked it back up before taking his hand again and stepped in place, keeping up with the tempo. Javon looked into her eyes and tried again. His mother's lips were moving, but Talin couldn't hear the words she spoke, although a stern look was evident on her face.

The last call was a spin and a salute, or bow, to their partners. When the dance was over, couples embraced, thanking their partners for a spirited dance. Javon pulled Shantel into him at her waist. She was stiff and didn't reciprocate. Quickly leaving the dance floor, she met Talin near the tables, and left Javon stranded alone in the crowd.

"You should stay and dance, Mom."

Music started again and the crowd continued their celebration. Javon approached the two.

"Thank you for the dance, Shantel," he said, bowing his head respectfully.

Yes, was all she said, turning and walking to the tables to grab a chunk of pineapple.

"Wow, you guys are good." Talin told him, not knowing what else to say in the awkwardness.

"Do you know the Quadrille?" Javon asked.

Talin shook his head.

"I'll be sure to teach you sometime. The ladies enjoy it."

Shantel glared at her ex, overhearing. Talin was aware his mother loved to dance, but wasn't so sure she'd enjoyed her partner tonight.

"Everyone come, please. Gather 'round!" Mr. George once again addressed the crowd. "I, Mrs. Boyce-Williams, Mr. Hunte, and our new Healer, Talin Boyce, would like to thank you for coming this evening. After we conclude the evening's formal activities, we encourage you to stay and celebrate as long as you wish. Do remember the Elimination that has been contracted for this Sunday so that we may show who the real Healer is to those who do not believe the truth."

The crowd applauded.

"For now, we shall show our appreciation to Healer Talin with our blessings."

Mr. George motioned for Talin to again take his seat next to Javon near the tree. He approached them, respectfully bowing his head to the new Healer.

"My best wishes to you Healer Talin," he said quietly. "The

Elimination will...challenge you. I suggest you seek out esteemed council. Good luck."

As Mr. George stepped aside, Talin felt a dryness in his throat. His gut churned.

A line of guests was forming in front of him. Each person that approached gave words of congratulations or blessing.

"Congratulations."

"It's great to have a Healer again."

"It's an honor to meet you."

"I am excited to see how our island changes with you leading the way."

"Call me sometime," the girl in the green and yellow plaid dress said, staring straight into his eyes. Mesmerized, he watched intently as she seemed to float back to her place in the circle.

Who is that? How would I call her?

"God bless you," said the Reverend, snapping Talin out of his trance.

Talin wasn't used to this amount of positive attention and none of it helped to settle his stomach, especially the young mystery guest in plaid. Sitting silently, he listened to each guest as they approached. Some touched him as if he was a god, some bowed their heads in respect, some came forward saying nothing at all.

"It's such an honor to be here," one of the women said, smiling from ear to ear.

"I knew your great-grandfather. He has chosen well," the last elderly gentlemen said.

Wait! Who was that?

Mr. George then closed by saying, "This concludes the evening's planned festivities. Please go forth in peace and safety."

The guests cheered, music played, and Talin's heart was racing.

18

TALIN SAT ON THE BOULDER, LEANING OVER, STARING INTO THE Drop. The pendants hanging from his neck gently swayed above the water like a pendulum. The sun had just risen, but the Sphere still held onto the pre-dawn glow. Only the strongest rays of light made their way through the thick foliage walls, scattering golden dapples across the lush grass and the still water.

"Good day, Healer Talin," he heard from behind.

Talin turned toward the familiar voice, "Good morning, Papa."

Papa Bois bowed his head.

Talin nearly laughed. "You don't need to bow."

"You are Healer now. You deserve respect."

"Can we be respectful without the bowing? It's really not my thing."

"Have you eaten this morning?"

"No, not really hungry."

"You had an eventful evening. How long have you been here?"

"A little while. I think everyone was sleeping in."

"What is on your mind?"

"Where do I start?"

Papa sat next to Talin on the boulder. "Anywhere you like."

"I'm the Healer, but I don't feel like it."

Papa didn't answer, only listened. The only sound Talin heard was the morning songbirds awakening.

"Now, after all this, I don't even know how long I will last with this Elimination thing tomorrow. First Onca threatens me, now Dewain."

"You are strong, and know enough to defeat either one of them."

Ya, right.

"Were you there?"

Papa nodded once.

"Did you see Amos and how he stole Mr. George's seal?"

"I did."

"And everyone talking about the fruit, did you hear that? It had to be from you."

Papa grinned.

"Where were you? I didn't see you." Talin asked.

"I have one hoof, it's quite easy to add three more."

"What? A goat? You were a *goat*?!" Talin shook his head. "I wondered once if you were actually Mr. George with the whole remember, return, reclaim thing. But, other things didn't add up." He paused. "First, he sells goats to Dewain for his stupid sacrifices, and didn't try to stop him from hurting them at *my* Induction, but yet he turns around minutes later and wants people to *bless* the goat...well, you apparently. He can't have it both ways."

"Sounds like something you'll need to address."

"What do you mean?"

"It's not a priority now, but something to think about for later."

"There may not be a later after tomorrow."

"Talin, why did you wish to become Healer?"

"I didn't. I was chosen."

"Yes, but why did you decide to accept?"

"I didn't want to let my family down, or my great-grandfather."

"What about your decision when the Sluice dropped you in the middle of the Lake?"

Talin exhaled, thinking back to when he nearly drowned, shoved by Papa himself into the Drop and surfacing at Hosea Falls, forcing him to make a decision about his new role. Talin had thought about how he wanted to make his family proud, show them he was worthy of something so special. He wanted to be respected, not bullied, feel important and needed. But most importantly, he wanted to protect the people and things he loved. And, part of that meant...

"Stop Dewain."

"So, you know who needs to win tomorrow then?"

It didn't feel quite as simple or straightforward as Papa made it sound. Papa continued.

"Why do you doubt yourself? Did you see the wonderful reception you received last night?"

"Yeah, Dewain was thrilled."

"Stop focusing on Dewain! Focus on you. The guests who attended were genuine. They were happy about your appointment. People above still believe in the choice Healer Kingston made. Not everyone is like the Dyllons. And not all the Dyllons are like Amos."

Like Marisha, Talin thought.

"You didn't happen to see Marisha there did you?"

"If Marisha were there, she'd have been standing front and center. She cares for you very much, but her situation is...complicated."

Everyone keeps saying that.

"What else can I help you with?"

Talin turned to face Papa. "I need to know what to do for the Elimination. I have to win."

"There will be an Earth Ritual, Water Rite, and Fire Summons, as in Eliminations past."

"Who makes the challenges?"

"The elders. They are likely discussing this today."

"Great. That means Amos. And the way he stole Mr. George's seal to force the Elimination, I'm sure Dewain will have the advantage. He'll know everything ahead of time! What about my Dad? He's an elder. Do I get to know the challenges ahead of time?"

"That, unfortunately, will be what you are up against. It's quite secretive."

"But *Amos* set up the Elimination! How is that a fair fight?"

"You do recall me saying that Healer Hunte was not fair, yes?"

Ugh!

Comparing Dewain to Healer Hunte, and Talin to Healer Kingston, was not exactly what Talin wanted or needed to hear. But was that what Papa meant?

"Speaking of that," Talin went on, "what happened last time? I really need to know. It might help me."

Papa rose from the boulder. "Come with me."

THEY ENTERED THE THEATER.

The tree remained—and all of the decorations that had been placed in Jumbie's branches by Talin and his mother the day before were also there.

Wow.

The ribbons, the strung lights, everything right down to the pile of offerings the guests had brought were there. A single table sat to the side, as the platform wasn't quite large enough to allow for duplication of the multiple tables at the original site.

"Are those...copies of the same offerings that everyone presented to Jumbie?"

"They are the offerings. Everything that is done above, affects us here below."

Talin thought back to the blood rains in the Realm when Dewain had sacrificed his goats at the base of the tree, then looked more carefully across the moat. At the base of the pile was his frangipani cuttings wrapped in his mother's bright red and yellow ribbons.

"So, you got them all from the tree?"

Papa nodded respectfully.

"Why?"

"No need for them to be stolen above. You may take your cuttings back when you are ready to plant them."

"What are you going to do with all the rest?"

"That's for you to decide." Papa motioned to Talin to cross the moat.

Talin waded across the water and approached the tree to look more closely at the gifts the guests had left. Many objects were handmade: pottery, wood carvings, fine cotton materials, jewels, spices, oils and herbs.

So much better than a bloody sacrifice, he thought. Then, he saw the weapon.

"What shall I do with the knife?" he asked Papa.

"Up to you."

"But they aren't *my* gifts, they're Jumbie's."

"Jumbie is a tree. You are a young man. Rule number five."

Make a decision.

Picking up the only knife that had been left, he inspected it. The handle was deep blue made out of some type of stone or gemstone. Wrapping his fingers around it, his hand fit perfectly. The butt of the handle was silver with the shape of a stingray etched into it. It had a matching silver guard, etched with a design that looked like water or waves. The blade was wide, about as long as his own dagger, and forged from the shiniest metal he'd seen yet. Glistening in the light, it seemed to be embedded with the dust of a million diamonds. He'd never seen such a material. A remarkable, and beautifully designed weapon, it could have belonged to a man or a woman and was quite heavy. He couldn't recall who'd left it and wondered why. But even as he sat underground, his gut told him it wasn't safe to leave it near the tree with Dewain and his friends nearby. His biggest fear was that Dewain would find the old crypt opening and tumble down onto a pile of treasures.

"Can we make a sheath for this?" Talin asked.

"Certainly. Leave it with me before you go and I will see that it gets done."

Laying the knife down on the edge of the stone stage, he asked, "So, do I need to do any training before tomorrow?"

"I think if we just discuss the past Eliminations and strategy, that will suffice for now. Not much more we can do to prepare you for tomorrow."

Settling himself on the edge of the stage across the moat from Papa, Talin sat to listen.

"The Earth Ritual will challenge you on the ground. Defensive skills, things of that nature."

"My knife work..."

"Not only that. Dewain will likely lure you with an animal sacrifice."

"Goats, again?!"

"Possibly."

"What happened at Healer Kingston's Earth Ritual?"

"Goats, of course. And Dewain knows you have a soft spot for animals. Be ready for anything. Do you know the tree by heart?"

"The branches you mean?" he pointed over his shoulder. "I think so."

"You must be certain. Dewain has only been in the tree twice that we know of. Do you know the locations of the roots, the ruins of the church, the cemetery plots?"

Talin had not thought of the surrounding area before, only the tree. "Um..."

"You will need to know every escape route, every inch of the ground you walk on."

"What's going to happen? Do you know what the ritual will actually be? Can't you find out? Dewain will probably know ahead of time because of Amos. I won't be able to see my dad to ask."

"All the better to impress the crowd when you outwit him."

"Can't you shape shift and go listen in on them talking?"

"My time is better spent with you."

"You're coming again, right? To help me?"

"I will be there, but again I will not be able to help you."

"Why couldn't you? No one would ever know it's you."

"The elders would know."

"Have they ever seen you, or just heard about you?"

"The stories have been passed from generation to generation. And you cannot risk a disqualification."

Can they even do that?

"You mean I'd lose..."

"Yes. All your training would mean nothing at that point. It would be quite difficult to reverse the outcome of an Elimination, even with my help."

Talin's gut twisted. "So, my great-grandfather had to prove himself and kill a goat?"

"I never said that. Healer Kingston was about treating the natural world with respect, just like you. But my gut tells me Dewain will try to get you to fight from the start."

"Ok, I've fought for goats before, so what about the Water Rite?"

"This, I'm afraid will take a little more practice. Shall we go above?"

"You mean...you're coming with me?"

"How would you like to get to the Falls? Walk or swim?"

"Oh no...you mean the Sluice! Oh, Papa, please, I don't want to—"

In front of him, the moat rippled and bubbled. Talin knew the sound.

Mama D'lo appeared above the water, bowing at her serpent's waist, her black snake mimicked her. "Oh my! What an absolute honor, Healer Talin!"

"Mama D'lo!" he exclaimed, leaning over the stage toward her.

"Oh, congratulations! Everyone in the Realm is so excited for you! How may I help you?"

Everyone, who?

"I suggest," Papa continued, "for the sake of time, you allow Mama to escort you through the Sluice to the Falls."

"But—" Talin backed away from the moat.

"Oh! It would, again, be my absolute privilege! Why yes, enter the water with me, Healer Talin!"

And have her try to suffocate me again?

"No, that doesn't sound very safe!"

"Not much in the Realm is truly safe for you right now, Talin," Papa pointed out.

"Oh, *now* you tell me."

"You have known this from day one with the over-ripened fruit, the Fire Marsh, and especially Onca. Shall I go on?"

"No." Talin bit his lip, staring at Mama D'lo. Talin really didn't want to take another trip underwater. It was the worst thing about being in the Realm— so far.

"Ok, ok..." he stepped forward. Staring into the moat, not knowing where else the water might connect to, he summoned his confidence from deep within him.

"I will meet you there," Papa said. He turned and walked away.

"Oh, what fun! Shall we?" Mama D'lo swished her tail and held out a hand as if asking for a dance at Prom.

No, not fun. Not fun at all.

"So, how do I...?"

"I'll keep the water out of your lungs. All you need to do is trust me," she said with a smile Talin thought quite cunning. Her scaly serpent flicked its tongue, tasting the air.

"Come-come now, if Papa didn't trust me, I'd have been dead long ago. Let's go." Her words carried a motherly tone he had never heard her use before.

If Papa trusts her, I should, too, he tried to reason with himself.

Cautiously, he splashed down into the moat. Then with the speed of a striking cobra, Mama's tail wrapped around his body, mouth and nose. Talin's eyes bulged as he was pulled underwater.

———

TALIN AND MAMA D'LO surfaced in the cave behind the Falls and Mama released her grip from Talin's body.

"Oh, I just love making the Bend! Isn't it exhilarating?!" her voice echoed in the dark chamber.

Coughing and sucking the damp air into his lungs, Talin sputtered, "No, *not* exhilarating."

"Oh, you'll get used to it," she waved him off.

What?!

"Now, you must take it from here. Swim to the beach, take the trail up to Dive Rock. I think you're familiar with it?"

He nodded, treading water and still catching his breath.

"I would love to come with you, it's so beautiful here, but I can't risk someone seeing me in the daylight."

The rush of the Falls into the plunge pool pushed moist air into the cave and into Talin's burning lungs. Water trickled down the rock walls surrounding him and the morning light flickered like flash bulbs through the heavy flow of the Falls. It was beautiful inside the cave in its own creepy way.

"Mama D'lo?"

"Yes?"

"I didn't thank you yet for finding my knife."

"Oh, it was my pleasure! I apologize for not finding it sooner."

"How did you know my dad would be here at the Falls?"

"I didn't, it was a wonderful serendipity while on patrol," she winked.

A what?

"Still, thank you."

She tipped her head down, eyes closed.

"Go on, now. Papa is waiting."

SWIMMING to the mouth of the cave to the side of the Falls, Talin was able to peer out while staying mostly hidden behind the rushing wall of water.

Oh no.

It wasn't what he saw, but what he heard.

Voices. Laughter. With the noise of the roaring water in his ears, he wasn't sure what was going on outside the cave, but he was sure of one thing—Dewain's voice.

No...

"Mama D'lo!" He turned toward her, "I can't go out ther—"

But she was gone—and Talin was on his own.

Turning again to assess the situation, he saw Dewain and his friends taking giant leaps from Dive Rock, one by one. He needed to get to the outcropping, where they were, but wasn't about to go out into the open right now.

"Haha! Don't worry, you got this Dewain!"

"Yah, sissy boy's going down!"

"Nobody will hold us back tomorrow!"

"I can't wait to see his face!"

It was obvious who and what they were referring to.

What am I supposed to do now?

He didn't see Papa Bois anywhere nearby. Was he supposed to go up the trail anyway? How long did he wait until the boys left? Today, though, was not a day for a challenge, there would be plenty of time for that tomorrow.

Grabbing onto the rock wall, Talin gave his legs a break from treading water and watched the boys splash about in the small pool, continuing with their shouting and banter.

"Careful Dewain, the current is really strong today."

"Nah, it's fine. I'm a strong swimmer. More than that twiggy Talin! 'Dey will call emergency and he'll be carried away, cryin' like a baby. I bet I won't even have to do the Fire Summons!"

"Yeah, he's probably going to drown!" they called back and laughed.

"No, I think he's right, Dewain. The current is really strong today!"

Talin could hear panic in the boy's voice.

The water was churning, sloshing back and forth like a giant wave pool. The suction tugged at Talin's feet, but he held steady on the edge of the rocks. The current was going to pull the boys straight to Talin.

The boys yelled, "What's happening?!" and raced for the shoreline. Struggling in the waves pulling and pushing them, one shouted for help.

"This is what happened when you pushed Talin in!" another sputtered.

"Shut up!" Dewain ordered. "You sissies! Just get out!"

"It's a riptide!!"

"We aren't in the ocean you idiot!" Dewain yelled back.

Is Papa doing this?

Looking again, Talin searched for Papa Bois as the boys struggled to swim to the rocky shore.

Maybe Mama D'lo is moving the water from below?

Talin dipped his head into the water and opened his eyes, but all he could see was the blurriness of the bubbles churning below the surface from the Falls.

Barely making it out of the choppy waters, the boys hollered, "Get up the hill and get our stuff so we can get out of here!"

Two of the four boys trekked up the trail, looking exhausted from the swim. Talin watched as they came in and out of view between the dense foliage lining the trail, grabbing their belongings before joining their friends and rushing toward the main public entrance.

After they'd gone, the waves slowly settled and the pool returned to its usual serene and blissful state.

Still not sure if it was safe to venture out, Talin waited a bit longer, taking in the sight of the birds soaring across the water then into the trees. Yellow butterflies fluttered outside the mouth of the cave.

He wished Marisha could've been with him.

Wasting no more time, as his fingers were starting to turn wrinkly, he slipped out of the cave, following the water's edge. Ducking behind hanging ferns and elephant ears, the sweet smell of tropical flowers filled his nose.

He slipped underwater, swimming a few feet at a time to avoid being noticed, just in case. Trying not to disturb the water as much as possible, he worked his way along the side of the pool toward the trail.

After getting out at the rocky beach, he walked to the trail head and was promptly harassed by a screeching owl diving and flapping at him. He swatted it away, whispering, "Shh, you're going to give me away, stupid bird!"

Don't these things only come out at night?

Wringing out his shirt, he looked around to ensure no one had seen him, and carefully climbed the wet rocks. Talin kept as quiet as he could, his wet shoes squeaking with every step. The owl followed, swooping down and criss-crossing the path ahead of him. But the owl refused to stay quiet and the screeching continued.

Coming to the top of the outcropping, the owl floated to a landing on the old fallen log and hooted.

"What?"

Then it disappeared into the trees.

Looking over the edge, Talin waited for Papa to arrive, wondering what the Falls had to do with the Water Rite, but having a pretty good idea. After his plunge from Dewain shoving him off this place not long ago, he could only imagine one scenario. If there was anything Talin disliked more than being pulled through the Sluice, it was falling—or jumping—from heights.

"I'm disappointed." Papa said from behind him.

Talin startled and whipped around, "Oh geez, you scared me."

"For one who is to protect nature and the creatures within it, you call a wise old owl stupid?"

"Oh, um...I—"

"Odd behavior for an owl wasn't it? Especially here, above ground, in the daylight."

"That was you?"

"Rule number four. Above *and* below."

Pay attention.

"I'm sorry. I didn't mean t—"

"Apology accepted. Let's continue."

Papa stood next to Talin on the edge of the cliff. Looking out, Papa asked, "Do you know how far it is to the water?"

Too far.

"Not exactly."

"Are you aware of the current in the cave?"

Very.

"Yes, and actually...when I got to the cave today, Dewain and his friends were here jumping into the water. The current nearly carried them into the cave. Did you or Mama D'lo do that?"

"Healer Talin, have you not realized yet? It's you. You have an aura about you with nature. One you must learn to control and use to your advantage."

"Wait. You're saying I did that?"

"When you entered the tree, after the Realm waited so many

years for a new Healer, you sparked the Evocations. When you entered the Lake for the first time, you caused the ripples to reach out in all directions. When you first entered this pool and were taken into the cave, that energy was from you."

Talin looked at Papa with a blank stare.

"But, Marisha said the current has always been strong—that divers couldn't explore the cave because of it—"

"It's a type of self preservation. The Earth and her beings know you are here. Very few are allowed to go where you have gone. It has always been this way in the cave, since before your great-grandfather walked these forests."

"What do you mean I should use this to my advantage?"

"Think of all the capabilities you possess. Use your surroundings. Be resourceful."

He'd heard this lesson before.

"Nature is your guide tomorrow. The creatures within the Realm will be there to assist you," Papa said.

"You'll be there, again?"

"I wouldn't miss it."

"Ok, so what is the Water Rite and why here?"

"There is less magic these days. At least above. The Elders have likely planned some physical feat surrounding the water."

Here it comes.

"I'd be prepared to swim, dive, or be dragged into the cave to see if you are able to escape the current. It could be something completely different."

Gulp.

Talin was not good at holding his breath. He was not fond of heights, or being shoved from them, or being asked to leap from them. The only thing here he was more familiar with than Dewain was the current. Even then, he wasn't completely comfortable with it. Good with a knife, Talin was confident he could win the Earth

Ritual with some effort. But he wasn't so sure the Water Rite would tip in his favor.

"I have to win all the challenges, or just two out of three?"

"Usually two of three. Depends."

"On what?"

"The elders, the crowd."

"The *crowd*?"

"You don't recall Mr. George inviting the entire island last night?"

"Well, yes, but I thought that was just to the tree. I didn't know till now the challenges would be at different places."

"The crowd will follow you wherever the challenge leads to, I assure you."

"And they get to vote?"

"No voting, but their reaction can sway the elders quite strongly if they wish to remain in good favor with the community."

Sounded like politics to Talin, something else he didn't understand or care much about, but he'd soon need to learn. The crowd seemed to look favorably upon Mr. George at the Induction. He had to have known Azacca Farms' success was based on the generosity of the people in the community.

"Where else will the challenges lead?"

"The Fire Summons."

"And that is what again, exactly?"

"The grand finale." Papa called down to the water, "Mama!"

Not long after Papa requested Mama D'lo, the water effervesced and a serpent surfaced amidst millions of bubbles in the pool below.

"Ah, I see you made it safely! How wonderful!" she said.

"Mama, could you help Talin to the beach?"

Ohh no. Not again.

"Oh, my pleasure! We just had great fun in the Sluice."

No, no we did not!

"We take the Bend, again! Jump, Talin!" she said.

"Wait! No, no, no, no. I'm not jumping. I'd rather take the trail down if I have to go back into the Sluice. Can't I just walk and meet you all there?"

"And risk running into Dewain on the way?" Papa asked with one eyebrow lifted, the other covered by a dreadlock that fell down over his forehead.

"Healer Talin, you can do it. I'll help cushion your fall." Mama swished her tail back and forth on the water's surface and bubbles erupted around her.

She hadn't made it sound that much more enticing.

"I'd go if I were you, before he returns to see if the waters have settled." Papa encouraged.

"Papa, please I *really* don't want to jump from here."

"It's good practice," he added cheerfully. "But it's time to go. Just don't swat at random things when you get there," he said with a wink and walked into the forest, leaving Talin alone atop the rock.

Talin looked over the edge. The water surface rippled, reminding him of the sprayers used to cushion a diver's entry into the pool at the Olympics.

"Quickly, now." Mama called.

If it's good enough for Olympians, certainly it's good enough for a Healer?

Taking a deep breath, Talin plugged his nose and jumped over the edge feet first.

CRASHING into the water knocked Talin's fingers off his nose. He spread out his arms and legs to slow his downward motion, then swam upward as fast as he could. It was difficult for him to tell how far he had sunk below the surface.

"Oh, that was spectacular!" he heard Mama cheer as he came up for air.

Talin gasped, "No! Not spectacular!"

"Ready?"

"No, can you just wait a min—"

Her tail whipped around his body again, and they descended deep into the pool.

SURFACING, Mama D'lo released her grip from Talin not far from the ocean's shoreline where he and Marisha had their one-on-one wave-diving lesson. Coughing to catch his breath once again, Talin's eyes widened when he realized where he was.

We're in the ocean?!

He quickly voiced his displeasure of the Sluice and how much longer this underwater trip had taken than others. "You nearly drowned me!"

"Oh, hardly," she laughed. "You're getting to be quite the pro! I'm having so much fun helping you! I haven't done this since...well, Healer Kingston."

"You did this to my great-grandfather, too?!"

"Why, how else would he get through the longest parts of the Sluice? Humans don't have gills yet, do they?" She leaned in, looking closely behind his ears, pushing his wet hair away with her hand. Her snake flicked its tongue on Talin's cheek, making him squirm and squeal.

"Ewe, no!" he said and pushed himself away from the creature with a splash.

"Oh, Healer Talin," her tone sounded like a scolding, "this little ol' thing won't hurt you." She pet the top of the snake's head, like one would the family dog, flattening its ears down on its skull. The snake's eyes squinted shut.

Bobbing in the surf, Mama stayed afloat effortlessly, but Talin was already tiring.

"Do I go to the shore now? I don't see Papa."

"Oh, you won't. He can't let everyone see him just sauntering about on the beach!" she laughed.

"What do you mean? He said he was going to go over the Fire Summons with me here."

"Oh, he must be shifting for you, then. I hadn't heard exactly why he asked me to bring you here." They both looked toward the shore for any sign of Papa Bois.

"Ok, well, I have no further instructions, and must be careful not to be seen myself. You enjoy your lesson, and I will see you soon." With that, she wiggled her ring-adorned fingers goodbye and was gone, leaving Talin to swim to shore.

Between strokes, Talin paused, peering up and down the beach for any flapping owls trying to get his attention. There were none. No wild hogs. No cats. No goats. He kept swimming.

ON SHORE, Talin walked to the base of the hill to sit and rest. Jumbie stood watch above the beach. Sand stuck to Talin's wet clothing, and he removed his wet shoes, setting them on a nearby rock to try to dry in the sun. He was surprised they stayed on after his trips through the Sluice.

Crabs peeked their big oval eyes out of their sand burrows and skittered out toward the ocean. A few locals walked by, tipping their heads as they passed to say hello. No one was sunbathing or swimming, which was unusual for a Saturday. Seagulls soared above the waves, as they did most days, looking for scraps of brunch left behind by careless visitors. Remnants of old bonfires dotted the expansive stretch of sand amidst a few scattered coconut palms and mangrove trees. Glancing in each direction, Talin kept a lookout for anything out of the ordinary that could be Papa in shifted form.

A brown and white pelican swooped down to the ocean to skim the surface of the water, then circled back toward the beach. Talin could have watched pelicans all day, gliding across the water then splashing down to catch their fish. But he thought it was odd when the bird landed in a nearby tree, as they have a difficult time grasping the limbs with their webbed feet. Sitting straight up for a better look, he saw a large nest in the highest branches. The pelican snapped its bill with a popping sound and ducked its head down into the nest, out of sight.

Just another pelican.

Talin slumped back down, waiting for a sign from Papa. The pelican popped its head back up from the nest and clacked its bill again. Over and over. Bobbing its head up and down, it seemed to be playing a kind of peek-a-boo from the nest.

Oh, great.

Talin walked down the beach, leaving his shoes to dry, trying to avoid bits of broken glass, bent beer bottle caps, and cracked seashells on his way to the tree some twenty yards away.

When he arrived at the tree, Papa was leaning against the shady side of the trunk.

"Not too annoying for you?" he asked.

"How did you change so quickly? Aren't you worried someone will see you?"

"Right now, you're just visiting with a gentle, old homeless man." Papa's cloak cleverly hid his one hoof and he stayed in the shade, his back toward the water. "This is where the Fire Summons will take place. I'm not sure if the fires will already be started or you will need to start them. Do you remember your firedust training?"

Talin nodded.

"You may need it. Also, if you are injured in the fire, you will need your pack with your remedies. And with so many spectators, they could be harmed if things get out of hand. Be ready to help."

"That's it?" Talin asked.

"And by that you mean?"

"I don't understand why I had to suffer in the Sluice again just for that."

"You seem impatient for someone who isn't very excited to participate in an Elimination."

"I'm sorry. I'm just so nervous."

"Understood, but I do have a reason I brought you here. Do you also recall your training in the Theater?"

"How could I forget?"

Memories of himself climbing Jumbie's branches blindfolded swirled in his mind.

"Nerves and fear make us forget training. So you must be aware of your surroundings at all times."

"Ok, but it's just the beach. It's wide open, nothing's here."

"Do you see the remains of the bonfires?"

Talin nodded.

"You do not have much time on this beach before tomorrow. I need you to walk and learn the distance between them, the distance between the nearest one and this tree. Be aware of exactly how far apart they are. And the scattered boulders down the shoreline and how high the tide rises this evening. Everything. Do you understand?"

"Mm hm. Right now?"

"Yes, now. But I cannot call out to coach you. I'll stay here in the shade. It is up to you. You must be aware and absolutely confident in each step."

The old man sat down in the sand and leaned against the tree, partially covering his head with a bit of his hood to hide his dreads and part of his face. To a casual passerby he'd likely appear to be something of a beach migrant. Hopefully no one would bother him if they walked past—at least Talin hoped.

"Go." Papa said.

Striding onto the sand, Talin started at the farthest bonfire from them and counted out his steps to the next as if he was tracking down a buried treasure. When he looked up at Papa, he was motioning with his finger for Talin to return to the tree.

"Not quite so obvious." Papa smiled.

FOR SEVERAL MINUTES Talin paced back and forth between all the points, the sun heating the sand under his feet. Papa quizzed him on how many paces it was between each of the fires, then asked him to walk them all again—backwards. He wanted Talin to appear as if he was out for a leisurely stroll, lost in thought.

"I didn't think acting would be involved."

"We are trying not to draw attention, but you need to know this. Your pacing is quite suspicious if someone is watching. Plus, acting comes in handy sometimes. Do you know how far the tide comes up?"

"I think so."

"Come back tonight to be sure. Retrace all your steps, without having to obviously count them. Be very familiar with the distances."

Just like being blindfolded at the tree.

"You make it sound so ominous."

"The Fire Summons is traditionally the most difficult of the challenges, because of the fire element. It is imperative you know where you are, spatially, at all times, to defend, to flee, to protect. It's the point when all Healers must really prove themselves. Especially if the battles are equal."

"Tie breaker."

Papa nodded.

The realization of what was going to happen in about twenty four hours was sinking in for Talin. "So, are we going anywhere else?" he asked.

"Not we...you."

"But, where else can I go that will help me?"

"It's not where. It's who."

"Well...who else can help other than you?"

"Your grandmother."

"You know my grandmother?"

"Not personally, but I knew her father very well."

Healer Kingston.

"She should be able to recount the history of her father's rule."

"But, she's so forgetful. I don't even think she knows who I am."

"We must always try, yes?" Papa rose from the sand. "Remember, come back tonight to check your steps with the tide. Commit it to memory. Oh, and give your grandmother my best."

"Go right now?"

"I brought you here so that you would also be close to home to avoid additional confrontation with Dewain. I'd say that was good planning. You've not much time to gather yourself before tomorrow." Papa tipped his chin up to motion for Talin to go.

Retrieving his shoes, Talin took to the hillside trail toward home.

***

APPROACHING THE HOUSE, he saw his mother was in the garden, bent over mixing fertilizer then filling the water bucket so she could water each row of her small crop.

"Hi, Mom."

"Where have you been?" She stood up, stretching her back.

"Sorry, I really needed to talk to Papa after last night."

"Do I dare ask why you are all wet?"

"It's probly better if you don't, but I went for a swim." He smiled.

She brushed the loose dirt off her gloves, removed them and opened her arms to Talin. He was glad to fill them. She didn't seem to mind, even while he was still damp with seawater. "Are you ok?" she asked.

"I think so. I had a question."

She stepped away from the embrace to look at him.

"When you're done here," he paused, "can we go see Nana Celeste?"

"Oh? Well...I guess we can. Why do you want to see her now? Tell her the news, you mean?"

She had cared for his grandmother as long as she could, having to place her in a care home when it became too much to handle. Shantel visited her mother as much as she could after that, often crying herself to sleep when she returned home. Talin had only visited a few times, too nervous and uncomfortable to go back with Celeste's dementia setting in. He was never quite sure how to act. Never really growing up around her, he hadn't gotten to know her that well—and he wasn't sure she even knew who he was.

"Papa suggested I see her."

"Well, honey, you know that she is very forgetful now. She may not remember you."

"I know, but I want to try."

"Ok, then. Go inside and clean up. I'll be in after I do the watering."

Running inside, Talin grabbed a few peanut drops as a snack from the kitchen, showered as quickly as he could, and slipped on fresh clothes. Grabbing the old photo album from its hiding place under his bed, he plopped onto the bed and munched on the crunchy peanut treat, turning to the page with the burial photos.

Now that he was Healer, staring at the old photos brought new perspective, feelings, and questions. It was an odd feeling going from regular teenager to living legend almost overnight. How would he get the community to trust him? And the elders, how would his relationship with them play out with him being so much younger and with less life experience, despite his new title?

Then more urgent questions surfaced. In the fall, did he finish school? How much time would being Healer *really* take up? Would Dewain always antagonize and hate him? Only time would tell.

Picturing himself in the photos placed more invisible weight on his shoulders. What would his own burial look like? What would his legacy be? Who would he pick as the next Healer? When did he do that?

He hoped his great-grandfather would be proud. So many people had told him that he would be, but there was only one person who might be able to help answer that question. He slammed the album shut.

19

THE DRIVE TO THE MONTSERRAT MEMORY CARE CENTER WAS quiet. Talin's mother hadn't quizzed him further about what he needed to see Nana for or about what he would say or ask, which was good as he hadn't figured it out himself.

The three-story building in the center of the capital city had once been the old hospital. A new, state-of-the-art medical facility had just been built when his family arrived on the island. Approaching the parking lot, the cinder block walls appeared freshly painted in a depressing dusty tan color. No bright Caribbean colors, no welcoming presence. Tropical plants lined the sidewalk to the front entry's double glass doors, but Talin didn't think it helped soften the drab sterility of the place, and he hadn't set a foot inside yet.

Pulling into one of the few parking stalls, his mother asked, "Are you ready?"

He nodded, feeling like a priest visiting the infirm for last rites.

"Let's go," she said.

Bells hanging on the inside handle of the front door cheerfully chimed, reminding him of sleigh bells.

"Good afternoon, may I help you?" a young woman at the front counter asked, hanging up the telephone. Residents' call bells rang in the background, and someone's television blared uncomfortably loud down the hall.

"Yes, we are here to see Celeste Joseph, please," his mother answered.

"Certainly. Visitors need to sign in here." She slid a clipboard over to his mother to sign. "Both of your names, please."

His mother signed as the receptionist confirmed his Nana's room number.

"Oh yes, Ms. Joseph is in room 333, but they've just had lunch, so she might be in the activity room. It's just down this hall to your right," she pointed.

His mother thanked her and they made their way down the hall. Talin wrinkled his nose. The air smelled of meatloaf, mashed potatoes, and urine. Several residents lined the hallway in wheelchairs, most sleeping, with their heads tipped to one side. Some moaned, reaching out for any kind of human touch.

In room #333, a curtain separated two beds. Talin saw a frail woman laying in the bed nearest the door, but it wasn't Nana. Nana's bed, closest to the window, overlooked a small flower garden and was empty.

They walked further down the hall to the activity room. Several residents sat at tables in their wheelchairs as an employee at the front of the room led the group in an arts and crafts session. Large pieces of paper lined the tabletops. Crayons, markers and colored pencils were scattered on the papers but within easy reach.

"Now, I want you to use your favorite color in your drawing. Is it an animal...a person or a place?" She walked to several residents one by one, asking what they were drawing and helped a few who had dropped their supplies from crooked arthritic fingers.

Shantel and Talin stood in the back of the room for a moment to observe, looking for Nana. The activity leader next approached the back row and greeted a petite woman with caramel skin and contrasting curly white hair. She was hunched over the table with an orange crayon in her hand.

"Oh my, what is this Celeste? It's beautiful." The woman leaned over next to Celeste, placing a gentle, caring hand on the curve of her back and smiled.

Talin's mother stepped up to the table. "Excuse me. May we interrupt and take Celeste for a visit?" she asked.

"Certainly, she'd like that very much," she said, then turned her attention back to Celeste. "This is beautiful. I think you should frame it."

"Hi, Mom." Shantel said, leaning over, hugging her mother's shoulders. "You've always loved to draw, haven't you?" The old woman smiled back, her dark eyes revealing some confusion about the surprise guest.

Gathering the artwork Celeste had made, Talin's mother handed it to him to hold, then took the handles of the wheelchair and pulled the artist away from her make-shift desk. They went to a nearby sitting room to talk. Talin looked at the picture of blue streaks that stretched across the bottom, red and orange scribbles twisted across the center of the page. There were brown vertical lines to the side. Maybe she wasn't done with the drawing.

The sitting room had large double doors that opened up into the same garden as Nana's bedroom faced. His mother parked the wheelchair by the window.

"Here Mama, let's sit here. I know how you love to watch the birds outside."

Talin took a chair next to her, "Hi, Nana."

"Oh, hello," she smiled sweetly as they exchanged pleasantries, a bird landing atop the bird feeder as she spoke. But Celeste wasn't interested in watching the birds, she looked across the room at a large fish tank and smiled again, her eyes lighting up.

"Do you want to see the fish instead, Nana?" Talin got up and pushed her chair in front of the tank then moved his chair to sit next to her. Shantel joined and held her mother's hand.

The saltwater tank held a variety of colorful local fish and live coral, even a small shark. Celeste smiled, reaching out with her free hand to touch the glass with a finger. Her eyes followed a single angelfish all across the tank and back the opposite direction.

"Mom?" Talin's mother asked, "how are you?"

"Do I know you?" she asked.

Looking up at his mother, Talin saw the hurt in her eyes and finally understood why she cried herself to sleep after her visits. His heart sank.

"I brought Talin to visit. Do you remember Talin?"

Nana turned to look at him. Reaching out her free hand, she cupped his face. "Oh my...Talin. Yes, you finally came?"

"I'm sorry I don't visit very often, Nana."

"I've been waiting for you." Gently pulling her hand away from Shantel's, she held onto Talin's hands with both of hers.

Confused, Talin looked to his mother. She shrugged her shoulders.

"Yes, Nana. I came to talk to you."

"You did?"

"I thought you could help me."

"Of course I can."

"I wanted to hear about your dad."

Shantel lowered her voice. "Talin, you shouldn't bother her with this, you see she is struggling to remember."

"Oh, my father? Did he come, too?"

"Um, no Nana. I just want to hear about when he was Healer. Do you remember that?"

"Talin!" his mother scolded again softly.

"Oh...the Healer. Talin? You're Talin? He talks a lot about you."

"Your dad talks about me?"

She turned back toward the aquarium. All of the fish had gathered in the far side of the tank, nearest Talin. Hovering in the water, they looked through the glass in his direction, tails swishing and gills puffing then flattening against their bodies.

"What is going on?" his mother asked.

He didn't know. Turning his attention to the drawing Nana had just completed, he asked her, "What did you draw? It's really good."

"Ohhh. That's you."

"Me?" Looking more closely at the picture, he thought not much in it resembled a human figure. There were only thick brown vertical lines and reddish-orange circles above horizontal blue scratches.

He wondered what was going on inside her mind, as it looked like a five-year-old drew it. "Which one am I?"

"Right there." She pointed to the vertical brown wax scribbles. "You look just like my father."

"Ohhh, I see it now," he said, trying to convince her that he could see his own likeness in her artistic skills that had obviously waned over the years, along with her memory.

"Hm!" she huffed, and patted her hand on his knee.

"Oh, Mom, you got some gravy on your shirt." Shantel said, apparently trying to change the subject.

"Oh no," she giggled, "we can't have that!"

"Shall we go get you a clean one?" she asked.

BACK IN CELESTE'S ROOM, she transferred from her wheelchair to the edge of the bed by herself. While Shantel looked through the too-small closet for a clean shirt, Talin was taking note of all the artwork hanging on the walls on Celeste's side of the room. None of it was there when he last visited, several months ago. But, it was clear she'd been the artist. The same bright colors and shapes adorned most of the drawings, some with more detail than others. The pictures spilled onto a cork board on the wall that held family photos his mother had brought previously.

"Talin, could you hit the call light? It doesn't look like her laundry's been done yet."

Talin leaned over near the edge of the bed to reach for the call bell, his necklace dangling from his chest between him and Nana.

"Ohhh, my!" Nana exclaimed, grabbing the pendants with fingers covered in smears of magic marker. "There it is, look! And it's hot!"

"What?" Talin took the pendants from her hand, "Oh, no...it's not hot, Nana. It's ok."

"It's *hot*."

"No, see," he said, holding it in his palm.

She bent her finger for him to lean down closer to her and whispered, "But, it will be."

She pointed to the pictures on her wall.

Talin looked at Nana. Her eyes were wise—but lost. He looked down at the pendants, fidgeting with them in his hand. Healer Kingston's stone was, indeed, slightly warm to the touch, but not hot.

The aid entered the room. "The call light was on, may I help you?"

"Yes, I was wondering if Celeste has any clothes in the laundry," his mother answered. "There's not a lot here and I'm afraid she's soiled her shirt at dinner. I wanted to get her into something clean."

"Certainly, I'll go check." She glanced over at Celeste. "Oh my, Miss Celeste, you've got marker all over your fingers. Let's wash that off before it's there for days again." Reaching for the bath wipes on the dresser, she grabbed one and gently washed off Nana's fingertips.

"Ma'am," Talin asked, "Can I ask you something? These

pictures...They weren't here the last time I visited. Did she just draw these?"

"Oh, Miss Celeste is our most famous artist. Aren't you, dear? She's quite insistent on having them hung in her room." She smiled, still wiping Celeste's fingers. "I think it calms her. She loves those circles in between the person and the fire. That blue she says is the ocean."

"Well, she did grow up on the coast and has always loved the sea," his mother added.

"Oh, yes. She speaks quite a bit about the ocean and what's your favorite, Miss Celeste?" She said, turning her attention to his nana. "The stingray, right?" She continued addressing Talin's question. "But the red and orange she puts on the page quite furiously, like a fire would be I guess. We've gone through several sets of orange markers and crayons just with her. Maybe something happened long ago she's remembering?"

"Yes. Fire!" Nana said, "It's the fire!" She pointed to Talin and then tapped her chest as if she was wearing a necklace herself.

"Fire? There's no fire Mom, you're safe here," Shantel reassured her.

The aid finished cleaning Celeste's hands, "There, that's better. I'll go check on the laundry for you."

Feeling more comfortable than his last visit, Talin continued asking about the artwork. Pointing to one above the headboard, he asked, "What is this one?"

"That's the water."

"And this one?"

"You. You're stopping the fire."

She continued randomly describing her artwork. Definitely a nature lover, many of her themes revolved around the outdoors. Some showed trees, the water, maybe a beach. But she seemed particularly obsessed with fire and water, which was in most of the pictures. But...a waxy-brown Talin was in every single one.

. . .

THE AID RETURNED with a small stack of shirts. "I'm sorry, these were the only ones that were dry, will that be ok?"

"Yes, ma'am, thank you."

"I'll be glad to change her for you."

"Oh, no. That won't be necessary, I've got it. Thank you, though."

Leaving Shantel to help her mother, Talin stepped out in the hall to give the girls some privacy. When he stepped back in, his mother tried to bring their visit to a close.

"Mom, are you tired after lunch? Do you need a nap?"

"I'll hang up your new picture before we go, where would you like it, Nana?" Talin added, reaching for her newest art piece.

"Oh, no. I made that for you."

"For me, Nana? But how'd you know I was coming?"

"My father told me."

Staring at his mother, both were silent.

Celeste just smiled, sitting back in her bed.

"Mom, why don't you lie down and take a nap? Talin and I will be back to see you soon, ok?" She helped her mother into bed and fluffed her pillow, then partially closed the heavy drapery to dim the sunlight streaming into the room.

"Talin, I'm going to stop at the nurses station for a moment, so if you want to say goodbye, I'll meet you there."

Shantel leaned over her mother, gently stroking her head with her fingers. "Mom, rest your eyes. We'll be back soon. I promise." She kissed her on the forehead, "I love you."

Turning to Talin, his mother reminded him, "Don't be long."

Talin sat on the edge of the bed. "Thank you for the picture, Nana."

She grabbed Talin's wrist, and stared into his eyes, "You have to stop the fire."

Talin assured her he'd try—quite certain she wouldn't remember who he was or what they talked about once he'd left.

He leaned down to give her a hug.

"Oh! That's hot!" she said as his necklace brushed against her. "Be careful!"

Talin smiled back, rolled up her artwork in his hand and walked out the door. On his way back to the nurses desk to meet his mother, he overheard the staff's hushed conversations about him in the hallway.

"Look, look, that's him!"

"Oh my gosh! He's so young!"

"His grandmother lives here?!"

"His Nana is Ms. Joseph."

"See, he has the necklace!"

"But the Dyllon boy is older and he's so much stronger."

"Are you going tomorrow night?"

Feeling like he was back in the school hallway again, he tried his best to ignore them.

HE STOOD next to his mother while she finished her conversation with one of the nurses.

"Yes, Ma'am, ever since she heard the staff talking about an Induction, she just wouldn't stop drawing. Last night, after hearing about an Elimination, she stayed up very, very late. Couldn't sleep."

Must run in the family.

"Has she felt ill?" his mother asked.

"No, there's been no change in her health. She's actually been doing quite well."

"How is her memory? Is it worse?"

"It's probably about the same. Sometimes these patients hear or see things that trigger their long-term memory but can't remember what they had for breakfast or if they have family. Her father was a local Healer years ago, yes?"

"Yes, it was Healer Kingston."

"Do you think she is drawing a memory of that since there's been talk of a—" she stumbled on her words as she made eye contact with Talin, "new Healer? She keeps saying she was there."

"Was where?"

"At Healer Kingston's Elimination."

What?

A frustrated giggle escaped his mother's mouth, "Oh, mother," she gently shook her head. "Well, we all know that's impossible, right? Thank you very much for your time, I appreciate it. I'll be back soon to check on her."

Bidding the staff good-day, she and Talin returned to the car.

"HONEY, I'm sorry this probably wasn't what you were expecting. Nana's memory has been declining for a while now."

"I know."

"Did Papa Bois know something? Why did he want you to come again?"

Not truly knowing, he was more confused than ever as his mother pulled out of the drive. Passing the Montserrat Memory Care Center sign, Talin couldn't help but think back to his world geography class. Nearby Montserrat was the least visited island in the Caribbean, and the wandering residents of the memory care center were each on an isolated island of their own, many rarely visited by family. It was a cruel parallel.

"Do you really think Nana was there," he asked, staring down at the picture Nana had gifted him, "at the Elimination?"

"Women weren't allowed back then. You know that."

But, she said...

"But…she was a bit of a rebel," his mother added.

"Do you think Papa Bois knew that she would know I was coming today?"

"I'm not sure. Maybe her mind is just playing tricks on her."

The red was obviously fire. Blue, the ocean.

"Did she know I was the next Healer?"

"I may have mentioned it a few weeks ago, but I didn't think she'd remember. It was just something to talk about. But remember, the staff talked about you, too. She could have overheard them, like the nurse said."

She said the brownish figure in the drawing was supposed to be him putting out the fire, but what fire? A circle hung in the middle of the page between "him" and the fire. Talin stared at the picture the rest of the way home.

When they made it home, Talin hung the picture on his bedroom wall. Sitting on the bed, he must have stared at it for another half an hour.

AFTER DINNER, as the sun began to set, Talin excused himself. Per Papa Bois' instruction, he made his way down the hillside to the beach so he could walk the steps between the burnt out fire pits and gauge the location of high tide with a better chance of going unnoticed after the sunset.

As he paced on the beach, he first counted methodically, then tried closing his eyes and "wandering" between the points in case anyone was watching.

The tide lapped onto the shore, reaching further and further up the beach. The waves retreated as soon as they touched the edge of the stones encircling where the bonfires had been. He walked the points, then jogged between them, both forward and backward.

He took a break and sat on a rock, staring out into the sea and waited for the green flash when the sun dipped below the horizon. Thinking about what could possibly happen here the following night would definitely keep him up tonight, yet again. He was going to run through his steps once more after sunset, but saw someone walking down the beach in his direction. Not wanting to draw attention to himself, he tucked the pendants inside his shirt and sat further back on the rock. The person moved closer, walking along the water's edge, kicking at the waves. Recognizing the silhouette, Talin missed the green flash again as the sun dipped into the ocean.

"Marisha?"

"Talin! What are you doing here?"

"Just wanted some time to think...before tomorrow. What about you?"

"Same," she said.

Scooting over to make room on the rock for them both, Talin waved her over. She accepted the invitation.

He couldn't help but ask the first question that came to mind. "Why weren't you at the Induction?"

Staring at the sand, she didn't look at him, "Like I said, things at home."

"But there were lots of other girls there."

"It's not that I'm a girl, it's that I'm—never mind."

"What?"

"Related. You know...complicated if I support the other side." She used air quotes with her last two words.

"Yeah, about that. So you heard," he used air quotes of his own, "our cousin, made an appearance then?"

"I heard."

"His dad stole Mr. George's seal."

She nodded. "I know."

"So, are you coming tomorrow?"

"I want to, but..." She said she didn't know yet.

"Do you know what's going to happen tomorrow?"

"For the challenges? I'm not sure. It's been pretty hush-hush around the house. They're careful not to let me hear anything."

"So, Dewain knows then obviously. How is that even fair?"

She didn't answer, but asked how it felt to be officially named Healer.

"I haven't had much time to enjoy it, seeing how I've already been challenged."

After attempting to reassure him that Papa had likely taught him everything he needed to know, Marisha offered her own words of advice.

"Just stop and think before the challenges. Dewain is cocky. He'll try to bully you," *That's nothing new.* "He may likely be drinking to show off and act like an adult."

"Sounds awesome. Papa's already given me what he can. He actually asked me to come down here tonight and make sure I knew how many paces were between these bonfires, the water and the tree."

"Maybe you'll be walking on hot coals."

"What?"

"What else would you do with fire pits on a beach? Do anything else today?"

Nana...

"Well, I went to see Nana today."

"Oh, I didn't think you liked to go there."

"I don't really. But Papa suggested I go. It was weird. She made me a picture, like she knew I was coming. Said it was me putting out a fire by the ocean. We think."

"Wow."

"Yeah, she had a bunch of these pictures all over her room. The nurse said that she'd heard the staff talking about the Elimination and she wouldn't stop drawing the pictures since."

"That is weird."

He further described Nana's artwork to Marisha, asking her

what she thought it meant. The circle in the air, the fire, the water. "I think it really bothered my mom, though."

"Well, it's her mom. How would you feel if one day your mom didn't even know who you were after thirty-some years?"

Hearing the words, Talin's chest heaved. Besides Marisha, his mother was the closest person to him. He hadn't thought about how that would personally make him feel until this moment.

"She seemed really confused today, even said the stone on my necklace was hot when she touched it."

"Poor Nana. I hope I'm not like that when I get old." Staring at the stars that had hung above them, she asked, "Can I see it?"

"My necklace?"

"Yeah, I've never really got to look at it much up close. Is that ok?"

Talin pulled it out from under his shirt, took it off his neck and handed it to Marisha.

Grabbing it by the trio of pendants, her eyes lit up. "Wow...Talin, it *is* warm!"

"Very funny."

"Seriously, how do you wear this? Is it like this all the time?" Tossing it back and forth between her hands, she finally held it by the rope and looked closer. "It's so cool. I can't believe this is the real thing." Twisting the leather string, she inspected both the front and back of the pendants. "Can I...try it on?"

"Sure."

Hesitating, she raised it up and over her head.

"It looks good on you," he smiled.

The compliment made her smile. She flipped her hair back over her shoulder and said, "I am Healer Marisha!" with a giggle.

Talin's grin could have lit up the night sky.

"I wonder if there will ever be a female Healer?"

"Who knows. Women can come to Inductions..." his eyes met

hers, pleading for her to come to his challenge with Dewain, "*and Eliminations now.*"

"Wow, it's getting hotter. What makes it do that? Talin, how do you stand—I...I should take this off." Marisha removed the necklace.

Taking the pendants back, he said, "Stop. It's *not* hot." Rolling his eyes, he put the necklace back over his neck. "First Nana, now you."

"But, the stone, it really is—"

Talin held up his hand for her to stop. "No, it's not." Talin couldn't feel any intense heat from the stone.

But it will be...

AFTER SITTING QUIETLY, looking at the sky as it continued to fill with stars, Talin thought more about the mysterious stone and how it had scarred Dewain's palm.

Marisha abruptly got up. "Well, I need to go."

"I'd really like you to come tomorrow."

"Me, too. It's not that I don't want to be there. But," she hesitated as she left, "just don't be upset if I can't, ok?"

Talin didn't get up.

"Good night then," she added. "Maybe I'll see you tomorrow?"

"Yeah."

Marisha turned and walked away, glancing back to look over her shoulder every so often. Talin remained on his rock, deep in thought about his Elimination. Marisha hadn't shown at the Induction, so he wasn't going to hold his breath that she would tomorrow night. He understood she was getting pressure at home to support Dewain, but both challengers were her family...

He couldn't dwell on it long. It was more important than ever that he focused. Letting himself get caught up in feelings wasn't going to help and it was obvious Dewain had no time for them. Talin couldn't let his guard down.

He walked the beach again, committing the locations of the fire pits and the tide to memory, and trying not to wonder about what Dewain was doing at this moment.

20

TALIN COULD HEAR THE CROWD OUTSIDE, EVEN WITH THE CLOSED window at his back. Sitting on the edge of the bed, he slowly turned the knife in his hand and stared at it. His heart racing, he couldn't will himself to look outside.

"Talin," his mother said, "are you ready?" The bedroom door opened and she looked surprised. "Is that really what you're wearing?"

Dressed in his usual cargo shorts and a comfortable tee shirt, he didn't answer—just stared, head down.

"Mom, do you really think I can win?"

Sitting down next to him, she said, "Hey, no matter what happens tonight, I am *so* proud of you. You know that right?" Her voice was comforting. Taking a breath, she continued, "If what you told me about Papa Bois is true and the things he's shown you, I don't see how you can lose."

Nodding his head, he didn't take his eyes off the knife, continuing to turn it, inspecting it.

"We should go." She stood up and extended a palm to him. He stood, putting his hand in hers and she pulled him into her arms.

"Now, put that knife away," she said, smiling.

Together, they went downstairs. Talin checked his pocket for the carving knife—just in case, and swung his pack over a shoulder. Tipping his head toward the office as they passed, he asked, "So where is he?"

"The tavern I imagine. Hopefully, this will all be over by the time he comes home."

"He doesn't know yet?"

"I'm sure he hears enough during happy hour. He's staying away from home longer and longer. It's only a matter of time before—"

Looking out the back door, Talin's mouth hung half-open. He'd never seen so many people gathered around Jumbie. So many, in fact, that the crowd spilled into the old cane field. He wondered if anyone was even left at the tavern.

"It's ok, Talin," his mother said. "They're all here for you." She gently lifted his necklace and rested it outside of his shirt, straightening it, knots in the back.

"I don't think so."

"Well, let's not keep them waiting."

THE CLOSER THEY came to the tree, the louder the crowd became. It seemed half the island had shown up to watch. Men, women, young and old, were all represented. Conversation mixed with laughter and playful banter turned to hushed whispers as Talin made his way through the crowd, his mother on his arm. He even overhead people betting with one another on who would win.

"Oh, there he is!"

"Shhh, here he comes."

"It's him, it's him!"

"I can't believe it!"

"Wow, now I wish I'd been at the Induction!"

"No way. I got fifty saying Dewain takes him out the first challenge."

Talin's stomach churned. The adults were just as cruel as some of his classmates in the school hallways.

Cell phones and cameras were pointed his way. Flash strobes popped in the dusk light as he and his mother moved through the crowd. Most of the decorations from the Induction were still in place, the strung bulbs lit and the generator running. About half the original ribbons dangled from the tree's limbs, the rest were being waved in the air by spectators. Guests had brought torches for additional light. Several drummers had gathered, beating their hands on their instruments, adding a festive sound. Talin wasn't feeling festive.

People lined up in every direction, at least four and five guests deep, many standing on the folding tables to get a better view. Children were propped up on the adults' shoulders so they could see. A few teens had climbed up onto Jumbie's roots. Vendors were selling drinks—even beer from pull-along coolers. To Talin, it looked more like a sporting event than a dangerous duel.

His mother held a firm grip on his bicep as they entered the main ceremony area in front of the tree. Portions of the crowd cheered. Others booed.

Mr. George was waiting near the trunk of the tree, wearing his best gold and cream colored embroidered vestments. Dewain and Amos stood to his left, both wearing materials of the brightest red. Amos wore a priest-like ceremonial robe and Dewain a red shirt-jac with gold threads that glittered in the light of the torches. His face was painted with black and red tribal marks, looking more like he was ready to play football than be in an Elimination.

Javon stepped forward from the crowd, approaching Talin and his mother, also wearing an elder's stole. But he wore emerald green.

"Thank you, Shantel." He motioned for her to step away. She squeezed Talin's hand, turned and walked away.

Talin and his father stood to the right of Mr. George and faced the crowd. The elders were clustered on one side, all wearing fancier ceremony vestments than they'd worn at the Induction. Robes of different colors adorned them, with embroidered stoles around their necks dragging in the dirt. Yellow, black and gold, green—and red nearest Dewain.

Rasta hats sat atop many of the elders' heads. Any man with dreads had matching beads in his locks. The cluster of colors looked eerily familiar.

Talin glanced at Dewain. As their eyes met, a sinister smile crossed Dewain's face. Talin suddenly felt out of place seeing his cousin decked out in the same festive costume he'd worn to his first unsuccessful Induction. Talin realized he looked like he was out for a leisurely stroll in his shorts and t-shirt, terribly underdressed for the occasion. Dewain's wrist and an ankle were wrapped in matching ribbon, and Talin knew it wasn't just for flair. Images filled his head—of Dewain's injured wrist as Talin cut it with a knife, and slicing his ankle only two nights ago. Dewain's group of friends stood nearby cheering and yelling.

Talin looked at his mother. Clasping her hands at her lips, she looked alone in a sea of people. Sadly, his stepfather was probably at the bar and Anya, his mother's former best friend, stood across from her—rooting for Talin to lose. Her only support was his aunt Luana, who draped an arm around Shantel's shoulder for comfort. He'd never seen his mother look so nervous.

Out of the mass of people waiting to watch history, Talin recognized only a few. The Reverend, Mrs. Ottley, and the neighbor, Mr. Browne, holding a leash with his black and white dog at the end of it, barking incessantly.

But Marisha...

She didn't come...

His confidence shattered, he stared at the ground.

Mr. George raised a hand to settle the crowd.

"Quiet! Quiet, please." A hush fell over the area as the sun was extinguished below the horizon. The air was still.

"Thank you all for coming on this very historic day. Since records have been kept of Healers on our island, this will be only the third Elimination held to date." The crowd applauded again as Talin imagined they did when gladiators were preparing to fight. Dewain's group of friends jumped up and down, yelling and pumping their fists in the air. Another raised hand from Mr. George signaled for them to calm their enthusiasm.

The Elimination challenges had not even begun and Talin's heart was fluttering inside his chest. Scanning the crowd, he tried to find Papa, or what Papa might have shifted into, for help or reassurance. No wild pigs, no owls or cats, no pelicans, and no goats—yet. Desperate to settle his anxiety sooner rather than later, he thought back to what Papa had taught him. Stepping away to meditate was out of the question. Even closing his eyes at any point this evening was not a smart option. As he focused on his breathing to relax the tightness in his chest, the words Mr. George said sounded distant.

"Although there has been some question on the validity of today's Elimination," he glared at the Dyllons, "the council has discussed the nature of the edict and, as you all can see, have elected to proceed."

Dewain's group continued their disruptive cheers, obviously fueled by adrenaline and ego, and likely alcohol as well.

"There will be one winner this evening, to be decided by the council," he motioned to the colorfully-dressed elder group nearby, "and that decision will be final. There will be no further challenges between the two candidates."

I'm not a candidate! You said I'm the Healer.

Palms moist, Talin continued to focus on breathing and paying attention.

"The winner will be named Healer...and the pendants Talin Boyce now has possession of will then be owned by the victor—"

Dewain let out a yell and leapt up, shaking his fist. "Yeah, those belong to me and *my* family!"

"Whoever that may be..." Mr. George added, with a glare at Dewain.

Talin felt a vibration against his chest and looked down. The pendants were shaking, emitting a subtle jingle.

Not on your life, Dewain.

Mr. George continued. "The rules are as follows. There will be three challenges. The victor must win two of three, unless overridden by the council. As senior elder, I will be the final vote in the event of a tie. Refusal to complete a task is an automatic disqualification and the remaining challenger will be announced the winner. There will be no help of any kind from the crowd. Challengers may have discussions and support from one or two individuals ahead of each challenge. Tradition calls for an Earth Ritual, Water Rite, and Fire Summons, all details of which have been voted upon by the council elders these past twenty four hours. These challenges will take place in different locations and you are all welcome to observe, so there will be travel involved. As per tradition, no vehicles will be made available to the challengers. They will be escorted by the elders on foot to ensure no trickery has taken place between locations. Any participants suffering physical injuries, rendering them unable to continue, up to and including death, will immediately be disqualified."

The crowd gasped. Talin heard his mother shriek and he turned to see her knees buckling from under her. Luana helped hold her steady.

"Any disruptions from the crowd or individuals will cause them to be forcibly removed from the sites. The competitors will not interfere with the completion of their opponent's tasks. All other regulations of the council remain unchanged." Mr. George turned to Dewain. "Are you ready to begin?"

That was fast.

"Let's go." Dewain answered in a familiar, low, threatening tone.

Mr. George turned to Talin. "Are you ready to begin?"

Mustering up as much courage as he could, he simply answered, "Yes."

"You may shake hands before you begin." Mr. George added with encouragement in his voice.

Dewain extended his hand, staring into Talin's eyes. Talin stepped forward.

What would Healer Kingston do?

Hesitating, Talin extended his hand, but Dewain pulled away.

"Do you see this?" Dewain said, raising his hand. He pointed to a round scar in the center of his opened palm, the same size and shape as Healer Kingston's stone pendant. "*You* did this. You and your little pendant. Oh wait, *my* pendant! I'll get it back fair and square. I guess you can enjoy it a few more hours." Laughing, he turned and strutted to his group of friends. They gave Dewain high fives and slaps on the back, causing the crowd to get riled up.

It was never your pendant. Never will be.

Recalling that he was nearly choked by his competitor, using the necklace's leather strap hanging from his neck, Talin realized the stone that Dewain had grabbed had burnt his palm, just as his nana had warned.

It's hot, she had said.

Talin tried not to let Dewain aggravate him before they'd even started. Focus, he needed to focus.

Not allowing the crowd to become too exuberant too early, Mr. George wasted no time starting the challenge.

"A Healer should be one that makes sacrifices. The Earth Ritual is exactly that—a prescribed procedure of a service or sacrifice."

Oh no.

Dewain laughed as one of his buddies jogged to the other side of the circle. The crowd parted and the boy took a rope from someone —a frightened goat at the end of it, stepping forward past the spectators.

"Oh, come on!" Talin said, turning to Javon.

"We give sacrifices to the spirits to express our thanks for our island and its traditions," Mr. George explained. "To seek forgiveness for our wrongs, ask for blessings, and discover who the spirits favor for this honored title!"

Dewain smirked at Talin, trying not to laugh as the animal was dragged to the center of the ceremony floor. Gasps from some of the crowd mixed with cheers from Dewain's supporters.

"Let me show you 'ow it's done, Talin!" he taunted.

"As challenger...Dewain, you will make your sacrifice first." Mr. George instructed, motioning for Dewain to enter the center of the circle.

Dewain drew his weapon and marched straight for the goat.

"No!" Talin yelled, his father grabbing his arm to stop his advance.

"Rules, Talin," Javon said, as Dewain reached the struggling animal.

"Talin!" A female voice screamed from the crowd.

Talin turned to see Marisha shoving her way to the first row of people as the goat bleated behind him. She gasped and froze, covering her mouth with her hands. Tears poured from her eyes.

"Marisha?" he struggled to pull away from Javon.

The crowd gasped and cheered.

"Awe, poor Talin, you're too late!" Dewain taunted.

Spinning back to see the tan and white goat bleeding profusely from its chest and still struggling against its single handler, Talin's blood boiled.

Dewain grabbed the goat's neck and snout, pulling up—his blade readied to slice its throat.

Knife drawn, Talin broke away from his father and pounced on Dewain as if he was Onca, but his own blade made contact with the animal's throat instead of Dewain's. Falling to the ground on its side, the goat struggled, kicking, unable to get up or cry out. Blood flowed.

"Ha! I didn't even have to distract you," Dewain scolded, as he and Talin wrestled on the ground, a dust cloud and cheering crowd surrounding them.

"Marisha! Get the goat!" he screamed.

She bolted onto the ceremony floor, only to be stopped by Mr. George. "No assistance from the crowd, Miss Dyllon."

"You can't save it now!" Dewain said, grabbing a handful of dirt and flinging it straight into Talin's eyes. Talin screamed in pain, losing focus, but not letting go of Dewain's red shirt as they rolled about.

"Hey, stupid, it was *your* knife that slit its throat! Not mine. Classic, just classic." Dewain's laughter continued, even in the struggle. "The necklace is *mine*, why don't you just give up and hand it over now? Save yourself more embarrassment."

Dewain was loving every second of the wrestling match and, unfortunately, gaining the upper hand. Talin's eyes burned and his temper flared, but he was able to maneuver away from Dewain and stand, stumbling towards the tree roots. He heard footsteps behind him and familiar voices yelling, "Get him! Finish it, Dewain!"

Unable to visually focus on anything around him, Talin placed the grip of his weapon in his mouth, hopped past a young spectator seated on the root under his stepfather's machete marks—and began to climb.

Ascending by feel only, Talin pictured himself blindfolded in the Theater and didn't stop climbing. The crowd gasped. Leaves began vibrating on Jumbie's branches.

"Get him, Dewain!" his friends encouraged.

The dangling ribbons shivered and shook, some falling down on the heads of the crowd below. Dewain entered the tree, just as before, trying his best to catch Talin.

"Just come down, Talin. It's over," he said, trying to hold on to the shaking branches, not nearly as adept as Talin at climbing.

A soft golden glow worked its way from the dirt, up the roots and into the trunk, on to the branches and exploded out every single leaf in the canopy, casting thousands of streaks of light across the crowd.

People started screaming, crying, gasping and calling out to the boys.

"It's the Evocation!"

"It's Dewain! The Healer!"

"No, the boy! Talin!"

"The spirits are choosing!"

"Someone stop them!"

The shaking became more intense and Dewain struggled to keep his footing. "Come down. We all know you aren't going to give a sacrifice so it's over!"

"I can't see! You've already cheated! Mr. George, this isn't fair!"

Mr. George did not interfere.

Laughing, Talin's own cousin continued, "No one said fighting was fair. That's why it's called a fight."

Tears of anger and frustration dripped down Talin's dusty face, slightly clearing his vision. He tilted his head back, sighing, wondering what to do and desperately wishing Papa Bois was there to help.

"Awe, Talin, are you crying?!" Dewain laughed.

While staring up into the canopy, trying to ignore the distractions below, Talin made out the murky details of an owl. He swore he saw it wink, even with his vision blurred. Its dark eyes were wide

—and wise. Shaking, it ruffled its feathers and hooted. The tree rumbled and bellowed, just as it did when his stepfather's machete had struck the trunk during the hurricane.

Below him, the crowd was anxious and confused.

"What is that?"

"What's happening?"

"Look! It's feathers!"

"Grab them!"

"It's da spirits!"

Talin kept blinking to focus his vision. Thousands of brown and white feathers resembling his pendant fell from the canopy, covering the crowd and the ground below. People were reaching into the air trying to catch as many feathers as possible. It looked like snow on a summer day.

Another rumble caused Dewain to lose his grip on the branches. Talin saw him struggling and called down, "Maybe you should jump down now Dewain, before the tree shakes you out...again."

Half the spectators were cheering for Dewain, and half for Talin. Over the noise, Marisha screamed, "Talin! The goat! Hurry! Help!"

"I'm not moving!" Dewain said.

"Then I guess I'll have to push you out myself!"

Starting his descent with blurred vision, Talin forced his eyes to water as much as possible, relying on his previous training to climb out of the tree mostly by feel and memory. Being taught to never attack in anger, he now had only one objective—help the goat. Dewain was simply in the way.

When he reached the branch Dewain was clutching, Talin did not slow his advance and shoved him to the ground. Dewain landed with a grunt. Mr. George grabbed Dewain's embroidered shirt, stopping him from chasing Talin as he rushed to the goat's side. Javon went to the center of the floor, kneeling next to him. The glow from Jumbie's branches slowly dimmed.

"Can you help it?" Javon asked.

Talin's vision became more clear from the added tears that now flowed freely, rinsing the remaining dirt from his eyes. He placed a hand on the goat's side.

No, no, no…

Obviously suffering and in pain, the animal's breathing was labored. Its nostrils flared, struggling for each breath. It no longer had the strength to kick and its chest heaved. The blood had slowed from its neck. There wasn't much time left.

Young children cried and their parents shielded their eyes.

"Talin, can you save it?" Marisha sobbed behind him, holding onto his mother and her sister in the crowd.

He could only imagine the awful, red rain shower happening in the Realm at this moment, just beneath his trembling fingertips. His stomach contents rose into his throat as he recalled the blood rains happening now below, and from his own hand. How angry would Papa be knowing it was Talin's blade that cut the goat's throat and not Dewain's?

"Just kill it, Talin. Put it out of its misery," Dewain encouraged. "Maybe 'den people respect you and take you serious."

The crowd yelled.

"Let him try!"

"Do something!"

"Save it!"

Mr. George stepped forward. "By order of Absolution, let this now be the challenge."

Talin could hear the elders arguing with Mr. George behind him, saying the challenges weren't equal in sacrifice and a vote would need to be taken. But, it was obvious—there was no time for that. Talin stared at the goat, thinking. What could he do?

Mr. George countered, raising his voice, citing one of the regulations within the council. As senior elder, he had the power to override and continue a challenge if deception was involved.

AKA cheating.

It was a rule, he explained, that allowed both Dewain and Talin to continue— Talin for interfering with Dewain's actions against the goat and Dewain for obscuring the vision of an opponent.

Otherwise they would both be eliminated and no winner declared. There would be two challenges left and one dead goat. Still, Talin didn't know if he could save it even if an exception was made.

Could you hurry up already?

Amos was the most adamant about the Absolution. "My son has clearly completed the task and won the Ritual. If Talin refuses to sacrifice another goat— as a matter of sportsmanship I'd even allow the one that lies here—then he has freely given the title of Healer to Dewain! I do not see this boy completing a proper sacrifice!"

There it was...set up to fail as suspected.

"Are you really going to challenge me, in front of a crowd of several hundred, while an animal needlessly suffers? And have your *own* son disqualified from the start?" Mr. George asked him. "I have called an Absolution to continue, benefitting both competitors! Do not interfere again, Mr. Dyllon!"

Talin felt the goat's breaths becoming more shallow under his hand.

The voices of the people were nearly frantic now.

"Save it! It's dying!"

"Let the boy make a decision!"

"The senior elder has the authority. It's the law!"

"Hurry!" a little girl cried.

Mr. George turned to the crowd, "Absolution for both opponents granted. Continue!"

Talin could tell in Mr. George's quivering voice and glistening eyes that the goat was of his stock. He wasn't a completely cruel man, was he?

Please! Help me, Papa!

Frantically taking his pack off his shoulder, Talin searched for anything that might help. Bandages, remedies, anything. There wasn't much left after his trips into the Sluice and not everything had been replaced.

"Marisha! Give me some water!"

"No help from the crowd, or did you not listen to the rules? There will be no more Absolutions granted going forward." Mr. George reminded him.

"Marisha is part of my team, with my Dad."

"She may not assist you."

Talin ran to one of the vendor's coolers and flung the lid open. The seller protested, "Hey mon, what are you doing?!"

"My job." Only beer was left.

Mr. George reminded the crowd once more they could not interfere and the man let Talin go about his task as he opened a bottle and dumped its amber contents out onto the ground.

"Hey! You have to pay for that!" the man hollered.

Javon motioned to the man, letting him know he would cover the cost of his lost beverage.

Talin partially filled the bottle with water from the melted ice, feeling all eyes on him, and ran back to the goat. He pulled ointments from his pack. First, periwinkle, to stop the bleeding. He scooped up the crushed powder in his fingers, dropping it into the bottle as best he could, covered the top with his thumb and shook it. Shaking out the milky, pasty substance into his hand, he coated the goat's throat wound and applied light pressure. He did not want to block the goat's breath, what little of it that was left.

Next, his favorite, the jackass bitters. Mixed the same way, he applied it to the chest wound as a disinfectant.

Javon was asking what he was doing, what the remedies were for and where he got them. Talin was too focused on his task to answer. He'd blocked out most of the surrounding sounds, thinking only about his apothecary class from Papa Bois.

Finally, he mixed a mimosa paste as a pain reliever and placed a small amount on the animal's snout to induce sleep— just in case it didn't survive. The least he could do was let it pass peacefully.

Then, gently stroking its head and ears, he waited. The goat's breathing still shallow, its chest hardly rising. The crowd was hushed except for the sniffles of children and the teen girls watching the suffering before them.

"For *real*? 'Ow long you gonna make it suffer before it dies?" Dewain taunted again. "Do I need to do it for you?"

"Shut up, Dewain." Marisha said.

"My challenge isn't over yet." Talin added.

Mr. George concurred.

Talin, again, overhead the restless crowd.

"How long are they going to wait?"

"Goat's dead. You can just hand over my fifty now, Jerome."

"Daddy, who won? The goat is dead."

"You need to pay for that beer, boy."

Trying to block out the hurtful comments, Talin grabbed a handful of feathers from the ground, using them to cover the paste in the wounds. Then a soft white glow emanated from the feathers on the goat.

What's happening?

He wasn't sure if anyone else saw it, as they all had begun to talk among themselves, buy beer from other vendors, or talk about the feather-coated ground while waiting for the goat to die. Moments later, the goat took a deep breath. The crowd shuddered.

"Dad, did you see that?" Talin asked.

The goat kicked a leg, striking Talin in the knee, but it couldn't stand.

"Marisha, come here."

She went to the center of the circle and Talin handed her the rope still tied to the goat. "Hold on, in case it runs."

"She's not supposed to be helping!" Dewain yelled.

"You had a goat handler at the start of this. Marisha is mine!"

Mr. George only held up his hand to silence the two.

Talin leaned over the goat, stroking its body and rubbing it. "Come on..."

The goat took another full breath and kicked again. Talin gently placed his hands around it, trying to lift it off the ground and help it stand. Legs weak, it slid back down onto the dirt and feathers.

Laughter erupted from the Dyllons. "Come on, Talin, just let me finish him off. We ain't got all night." Dewain said, pulling out his weapon and taking a step forward. He was stopped by a gust of wind so strong it blew out some of the torches and hats off the guests' heads. Feathers were strewn about the site. People scrambled to catch their caps, confused.

"The spirits!" many shouted.

A swirl of brown and white feathers lifted into the air and surrounded Talin and the goat, just like the fish had in the Lake, healing his injured ankle.

The goat shook its head, ears flapping, then the wind stopped. Feathers floated to the ground like snowflakes.

Talin tried lifting the goat again and it stood. Staying on its feet, it flicked an ear and took a single step toward Marisha.

The crowd went wild, yelling at each other.

"Did you see that?!"

"The wind spirits!"

"It's a miracle!"

"*He's* a miracle!"

"It was magic!"

"No, it's Obeah, witchcraft! Stop the challenge!"

"The spirits, they're back!"

Mr. George took control, announcing, "And now, the elders would like to invite you to Hosea Falls for the Water Rite!"

A mix of responses erupted from the crowd. Applause, cheering, boos, yelling and grumbling.

Marisha turned to Mr. George, "But wait, who won? Talin healed the goat!"

"No winner will be declared." Mr. George said.

Not surprisingly, the Dyllons were also not pleased.

"*I* won this challenge, you old man!" Dewain spouted as Javon and Amos exchanged scowls. "He did not complete a sacrifice, as agreed ahead of time, by *your* council! I did!"

Mr. George stood firm in his Absolution of both boys.

"*Both* of you started this challenge and gained an Absolution. There will be no winner declared for this Ritual! At the end of the night, if there is a draw, the council will make the final decision about who of you succeeded. The actions of a Healer— or that expected of a Healer—will be taken into consideration!"

Marisha beamed at Talin and knelt down to scratch the goat, who took another timid step forward.

Mr. George turned away. "Follow me."

21

"I'VE BEEN PROMOTED TO GOAT WRANGLER NOW, HUH?" MARISHA teased, as she led the young goat.

Talin didn't answer, just smiled, completely thrilled that she had made it to the Elimination and was walking by his side.

"It's OK, it's the best position I could have." Marisha winked and picked up the goat, cradling it in her arms.

Javon, Shantel, Luana, several elders, and a slew of spectators walked beside them, cutting through a neighborhood on the roughly twenty minute walk to the Falls. Dewain, his father, and the rest of his family were at the front of the group carrying flashlights and torches. A large portion of the crowd went ahead in their cars or golf carts. The younger people rode their bikes or mopeds alongside the mass of people, wearing neon glow-in-the-dark plastic necklaces around their necks and wrists.

"I can carry her for you if you want," Talin offered.

"Oh no, thank you. It's ok. I got her." Readjusting her grip, she snuggled the goat into her chest. It had to have been thirty or forty pounds but she handled it well. She gave it a delicate kiss on the forehead. "I want to carry her. I caused this."

"You didn't cause anything. Dewain took advant—"

"Talin, stop..."

"It was my knife that—"

"Shhh."

Standing on their porches, residents waved to the group, shouting blessings and good luck to both Talin and Dewain. Many offered a bottle of water or other gifts as they passed. The elders refused for both challengers, but gladly took the offerings for themselves.

I can't have water? That wasn't in the rules.

But not everyone was celebratory or wished them well.

"Talin Boyce? Just like 'is mother," a middle-aged woman shouted at them, "he'll run off scared of the Dyllons. Healer Dewain! Go, go! Healer Dewain!" She shook her fist in the air. Dewain gave the woman an approving nod and smiled.

Talin looked at his mother, who was holding her head high, clutching Luana's arm as they walked. She did not address the woman shouting at them, didn't even turn her head.

"Ya, no winning, that Talin boy, considering his father is running around with the town tramp! He'll end up just like 'em! You know what 'dey say."

What? My father...town tramp?

Talin was certain these ladies couldn't have meant Javon, could they? But, his stepfather, gone more than he was home, not to mention the unfamiliar perfume Talin had noticed recently...well, that was something different. Did they even know who his real father was?

He saw his mother's proud shoulders drop.

"The drunk!"

"Yah," the woman's neighbor hollered back, "probly La Diablesse got hold of him down at the bar!"

"She'll never let him go now!"

"Yah, he probably wind up crazed, lost in the woods—"

"Dead!" Both women broke into laughter.

La Diablesse?! Who's that?

"Keep walking, Talin. Don't say anything. They just want to upset you," Marisha said.

"Wait till her Lilliana meets that Boyce boy, she'll take care of him, too!" Again, laughter erupted from the women.

"Who's Lilliana?" Talin asked Marisha quietly.

"Like La Diablesses' daughter or student or something. Walk faster so we can get out of here."

Trying to ignore the taunts flooding his ears, and the increasing dryness in his mouth, he thought about the upcoming challenge. Only a brief lapse in rule number four, *pay attention*, had caused significant harm to the goat, nearly killing it. He simply couldn't make another mistake.

Controlling his anger and not interfering with Dewain's "task" would be next to impossible if it involved harming another living creature. Still, he couldn't afford to lose the Elimination either. He would have to find another way if it happened again. Rules inside and outside the Realm had proven to be similar—but also very different. Somehow, he felt confident that the subsequent challenges wouldn't involve goats, considering the Falls was their next destination.

As they entered the protected forest, the spectators following them thinned, per the request of Mr. George. A majority of the crowd were directed to the large parking lot nearby for tourists, as it was a short hike to the rocky beach entry at the Falls and where the bulk of people had room to watch. The Elimination participants, elders, and a handful of spectators continued up the lush hillside and past the aged double gates of Hosea Preserve.

Stepping onto Dive Rock, Mr. George brought Talin and Dewain forward nearest the edge. All others stood back several feet, crowded amidst the tropical foliage. Just over a dozen people, and one goat, were on the rock. His mother stayed below on the beach to watch.

There's no room up here to do anything but jum—

Oh no.

Marisha stood next to Javon, set the goat down and grasped the rope tight. The moon was hidden behind white clouds overhead, and torches and flashlights lit the slab. Everyone was acutely aware of their footing this high up.

Talin looked over the edge. The crowd below covered every boulder on the rocky beach and partially up the inner trail. The area was lit up by vehicle headlights, flashlights, torches—and flashing red and blue light bars.

"Are those fire trucks and ambulances?" he whispered, tugging on his father's sleeve.

Overhearing, Dewain chimed in. "Beach rescue. Don't worry, they aren't here for you. They're here to protect *me*," he chuckled.

The basin was cloaked in darkness, except for the emergency colors reflecting off the water and bouncing off the surrounding plant growth, making Talin dizzy and disoriented.

"Continuing the Elimination, the Water Rite will challenge a Healer's confidence," Mr. George explained, his voice booming, but likely not loud enough to be heard on the beach below.

Please, no, not in the dark...

As Mr. George continued explaining the challenge, Talin looked over the side again, struggling to judge the distance down to the water with the flashing strobes. On earlier trips to the Falls, he'd guessed it was twenty-five to thirty feet. Tonight, it looked more like a hundred.

This isn't fair.

Dewain had leapt many times from the outcropping but Talin had jumped only once—pushed the other.

"We shall cast stones to see who leaps first." Mr. George announced.

Wait, what? We're starting already?

Having been distracted again, Talin wondered if he'd missed any important instructions. Was there something specific he had to do, before, during, or after landing in the water? He couldn't mess this up.

Mr. George reached into his pocket, removing two similarly sized, and near-identical looking stones, holding one in each hand.

"One stone for each challenger. One is lava rock from this sacred place. The other, granite from the old quarry on the north end of the island, much different in weight." Placing them on the ground in front of him, he crossed the rock slab to the trees and plucked off two large leaves. He walked by the line of attendees gathered in the small space, hands behind his back like Papa Bois. Inspecting the guests, he stopped at a young girl in a green and yellow plaid dress.

"Miss, thank you for coming. You look quite lovely tonight."

"Thank you," she said, curtsying.

"What is your name?"

"Lilliana."

Extending his hand to her, he said, "Beautiful name for a beautiful lady, on a beautiful night. Lilliana, would you be so kind as to help select the stone?"

She nodded, taking his hand as he led her to back to the rocks. Gazing at Talin, she swished her dress and spun to face the small crowd, thoroughly enjoying the attention.

She looks familiar.

Mr. George covered each rock with a leaf, instructing Talin and Dewain to turn their backs to the rocks and face the Falls.

"Lilliana, would you mix the rocks and cover them back up?"

Talin heard the gentle sliding and tapping of the rocks being moved on the slab, and felt Lilliana's skirt brush firmly against his leg. A shiver ran up his spine.

"Nicely done, thank you. You may return to your place."

Talin and Dewain were allowed to turn back around, and Mr. George continued. Lilliana was staring right at Talin.

"As challenger, Dewain please choose your stone."

Dewain pointed at the stone nearest him. Mr. George retrieved both, careful not to give away the differences in weight between them and turned toward the pool. He held the stones out over the edge of the water.

"The challenger to leap first will be determined by whose stone reaches the water first."

Then he dropped them.

Talin held his breath.

About three seconds later, cheering erupted from the beach. Talin never heard either rock hit the water.

Mr. George leaned over the side, looking down toward the rope swing. An elder on that boulder raised his right hand, Mr. George nodded.

"Mr. Dyllon, you will leap first."

Moving away from the edge, Mr. George stepped back with the observers, giving Dewain room to prepare for the leap. Dewain lowered his voice, discussing something with his father and received a manly slap on the shoulder along with what Talin assumed were encouraging words.

"Don't drown, Talin." Dewain teased. "It'd be a shame if I couldn't get my necklace from the bottom of the pond." He took two cocky steps and leapt off the ledge, waving his hand as he fell from sight. Car horns honked as Dewain's fans cheered below. Then he splashed into the dark water somewhere below.

A lump formed in Talin's throat.

Mr. George stepped to the edge again to look at the man by the rope swing below give another hand signal.

"It's good," he said, and backed away from the ledge.

Of course he's good. He does this for fun.

"Mr. Boyce, you may now take your leap."

Talin turned to Marisha and his father, "I don't know if I can do this. I can't judge where the water is."

"Yes, you can Talin," she said.

"If you decline, Dewain will be Healer. Do you want that?" Javon reminded him.

"No," Talin said, but he didn't want another broken rib either.

"You have to jump. Dewain is ok, you'll be ok, too," his father encouraged.

At least it's better than killing goats.

If he jumped, the fall would be over in mere seconds, and then there would only be one challenge left. The sooner he jumped, the sooner the night would be over, one way or the other.

Chanting had begun below.

"Ta-lin! Ta-lin! Ta-lin!"

"See, they believe in you, too!" Marisha encouraged.

Maybe. They might just want to see me die.

Talin stepped to the edge. Taking a breath and closing his eyes, he rehearsed the jump in his mind. Recalling Papa Bois' instructions of striking the water feet first or palms flat with elbows locked, depending on how he landed, was only minimally comforting when he couldn't even judge when he would hit the water. If Papa was there, he would likely be giving a lecture about how many more dangerous things Talin had survived in the Realm compared to jumping off a ten-meter dive platform.

"Ta-lin! Ta-lin! Ta-lin!" the crowd continued.

Opening his eyes and staring into the water, a rush of bubbles caught his attention. A dark swirling form was below the surface. The flashing strobe lights made it difficult to tell what it—

Mama D'lo!

"We haven't got all night, are ya gonna jump or not, boy?" an impatient spectator heckled from behind.

Talin hoped no one else had seen the bubbles, and knew he

needed to jump before they had. He gave his pack to his father for safekeeping and made sure his knife was secure in its sheath. Standing on the edge of the platform with renewed confidence, he took a breath, and a giant step over the side.

WIND RACED past him as he tried to keep his body upright, legs together and straight. Noise from the crowd, the rumble of the Falls, car horns blaring, and the intense flashing lights were not helpful as Talin struck the water. He entered feet first, leaning slightly to the left. Pain shot through his left side and ear, again.

Bubbles from Mama D'lo rushed upward around him. Wrapping her muscular tail around his face and body, she dragged him deeper down.

Mama D'lo, please I need to breathe!

Moments later Talin surfaced with Mama D'lo releasing her grip on him in the darkness of the cave behind the Falls. A rush of damp air entered his lungs.

"Oh, Healer Talin, that was just lovely!"

"Not lovely," he said, wincing in pain and trying not to cough with each breath. It was difficult for him to remain afloat.

"Oh, but the crowd loved it! Didn't you hear them? We can wait here a few moments while you catch your breath."

"I could have died!"

Quickly realizing what could have happened had Mama not been there, he changed his tone. "I'm sorry. Look, thanks for breaking my fall. But I *can't* wait. I need to go back out there right now."

The yelling and screaming outside the cave had already begun, but he couldn't make out exactly what the people were saying.

"You look hurt. You can't stay afloat for long against the current out there."

"I can manage. Or you could help take me back out there."

"Oh, no. Too many eyes on me. I can't risk everyone seeing me. See all the spotlights on the water now? You'd be disqualified for having help during your challenge."

Talin was surprised she knew of the Elimination rules, but then again, like Papa, she'd been around many years…

"Well, I don't want to be disqualified with people thinking I'm dead, either."

"You think they really think that?"

"Yeah!"

"Let's just hide along the edge and listen. I always love hearing people's reactions to the jumps."

They moved to the mouth of the cave, near the rushing Falls. Large leaves and vines provided perfect camouflage, which was even better in the dark.

Paddling out of the cave, away from the rush of the Falls, they hugged the edge of the lake. Talin moved slowly toward the area below Dive Rock, ducking his head behind leaves that were larger than his entire body. Mama D'lo stayed underwater, only surfacing with Talin behind the same thick plant life, until they were both close enough to hear the details of the commotion more clearly.

"Where did he go?"

"Did he drown?"

"Nah, the kids do this all da' time!"

"Dewain is fine, why is the boy not?"

"Can he not swim?"

"He's hurt! Send the divers!"

"He's not coming up! SOMEONE HELP!"

There was chaos on the beach as the rescue team gathered their gear. He thought he heard his mother wailing and Marisha yelling his name, but he could definitely make out Dewain's distinct laughter. "See! I told you I was Healer! Have the divers find my necklace!"

Mama D'lo giggled. "So much drama!"

Talin found nothing about this comical. It was terrifying.

"Mama, please, they think I'm dead! I need to go out there, so I can get back to the beach where we went yesterday. It's the final challenge!"

"Oh, it will take them some time to walk back to the beach, my dear."

"But not if they think I'm dead! They won't even *go* to the beach, and they'll make Dewain Healer!"

"You really think those people up there on your team are that foolish and empty-headed? Your father likely knows I returned your weapon before your Induction? He knows of me, the stories. And have you not told that gorgeous Dyllon girl about me already? Oh, I would so love to meet her! Doesn't she trust you? Believe in you?"

Talin stared blankly at Mama and the slithering snake perched atop her head.

"Let them help you, Talin."

"But they think I'm dead."

"No, my dear. *They* do not. Have a little faith."

She glided her tail beneath Talin, helping him stay afloat in the water and said, "How about we get that rib looked at before we go to the beach, eh?"

22

COUGHING AND OUT OF BREATH, TALIN WAS PUSHED UP ON THE bank of the Lake, after another painful trip through the Sluice.

Looking around suspiciously, he sensed this would be a perfect opportunity for Onca to pounce, as he would definitely struggle to fight back.

Easy pickings.

Already concerned with trying to make it to the last of his Elimination challenges in time, he certainly did not want to tangle with Onca on top of everything.

"Good evening, Healer Talin," Papa said, approaching.

Grabbing his rib, Talin struggled to take a deep breath. "Hi, Papa. Can you help my rib again, so I can make it back to the beach?"

"Most certainly. Lie flat here, relax."

Talin stretched himself out on the soft grass, belly up, staring up at the moon.

"What happened during your dive?" Papa asked.

"I don't know. Everything was so hectic with all the people and the lights. I couldn't see the water so I landed a little sideways."

"Well, no one is perfect, are they?"

Rubbing his hands together, preparing to heal the rib, Papa suggested Talin take this extra time to settle and center himself for the remaining challenge.

Warm hands pressed into Talin's chest, dulling the pain.

"Wait," Talin said, sitting up. "Were you there watching?"

"Lie down." Talin did as instructed. "Of course I was there. I wouldn't miss it."

"Did you wink at me in the tree?"

Papa let out a chuckle, but neither confirmed nor denied Talin's suspicions. "Lie back, close your eyes."

Talin relaxed as best he could, trying to take deep breaths, while Papa pressed and moved his hands over his chest in different directions.

When Papa was finished, he asked, "How do you feel?"

"Better." Talin sat up to stretch, his hand moving to his sore rib. "How did you make all those feathers fall from the tree?"

"Oh, the feathers were not me." He winked again.

Eyes wide, a feeling of warmth flowed through him. If not Papa Bois, there was only one other person it could have been.

But...

"So, are you ready for the final challenge?"

"Yeah, if there is one."

Mama D'lo, still afloat near the shore, had been uncharacteristically quiet until now. "Healer Talin, there *will* be a Fire Summons, and *I* will take you."

"Oh, not the Sluice, *again*! Papa, *please*," he begged, prompting another chuckle from Papa.

"Thank you, Mama. But I think our Healer could use a break. I'll ensure he makes it to the Summons in enough time." Relief washed over Talin, his shoulders relaxing under his Sluice-soaked shirt. "But, I would like you to stay close during the challenge."

She and her serpent gave a respectful nod, then she bid Talin good luck and safety before retreating into the Lake.

"She's coming to the Fire Summons?" Talin asked.

"Mama D'lo is quite fond of you, I'm sure she'll want to be there, as she was at the Falls."

"Well, I'm glad she was there. I'd probly be a lot worse off if she hadn't been. I just don't want her to cause panic on the beach with so many people watching. She stayed away from there yesterday when hardly anyone was there."

"You forget, Mama has been around for many years, and she's been spotted a few times. But she knows how to handle herself and lay low. Besides, the crowd will be focused on you, not the water."

"If you're feeling well, you should make your way to the beach now, before the pains return. It won't last all evening."

"Ok." A sigh escaped him. "Any last words of advice?"

"You have all the training, knowledge, and support you need to succeed. Remember, your battle begins with a clear mindset and ends with a calm spirit."

Talin had heard this before.

Papa extended his arm toward the tree. "My best to you, Healer Talin." He bowed his head.

At Jumbie's base, Talin glanced back toward the bank, but Papa was already gone.

PUSHING his way out of the portal, Talin looked carefully over the root. All the guests were gone, but the white lights still hung, the generator rattling from behind the tree. In the distance, he heard voices. He stepped over a root and walked to the trailhead by the church ruins. He saw the crowd gathering at the base of the hill, lining the beach for hundreds of feet. Young children again sat atop their parents' shoulders and several in the rear brought binoculars, hoping for a better view of the event. Others lined the trail to get a higher vantage point. Again, a fire truck and ambulance sat in wait, lights flashing. Several fishing boats appeared to be anchored in the shallow waters, packed full of passengers holding flashlights and lanterns, casting a flickering light across the sea. He'd wondered if Mama D'lo was already among them in the water.

The fire pits sat aglow in the middle of the crowd, ready for the final challenge. A strip of something black between them emitted a haze of smoke.

What is that?

Talin took a breath and rubbed his side. He hoped the injured rib would hold up just a little longer as he began the walk down the trail to the beach.

"Excuse me, sorry," he said, passing spectators on the trail. "Excuse me."

"Oh my gosh! It's him!"

"He made it!"

"He's alive?!"

"He's coming! He's coming!" they all called down to the shore.

"Hey, wait! The boy is here! He's here!"

The crowd turned his way, many of their eyes wide in surprise. One by one, they clapped, the sound growing louder. Cheers and chants mixed with the applause.

One voice could be heard above it all.

"Talin! I knew it! I knew it!" Marisha ran through the crowd, shoving her way through the sea of people and wrapping her arms around him, nearly knocking him over.

Ouch.

"Come on, let's go. Everyone's waiting!" She pulled him onto the beach, the crowd parting as they moved forward.

"He really made it?!" people whispered among themselves.

"How did he get here?"

"I didn't think he was coming back!"

"I thought he was dead!"

Screaming, his mother came running toward him and pulled him into her arms. Tears streamed as she hugged him.

"Oh, God, I thought you were dead! We all thought you were dead—"

Marisha cleared her throat with a smile.

"Well, except Marisha." She pulled away to look at him. "She convinced everyone—I don't know how—but she knew, she knew you would show up and be ok. *And* your father." Her words tumbled out so fast she barely took a breath. "And I, I just wasn't sure. I'm so sorry. And just when I thought you weren't going to come back, you—how did you get here?!"

"Mom, it's ok. I'm here."

He winced when she hugged him again. "Ouch. Easy, Mom."

"Oh good heavens, you're hurt. Are you ok? Can you go on? What happened?"

"I'll be ok, just a little sore."

"It's such a touching family reunion," Dewain interrupted, dramatically rolling his eyes, "but can we get on with it?"

Talin looked toward the bonfires near the water's edge, the waves were rolling in and out along the shoreline just as they had the night before. Mr. George waited between the flames with Javon, Dewain and his parents.

"Shut up, Dewain," Marisha spat again.

"And what you goin' to do about it? Why don't you pick a side? Like, maybe, *family*?"

But, I'm family, too.

Marisha's parents stepped out of the crowd near the Dyllons, both holding red ribbons in their hands.

"Young lady, you were instructed not to come here," her mother scolded. "You will leave right now."

"I'm not going anywhere," she said, pushing herself against Talin's side, gripping his arm. "Apparently, it wasn't a problem earlier tonight—until you all thought he was dead!"

As her father grabbed her arm, attempting to drag her away, the crowd booed and hollered.

Mr. George stepped forward, raising a hand. "Quiet!"

Everyone stopped, turning to look at him.

"Miss Dyllon has been appointed by Mr. Boyce as his assistant. She is required to be present for the completion of the challenge. Mr. Dyllon," he turned towards Marisha's father, "if you, siding with your brother Amos, choose to break apart the opposing challenger's team, you risk forfeiting the challenge for your own challenger. I'll remind you this last time, there will be no interaction from the crowd! Choose wisely."

"Yeah, that's not 'appening tonight," Dewain said, stepping in front of his uncle. "No worries about it. He's not goin' to win anyway." Fire reflected in his eyes.

Marisha's father stared at Talin, jaw tight and fists clenched. Anya glared at Shantel. There was no mistaking the tension between families.

Rowdiness from the crowd erupted again, many picking a side like a sporting event. They physically moved nearest the challenger they chose to support.

"Let's proceed, shall we?" Mr. George asked.

The crowd yelled, waving ribbons and chanting for their chosen opponent. Thinking it was a fairly even split, Talin was quite happy with his supporters, as the majority had mostly cheered for Dewain up until now. It felt good.

Talin walked toward Mr. George and his father, flanked by Shantel and Marisha. Cheering, the crowd ushered them on.

A familiar young teen in a checkered dress stepped away from the spectators. Moving alongside Talin and the girls, Lilliana leaned in exceptionally close to Talin, "I like what you did with the goat back there," she whispered in his ear. Her fingers pointed to the top of the hill. "Like magic!" she said, then let her fingers dance across his shoulders, lingering a bit too long.

Marisha swatted Lilliana's hand away from Talin. The girl flashed a smile and raised her eyebrows. Her amber eyes flickered, turning orange like the fires, stealing away Talin's attention. He stared at her, never breaking eye contact as she faded into the crowd. Marisha gripped Talin's arm tighter and squeezed hard.

"Ow!" he said, bringing his attention back to the crowd and Marisha, who wore a displeased scowl on her face.

"Talin, focus!"

WAITING next to Mr. George was Javon, wearing a proud smile on his face and holding the goat's rope. Passing the rope to Marisha, he placed a firm hand on Talin's shoulder.

"I believe in you," he said, "all of these people do."

Not all of them.

Javon and Anya exchanged cold looks.

Mr. George wasted no more time after Talin's delay in arriving.

"Thank you all for attending the Fire Summons, our final challenge of the evening. Currently, no winner has been declared for the Earth Ritual and Mr. Dyllon has won the Water Rite." Dewain's crowd clapped and cheered, while boos sounded from behind Talin.

"If Mr. Dyllon wins the remaining challenge, he will be named Healer. If Mr. Boyce wins the Fire Summons, causing a tie, a winner will be declared for the Earth Ritual after consultation with the elders. The winner of the two challenges will then be named Healer. All decisions will be final."

Saying a silent prayer, Talin focused on Mr. George's instructions.

"The Fire Summons consists of two parts. First, Summoning of Fire, the second, the Release of Fire."

Papa didn't tell me about that! What's a Release?

"We will begin with the winner of the last challenge. Mr. Dyllon, your challenge is a firewalk." Several elders came forward with shovels, stirring the black strip of hot coals between the bonfires as Mr. George continued. "You will walk, not run, across the coals. Each step must be deliberate." The flames flickered and popped. Embers floated into the air and disappeared. Talin's skin glistened from the heat. "Refusing the challenge will result in your elimination."

A cackle escaped Dewain. "Ha! So much easier than I thought!" he told his friends nearby.

Seven.

The number of paces between the fires, if he walked it, half that if he ran with a broader stride. But they had to walk. He'd taken on well more than ten fireballs in succession from Papa and he'd learned about walking hot coals in science class. A controlled walk was better than a stomping run. He could do this, and hoped Dewain had missed that days' lecture on heat conduction.

The elders stirred up chunks of charcoal and burnt wood. Fire leapt up from the glowing coals. Finally, they sprinkled ash on top to settle the flames.

Cameras and cellphones were readied as Dewain removed his shoes and bounced in place, shaking out his arms and hands. Deepening and lengthening his breaths, he focused his gaze on the glowing path in front of him.

The elders stepped away from the smoldering ground.

"You may begin."

Dewain's fans roared with applause as he stepped up to the coals. Letting out a yell, he pounded his chest. He stepped onto the coals, then stomped all the way across. Making it to the other side he hopped about, wincing, and tried not to holler as his buddies congratulated him. They helped him into the ocean a few steps away to cool his feet and continued their celebration, splashing about. Spectators joined him and the people in the offshore boats cheered and revved their motors. Jet ski riders buzzed in circles close to shore, splashing Dewain with their wake.

"Mr. Boyce. Are you ready?" Mr. George asked.

Already barefoot, Talin nodded. The elders stepped up to the hot coals, mixing them with their shovels. Flames and embers shot up as the wood and coals were freshly mixed. Then the men stepped away.

Mr. George nodded for Talin to proceed. Dewain came out of the water with his friends to watch.

"But, there's no ash," Talin said. *They sprinkled ash over the coals before Dewain went.*

"Proceed, Mr. Boyce."

Talin stood staring at the flickering orange path in front of him. He had learned one of the tricks to the spectacle was the layer of ash atop the smoldering coals. Without it, he risked serious burns.

"Mr. Boyce, please proceed," Mr. George prompted again.

Dewain and his friends pointed and laughed, making it clear they were aware of the trickery.

"Mr. George, how is this fair?" Talin asked.

There was no answer. He stood waiting for Talin to walk.

"Talin, you can do it!" Marisha encouraged.

The crowd encouraged him, chanting, "Ta-lin! Ta-lin!" and pumping their fists in the air.

Looking back at his family, they all nodded in support. The longer he waited, the more he risked severe burns. Taking a breath, Talin gently stepped onto the hot surface and moved one foot in front of the other. Pieces of burnt wood shifted under his feet, urging him not to delay. His pace was brisk.

One, two, three, four, five, six, seven.

Reaching the other side, he pressed his feet into the cool, damp sand and exhaled in relief.

The crowd erupted.

Javon was first to congratulate him, quickly followed by his mother, Luana, and Marisha.

The tide swept in over his feet, soothing them and dousing the hot coals he'd just crossed. Smoke and steam rose from the sizzling ground. The puddles of water left behind boiled.

"Very well," Mr. George said, taking control of the crowd. "Everyone please take their places for the Release of Fire."

Just when Talin thought it would be over, it wasn't. The soles of his feet had already started to blister.

I'm gonna need Papa after this.

"Just as the Fire Summons is symbolic for a Healer to be one with the elements, he must also know when to let the forces of nature carry on without him."

As Mr. George spoke, the elders formed two lines on either side of the partially washed out fire walk, all holding palm fronds. "The Release of Fire is an exercise in being close with the fire element and knowing when to step away and surrender. Man is never stronger than Nature. You will now be tested on this ability."

But I never summoned the fire, and now I'm supposed to release it by getting closer to it?

A drumbeat began at the back of the crowd. An elder used a nearby torch to light the palm fronds on fire. Holding up the flaming branches, the men stretched them across the blackened path to each other, forming a make-shift tunnel of fire.

"Mr. Dyllon, you will enter one end and retreat through the other. The elders will lower the fire and you will enter again. With each pass the fire will be lowered. Let us know when it is time for you to Release the Fire."

Talin turned to Marisha as Dewain approached the flaming tunnel.

"Just think of it as limbo, but with a flaming limbo stick. You're smaller than him, can go lower, you can win this," she whispered.

"I'm used to jumping over hurdles, not crawling under them."

"But you can crawl into the smallest hole in the root of a tree?" One eyebrow was up.

She had a point.

Dewain had completed his first pass when they finished speaking. He marched back and forth as the elders lowered their branches each pass. Some had to have their fronds replaced by assistants as they had burned too fast, but the drill did not stop. Sounds from the crowd reached new decibels as Dewain continued. Beads of sweat collected on his reddened forehead. Soon, he was crawling on his belly, covered in sand and ash from the burnt and washed out firewalk. The fronds were mere inches from his back and as he came out the end, a flame was blown by the sea breeze, catching his fancy red shirt on fire. The crowd gasped, women screamed.

Frantically ripping off his shirt, Dewain looked like a panicked teenage girl who just walked through a spider's web.

"Is this your final pass Mr. Dyllon?" Mr. George asked.

Dewain confirmed. His friends helped him brush the bits of debris off his chest. Firefighters that had been standing by approached to check him, but he refused to be examined and assured them he needed no assistance.

MR. GEORGE SIGNALED for the elders to replace their fronds with new ones. "Mr. Boyce?" he motioned to the tunnel as fresh palm leaves went up in flames.

Standing near the flaming entrance reminded Talin of the Fire Marsh. Except he wasn't jumping from rock to rock trying to escape from billowing flames, he was walking right through them, hoping to remain as close as he could, for as long as he could.

Burnt leaves broke away from their stems and fell to the ground. *It's only seven steps each way.*

Talin walked through. Intense heat surrounded him. When he exited, the cheering crowd brought his confidence up and he turned to enter again.

"Ta-lin! Ta-lin!" the people chanted louder and louder. Fronds lowered and more embers fell onto his path. He marched through again and again.

One, two, three, four, five, six, seven.

Sliding on his belly like a lizard, he was halfway through one of his passes when he heard, "It's not low enough!"

Suddenly, his body was slammed into the sand and ash. Flames thrust down and several men toppled on top of him. Smoke filled the air. Dozens of people were screaming—but only one was laughing.

The ground rumbled beneath him, just as it had during the Inductions and the Earth Ritual.

What's happening?!

"Help him!"

"He's going to burn!" the people yelled.

"Talin!" Marisha screamed for him. "Nooo!"

Talin couldn't see anything with all the smoke surrounding him. Flames popped and crackled. His lungs burned, coughing followed. But the weight of the men on top of him lifted.

Thousands of glowing embers rose into the air and began swirling around him like a cyclone, faster and faster. He crouched close to the ground, covering his face, to avoid the firestorm. Above the chaos he heard a familiar sound—the crackling roar of a jaguar.

"Talin! Behind you!" his father yelled.

Talin rose and turned, the smoke and embers clearing as quickly as they had formed, revealing a big cat engulfed in massive flames.

And he was ready to pounce.

First Dewain, now Onca.

Onca faced Talin, pacing on the remains of the firewalk, flicking his tail like a whip in Talin's direction. As Onca stepped into one of the firepits, the inferno shot high into the air as his flames mixed with the bonfire's. Everyone was screaming. Some fainted. Some ran. Panic filled the crowd that remained. His mother was wailing not far away, "Talin!" She clung to Luana.

Talin stumbled backward to avoid a swiping paw and scurried back. His eyes watered. The soles of his blistered feet throbbed in pain from standing on smoldering palm leaves. Waves doused the remaining flames bit by bit as the tide moved in and out and the ground continued to shake.

"Run! It's a spirit!"

"Quick! Someone get the Reverend!"

"Told you he's not da' Healer. Black magic! Against da rules!"

"Help!"

"My camera, my camera is jammed!"

"Mine, too!"

"And mine!"

Talin was three and half paces between the fires.

"You like to play with fire do you, Talin?" Onca said. "I told you I would come for you. But I'm not sure Healer Kingston would approve of all the antics."

Can anyone else hear him talk?

"It's just so fitting that you and I should meet at an Elimination, just like he and I did. Step aside, and don't make this more embarrassing for yourself. You have lost. Dewain will now take over here where I left off, and I'll take the Realm."

As the shaking ground settled, Talin's temper did not. Dewain and his friends laughed, Amos flashed a sinister smile.

Why are they not afraid?

Everyone was watching.

"Listen to the crowd. They want Dewain. Not you, fool," Onca continued.

Cheers and boos filled the air. Talin could only assume the crowd must have been able to hear Onca speak.

Not sure how much longer he should let Onca continue, he didn't know how to make him go away either. There wasn't enough firedust to produce even a small amount of ice to put out the flames that surrounded Onca in the bonfire. His weapon was useless in this situation. Talin felt his chest burning. His necklace's leather strap was warm around his neck.

Javon had asked him—begged him—to not let Onca escape from the Realm. He'd failed and everyone saw it. Maybe Onca was right, maybe he should stop fighting and let Dewain lead the people.

"Talin! The necklace!" Marisha shouted.

Looking down, Talin saw Healer Kingston's stone glowing like the red hot coals from the firewalk.

"Awe, getting a little sentimental are we?" Onca chided.

People started pointing and yelling.

"It's him! See? He is the Healer!"

"Healer Kingston has chosen!"

"Nah, mon, black magic!"

"How did he do that?"

The longer Talin stared at the stone, the hotter it was getting on his chest. He held it away from his body by the leather strap to avoid more burns.

"Can't take the heat can you, boy?" Onca leapt over him and into the opposite bonfire with a snarl. The onlookers gasped. Embers floated down atop Talin. Catching one in his palm, he wrapped his fingers around it and blew into his cupped hand, forming a fireball.

Bending down to the tide rushing over his feet, Talin splashed the ball with sea water, and threw the block of ice straight at Onca.

The ball struck the cat's shoulder, sizzling.

Onca winced only slightly, but the crowd cheered.

"Is that all you have? A tiny little hailstone?" Onca lowered his head and let out a fierce roar that sent a rumble through Talin's chest.

The stone pendant, hotter than ever, had left a scorching black circle on Talin's shirt.

"The water, Talin! Send him to the water!" Marisha instructed.

What?

The goat let out a bleat and stomped its hoof in the sand, staring straight at Talin. The pendant was so hot now, he removed it from around his neck, holding it by the warm leather strap. Papa's words replayed in his head.

Extinguish him with the sea...

Talin moved several steps away from the charred firewalk.

One, two, three, four.

Onca was now between him and the ocean.

"Onca, go away!"

"Oooh, such threatening words." Onca stepped out of the fire and onto the beach to pace in front of Talin. "Are we finally ready to battle? We even have witnesses. Lovely of them to stay."

Talin ran to the nearest spectator and grabbed his torch. "I need your torches! All of you! Help me!"

Onca roared, "They cannot help you! You heard Mr. George!"

Talin looked to Mr. George, but he said nothing and stared at the cat. It looked like he was in some sort of trance, or willing himself to stand in place and not flee with fear like many in the crowd had. Or he chose not to interfere.

"I need your torches! If I'm to help you as Healer, I need you to help me!"

"No, Talin, this is on *you*!" Dewain shouted, "Plus, I want to see this!" He watched Talin's hand, wrapped around the pole of the torch, pendants dangling.

Talin held them tighter.

The people yelled at one another, each supporting their side, tempers flaring.

"Things are different! Rules change." Talin tried convincing the drunken crowd. "What do you want your leader to do? You want him to just stand around doing nothing or respect what is *right*?"

"Enough!" Onca roared, flames shooting out of his mouth like a dragon. Flames shot over Talin's head into the crowd. Ribbons and banners blazed as they caught fire. The screaming grew louder. A little girl cried as her shirt erupted in flames, her mother screaming and wailing in a panic.

Talin's hurt ear rang and throbbed from the deafening noise.

"People are burning! Do something!" his mother sobbed, gripping Luana to keep from collapsing.

Onca glowed a more intense orange than he'd ever seen, the same color as Lilliana's eyes. The red and blue strobe lights from the fire trucks reflected off the water with the boaters' lights, mixing into a strange blue-violet.

The colors reminded him of the blue in Nana's drawing. Tiny embers began to spark from Healer Kingston's stone and Talin thought it might explode.

"He's going to attack and their blood is on your hands now, Talin!" Dewain taunted.

No, it's not.

"Bring your torches with me, NOW!" Talin commanded his crowd, turned and ran at Onca. Several men from the group followed.

"The picture, Talin! This is Nana's picture!" Marisha screamed, "Throw the pendant!"

Onca backed away from the crowd, putting a small distance between himself and Talin. "Your little fires are nothing compared to me!" His tail flicked over the heads of the men, causing thousands of embers to swirl around the group. The wind intensified, pulling up grains of sand from the beach. Talin felt like he was surrounded by a swarm of stinging bees as it pelted him. But the crowd pushed forward, slowly forcing the cat closer to the water's edge.

Talin held tight to the leather strap of the necklace and wound it in circles like prepping for a fastball pitch, then slung it as hard as he could at Onca.

Striking the big cat in the shoulder, the pendant burst into dazzling orange and blue flames. Onca stumbled back into the water, splashing, snarling, roaring.

The cyclone of embers surrounding the small group scattered away into the night like fireflies. The ocean sizzled and boiled under Onca's paws and he sank deeper. A serpent's tail burst from the water, wrapping around the floundering cat, pulling it under.

Only a swirl of bubbling water and steam remained.

He was gone.

ALL WAS silent for a moment as everyone stood looking in awe at the smoking sea. One by one, the crowd began to whisper and talk among themselves.

"What happened?"

"What was that?!"

"It was a mermaid!"

"No, it's the Massacooraman!"

"More spirits!"

"Anaconda!"

Then the chanting began again, "Ta-lin! Ta-lin!"

Celebratory cheers filled the night air. The men who had helped Talin push Onca back to the water's edge with their torches grabbed him, holding him atop their shoulders like a god. Talin could see down the beach where the frightened onlookers had run and they were dashing back to the bonfires. Small children waved ribbons and flags, dragging their parents behind them to return to the beach.

The men carried Talin back to the firepits and set him down next to his parents, Mr. George, and the Dyllon family. Talin had never seen a smile as broad as his father's. Tears covered his mother's face and her lips quivered. The celebration continued behind them.

Mr. George raised his hand. "Quiet! All quiet! Our evening has come to a close."

The villagers grumbled, immediately demanding a winner. The majority of the group shouted Talin's name as Healer.

"Quiet!" Mr. George continued, having difficulty calming the celebrating crowd. "No winner was declared for the Earth Ritual due to interference on the participants' part. An Absolution was granted."

More grumbling from the crowd.

"The winner of the Water Rite was Mr. Dewain Dyllon."

Dewain 1. Talin 0.

A few people in the crowd cheered for Dewain, but there was an overwhelming amount of boos and yelling, the first Talin had heard all evening.

"But Talin returned! He came back!"

"It's a miracle!"

"No, it's Obeah! No one goes into the cave and is able to come back out!"

"Dewain had a fair win!"

Mr. George continued, "For the Fire Summons, there is no declared winner."

But...

Dewain gloated with his friends, high-fiving each other and exchanging slaps on each other's backs. But an angry mob pushed forward toward Mr. George, raising torches above their heads and shaking their fists. Threats were made. Beer bottles flew past him, just missing his head. This was the first time Talin thought Mr. George looked truly unsettled, even more than when he was staring at Onca and did nothing to interfere with the challenge. Demands of an additional battle were made.

I don't want to do this again.

"I understand you are all very upset about tonight's events. So, in respect, I will confer with the elders about the winners of each challenge and will return to you shortly." He waved to the elders, and walked away to a nearby tree.

Someone in the crowd encouraged the spectators to settle, relax with drinks, and wait.

Talin's mother hugged him tightly and let out a sigh of relief. He felt her tensed shoulders relax. "You were wonderful," she said.

"Talin, can you come over here?" Marisha asked, standing next to the little girl whose shirt caught on fire. Handing him his pack, she said, "Do you have anything in here? Her neck is burned."

Opening his bag, he asked the girl if she was ok. She nodded.

"Really, Mr. Boyce," a man said that Talin assumed was the girl's father. "You've done enough tonight." He did not seem pleased.

"May I see her back?" he asked.

The little girl's mother stepped forward. "Yes, please," she said, her eyes pleading.

Talin nodded to Marisha and she lifted the girl's shirt in the back for him. "What's your name?" she asked.

"Sasha."

Her neck and back were extremely red, but no blisters had formed yet.

"Oh my, that's so beautiful," Marisha comforted her, "did you know that means helper of mankind?"

"How did you know that?" Sasha's mother asked.

Marisha shrugged.

"And your name means the claw of a bird," Sasha told Talin.

He smiled. "Yes, that's right. You are very smart to know that."

Finding aloe in his pack, Talin gently placed it on her shoulder blades and neck, but allowed Marisha to spread it evenly and lightly, then lowered her charred shirt back over it.

"It feels better," she said.

"I'm so glad." Marisha smiled.

"You helped me, just like you helped the goat!" Sasha said proudly.

"Thank you so much," her mother said.

"You're welcome." Talin closed his pack and shouldered it. "It should be better tomorrow."

"Thank you for coming," Marisha told Sasha's parents, then took Talin's arm and walked back to the fire pit. The elders still stood in a huddle under the tree in a heated discussion. A fair amount of shouting was heard, hands flailed and pointed. Amos and Javon exchanged shoves.

"I can't believe they brought her," Talin said, "she has to be what, seven, eight?"

"Talin, you *still* haven't grasped what a big deal this is, have you? I talked to someone who came from the neighboring island to see this. As of tonight, you're practically a legend."

He chuckled. "No legend."

"Talin! You healed a nearly dead goat, came back from the dead, and—"

"I wasn't dead."

"Well, I know, but they didn't! And, you just defeated a real life flaming jaguar that, up until now, people thought was only a myth. This is huge!"

"So, how did you know I would be back?"

Smiling, she said, "It was obvious when Dewain shoved you off Dive Rock, and you got sucked into the cave, but came back after that. When I saw it happening again tonight, I knew you'd be ok. But, Dewain, you should have seen his face. He was scared. *He* knew you'd be back, too."

She went on to tell him that she'd begged Mr. George to continue the Elimination. Apparently, it took some persistence and a fair amount of Marisha's strong will and fiery temper for him to agree.

"Thanks...but now I'm not so sure it will even help by the looks of it." He motioned to the elders still in a fierce debate. "Dewain has won one challenge and I've not won any. That's not enough."

She took a breath. "Have faith, Talin."

"And I've lost the necklace," he added. "Dewain will be extra angry."

They walked back to Talin's mother, where she held the goat's lead rope. "Well, it looks like we'll be adding another family member tonight," she said.

Talin reached down to pet the goat.

Mr. George returned to the anxious crowd, the elders following, then lining up behind him. A hush came over everyone without being asked. All attention was on Mr. George.

"The elders have come to a majority decision. The winner of the Fire Summons is Mr. Talin Boyce."

Cheers rang out. Dewain's brow furrowed, his friends complained.

One to one.

"So, it's a tie," snipped Dewain. "Are you going to name a winner of the Earth Ritual then?"

"Talin Boyce has been named winner of the Earth Ritual."

The crowd erupted on both sides.

"And," Mr. George raised his voice above the crowd, "the ruling of Mr. Dyllon's win at the Water Rite has been reversed."

What?!

Everyone erupted in chaos. There was cheering, yelling, cursing, and shoving matches that broke out in small groups. Dewain was wide-eyed. Talin's family scooped him up in their arms and jumped up and down, celebrating. Supporters emptied their drinks onto each other's heads. The children clapped and threw their ribbons. Someone grabbed a nearby cooler and dumped the icy water on Talin's head, dousing him, his entire family, and the goat.

"You won all *three*!" Javon repeated. "All three!"

"I *demand* a new challenge!" Dewain spouted.

"There will be no further challenges, per the rules of the Elimination, announced at the start of the evening."

"You *changed* 'da rules! I was announced as winner of the Water Rite, why was it reversed?!"

"Seeing Mr. Boyce's return from the current of the Falls shows superior strength and connection with the water element. The elders' reversal stands and will not be changed."

"But you said no winner would be announced for the Earth Ritual, now he's won that, too!"

"You were both afforded Absolutions for that challenge, but Mr. Boyce showed the true spirit of healing. Your performance was one filled with ego, not true sacrifice."

Dewain puffed up against Mr. George's chest, "You're a crazy man! You know 'dat? How could he have won 'da last challenge then? *He* killed a living creature!"

"Mr. Boyce has rid this community of the former Healer Hunte, who has harassed, bullied, and threatened this island for many years!"

"Yeah, and he broke the rules asking for help from everyone here! You saw it yourself!"

"This is the true nature of a Healer—helping the community, working together for protection, doing what is right and not forcing others into unsafe conditions! Even then, he did not back away when true danger existed!"

"That's a load of crap! I could have done all that, but I did the challenge as instructed! This is rigged! It's all rigged!"

"Mr. Dyllon, you asked for an Elimination—with my stolen seal I might add—I apologize if it did not end as you intended! You are now excused!"

The crowd cheered at the announcement, shouting for the Dyllons to leave. Very few protested for them to stay.

"Are you going to let him get away with this?" Dewain hounded his father.

"We go. There's nothing more I can do," Amos told him quietly, glaring at Mr. George.

Dewain strutted up to Talin. "You are not Healer," he shoved Talin's chest. "You 'ave no relic, no necklace. You threw it in the fire! So, you like to fight fire with fire, do you? I show you. This is not over! I will *prove* you wrong. You see."

Dewain finally walked away, his three friends and parents following. Everyone watched as they walked down the beach toward town. Then Mr. George announced, "I present to you all, Healer Talin Boyce!"

The crowd roared with applause and whistles.

"Now, we celebrate!" he added.

"Let's go to the tree, everything is already set up!" Marisha suggested.

Mr. George agreed it was a grand idea, making the announcement to everyone, and a sea of people swarmed the trail leading back up the hill.

23

D<small>RUMBEATS WERE CARRIED IN THE AIR AS THE CELEBRATION GOT</small> underway. Dancing, laughter, and spirited conversation filled the space. Children jumped up, reaching for the remaining ribbons in the tree's branches, and giggled while playing hide and seek within Jumbie's roots. They didn't seem afraid to be around the tree or touch it.

His mother kindly asked those selling alcohol from their coolers not to do so on her property and everyone respected her request. The man that Talin took the beer from earlier approached and congratulated him, saying no one needed to reimburse him for the drink. Bottled water was the drink of choice, and the children enjoyed juice boxes they had brought. Shantel had made a trip to the house with her sister and Marisha to bring back whatever leftovers she had from the Induction to share. Lots of desserts and drinks were spread on the table, and again, everyone raved over the fruit from the Grove, without knowing where it had come from.

If they only knew...

Shantel had tied the goat to a table leg. She kept a watchful eye on it as it grazed along the edge of the dirt in the grass as she danced with Luana. The white lights still strung from Jumbie's branches highlighted his mother's joyful smile. Javon cut in midway through a dance, and she did not decline.

The song of the tree frogs competed with the generator, which Talin was surprised hadn't run out of gas yet.

Marisha pulled Talin onto the dance floor, where he tried his best to entertain her, feeling as if he had two left feet. She led the dance, prompting Talin to spin her around. She laughed as he twirled her.

"You could use some dance lessons," she teased.

CELLPHONES AND CAMERAS lit up once again and Talin was bombarded with a steady flash of strobes and selfies from complete strangers. A reporter from the newspaper asked for an interview, and he uncomfortably stumbled his way through it. The local news station interviewed his parents and Mr. George, but Talin lost himself in the crowd or the tree's roots when the cameras turned his way. Realizing what real Hollywood celebrities must feel like, he wasn't a fan.

Maybe it will settle down in a few days.

Overwhelmed by all of the attention and congratulations, Talin asked Marisha to step away with him. They snuck to the back side of the tree, between the tallest roots, underneath Dewain's broken branch, and sat.

"You ok?" she asked.

"Yeah, tired. Just need a break."

"Well, a lot happened today," she smiled.

"Tell me about it." He paused. "Hey, how'd you know I had to throw the pendant?"

"At Onca? I didn't. Your nana did."

"But, you didn't even see the picture."

"Yes, but you told me everything about it. I couldn't stop

thinking about it all last night. You forget, I'm really good at puzzles. And I *told* you the necklace was hot, didn't I?"

"But it wasn't. Not then anyway." Then he thought back to what Nana had said. *It will be.* But, how did she know?

Hearing the crowd erupt in laughter and yelling on the other side of the tree, Talin stood up to glance over the root, checking that everything was ok and that no one was looking for them.

Marisha stood up next to him. "What is it?"

"Nothing. Just making sure nobody came over here. But...how did Nana know that's what would happen tonight? How did she know I was coming to see her yesterday?"

"I don't know, but I've heard that women in families of Healers sometimes have a type of clairvoyance."

"A what?"

"Clairvoyance. You know, like see the future, read minds. Sometimes they have vivid dreams that tell the future. You've never heard of that?" She leaned back into a root.

Talin stared out into the cemetery.

"What is it? What's wrong?"

"My mom has had dreams like that."

"Really? Well, that would definitely make sense since her grandpa was Healer."

"No, that's not it."

"Then what?"

"She also told me Anya dreamt that Dewain was Healer."

"Oh. Well...maybe the dreams are wrong sometimes, like the dreams themselves are trying to choose, because that obviously didn't happen tonight." She flashed a smile.

"But, mom said she dreamt that I was Healer."

"See? There you go. She was right!"

"And...that there was a large fire she couldn't save me from. Then she'd wake up crying in a sweat."

"Well, that could have been Onca tonight and her not being

allowed to help you?" She shrugged her shoulders.

Maybe his mother's dream really was about Onca's battle tonight. Her own mother even had a similar vision of flames being pushed toward the sea; she'd tried to show them in her drawings...

Was Nana a clairvoyant, too?

"Speaking of which..." she asked, "What are you going to do now that you don't have the necklace? It's a shame it's gone."

"Mama D'lo got my knife back right before the Induction, after I lost it in the Lake, and she helped pull down Onca. Maybe she could help me get it from the ocean—if there's anything left of it."

"That *was* Mama D'lo?! I *knew* it!"

THEY TALKED MORE about the evening, the necklace, how he felt to be named Healer, and his family's capability for clairvoyance. Marisha suggested Talin speak with Mama D'lo as soon as he was able to about the necklace, afraid Dewain would don his snorkel gear and go look for it himself not far offshore.

"Well, I'm really proud of you, Talin." She stepped in front of him, her hands on his shoulders. "And it's really cool that you are the Healer." Leaning in closer to him, she gazed into his eyes. "And you're my best friend, not my cousin." She wrapped her arms around his neck and kissed him on the cheek.

Talin's heart pounded. Warmth filled him when she'd said the words 'best friend', even though they were still related. It was all he ever wanted.

But then she whispered into his left ear, "I'm adopted."

Terrifying screams erupted from the celebrating crowd behind them. With his hurt ear still ringing, he wasn't sure if he understood what Marisha had just said.

He pulled away and they both ran, stumbling out from behind the roots like drunken sailors.

Everyone was panicking.

"What happened?" he asked a woman running by. They pointed further up the hill, beyond the cemetery. Her mouth hung open, unable to speak.

Massive flames shot up in the distance.

"Fire! FIRE!" people screamed.

Talin weaved through the scattering crowd, looking for his parents.

"Help! Someone, please help!"

"Call 911!"

"No! The island! Our treasure!"

The firefighters that had been standing by all evening raced to their trucks. The other men ran to their vehicles parked in the cane field, others piled into ATVs and sped off toward the flames. More tears flowed from the local women, some falling to their knees in anguish. "Dear God, please no!"

Talin found his mother sobbing by the table, her hands fiercely clutched onto Javon's shirt, her head buried in his chest, "Everything! Everything he worked so hard for. It will be gone. All of it! Gone! No! What am I going to do?!"

She wailed and slid to the ground.

What? What will be gone? Who worked hard for?

Javon helped Shantel to the ground, sitting next to her, cradling her in his arms to comfort her–without success. Looking up at Talin, gray ash began to fall from the sky, he said, "You need to go. *Now!*"

"Go where?!"

A bullhorn sounded in the distance. A chill rushed through Talin's body. He knew immediately who'd blown it.

Oh no.

The horn sounded again, this time with seemingly more urgency.

"Oh my God, Talin," Marisha said, staring at the billowing smoke and flames, "It's Hosea Preserve."

THANK YOU

Thank you for reading Talin and the Tree- The Elimination. If you enjoyed the story, please consider leaving a review on the platform you purchased it from.

Reviews are very important for Independent authors and I would appreciate even a starred review.

For more information on upcoming books in the series, give-aways, and more, sign up for Talin's Tribe at:

www.authorstephaniedossantos.com

DO YOU, OR SOMEONE YOU KNOW, NEED HELP?

If you or someone you know needs help recovering from alcohol addiction, take the time to contact your local chapter of Alcoholics Anonymous for assistance.

Please help the victims of bullying. There are many anti-bullying resources online or at local school districts.

Together, we can help.

ACKNOWLEDGMENTS

As with Book 1, there are so many people who brought this book to life, if not more! Without them, you would not be reading the story in your hands now, and wondering what happens next to Talin during his underground adventures! Sorry about the cliffhangers! Although many readers don't take the time to read this section, it's still important to acknowledge them here.

To my husband, **Rogelim**, for all the encouragement in my attempt to make writing my full-time career. We'll get there!

To Mom and Dad, **Tom and Margie**. You both know :) & Mom should be credited for many surprise bits in the story - keep 'em coming!

To my black and brown dogs, **Blitzen and Trevor** for sitting at my side while I wrote instead of playing with you. Dogs are better than most people, and you are the best. I know you can't read this, but I'll read it to you! <3

To **Tracy Noe** for being an awesome beta-reader and supporter of my writing! You are a wonderful, supportive friend and I am so thankful that you came along to be part of Talin's journeys! Book 3 is on the way!

To **Dr. M. Maxwell**, for constantly asking me about the progress of Book 2 and keeping me motivated to keep writing. Your input about Talin was very insightful and much appreciated. Hopefully I have done him justice for you in accepting his new role as Healer! Stay tuned more crazy adventures.

To **Pam Sourelis**, for being an invaluable developmental editor! Your insights were spot on and I appreciate all the time you put into pointing out discrepancies and areas for improvement! Talin and I look forward to working with you more!

To **April Faulkner**, for the AMAZING final copyedit/proofread. I can't tell you how much I appreciate your time and work on making this book not sound like a first draft. (It still might LOL!) But, again, you have saved me much embarrassment We will meet up someday soon! You're the best!

To the amazing crew at **Deranged Doctor Design** for the wonderful cover designs, logos and swag! Thanks for incorporating all of my input and making awesome covers that always get me many compliments!

A lifelong love of writing began with poetry, short stories, and school magazines. This transformed into freelance work at a local newspaper...before life got in the way.

After a 20+ year career in the medical field as a Registered Nurse and Paramedic, she has returned to her love of writing. She brings themes of love, nature and the mystical, travel and transport to her books, as well as good overcoming evil.

Talin and the Tree is her debut fantasy series, published under BlackDog BrownDog Press. When not writing or traveling, she can be found training her dogs, or pursuing other creative endeavors such as photography and painting. She resides in central Texas with her Brazilian husband, black and brown dogs, and quarter horse.

Sign up for the newsletter to be the first to hear about new releases and giveaways at:

www.authorstephaniedossantos.com

Email: stephanie@authorstephaneidossantos.com
www.tiktok.com/@authorstephaniedossantos

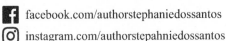

facebook.com/authorstephaniedossantos
instagram.com/authorstepahniedossantos

ALSO BY STEPHANIE DOSSANTOS

Talin and the Tree - The Legend - Book 1

Want a free book?

Talin and the Tree - The Healers' Chronicle Prequel ~
Sign up to the newsletter at www.authorstephaniedossantos.com

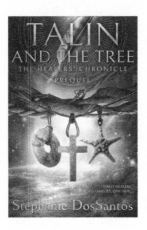

Made in the USA
Coppell, TX
12 October 2022

84488279R00208